Indian Country

ALSO BY SHOBHA RAO

Girls Burn Brighter
An Unrestored Woman

Indian Country

A Novel

SHOBHA RAO

CROWN
NEW YORK

CROWN
1745 Broadway
New York, NY 10019
crownpublishing.com
penguinrandomhouse.com

Library of Congress Cataloging-in-Publication Data
Names: Rao, Shobha, author.
Title: Indian country: a novel / Shobha Rao.
Description: First edition. | New York, NY: Crown, 2025.
Identifiers: LCCN 2024038935 | ISBN 9780593798959 (hardcover) |
ISBN 9780593798966 (ebook)
Subjects: LCGFT: Novels.
Classification: LCC PS3618.A694 I53 2025 | DDC 813/.6 — dc23/eng/20240823
LC record available at https://lccn.loc.gov/2024038935

Hardcover ISBN 978-0-593-79895-9
Ebook ISBN 978-0-593-79896-6

Editor: Amy Einhorn
Editorial assistant: Lori Kusatzky
Production editor: Abby Oladipo
Text designer: Amani Shakrah
Production: Heather Williamson
Copy editor: Maureen Clark
Proofreaders: Robin Slutzky, Rita Madrigal, and Emily Moore
Publicist: Gwyneth Stansfield
Marketer: Chantelle Walker

Manufactured in the United States of America

1 2 3 4 5 6 7 8 9

First Edition

The authorized representative in the EU for product safety and compliance is
Penguin Random House Ireland, Morrison Chambers, 32 Nassau Street,
Dublin D02 YH68, Ireland, https://eu-contact.penguin.ie.

For Srinivas Inguva

They drove away and left it lonely and empty in the clearing among the big trees, and they never saw that little house again.

They were going to the Indian country.

— *Laura Ingalls Wilder*

Indian Country

The Cotton River,
Custer County, Montana

Porcupine said, "Can't we do something?"

Older Brother, turning to him in the wind, said, "You know we can't."

Meanwhile, Younger Brother, ignoring them both, bent down as far as he could and tried to warn her.

Older Brother, Younger Brother, and Porcupine were standing on the banks of the Cotton River. They had been standing there for a long, long time. From where they were situated, they could see the dam and the reservoir along which the woman and her daughter were having a picnic. They could see the notch too — the cut, made just the other day, at the top of the dam to drain it — and the burial site on the opposite bank. And yet, even though they saw these things, not one of them — not Older Brother nor Younger Brother, not Porcupine — could do a single thing to alter what was to come.

But that has never stopped anyone from trying, has it?

While Younger Brother was bent down, trying to warn her, the woman was thinking of other things. She was thinking of the adage *You can't step into the same river twice*, but it seemed to her that that's all she'd ever done: step again and again into the same river. The Cotton River. All her life, she'd made the same mistakes, over and over.

Not anymore.

The divorce was final. After six years, and the child they shared, she was done being married, done getting beaten up. She'd gotten full custody, with her ex-husband getting supervised visitation. He wasn't all too happy with the parenting plan, or with the divorce. He'd stamped out of the courthouse after the hearing, and when she'd gotten outside, she'd seen him sitting in his truck, the F-150 Raptor he was so proud of, and swigging straight from a bottle of vodka. He'd always been a drinker, but in front of the courthouse? Despite everything, she felt sorry for him. There was a sadness in him. Understandable, in its way. His family's ranch lost to the banks, his mom running off, his dad busy with his new family, but her ex-husband's sadness, in her estimation, reached further back. It had a depth and a density that she'd never been able to make sense of. As if he were haunted not by something that had been done *to* him, and plenty had been done to him, but by something far more elemental, more unbearable. It was as visible to her as a limp would be, or a scar on his face.

And now it all made sense. All his sorrow. The last time she'd spoken to him, she'd placed the finger bone between them. She'd known instantly what it was when she'd found it on the banks of the reservoir; he had too. He'd said, "I've known you since high school. We have a kid. Doesn't that amount to something?"

It did, but that still didn't mean she wanted to stay married to him.

This Saturday afternoon picnic was her celebration. The start of a new life. A rebirth, she called it. A new apartment, a new job, and finally enough money to enroll her four-year-old daughter in daycare. After years of working dead-end jobs, a steady one that paid all the bills was a blessing.

She parked her run-down Toyota Tacoma among the sagebrush and the wild grape vines. She got out of the pickup, took a deep breath, and then lifted her daughter out of the car seat. They walked holding hands to the river's edge, and then she laid out the blanket and the bags of food, along with a few beers for herself. After the heartache and agony, and the long days excavating the burial site, the pop of the beer can, the fizz that followed, was celestial music. And this: the constant easy motion of the river, the sun on her neck, the flow of light and heat and water.

She looked out over the Cotton River. She looked at the dam, just past where she'd laid down their blanket, and then at the burial site. To think she was here yesterday, working. She'd lived here all her life and had not once imagined that the dam would be gone; that the river, one day, would run free. Her gaze, without her bidding, flickered to the water rushing through the notch. She smiled to herself. Funny to think that taking down a dam, a structural and civil engineering marvel, was as simple as punching a few holes in it.

She liked Sagar, the engineer. She liked how he looked at the river, his eyes soft, gentle — not at all how she'd imagined the eyes of someone who did calculations all day. She wondered what he did on the weekends.

Her daughter squealed. Yelled out, "Mama, catch."

The bright red ball bonked her in the face.

She laughed. She said, "Later. Here, come eat your sandwich."

The little girl picked up the ball, which had rolled back toward her, and plopped down next to her mother. She said, "Mama, I almost forgot! Lily killed a frog yesterday. On the playground. It was a little one, and Lily killed it. She stomped on it until it died. I told her not to, but Lily didn't listen. Mrs. Nelson said it would go to heaven. And then the class watched as she buried it. She made Lily say nice things about the frog. Can we buy the frog some flowers, Mama? Can we?" The woman looked at her daughter. How could a body so small hold so many words?

How much later was it? An hour? Two? A pickup. A swirl of summer dust. Just on the edge of the cottonwoods. Probably some kids, drinking and carousing on the last Saturday before school started. But her gaze held.

The dust settled.

Then came three questions the woman had never considered, not in this order: the first, How good was her sight line? The second: How many bullets did she have? And the third: What good was a gun when you left it in the truck?

Janavi and Sagar were at Reynolds, Mansfield's local grocery store, when Sagar's phone rang. They were in the deli section, staring at the trays of hot food behind the glass case. Specifically, at a pyramidal stack of corn dogs. Janavi, perplexed, said, "What do you think they are?"

Sagar shook his head. "I don't know."

They looked like mango popsicles to Janavi, but obviously they weren't.

When his phone rang, Sagar looked at her, as if it might be her phone, but Janavi said, "It's yours." She began to walk away, maneuvering the cart toward the produce section, when she stopped at the tone of Sagar's voice. She'd never heard it lift like that. She'd never heard that timbre. Sagar was saying, "I don't understand . . . but I don't . . . are you sure?"

Janavi turned and looked at him. Who could it be?

Probably it was someone from work. Who else would call him? It couldn't be good news. Not on a Saturday night. Sagar held the phone to his ear for a long while without saying a word. Then he seemed to nod, mumble something, and hang up. He stared at the phone in his palm. When she walked back, Sagar looked up at her, and in yet another voice she'd never heard, he said, "She's . . . she's dead."

Janavi looked from the phone to his face. She said, "Who?"

He didn't answer. His face was stone.

She blinked. The horror of the cold fluorescent lights, the empty aisles, the anemic music drifting down like ash. An older woman walked past, glaring at them.

When she blinked again, all the blood in Janavi's body rushed to her feet, because she knew in that moment that their lives in this new country, so fragile already, were now imperiled. The prairie, the grasses, and a river that was nothing like the Ganga — the holiest river in the world. Here, on the Cotton River, there were no ghats, no temples; no one sat by this river and prayed for enlightenment. She'd thought this when she and Sagar had been sitting under the cottonwood trees, her head against one of their trunks. And though she couldn't have known it, Younger Brother had been charmed by her, and he'd said, into the breeze, "We've never seen her before, have we? She's lovely."

Porcupine had agreed.

Younger Brother had said, "I wonder who she is."

Older Brother, who'd been thinking of other things, had looked at Younger Brother. He'd thought, How gentle you've become. Then he'd looked out over the Cotton River Valley, at the land and the waters that held all memory, and had said, "No, we haven't seen her before. But she's here now, isn't she? From a different place, a different kind of Indian, but that doesn't matter. She's here now."

Part I

Chapter 1

Janavi was in Shivdaspur, near the locomotive works, when she saw the little girl. She was wearing a short gray frock; it might've been blue or green at one time, but like the clothing of all the slum children, it was now the blotchy gray of soot and poverty and privation. There were no other children nearby, which was surprising; they usually traveled in packs. The girl was young, five or six at most. What was she doing? Janavi couldn't tell right away because the child's back was angled away from her, and she was hunched over, but as Janavi's training had taught her, she knew enough not to approach unannounced. She waited. There was no bus stop, but she stood — her stance, her posture, her impatience — as if she were waiting for a bus to turn the corner.

Janavi had started at ChildDefense six months ago and had finished her training, but she still saw street children everywhere. She'd lived her entire life in Varanasi, among its ghats and its temples and its slums and its shops and of course its river, the River Ganga, and yet she could not remember there ever having been this many street children. There had to have been — their numbers couldn't have exploded in six months' time, but as one of her workshop leaders had taught her, human eyes only see what the mind allows them to see. There were exceptions, certainly, things the eyes and the mind would rather not see but are forced to. That fell under the section of trauma, which they'd covered on the last day of her training.

Her boss, Ms. Sujata, had hired twenty-three-year-old Janavi only because four of her six social workers had resigned in a two-week period. Janavi, in her interview, had said, "I can start right away, madam. Today. I know English, and I know Varanasi. Oh! And I have a big heart."

Ms. Sujata had looked at her evenly and said, "Everybody has one of those. What these children need is one that can't be broken."

Janavi had assured her hers wouldn't. But it did break, with every child she met. Though, in a strange way, every child she spoke to also made it stronger. After the first month, she'd stopped crying herself to sleep and wanting to take every one of them home with her, but this girl . . .

She finally angled away from the corner she was hunched by, and Janavi saw, huddled against the edge of a wall, a tiny pink piglet. It was the tiniest piglet she'd ever seen. It could've fit in her hand, and maybe even in the little girl's hand. When the girl saw Janavi looking, she scooped up the piglet in her arms and started walking away. Janavi called after her, "Wait."

The girl kept her pace.

"Wait! Does the twenty-seven bus go down this road?" That was a mistake. A rookie one. Street children were the smartest children — the smartest *people* — Janavi had ever met. They were nowhere near the twenty-seven line and the girl knew it. Janavi tried again. She yelled out, "I have something for the piglet."

The girl slowed.

Janavi rummaged in her bag. *Did* she have something? An unopened packet of glucose biscuits! She handed it to the girl. She said, "What's your name?"

The girl was paying her no attention. Janavi hoped that she might open the packet and feed the piglet right there, but instead she started to walk away again. "What's the piglet's name?"

The girl turned and said, "Bulbul." Songbird.

Janavi smiled. "That's the perfect name for her."

"Him."

"Him."

Janavi took out a piece of paper from her bag. She said, "Can you read?"

The girl shook her head.

"Can you remember?"

She shrugged. Janavi gave her the address for the home that was run by ChildDefense and asked her to repeat it. She stayed silent. Janavi said, "What if Bulbul needs food? Or gets hurt? What if he needs a warm place to sleep?" The girl was quiet, perhaps thinking it over, and then she repeated the address back perfectly.

Janavi watched her leave with the piglet and knew three things. The first was that she'd finally found her calling. After slogging through college and after the debacle of the call center, it was now, on this twilit street, that she knew what she was made for, where the years had been leading. The second thing she knew was that Bulbul would soon get too big to be loved by the little girl. And the third? The third thing she knew was that the girl, if not already, sooner or later, out of hunger or fear or some other threat of extinction, would turn to begging or sex work or the drudgery of digging through rubbish heaps.

That night, when she got home, she researched everything she could find on piglets and their growth rates and even what they liked to eat, so that she might carry a snack for Bulbul in her purse. But then she felt foolish (All this for a piglet? And a girl she may never see again?) and turned off the computer. Even so, she decided to carry a carrot or two in her purse from then on, in case she ever saw the little girl and Bulbul again, and then she wondered, *Will* I see her again?

She guessed not, but she did.

A month or so later, in October, while Janavi was at the ChildDefense home, filling out paperwork, the little girl walked in. Janavi stared at her, and then she bent down and quickly checked her for blood, bruising, infection. Finding none, she exhaled and said, "You can stay here for as long as you like."

The girl, instead of looking around or at the ground, as most children did, looked straight at Janavi. She said, "Bulbul died."

The news pained Janavi in a bigger way than she could understand. She said, "He did? How?"

"He jumped down, out of my arms. And he ran onto the road. Lahartara Road. And then — "

Janavi's heart seized.

The little girl became a blur.

Lahartara Road.

It happened only for a few days in October when the axis of the earth tilted just so. The sun, in its rising, on one curve of Lahartara Road, blinded the drivers as they rounded it. Janavi's amma had been killed on that curve, at sunrise. Her amma wasn't the only one. An old man had died, struck by a scooter, and a young American woman who'd looked in the wrong direction before stepping onto the road. Several animals had died, of course, dogs, cats, any number of small rodents, a couple of goats. And now, Bulbul.

Once, an autorickshaw driver struck and killed a cow at that curve. Being Hindu, the driver was inconsolable. He went to the Shiva temple that very night and cracked open 101 coconuts, each by hand, and prostrated himself in front of the lingam until the gray stones of the antechamber ran sweet with milk. It collected in syrupy pools. Flies converged. The autorickshaw driver swatted them away and vowed to the

Lord Shiva that he would make an offering of 101 coconuts every year on this day for the rest of his life. And he did, for the first five or six, maybe seven years. After that, the usual: marriage, family, children, the day-to-day and year-to-year work of being alive, being humbled, being human, and so naturally, he forgot. He remembered only some twenty-five years later when he couldn't find a marriage match for his daughter, who'd been born with a slight lisp. He came upon her weeping in the kitchen one night, and that is when he remembered. He went to the temple the very next day, offered Lord Shiva 101 coconuts, and within three months, his daughter was married.

The summer before Amma died, she took seven-year-old Janavi and her sister, Rajni, eight, to the house of relatives who lived on the other side of town, a distant cousin or aunt whom Janavi had never seen before. There was a puja of some sort going on when they arrived, the entirety of which Janavi spent yawning or watching the flight patterns of the flies that hovered over the prasadam or poking at Rajni until her sister complained to Amma, at which point Amma smacked Janavi's arm and told her to sit still. After the puja ended, well past lunchtime, the distant cousin or aunt gathered all of Janavi and Rajni's boy cousins and herded them to the canopy tent where the food was being served. The Brahmin who'd conducted the puja, along with a few menfolk, were already seated. Amma led Janavi and Rajni to the tent, and without a trace of humor or equivocalness, said to the distant cousin or aunt, "Why aren't my girls being seated? Why aren't *any* girls being seated?"

The woman looked at Amma. And then at the canopy tent, where mounds of rice were already piled high on the banana leaves. "There's no space. See for yourself."

"Ask a few of the boys to get up. Better yet, ask the Brahmin to get up."

The distant cousin or aunt gasped, scandalized. "I couldn't possibly. He's a man of God, and the boys . . . they're . . . they're children."

"So are they," Amma said, indicating Janavi and Rajni, and then she said to them, "Let's go."

They must've gone to a restaurant afterward, or to the nearest street stall for snacks to hold them over until they got home. Janavi couldn't remember. Though what she did remember was how tightly her mother had gripped her hand as they'd walked out of the house, and the look on her mother's face — hard and fierce and calm — when she'd said, *So are they*.

The only other clear memory Janavi had of her mother was from another meal: dinner on the night before she died. Janavi and Rajni were squabbling over the last piece of fish. Fried to a golden brown, spiced perfectly, the layers of the fish steaming and white and succulent. It was their amma's signature dish. Their amma said, "Cut it in half," but they each wanted the whole piece. Their papa, who, through bad business dealings, had squandered away a formidable fortune, fed his family on a small income generated by a sugarcane plantation and a rental property he owned outside of Chelluru and an office job with a shipping company. He was reading the paper. Their amma, after watching them for a moment, took the piece of fish, placed it on Rajni's plate, and said, "Eat."

Little Janavi opened her mouth to bawl but was so outraged that nothing came out. She leapt from the table, ran to the kitchen, and crawled into a small niche between a shelf and the sink. Her amma came in carrying dishes. Janavi felt her gaze but refused to look up. Her amma bent down. She said, "Janoo, come out from under there."

Janavi didn't move.

Her amma said, "Do you know how much I love you?"

She sniffled. "Then — then how come you gave Rajni the last piece?" Her amma smiled. She brushed the hair back from Janavi's face, her hand cool against the heat of her misery. Janavi lamented, "*I'm* the baby."

Her amma took her chin in her hand, raised her face to meet her eyes, and said, "Yes, you are, my girl. But you have more fight in you."

Janavi said nothing. More fight? She understood, without under-standing.

Her amma then went into the dining room, came back with the plate Janavi had abandoned, and proceeded to mix the leftover rice and dal. She shaped the rice into round balls with her hand, and then fed them — each of the little balls, one by one — to Janavi. Janavi, chewing, tasted the salt from her tears, she tasted the spiced goodness of the dal, but what she tasted most was something of her amma. No bite of rice, eaten by her own hand or any other, nourished or comforted or quieted her heart, her hunger, in the same way. Janavi ate until the dal was finished, and then she asked for yogurt rice, and this too her mother scooped into balls and fed her, and when even the yogurt rice was fin-ished, Amma handed her a glass of water, but Janavi said no, she didn't want water. She didn't want to wash it out of her mouth, whatever it was her amma had imparted. Did she know it would be the last bite her amma would ever feed her? Is that why she wanted to safeguard it, bank it like embers against the coming cold? She had no answer, but the next morning, Amma died. No one knew why she'd been up at that early hour, or where she'd been headed. All anyone could tell the police was that they'd heard the screech of brakes, a thud, and not much else. Her body landed fifty meters away, on a grassy hillock. Rare for Varanasi: a grassy hillock. The city, which had stood for over three thousand years, with its narrow alleyways and motionless sadhus and hundreds, no, thousands of temples, didn't leave much room for grass, though even the few patches of grass bent to one goddess and one goddess alone: the River Ganga. Carrying in her waters life and death in equal measure, though truly, what she carried more of was death.

At least, that's what Janavi decided that night, as she considered the body laid out in the sitting room: that death, in its drift, would always vanquish life. And what was more, the body before her was no longer her amma nor had it ever been. It was not anything. Which is why, when she turned to Rajni, and then to her papa, she said, "When is Amma coming home? She's late for dinner." Rajni, crying, whose hand Janavi was holding, said nothing. Neither did her papa, so Janavi looked at her amma's face, unmarked by the accident, and studied every detail. She knew, even at the age of seven, that she would need these details later. And so, she committed to memory the small scar above her eyebrow where her mother had tripped and landed on a bottle cap. The aching elegance of her nose. The lips slightly parted as if the words, all the ones left unspoken, were waiting patiently for the God of life, birth, and breath to animate them.

And the last thing Janavi did?

Without letting go of Rajni's hand, she laid her free hand on Amma's chest. Still and cold and quiet. As if her heart were a small animal, burrowed deep underground and afraid to emerge. Is that what the heart was? Is that what death did? No matter. Janavi looked again at Rajni. People often mistook them for twins; they were only a year and fifteen days apart. And yet, Amma was right: Rajni was the gentler, the more sensitive, and thereby the weaker, which made Janavi suddenly and fiercely protective of her. She looked at her amma, bent down to her ear, and whispered, "Don't worry, Amma. I'll take care of her."

Janavi and Rajni weren't allowed to attend Amma's cremation ceremony. "Bhaiya, they're too young. Far too young," her chachi said, and Papa agreed. Janavi wanted to pinch her chachi; she protested, pleading, "I want to go with Amma," but she and Rajni were left behind with a neighbor. The neighbor, a kind elderly woman who smelled of Zandu Balm, listened to the radio all day. ("Why would she listen to *that* when she has a television?" Janavi asked, but Rajni was just as perplexed.) For lunch, the neighbor lady limped into the kitchen and reappeared with two plates of rice and kadhi. She set them down in front of Janavi and Rajni. Rajni began to eat immediately, but Janavi stared at her plate. The old woman looked at her and said, "What's the matter? Why aren't you eating?" Janavi said nothing. Rajni prodded her under the table, but still she said nothing. How could she? How could she explain that she was waiting? Yes, she knew Amma was dead, and yes, she knew death was final, but she was still waiting for her to sit down next to her and to take the rice and kadhi in her hand and shape the mixture into a ball and then bring the bite to her mouth and feed her. Death could do that, make both things true: the knowing and the waiting.

A few weeks after her amma died was the first time Janavi yanked on a classmate's braid, sending the little girl crying to the teacher. The teacher pulled Janavi by the ear to the front of the class and said, "Say I'm sorry." Janavi refused. She was in third class, and the teacher repeated, "Say it." Silence. Sometime later, while playing in the schoolyard, Janavi punched a boy in the face. Why? According to the other children, there was no reason why. She simply walked up to the boy and punched him, causing his eye to swell. Again, Janavi offered no explanation. In music class, when everyone was seated in a circle discussing chords, the teacher looked up to find Janavi spinning a wooden drumstick on the ground. He asked her what she was doing, to which Janavi replied, "Whoever it stops on next is the one I'm going to hurt." The school suspended her for three days. For those three days, Janavi sat cross-legged on the floor of her room, a pair of scissors in her lap. She watched the smooth cool stone for ants. If one happened to walk by, she picked it up between her thumb and index finger and snipped it in two. She dropped the halved body on the ground.

On the night before she was to go back to school, she told her papa she was having nightmares.

"What kind of nightmares?" he asked.

"The terrible kind," she said.

Her papa waited. He looked different; in a show of mourning, as was the Hindu custom when a close relative dies, he'd shaved his head after Amma's cremation, and now his head looked to Janavi like a gulab jamun with a fuzzy top.

Rajni was on the other end of the bed, picking at a loose thread. "What happens in the dream?" she asked.

Janavi said, "Amma dies. Again and again. Every night." She said this, looked at her papa, and then her seven-year-old body folded into itself like crumpled paper.

Since Amma's death, their papa had begun to work at his job in earnest. He'd already been promoted once, to head clerk. It was not for the money; Rajni had been promised, at five, to the son of old family friends in Rajahmundry, a well-to-do family who traded in mangoes and tobacco and textiles. The betrothal stood, even with the faded fortunes of their would-be daughter-in-law. As for Janavi — by the tilt of her head, the steadiness in her eyes — anyone could see, even as her papa patted her head as she wept, that she'd be all right in the end, with or without a dowry. So why his newfound dedication to his job? Perhaps it was sorrow. Or boredom. Or both.

Her papa held her, shushed her, and for lack of a better idea, told her time would lessen her grief, as time did.

Except, time didn't.

In the years that followed, Janavi turned inward. She became withdrawn, sullen, mumbled one-word responses to even Rajni; she was not moody as one would suspect, because she had no moods. What she had was only a dull feeling of forgottenness, being out of step, and being awfully alone. Nothing tasted of anything, smelled of anything, and nothing she looked upon tempted her to look again, or to look longer.

When she was thirteen, six and a half years after their mother's death, as she and Rajni were walking home from school one afternoon, they passed near the Ganga. Usually, they bypassed the river and the ghats and cut through the alleyways to get home, but today, maybe because Janavi saw river light dancing on a stone wall, or maybe because

Amma seemed to beckon her with an unseen finger, she turned toward the river. Rajni followed.

They arrived at Scindia Ghat. Janavi had never been to this ghat before and she stood on the top step, looking out at the fast-moving river and the sinking temple and the distant sandbar and the worshippers and the vagrants and the fishing boats and the barges and the ferries and felt nothing. What was there to feel? Even the brilliant red and orange and green of the sky passed over her and was, in her mind, already the blank darkness it would soon become. Somebody behind her yelled, "Get in," and Janavi turned her head. Was it Rajni? It wasn't, and besides, it had been a man's voice. Who had said it, and were they even speaking to her?

The last time Janavi had waded into the Ganga was during a mela. Her amma had held her hand and led her into the water, through the hordes of people and the floating flowers of the festival. Her amma had said, "I won't let go," and yet she had, hadn't she?

Just to spite her amma, Janavi descended the ghat. Rajni cried after her, "Janoo! Don't." Janavi ignored her, abandoned her chunni and her bookbag on one of the steps, and walked into the river.

The water was as cold as her heart had been.

She wanted her amma to see her now. Standing alone in an unfeeling river, waist deep in swift water, with no memory except for the shape of a nose, a scar, lips that parted but spoke no words, certainly not a goodbye. She wanted tears, anguish, but neither came. I'm not a cinema heroine, she thought, to make them arrive on demand. And then she thought, I should've brought an onion. She smiled, and it was this smile, or maybe an undertow, that led Janavi to take another step into the Ganga. And then another. She was neck deep.

She heard Rajni calling to her, her voice panicked. Janavi was now eye level with the water, and nothing prepared her for the seduction of a river in full spate; the silken gold rush of the water heaving against her with the strength of a mother's hand, with the force of a mother's love. To join her, to simply take another step and join her.

Join her.

The idea landed with the thud of a heavy burlap sack. And why not? The decision — to join her — came as if it had been waiting there, always, with a totality and a power that stunned her. She understood, in that moment, the undeniable, the arrival of an answer to the puzzle of her life.

She turned to take a last look at her sister. To wave goodbye. The ghat, which had been crowded just moments ago, had nearly emptied, leaving only Rajni, still standing on the top step, frantically waving, calling, and a little girl and her dog, both seated on the step nearest the water. Or maybe it wasn't her dog, because as Janavi watched them, the little girl got up and left and the dog remained. It spoke. But how could it? It said, very clearly, You lied. You broke your promise.

What promise?

The promise you made to your amma.

How could the dog know about that?

It said, You promised to take care of her, but you aren't, are you?

The dog stood for a moment and then walked away. Janavi watched as it trotted into an alleyway, though its question remained. It exploded in the evening air. Rang against the stones of the ancient city. Rained down on her without warmth. She looked at Rajni. Standing alone now on the ghat. Fourteen years old, and yet still holding in her face, her posture, the fragility she'd held at the age of eight. Motherless.

She *had* broken her promise, hadn't she? She wasn't caring for her. She never had. She'd squandered the first few years after her amma's death on cruelty and the past few on apathy. When she looked again, the dog was gone. The girl was gone. But what remained was Rajni. And Janavi's resolve.

A re-promising of an old promise.

She turned back to the water and *now* the tears came. Unstoppably.

Janavi cried for her dead mother, she cried for her grief-stricken sister, but she also cried for the lost years. As the waters of the holy river surged around her, she thought they were surging with her shame, but really, they were surging with her life.

As it turned out, Rajni was doing just fine on her own, arguably better than Janavi. Her sister had lots of friends in high school. She grew more and more beautiful by the day. And there was a sweetness about her; everyone flocked to Rajni like birds to a tree.

When they were in high school, Janavi in ninth class and Rajni in tenth, at the Central Hindu Girls School in Bhelupur, Rajni secretly started dating a boy from the Boys School. Their papa didn't know about it, of course, and the only reason Janavi learned of the relationship was because Rajni's friend Meena came over unannounced on a Saturday afternoon and asked if Rajni was home. "I need to buy hair clips. And a new lipstick if I can find a good color." Then she twirled a strand of hair and said, "It's hard. When you're this fair-skinned." She looked at Janavi and smiled. "Well, you wouldn't . . ."

It was true that Janavi was a few shades darker than Meena, darker even than Rajni, but her papa had said to her once, "You're your amma's color," and that was enough for Janavi.

"She's not home."

"She's not? Where is she? She said she'd be home."

Janavi shrugged.

Meena looked crestfallen, pouty, but then her face suddenly brightened, and she said, "*I* know. She's with Ravi, isn't she?"

"Ravi?"

"I know she is. I know it."

Janavi said nothing, wondering who Ravi was.

"Have you met him? He's the batter. On the cricket team for the Boys School. The best batter in the school's history. That's what Rajni says, but what would she know?" By now, Meena was smiling, practically swooning. "His arms. You should've seen him at the test match." She smiled conspiratorially. "I know she's with him. What are they doing, I wonder . . ." Janavi wanted to punch her.

When Rajni came home, just before dinner, Janavi was in their room, the one they'd shared since childhood. She was flipping through a magazine, *Stardust*, and when Rajni came in, she pretended to be engrossed in an article about the newest Bollywood starlet. Rajni threw her bag on her bed and said, "What's for dinner? I'm starving."

"How should I know? Ask Kumari."

Kumari was their cook. Their papa had gotten an accounting certificate and had been transferred to the main financial branch of his shipping firm. His increased position and salary meant they now had a full-time maid and cook, an old widow from Chunar whose son lived in Varanasi. She'd moved from Chunar a decade ago, after her husband had died, hoping to live with her son and his new wife, but they'd kicked her out of the house. The new wife hadn't liked her smell, Kumari told Janavi and Rajni, and she hadn't liked how she'd folded her saris. When the daughter-in-law had thrown her bag out onto the street, Kumari said, "My beta just stood there. Didn't say a thing. Not one word." Then she looked them each in the eyes and said, "Whatever you do, don't have sons." Janavi couldn't understand it. She liked Kumari's smell. She smelled like cardamom and amla oil and new cotton and the sweetness of burnt sugar. Just how an amma should smell.

Rajni looked at her. "What's wrong?"

Janavi put down the *Stardust*. "Were you with Ravi?"

Rajni, who had been hanging up her kurta, stopped. Her back was to Janavi. She said, "Who told you about him?"

"Meena. She came by. She wanted to go shopping with you."

Rajni swung around. "Please, Janoo, *please* don't tell Papa."

"Why didn't you tell me?"

"I didn't want you to have to lie to him too. Besides," and here she grew shy, "we haven't dated for that long. He's a batter, you know. For the Boys School."

"I heard."

Rajni looked at her pleadingly. "We're going for ice cream tomorrow. Do you want to come?"

Janavi feigned disinterest. "I don't know. What time?"

They met Ravi at the Amul Ice Cream Parlour on Sigra Road. Janavi and Rajni arrived first. Janavi got chocolate and Rajni got pista. They waited. Janavi tried not to look toward the door, but with Ravi, there was no need to look, he was a boy who was *felt*. A boy? He was nearly a man, with his stature and his facial hair and his cologne, or maybe his soap, that swept into the shop with the briskness and unapologetic gusto of mountain air. He sat down. He smiled at Rajni, and then at Janavi. She would've called it a winning smile, but she knew that, despite his adolescence, or maybe because of it, he was so used to winning that the smile was simply a confirmation, not an eagerness.

"Sahil might meet us later," he said. "At the school. You want to head over?"

"Don't you want some ice cream?" Rajni asked.

Again, that smile. "Look what my dad got me." He reached into his duffel bag and pulled out batting pads. They were leather, a spotless, sparkling white. "They're the best for impact protection. Expensive too. And feel. Go ahead. Feel how lightweight they are."

Rajni touched them reverently. Janavi stared at her. Her sister had never given a hoot for cricket and yet here she was, caressing the stupid pads as if they were a baby bunny rabbit.

"We're playing this afternoon. I'm good, but with you there . . ." He and Rajni looked at each other, as if only they shared a great and mystical and annoying secret. "Want to come?"

Rajni nodded eagerly. When he looked at Janavi, she looked right back and said, "No."

Rajni filled her notebooks with her and Ravi's initials enclosed in hearts. Janavi found one page filled with practice signatures for when she took his last name: a hundred Rajni Deshmukhs in varying degrees and styles of ludicrous curlicues. Janavi rolled her eyes, crumpled up the page, and threw it into the trash bin. It was as if Rajni had completely forgotten about being betrothed or was ignoring it. She thought, Where has my sister gone?

The relationship continued for another few weeks, swimmingly it seemed, until Janavi found Rajni weeping in her bed. Janavi had been running errands for Kumari, buying cilantro and ginger at the market, and when she returned, she stood in the doorway, alarmed. "What is it? What's wrong, Raju?"

Rajni lifted her face. She choked back tears and said, "He — he cheated on me."

Janavi knew she should've punched him then and there, at the ice cream shop. She went to her sister's side. "What happened?"

"He . . . I don't — I can't. It's too awful."

"He's a chutiya. Tell me."

Rajni raised her tearstained face. "He kissed Meena." She sniffled. "And then he bragged to the whole school about it."

Janavi went to the kitchen and asked Kumari to warm up some milk. She brought a glass of it to Rajni. The next day, she went to a cricket match at the Boys School. She searched out Ravi. She even waved to him when he looked in her direction. He waved back, a confused expression on his face. After the match, she waited until all the equipment was piled up and the players had gone off to an adjoining field. Then she rifled through the pile of duffel bags. She'd know them anywhere — the batting pads. She took out a bottle of kerosene she'd brought along and then she took out a match and then she set Ravi's duffel bag, along with his pads, on fire.

By the next morning, the story was all over both the Boys School and the Girls School. That night, once their papa said good night to them and turned off the light, Rajni, out of the dark, said, "You shouldn't have done that."

"Done what?"

Rajni sighed. "Meena saw you. At the match."

Janavi said nothing.

Rajni turned toward her, though Janavi stayed on her back. She said, "Janoo, you shouldn't have done it."

She couldn't stand it anymore. She felt like the little ants, just before she had snipped them in two — helpless. She flung herself onto her side and said, "He *hurt* you."

Rajni was silent. Janavi thought she might've fallen asleep, but after a moment, she said, "You have to grow from heartache, Janoo. Not be made smaller by it."

Janavi didn't know at all what Rajni meant, but she grasped then what Amma *hadn't* said, and maybe hadn't even known: Janavi might have more fight in her, but Rajni had more sense.

Chapter 2

If Sagar had bothered to notice, the signs were all there on the day his life changed. On his way to work, as he was waiting for his morning cup of tea at a stall in Sonarpura, a wayward goat butted him against his leg just as he reached for the cup, making him spill the tea across the front of his shirt — slightly scalding the inside of his forearm. While he was wiping away the tea, Sagar caught the distinct and briny scent of the sea, so distinct and so briny that he looked down at his ankles, fully expecting to see seaweed tangled around them. But there was no seaweed, of course. And no sea. The goat, in the meantime, had turned its head to eye him, maybe to tell him of the continents he would soon cross, but Sagar only looked back at the goat and thought, Why do I smell the sea? Why? When Varanasi is nowhere near the sea.

Varanasi. Banaras. Kashi.

He was in a city that demanded more than one name. A city that would not be appeased by a single utterance. It was his first winter here and walking in the early mornings through its ancient alleyways, enveloped in white mist, Sagar looked up at the sky of pale brass, remote and unreachable, and it felt to him as if he were looking up from the bowels of the earth. Cows blocked the way, and the small stalls selling wares were setting up shop, while boys weaved through the alleys, on some errand or none at all except the irrepressible urgency of boys, and in their midst were shuttered some of the oldest monastic orders on the planet. He felt the thickness of prayer and deep meditation choking the passageways like incense that left one breathless and flinging open windows, but here, in Varanasi, the only window was the Ganga.

He finally stumbled out of the maze of narrow alleys and there she was: the holiest river in the world. He stood on one of the ghats and watched as the red ball of the sun rose out of the mist, and for one instant, maybe two, the sun was the subservient, the single locket dangling from the wide, languid necklace of the river. This was the moment he loved best: the moment when the Salat al-Fajr rang from the minarets. He woke early, punctually at five, and walked slowly, arriving just as the sun rose. He'd grown up in Rajahmundry, on the banks of the Godavari, a magnificent river in her own right, but it was not until he'd finished his engineering degree at Andhra University, and had been posted here, to Varanasi, that he'd understood what it was to witness a body of water sweep away everything — corpses, the trembling light of small aartis at dusk, flowers, ashes, sweetmeats, sewage, waste of all kinds, the submerged sins of countless Hindus, millions sometimes on a single day — and so why not too his words?

He was stationed in Varanasi by the Central Water Commission. His job was to study the load and size of the sediment in the Ganga, in preparation for drainage channels that were being planned downriver, near its meeting with the Gomati. At midday, when he was taking his measurements, in a hired boat or along one of the sandbanks, Sagar looked out at the glisten and glitter of water, its sparkle, its strewn gems of noon light, and saw not the river but the riverbed. Everyone assumed it was the sun alone that made water sparkle, but it was also sediment, the dance of it with water and slippery aquatic organisms and veiled underwater vegetation. It was sediment too — the unseen, the unworshipped —

that caused the luster and the ripple. He'd lose himself, as any man in his twenties would, imagining beneath the quivering skein of divine perspiration the body of a woman. Lying prone. In his mind, she was just as fickle, just as inconstant as the stories revealed all women to be. Why else, in the early 1800s, did British irrigation engineers, attempting to shift a channel of the Ganga near Murshidabad, find that it had altered its course westward by over five miles in less than a year? And then shifted again, a few years later, this time eight miles to the southeast? Why else, aside from the inherent faithlessness the stories spoke of?

When he returned to the office after his tea break, his boss, Mr. Mandal, asked why his shirt was stained, and when Sagar told him about the tea and the goat and the smell of the sea, Mr. Mandal, who'd taken a keen interest in interpreting dreams and visions since the age of five, when he'd dreamt that his pet rooster had circumnavigated the earth and come back to tell him the secret to life, said to Sagar, "It's not the sea or the goat you need to worry about, my lad. It's the seaweed that caught your ankles. *That's* what you should worry about."

Sagar didn't tell him he could still feel it gripping his ankles, as cold as metal.

That evening, as he did every evening, he walked to a canteen for his dinner. The sky was low and dull and gray. The alleyways shadowed and hushed. Being a man of habit, he ate at the same canteen every night — even though the dal was watery and the puris were never puffy. He didn't care. He liked to sit at a table facing the alley and read *The Times of India*, or on occasion the latest issue of the *International Journal of Hydraulic Engineering*, or some other scholarly article. But this evening he noticed neither the dal nor the soggy puri. He put the journal aside. He was thinking about the chickens. The ones his landlady had been killing. The one modest room he let from her was upstairs, while her two rooms, along with a kitchen and the toilet, were downstairs. For how congested Varanasi was, the grounds of the house were palatial.

There was room enough in the garden for a tamarind tree, a peepul tree, and a chicken coop. The wall surrounding the house was draped with flowering night jasmine. He'd emerged from his evening bath and found her slaughtering all her chickens. But *why*, he'd asked. Because they're eating their own eggs, she'd said. They're lost to you, she'd continued, once they realize how tasty the eggs are, how filling and delicious, a feast, really. And who would give up a feast? Anyway, the problem is not just these chickens and their love of eggs, but they'll teach any new chicken or baby chick you put in the coop to eat the eggs too. So you see? There's no choice, they have to be killed.

There's no choice, he repeated to himself, staring out from the canteen at the gloomy winter evening, They have to be killed. And the image came back to him of the tub of bright yellow and pink and gray innards, slippery with mucus, and the pile of chicken's feet, which, once separated from the body, looked as if they should belong to a creature far more Paleolithic, far more predatory than a common chicken, and of course the feathers, their tips broken and strewn as if fallen weapons on a blood-soaked battlefield.

Here then was a day with two omens: seaweed, slaughter.

He went to pay his bill, and when he came back to collect his things, he found a cow munching on his journal. He ran over to it and after a mild struggle, ripped the journal out of its mouth. The cow ambled away, a little sad but unperturbed. Sagar flattened out the sodden, ripped pages, mumbling, "That's what's wrong with this country . . . everywhere you look, cows and goats and . . ." He straightened out the crumpled sheet and saw that it was the listing of job openings. And there, just where the cow had been forced to stop chewing, was a large advertisement inside a thick, black-lined box. The heading read: HYDRAULIC ENGINEER, COTTON RIVER, MONTANA, USA.

Sagar looked at it. He was about to close the journal and tuck it into his bag, but he didn't. Instead, he read the full listing — he had nearly every qualification it required and more that it didn't. He read the heading again. Cotton River. What an odd name. And where was Montana? It must be a state in America, though he'd never heard of it.

When he got home, he looked up the Cotton River, in southeastern Montana, on his computer. Then he looked up all of Montana, and even read up on the Montana Territory. He was fascinated. By the history, and the Indian Wars, and Red Cloud's War, and the mining of everything — as far as Sagar could tell — every metal, mineral, and rock the earth had ever concealed. He pulled up a map of the United States. He stared at it. What was he looking for?

He didn't know, but he was enchanted, and when he woke the next morning, his mind was made up.

After three rounds of phone interviews, Sagar was offered the position. The Cotton River Dam Removal Project was what Sagar would be leading, and the Department of Natural Resources and Conservation (DNRC), located in a town called Helena, was the division he'd be working for. It was true that he'd fudged a bit on his CV and inflated his role in the only other dam removal project he'd worked on, on the Majuli River, a tributary of the Brahmaputra. That had been a few years ago, and Sagar had been one of the assistant engineers, not the lead engineer. In fact, he'd been one of seven assistant engineers on the project. When he interviewed with the DNRC, he'd simply left that part out. Regardless, he got the offer letter, and with consulates and bureaucracy and visas still to contend with, he wouldn't start the job for another six to seven months.

He would have to tell Mr. Mandal and his colleagues, and tender his resignation with the Central Water Commission.

He would have to phone his friends. Tell his landlady. Say goodbye to the waiters at the canteen.

He would have to tell the little boy who lived next door and came over sometimes asking for biscuits or a toffee.

He would have to tell his parents.

And Sandeep. He would have to tell Sandeep.

The afternoon light swung from the trees. The leaves spun like tinsel. Even the water seemed a swollen, luscious berry, blue and bursting with juice. At least to Sagar's eyes. He was twelve, his brother Sandeep was seven. They were with family friends, picnicking at the waterfalls at Pinjari Konda. The older boys, once the food was eaten and the adults were lying around on blankets — the men talking about their lands and the meager rains, the women about their nettlesome servants — wanted to go swimming. "Take your brother," Amma called out.

Sagar whined. "Do I *have* to?"

"Yes."

"He just slows us down."

"Then slow down."

Sagar rolled his eyes. The other boys, three of them, had already started for the swimming hole, on the Yeleru River. Sandeep leapt up and ran after them; Sagar followed. When they reached it, they scrambled up onto the high boulders, throwing off their clothes, burning the soles of their feet on the hot stone. Below, the river flowed smoothly by, cold and inviting. The boys, one by one, dived into the water, coming up squealing from the tickle and twirl of it. They took turns, as if the afternoon, summer itself, were an engine that would never stop. Sandeep, though, held back. He glanced over the boulder, leaning forward only with his head. He looked at Sagar, standing behind him, and said, "From here? But Annai, why can't I just wade in?" The other boys yelled up from the water, taunting him. Sagar said, "Stop being a baby. Jump."

Sandeep turned and peered over again, his toes gripping the stone.

Sagar would remember it — the tender curve of his little brother's body. The knobs of his still-growing spine as tiny as almonds. His thin boy legs. The pitiable shape of his shoulders, as breakable as chicken bones. He would remember the sounds of the other boys, their limbs splashing in the river, and the wind in the trees on the farther shore.

Why did he do it?

He would never know why, but he took a step, raised his arm, and pushed his brother into the river. He jumped in after him, only to find when he surfaced that Sandeep had not. He scanned the river frantically, bobbing up and down, and then dived under. Minutes passed. Hours? One of the boys ran to tell the parents, and by the time Sagar dragged his brother out of the water and onto the rocks, his father was running toward them, screaming.

He'd landed in a way that had impacted his neck and shoulder, damaging the nerves. The brachial plexus nerves, the doctors said. Surgery didn't restore function, and Sandeep never regained the use of his right arm. He could write with it, and move it close to his body, but the greater arc of it was diminished. Nothing past the line of his shoulder. And lifting it above his head? Impossible.

Sagar spent the rest of his childhood trying not to look at his brother's arm, but it seemed to him that it was all he ever saw. Sometimes, in his sleep, he'd throw his arm over his shoulder — a thing his brother could no longer do — and wake up weeping.

Sandeep, when he'd come to, had looked up at his father, his eyes welling with tears, and said, "He pushed me, Papa. He pushed me." Papa turned to Sagar. The slap that followed, even years afterward, stung his cheek and shamed him to the core.

He wanted to say, But I saved him too, didn't I?

By the time Sandeep reached high school, he was failing in his studies. Their parents hired an army of tutors, but still he was held back twice. His tutors reported that he was lazy and needed to apply himself; his teachers were slightly less artful and said, What does his arm have to do with his brain? Under the guise of pursuing his studies, he went to a donation college and developed a drug habit. Mostly hashish, though the bag of white powder Sagar found in his room couldn't have been hashish. There was a pregnancy scare, too, with a few phone calls from an angry father, but it came to nothing. He finally graduated after six years with a BA, though Sagar never fully understood what his degree was in. Through all this, their parents didn't discipline or reprimand him in the slightest. It was as though the injury to his arm had released him from all the duties of a child, a son, and turned him into the recipient of endless clemency. On the other hand, Sagar seemed to bear the brunt of two sons. The guilt of many more. Was he imagining it? That every time he raised his arm, his father glared at him, and his mother looked away?

After college, Sandeep went off to Manali, presumably to find God, though Sagar was fairly certain that all he'd done in the wilds of Himachal Pradesh was seek out a purer grade of hashish. If he'd said this to Sandeep, said, You didn't want to find God, you just wanted to do better drugs, Sandeep, he knew, would've laughed and said, Aren't they the same thing? When he returned from Manali, with long hair and a beard and the air of someone who mistook a few cold nights in northern forests for spiritual clarity, his arm injury seemed to have worsened. But how could it worsen? The nerves couldn't be *more* dead. Still, his father and Amma fawned and cooed over him as if he were a newborn. Or a hero wounded in war. Sagar had enough and applied for the position with the Central Water Commission in Varanasi. It was as far away as he could imagine — Andhra Pradesh to Uttar Pradesh.

And now here he was, going to Montana.

After he got the offer letter from Montana's Department of Natural Resources and Conservation, he flew to Rajahmundry, with a layover in Bhubaneswar. When he looked down from the window of the airplane, he saw below him the vast Gangetic plains, unfurling to the Bay of Bengal, and then, on the journey south-southwest, the lush Godavari delta. His parents still lived in the house he and Sandeep had grown up in. When they'd been boys, the house had been on the outskirts of Rajahmundry, adjacent to land his father had owned, but now the house was practically in the center of town. His father had sold off the land surrounding the house and reinvested the proceeds in mango orchards and tobacco fields farther out, some as far away as Peddapuram, and even in a small textile mill. When Sagar arrived, Sandeep was out with friends. He'd been out of college for years, but hadn't ever bothered to look for a job, and though unspoken, the truth was always there: he never would.

Sagar told his parents that evening, after dinner.

His amma said, "So far away too. Where did you say?" Sagar showed her on the map. She shook her head sadly and said, "What is this place? Only villages there." His father poured himself a whiskey and asked more pointed questions. What would he be doing? How long was the project? What was the salary? When he told them the salary, his father looked unimpressed, though he must've been. It would take him ten years in India to make what he would in one year in Montana. He said, "Which river did you say?" When Sagar told him, he took a sip of his whiskey and said, "Never heard of it."

Sagar felt the familiar heat rising from his stomach to his eyes. He looked gratefully at his amma when she said, "How long will the project take?"

He smiled. "A few years. And then I'll be back."

His mother shook her head. "No one comes back from America."

His parents went to sleep. Sagar sat on the terrace and looked at the stars, the almost-full moon. He caught the scent of lantana and pomegranate blossoms in the air. He felt the tug of the Godavari River. Maybe even the Yeleru. When had he fallen in love with rivers? It was so long ago, it felt ancient. As ancient as those stars. Perhaps he was born with it? Born with river water for blood.

He remembered that his boyhood history teacher had taught the class about the age of conquest, exploration, and the New World. How Columbus had landed and called the people Indians, thinking he'd arrived in India. And of how exploration was always rooted in gold. The search for it, the stealing of it. Sunken Spanish galleons, his teacher had said, littered the floor of every ocean. Their hulls full of treasure lodged into the sediment of every sea. Sagar, eight or nine at the time, knew enough to know that every waterway, no matter how minor, eventually emptied into the sea, so why not? Why couldn't the treasure chests full of gold, at least a few of the coins, be in the Godavari?

Every chance he got he took to searching the riverbed. Swimming as far down as he could before he had to come up for air. Choosing different segments of the river; ticking them off on a homemade map. He hadn't counted on the Godavari being so deep, so he was never more than a few meters from the shore, but he was determined, systematic, ordered. Those Spanish galleons had to be somewhere. And they belonged to him anyway, and people around the world who looked like him. That, too, he'd learned in history class.

Once, he found a shiny locket, but it turned out to be made of tin. Another time, a beautiful string, colorful and sparkling, but it was only a necklace of plastic beads. He dredged up innumerable bottle caps and candy wrappers and aluminum cans. When he was older, he swam in the Bay of Bengal, the boy in him still secretly searching for the lost treasure chests and their mountains of gold. He wondered sometimes if *that* is why he'd become a hydraulic engineer, specializing in the study of sediment and riverbeds and ocean floors — for the Spanish galleons.

On this summer evening on his parents' terrace, with the fragrance of lantana and pomegranate blossoms wafting in the air, and the moonlight streaming and streaming, pouring like an avalanche of light onto the chair in which he was seated, he thought, Montana. Maybe that's where I will find them: my Spanish galleon, my treasure chests of gold.

Sometime in the night, or maybe early in the morning, he heard Sandeep come in.

The next morning, during a breakfast of idlis and vadas with coconut and ginger chutneys, his father said, "Seems as if your mind is made up, but we can't have you going alone."

Sagar looked up, mid-bite. "What do you mean?"

"Marriage. We'd like to see you married first."

Sandeep glared at him across the table. "Go where?"

Sagar told him about the Cotton River dam, and how he'd be leaving for America as soon as he got his visa. Sandeep lifted his coffee cup, more carefully than he needed to. He said, "Lucky for you."

Amma turned to him and said, "Deepu, have more idli. Just one more."

Sandeep said nothing; he didn't even turn to look at her.

After breakfast, Sagar took his coffee back to the terrace and thought it over. It wasn't so far-fetched. He was already promised to the daughter of old family friends. It was simply a matter of setting an auspicious wedding date. He'd been promised at a young age, eight years old, and it was the way things had always been done in his family, for generations: The eldest son was given in marriage to the eldest daughter of a suitable family. Not just to maintain their wealth (which, in this case, didn't much apply since, from what he understood, his betrothed's father had lost most of his money in bad dealings and his own father's mango orchards had been infested with mealybugs), but primarily to keep pure their aristocratic bloodline. Antiquated, yes, and for many years, starting in adolescence, he'd resented the arrangement. Hated that he couldn't choose, and that Sandeep could. But he'd grown to understand, or maybe decide, that among the many reparations he'd had to make for causing his brother's injury, this was yet another. He'd once caught a peek of his future wife, Rajni, at a family wedding. She'd been talking with a group of women, and at one point had lifted her hand to her cheek, unconsciously, and Sagar, in that moment, had blushed, thinking, One day. One day, far or near, she'll be in my arms.

That night, he told his parents he would marry. He said, "Do they still have a house in Chelluru?"

His amma said, "Yes, but they don't live there. They're in your town."

"Varanasi?"

"They've been there for ages. Since before Auntie died."

Sagar was astonished. "Why didn't you tell me?"

"I did. I thought I did . . ."

His father said, "No matter. It wouldn't have been proper for you to go around visiting anyway. I'll phone today. We'll set up a good day to meet. Find a muhurtham."

Sagar said, "Do you think we can do it, the wedding and all, in six months?"

"Easy," his father said. "We have the boy. And we have the girl."

Chapter 3

When Janavi graduated from high school, she considered her options. She could follow in Rajni's footsteps and pursue a degree in Sanskrit at Banaras Hindu University, or she could follow in her father's and study accounting or economics. She chose neither and instead decided to study English. She'd liked her English classes in high school, and now with the internet and globalization and India poised to become the next big technological hub — all things that her papa talked incessantly about — it seemed to her a sensible degree. Her papa, when she told him, said, "I was thinking computer science, or an IT course. Though I suppose, unlike your sister, studying a living language is better than studying a dead one." But by the end of her third year, she was listless. She would soon have to choose a specialization, and her choices were medieval literature, British literature, or rhetoric and composition. Janavi contemplated her choices. They all seemed to her equally dismal. She realized that what she liked most was *speaking* English, not reading it. And spending years studying a poem about a monster, its mother, and a dragon seemed pointless, unless she was willing to do a PhD in the monster, its mother, and the dragon.

In the meantime, Rajni had graduated and gotten a job as a Sanskrit lecturer at Adarsh Inter College. She took the bus every morning and came home exhausted every evening. Then she graded papers and exams late into the night. Yet even with her grueling schedule, she seemed happier than Janavi had ever seen her.

Janavi told her papa she'd lost interest in her English degree one night while he was in his study, poring over a map. She expected him to be angry, but instead he looked up and said, "I suppose I'll have to get you married now." It was clearly a joke, since of course Rajni would be married first. And since they didn't have to search for a boy for Rajni, it would be relatively painless. In fact, Papa told them that the boy had recently gotten a job in Varanasi. He patted Rajni's head with affection. "Isn't that wonderful? You won't have to leave your job after marriage," he said, smiling.

Rajni looked down at her hands without a word; Janavi assumed it was because she was shy, and so she teased her sister until Rajni shooed her away. As for Janavi, the thought of marriage annoyed her — the subservience, the dowry, the boring rituals. *She* would pick her own husband, and not for a long time to come. She wanted to make something of herself first.

The night Janavi told her papa, the map he was studying was a very particular kind of map — a nautical chart. Over the years, he had grown more philosophical. He'd started feeding the neighborhood cats. He was now an accountant for a shipping company based in Mumbai, and every evening he'd sit for hours and stare at the routes of the ships that carried his company's cargo. He'd spread the nautical charts out on his desk or the granite floor of the sitting room, and once, when she was ten, he said to Janavi, "Do you see that? Right there. Can you read it?"

"Bering Sea," she said, mispronouncing it *beering*.

"That's right. Almost right."

"But what are these? All these little numbers?"

"They're all kinds of things. The depth of the sea for instance, right here. And here," he said, pointing to a circle with a dot inside it, "is the location of a rock. It could be dangerous, you see, for a ship to hit that rock. So, it's marked with a circle."

"And these arrows? Around the rock?"

"They're the direction of the current. And this number — this number is the speed of the current. In knots."

Nots?

She said, "Why do you like them so much? These maps?"

He was silent, and then he said, "You know that Amma's ashes were released into the Ganga, don't you?"

"Yes."

"Do you know where she went? Do you know what the Ganga flows into?"

Janavi considered for a moment. "The Bay of Bengal?"

"That's right. And what does the Bay of Bengal flow into?"

"The Indian Ocean!"

"And the Indian Ocean?"

They both turned to look at the nautical chart. Janavi said nothing, and neither did her papa.

The Sociology Department accepted all her English credits, so she transferred there. She got her degree and started applying for jobs. Weeks went by without a single call or interview. Disheartened, she considered plodding through graduate school to get her master's in sociology, but her papa suggested going into the tech field. "Papa, you've been telling me that since high school," she said. "You know I don't like computers." You don't have to, he said. Because this, he said, was a different kind of computer job. One of his colleagues had mentioned it as a field Janavi might be interested in — the field of BPO, or business process outsourcing. Namely, working at a call center.

The colleague had explained what he knew about them, and her papa said that with the English she already knew, she might be the perfect candidate. When Janavi looked into call centers, she found that what her papa and his colleague had said was true: She could make good money and get to use her English, and what was more, training only took a few months. In fact, she found a four-month call center training course that was far cheaper than getting a master's degree, and she would be part of a vibrant new field!

Janavi signed up for the course.

Her instructor, who was only slightly older than she, was named Tejas, and on the first day, he spoke about two things: MTI and accent neutralization. MTI stood for mother tongue influence, which Tejas explained was the Indian accent, with all its vocal peculiarities. "You all have it," he said, "and we are here to get rid of it." Accent neutralization was the other aim of the class, and that meant not only getting rid of the Indian accent but getting rid of *all* accents. "That way," he said, "you can speak English to anyone in the world and be understood. Perfectly. American. Canadian. Scottish. Irish. Doesn't matter." Then he pointed at Janavi and said, "What's your name?"

"Janavi."

"You are now Jane."

"As in Austen?"

Tejas looked at her with confusion, and then with contempt. "Say the word *parent*." When she did, he said, "You see? You see how her mouth widened? And she elongated the *a*, in the *pa*? Unnecessary. It will be gone in no time."

He was right: It was gone in a month.

At the end of the training course, Janavi applied and got a job at a call center on Vidyapeeth Road. On her first day, she walked in, saw the expanse of cubicles, row after row after row—there must have been acres of them, each with a lowered face, a headset over their ears, and each of them feeding the unnerving murmur of hundreds of accent-neutralized voices—and her heart sank. She thought of conveyor belts, she thought of slaughterhouses, and then she thought, I don't belong here. Her boss was nice enough. His name was Kiran, but he went by

Chris. When he called her Jane, Janavi winced. He noticed and said, "You'll get used to it."

She didn't get used to it, not for the entire week that she worked there.

On Friday morning, out of fatigue and boredom, she pressed AEW on the blinking light — which held off the caller — for fifteen seconds longer than was allowed by the call center's rules. And worse, she did it twice. Kiran called her over to his slightly larger cubicle and asked her what the problem was.

"There is no problem," Janavi said.

"You held off two calls. Each for more than fifteen seconds. Why?"

Janavi shrugged. "I needed a break."

"You have allotted breaks," he said. And then he said, "I'll have to cut your pay."

She looked past him to the sea of bent heads. She said, "It was only fifteen seconds. It's absurd to reprimand me for a mere fifteen seconds."

"You know what those fifteen seconds are to the American person on the other end? Sitting in their house. Listening to the hold music. Maybe they have a party to go to. Maybe their boyfriend is coming over. We could lose them. A customer — those fifteen seconds is a customer."

"It's inhumane."

"What is?"

"To dissect a life into fifteen-second intervals."

Kiran rolled his eyes. "Jane. Grow up. It's not inhumane, it's adulthood."

Janavi went back to her cube, gathered her things, and walked out.

That night, while Janavi was lying on her bed, Rajni came into the room and asked if she could borrow her white chunni, the one with the silver embroidery. They rummaged in the almirah, and when Janavi handed it to her, Rajni was delighted. She said, "I'll wear it with my Rajasthani jewelry," and modeled it in front of the mirror. She seemed to be doing a lot of that these days: dressing up and going out in the evenings. She turned, saw the look on Janavi's face, and said, "What? What's the matter?" Janavi told her about the job at the call center and how she'd only lasted a week.

Rajni laughed. "You're lucky to get out alive," she said.

"But what will I do now?"

Rajni looked at her. "Anything sounds better than that place."

Browsing the internet, Janavi saw an ad for a position with an organization called ChildDefense that worked with street children, providing them with resources and education and housing. She submitted the application. She applied to other jobs as well. She waited. Then one day her phone rang. The executive director of ChildDefense, Ms. Sujata, called her in for an interview. After they'd talked for a while, Ms. Sujata said, "You're young. Maybe too young."

"No, no, madam," Janavi protested, "I can do the job."

Ms. Sujata eyed her. She said, "Most people don't make it past the training course."

"I will. I know I will."

"How do you know that?"

Janavi wanted to say, Because I've never quit anything before in my life, but obviously, that was untrue: She'd dropped out of the English program and left the call center job. So, she said the next true thing that came to her head: "Because there is nothing in the world more beautiful than a child."

Where had that come from? Janavi couldn't say, but she knew she believed it with all her heart. Maybe because she yearned for the child she'd once been, before Amma had died, or maybe because her amma's words still echoed inside of her, *So are they*, and Janavi had understood in that moment that regardless of whether a child was a boy or a girl, born into a slum or into the richest family on earth, each was equal to every other.

Ms. Sujata's expression softened. She might've been charmed by what Janavi had said or amused by her innocence. Either way, she hired her, and Janavi started the following Monday. She roamed all over Varanasi — the railway and bus stations and the neighborhoods and the slums and the marketplaces, talking to children and laughing with them and taking them by the hand and wiping away tears, mostly her own. At the end of her first week, she was so depleted and agitated and fulfilled and fuming that she walked out onto Assi Ghat and screamed at the top of her lungs at the water and the birds and the boats and the sky.

She couldn't imagine a better, more meaningful job.

One evening, Papa called Janavi and Rajni into the living room. Janavi said, "What is it, Papa?"

He smiled and told them that the groom's family was ready. Janavi saw Rajni's eyes shoot up and stare at her father. She said, "Ready for what?"

He laughed. "To marry you, my dear. What else?" He then told them they were coming to set the muhurtham, the time and date of the wedding, at the end of the month. That was only a week away!

The next few days were a rush of activity. Arrangements had to be made. Orders placed. The priest had to be called. Janavi and Rajni and Papa went shopping for saris. She and Rajni would wear them for the marriage viewing, which was to happen in three days' time. They went to Luxa Road and trudged through every sari shop in and around Rathyatra Crossing. They stopped in the afternoon for tea and pakora, and then they shopped some more. Janavi couldn't help but notice that Rajni, throughout the day, seemed distant, melancholy, and she thought, She's scared. And then she thought, *I'm* scared; marriage, after all, was no small thing, and what if her new husband was cruel or unfaithful or unpleasant? What could Janavi possibly do?

She tried to make her sister laugh. She told her stories of the children she worked with and their antics. She pointed out a little goat that had stolen a packet of kachori and was munching on them behind a doorway. She draped and twirled in the bright silk saris, covering her head with one end and batting her eyes at Rajni, pretending to be a shy bride. In the end, they bought a forest-green sari with a fuchsia-colored border for Rajni, and a marigold-colored one with a red border for Janavi. Janavi wouldn't be able to be seen by the groom's family until after the muhurtham was settled, of course, so that the future groom wouldn't favor the younger sister, but that was only protocol. A small thing. Unheard of.

The following day, their papa ordered sweets and namkeen and fresh flowers.

Then he confirmed the time the soon-to-be groom and his family would arrive with the priest: four o'clock on Saturday afternoon.

Everything was ready.

Theo Mortimer

Ganges River, 1814

Theo Mortimer arrived in India in 1814, at the age of seventeen. He disembarked from the *Marquis of Wellington* at Calcutta and stood, unmoving, in the teeming crowd of porters and deckhands and passengers and beggars and harbormasters and sailors and even a parrot singing in Arabic and realized that he had never felt so alone. His father, who had been a vicar near the village of Stoke, in Kent, had died of a weak heart, but had left behind a horde of relatives with hearts as strong as bulls, snorting and snuffling their way into old age. All four of his grandparents, two great-grandparents, over two dozen great-aunts and -uncles, and any number of cousins and distant relations surrounded young Theo's early life, so that when he landed in Calcutta, and stood alone in the middle of all these people, he understood for the first time what it was to be wet wood thrown into a fire. So much smoke, but no heat.

To allay his loneliness, Theo threw himself into his duties — first as a cadet at Fort William, followed by a brief stint of fighting during the siege of Bhurtpore, and then as an officer for a canal-building project on the Ganges. The much-debated canal —

whose cost was estimated to run into a few million pounds — was finally commissioned by the government after a period of flooding that killed thousands, followed by a longer period of famine that killed hundreds of thousands. For, as all empires can agree, of the many resources to be exploited, exported, and enslaved, labor was the most lucrative; you couldn't let too many of them die. Once the Crown approved the project, Theo set to work. He was now promoted to assistant to the superintendent of canals, working under Sir Robert Fernsby, a man who'd been stationed in India since the 1770s and considered the colony — with its unbearable heat and its legions of unwashed, unmannered subjects — no better than a flea-ridden dog. He once said to Theo, over a dinner of liver and potato hash, "You can't kill it, of course, but remember, my boy, you bloody well can't be kind to it either."

The canal, which was designed to irrigate the lower Ganges delta, south of Varanasi, encountered many challenges, from the variance in soil textures, ranging from stone boulders to sand to beds of clay, to seasonal swings in drainage, differing profoundly between the dry season and the monsoon, but of these challenges, the greatest of them was that, at a few points along the canal's 140-mile route, the land was so steeply sloped that the velocity of the water, traveling down these slopes, actually raised the bed, carrying forward huge quantities of silt. Theo, sitting up late one night pondering the problem, listening to rain drip from the eaves, reading and rereading a letter from his brother saying that their mother had died, wondered if she had ever sat in darkness and listened to rain. If she had ever heard it with such precision that she could measure distance — from the roof to the ground, from the head to the heart — by its falling.

And then Theo thought, Waterfalls.

His idea of constructing small waterfalls on the steep slopes, along with a series of sluice gates, reduced the velocity of the water, which in turn reduced the deposit of silt considerably. Theo's innovation won such universal acclaim that a renowned Italian hydraulic engineer wrote to him congratulating him on his ingenuity, he was elected to the Fellowship of the Royal Society, and last, but not least, Sir Fernsby threw him a ball. And it was at this ball that Theo Mortimer met Clarissa Hughes.

Clarissa Hughes, the daughter of a deputy governor for the East India Company, was not the most beautiful woman at the ball, but she was the most attractive. What made her so? Not her dress, which was of a pale-green color and not very flattering. Nor her bosom, which was modest and unimpressive when pitted against the voluminous and powdered décolletage of her companions. What then? When Theo noticed her, she was talking to three of those well-endowed companions. The group stood along the far side of the ballroom, and Clarissa, Theo could clearly tell, was regaling them with a story that lit up the faces of her companions — all of whom were quite pretty, and utterly enthralled. Though he couldn't hear a word, Theo watched her, also rapt. Her face, lit by candles, perspiring slightly, seemed mundane and magnificent, both at once. How could that be? And then Clarissa did something. She did something that Theo would never forget and would never forgive. In the telling of her story, at some point of climax, Clarissa lifted her arm (perhaps her loveliest aspect) and swept it in an arc across her body, as if she were sweeping away everything — plates, glasses, food, wine, cutlery, flowers, napkins, everything — off a table. Theo held his breath. So, it seemed, did her companions. Such an amazing, assured, and grandiose sweep! What could possibly come next? In that moment, Clarissa and her companions were interrupted by a man (a cavalry officer, Theo recognized him from a brief meeting) asking one of the young ladies (not Clarissa) to dance.

Theo sighed. As it turned out, he was never to find out what came next in the story. But what came next for Theo? The obvious: He fell in love.

Given Clarissa's standing, with respect to power and wealth, against Theo's modest income and relatively unknown family, a marriage between the two would seem out of the question. But convergence is everything. The ball in his honor, the waterfalls, the sluice gates, the Italian engineer, the Royal Society, the ego. They all came together in a crescendo of confidence, perhaps even arrogance, and found Theo at the Tollygunge Club, asking Clarissa's father for her hand in marriage. William Hughes agreed. The young man, he later told his wife, seemed so damn *dogged*. When his wife raised an objection, Clarissa's father held up a hand and said, "*That* is what I want in a son-in-law, my dear. Doggedness. There is, in my estimation, no greater determinant of success in life."

They had a garden wedding and honeymooned in Ooty.

After the wedding, they settled in Varanasi, on a lush estate along the Ganges. Two years later, little Lillian was born. Theo adored her from the start, as he had adored nothing else — with a passion that was unrelenting, that no waterfall or sluice gate could restrain. But the baby was sickly. She refused to gain weight. They took her to the best doctors, even to a few native healers, but none of them were able to help. After three years of near-constant worry and excruciating anxiety, it was decided that Clarissa would take little Lillian to England for treatment. They set sail in late winter; the night before their departure, Theo bent over Lillian's sleeping body, hardly heavier than when she'd been born, took her small hand in his, and wept.

The plan was to meet them in London, but he couldn't take furlough for two years; when he finally arrived at the home Clarissa had rented in Mayfair, he found that Lillian had died during his ship voyage. And what was more, Clarissa was pregnant again, by a man she refused to name. Theo looked at her. He couldn't recall why he'd married her. He said, "How did she die?"

"Marasmus."

"Marasmus? What is marasmus?"

"How should I know? Talk to the doctor."

Theo grabbed her arm, the very arm that had arced so gracefully, telling a story whose end he would never know, and said, "You don't know how our daughter died?"

"Starvation," Clarissa hissed. "She died of starvation."

Theo let go of her arm. Starvation? He, who had built a canal to irrigate fields that fed millions, could not save his own daughter from hunger.

After he returned to India, Sir Fernsby called Theo into his office and told him there was a problem. "What sort of problem?" Theo asked, thinking that the canal needed repairs or the slopes needed to be flattened, but instead Sir Fernsby said, "There's a wolf maundering about."

A wolf?

"Killed some livestock, apparently. Causing a ruckus."

"I didn't know there were wolves so close to Varanasi."

"There aren't. Probably a fox. The natives are too stupid to know the difference."

Theo nodded, but he was thinking of the ball, of the tiny sliver of a moment before he'd noticed Clarissa. It was then, and only then, that he'd been a man: strong, a solver, a god. God enough to wed water to land, and land to water, pronouncing them famineless, floodless, fruitful, one lying beneath the other like a new bride. He'd known such power; he'd been that powerful. And yet, here he was now.

"Send one of your boys," Fernsby said. "Tell him to kill it. Hell, tell him to kill *something*."

"I'll go."

Fernsby raised an eyebrow.

"I'll go tonight."

"Have you ever been on a hunt?"

"Well, no. But in Bhurtpore — "

"No tigers, no elephants, no boar?"

"No."

"No deer?"

Exasperated, Theo said, "With all due respect, Sir Fernsby, hunting a tiger is hardly the same as hunting a wolf. And then, one famished enough to come near the villages."

Fernsby smiled. "Hunting is hunting, my boy. The smallest creature, a rabbit say, can demolish your pride."

Theo nodded again. He set out that night. He went on horse-back, riding along the outskirts of Varanasi. First through the fields, policing the penned livestock, and then back home during the early morning hours. But the goats bleated at the sound of his horse, and the cattle and the pigs shuffled and grew scared, so after a few days, he started to walk, the rifle slung over his shoulder. A wolf, a fox. It did not matter. Kill something, Fernsby had said, and Theo intended to. He walked. He walked and walked. He was nearing home — the sun beginning to rise, the scent of the Ganges heavy, sodden like wet leaves — when he looked out at the sandbar, the one beyond the Shiva temple that was being built by the Scindias, and decided to row out to it. Why? He could never again remember why, but there was a boat tethered to a pole stuck into the water and Theo simply climbed into the boat and began to row. When he reached the sandbar, he looked back at Varanasi, and thought, Three thousand years. Roughly. Why stand for three thousand years when a thing as trivial as a wolf can terrorize you? And then, as if he'd conjured the very thing he'd mocked, he turned and the wolf — *Was* it a wolf? He couldn't see clearly. Not in the gray gloom of a winter morning, but there it was: silver, *actually* silver, metallic and molten against the mist. Not a hundred yards away. Looking back at him. Simply looking.

What did it see? What was there to see? The only things there are ever to see: man, water, memory.

Theo raised his rifle. How had a wolf gotten onto a sandbar? No matter. Theo aimed. He squeezed the trigger. The wolf fell. And in the moment that it fell, the sun, too, was stricken. Plunging back into the horizon as if it, too, had been shot.

Theo walked toward it. And in the exact number of steps it had taken to reach Clarissa, he reached the wolf. When he looked down at the body, and met its glowing red eyes (dying, diminishing), he began to weep. Not from regret (though he felt it) and not from sadness (though he knew he would always feel it), but because he understood in that moment that his daughter was dead. And that what had taken her was the kind of demon that you fed and fed but was never sated; that you coaxed with every love imaginable but was never nourished. But this wolf? It was not that demon. And as Theo knew, you can't slay a near demon and you can't slay a far demon, you have to slay *the* demon. Nothing less. And what more did he know? That what he had slain was not a demon at all, near or far. What he had slain, Theo knew, was a god.

Chapter 4

Sagar left his parents' house in Rajahmundry and returned to Varanasi alone. The plan was that they and Sandeep would come later, after making arrangements to view Rajni. He arrived back at his flat in the evening, and though he was tired, he couldn't resist, he had to go see her, the River Ganga. On the way, he bought a packet of samosas and a cup of tea, and then he sat down on the steps of Scindia Ghat. The river was silver and indigo, and as he sat drinking his tea, it turned to black ink as the moon rose higher. The stone steps still held the heat of the day, and he saw, across the sandbar, the lights of Mata Mandir and the apartment blocks in Ratanpur.

In his pocket was a photograph of Rajni his amma had given him. "It's from a few years ago," she'd said, "but I hear she's even more beautiful now." He took it out and held it in his palm.

He didn't know what he feared more: marriage or moving to Montana. In a way, marriage too was a new country, perhaps the most unknown and alien of all. And though he held Rajni's photo in his hand, and though he'd seen photos of the Cotton River and the Cotton River Valley and Mansfield (which was the town where the dam project was headquartered), he couldn't imagine either. Neither she nor the place they would soon move to made any sense. To contemplate them was like walking into a theater in the middle of a foreign film.

In the days before his family arrived, he spent all his free hours at the Ganga. His favorite time was still the morning, before work, when the white river mist, as he made his way to the ghats, swirled around him and the world became unreal. Without solidity. The little boys who shouted and whooped as they raced in front of him, what seemed to him just a few meters away, within arm's reach, disappeared as soon as he turned a corner. And the cows lowing their long mournful lows, their eyes and their noses wet with the same mist that enveloped them, ambling past him, just at the end of the alley, their white bodies as sluggish and aglow as desert caravans — they, too, evaporated when he reached out to touch them, simply a thicker mist within the mist. He thought on some mornings that he might wander like this for months, years. How would he know the passage of time? How is it measured if one never sees a hummingbird dart, or watches a continent drift?

He knew he would miss them all: the mystics and the worshippers; the ambling cows and the sleeping dogs; the bodies of the dead, the funeral pyres, the lost faces of the living; the fishermen and their nets, hopelessly tangled and knotted, slumped in dismal mounds on the shore, and yet, when swung from the stern of a fishing boat, the arc of them so graceful and so silver and so alive, they could've been the wings of a fabled, storybook bird. He watched them pull in the fish. He watched them with such interest, such passionate longing, he began to understand he was trying to memorize everything, every detail, for when he was in Montana, for when this moment would be as fabled as those birds.

His parents arrived. Sandeep had stayed behind. He was disinterested, he'd told his parents, in these farcical, fusty traditions. His parents brought with them a new set of clothes for Sagar — a tailored shirt, slacks, and Bata shoes. His mother insisted he try them on so she could make sure they fit him. They also brought a silk sari and sweets and a gold bangle for Rajni.

The next day, Saturday, was the viewing.

All along their taxi ride, his amma tinkered with her sari, her jewelry. "I hope they appreciate how we're sacrificing," she said. "We could've had our choice of brides, and dowry. All that money. How? How did they lose it? There was so much."

She'd asked the same question off and on for years.

His father was looking out of the window. "Ramachandra has more ideas than sense. That's how." Rajni's father was his father's childhood friend. They'd grown up in the same village. They had a great-great-great-someone in common. The friendship had endured, and yet Sagar could hear the slight disparagement in his father's voice.

When they arrived, and after the tearful embraces and exclamations of "It's been too long" and "You haven't aged a day" and "Where has the time gone," they were shown into the sitting room. It was a fairly large room, and the sofa, where all three were seated, was facing a reed mat laid out on the floor. They were served coffee and plates of snacks. Sagar nibbled the almond burfi. He was nervous. His future wife! Her eyes — he wanted to look into her eyes.

"Uncle, I have to tell you something."

Rajni's father looked at him.

"I've taken a new job. I — we won't be living in Varanasi after marriage. I wanted to tell you before — "

"Why, that's wonderful, Alludu-garu." He was already referring to him as son-in-law. "A dam project? Where in India?"

His father said, "No, no. Not India. In U.S. Some state — what is it called? Yes, yes. Montana."

There was silence, and then, after a long moment, Rajni's father said, "Why, that's even better. U.S.! One could only hope to have such an intelligent, accomplished son-in-law." Though he was smiling, Sagar saw a hint of sorrow pass across his face, or maybe in his voice, and why wouldn't it? To learn, so abruptly, that his elder daughter would soon be whisked away to another country? On the other side of the world? Any father would be sad.

After more chatter, Rajni's father excused himself, and, after a few minutes in a back bedroom, Sagar guessed, led Rajni down the hallway into the living room. She sat down on the mat; her father sat down in a chair next to the sofa. A female relative, or maybe a neighbor, sat next to Rajni.

Sagar, nervous, studied his hands. His mother nudged him. He looked up and was overwhelmed. Such a lovely woman. She was in a green sari, and its pink border perfectly reflected the blush in Rajni's cheeks — or what he could see of her face, since her head was bent low.

Her father turned to them. "Isn't she a beauty?"

All three agreed.

His amma said, "Where are you working, dear? Your father says you're working as a lecturer."

When she told them, her voice was deeper than Sagar had expected, but sweet to hear, and strangely, also tinged with sorrow, though it was unlike what he had heard in her father's voice — her sorrow was sharper, splintered. Had her father told her about Montana when he'd gone to get her? He must have.

His father asked Rajni what her salary was, and when she told him, he said, "Well now, that's respectable. I'm sure you'll have no trouble finding a job in U.S. An even better job."

Rajni said nothing. Sagar looked at his father, annoyed. He had explained to him that Rajni wouldn't be able to work in America, not until she got a work permit, which might take months. Oblivious, his father said, "Go ahead, Sagar. Ask her something. Go ahead."

Sagar struggled to think of a question. One that was meaningful. Intelligent. And not insulting to *her* intelligence. He thought, Maybe something to do with Sanskrit . . .

Rajni's father jumped in. "Why don't we give them some private time. That way they won't be so shy." He turned to Sagar. "Why don't you two go out to the back garden? The guavas are coming in. Go on, Beti, show Sagar the tree. Have a chat. Go on."

Rajni led, and Sagar followed her to the back of the house and into the garden. The guava tree was at its center and reached nearly two stories high. There were a few flowering trees at the perimeter of the garden, and a bench, but Rajni went straight to the guava tree and leaned against its twisting trunk. She looked not at her hands or at the ground, as he thought she might, but straight at him.

He nearly stepped back.

Her eyes. He thought of dense undergrowth. He thought of the surface of the moon. He thought, Look away. Look into the leaves. Look for the guavas coming in. He said, "Your father is right. The tree is full of them." And then because he could think of nothing else, "When was it planted?"

Rajni said, "When we were children." And then she said, "Forgive me. I know. I know that — "

Her courage seemed to be failing her. Sagar wanted to reassure her, but he had no idea what she meant to say.

She finally blurted it out headlong, in a torrent. "I — you see, Mr. Sagar — I have to ask, it's a strange request, I know, but I have to ask you — not to marry me."

Sagar smiled, from the shock. Or maybe she was joking? "I'm sorry — I don't . . ."

"Please don't agree to this marriage."

"Don't agree? I don't understand. Our families — it's been decided. Is it because of America? Do you not want to go?"

Now she looked down at her hands. She was silent. Something rustled in the guava tree. "The truth is, Mr. Sagar, I've fallen in love. With a colleague. We hope to marry. But obviously . . ."

They stood in silence.

What was he supposed to say?

Finally, he said, "I see." The words were two kites falling to the ground. Two bells, aching to be rung. "You should. Of course you should. I'll just — it's simple, really. I'll tell them we've decided not to — "

"No! You can't."

He opened his mouth, but nothing came out.

She said, "My sister. If I bring this shame upon my family, go against my family, you know just as well as I that she'll never be able to marry. It'll be her ruin. It'll be all our ruins."

He looked at her, perplexed. "I don't understand. What is it you want me to do?"

She looked at him again. This time her eyes pleading, afraid, as if they were two rivers emptying into a strange and precarious sea. "Tell them you like my sister. Tell them you prefer her to me. That way, our family's honor will be saved. And we can all marry . . ."

"*What?* Your sister? Who is she? I haven't even — "

"She's more beautiful than me." Her voice was firm — firmer than he would've guessed it could be. "One other thing," she said. "Please, Mr. Sagar, you can't speak a word of this to my papa. Promise me. Promise me you'll never speak of this to him."

He was flustered. Speechless. It was surreal — this moment, this woman, this tree. Who was this sister? Obviously, he couldn't marry her. It was ludicrous to suggest — maybe there was something wrong with her. Maybe they were trying to foist someone disturbed or damaged or deranged onto him. He said, "I'm sorry, but I can't do that. I don't know her in the least."

"You don't know me."

He was silent. He wanted to say, But in a way, I do. He'd known *of* her since he'd been a boy, and that seemed to him a kind of familiarity. An absent companion through the years of his life. "Miss Rajni," he said, "I understand your dilemma. I do. But I'm sure we can convince our families to — "

"Our position is far different from yours."

Did she mean her and her sister's? Or the position of all women?

"Please."

Sagar was looking at her, but he was thinking about sediment. What moved it from one place to another? Erosion. And what was erosion but the wearing away of something? Something you might've believed in all your life? "It's not that easy," he said.

"No?"

They stood. His mind went blank. And before him were only the green of the leaves and the green of Rajni's sari and the green of the choice he was too paralyzed to make.

She clearly took his silence for acquiescence. She turned and walked to a nearby window. She said, "Janoo? Are you there? Come. Come to the window. I need something."

A pause. And then a shutter creaked open.

"What is it, Rajni? What do you need?"

He looked at the woman in the window. Her arm lifted to the open shutter. She was positioned a bit to the left of the window, and the room behind her was hidden in shadow. Her yellow sari, against this darkness, devoured all the light in the garden. Looking at her, he felt as if he were looking at the painting of a woman hanging in a museum. He blinked. She was beautiful, yes, in a way more feral than her sister, more determined, but he couldn't possibly marry a painting. He said, "I want to talk to her."

He saw Rajni stiffen, as if the request were beyond her powers to give.

"I can't give you an answer without first talking to her."

Rajni hesitated, and then she moved to go back inside. She said, "I'll say you asked for more tea. Hurry." She glanced once at her sister, and he saw her smile, but the sister didn't smile back.

Chapter 5

Both Rajni and this man Sagar were looking at her. Why were they staring at her like that?

Rajni called her to the window, and then she went back to standing under the guava tree, next to him. Both waiting, it seemed.

Her sister looked confident. He looked uncomfortable. As if his clothes were itchy. He looked away after a moment, almost embarrassed, and Janavi thought, Why is *he* embarrassed?

She looked again at Rajni.

When she'd been helping Rajni dress, before the viewing, she'd said to her, "It's so sudden. I wonder why they want the wedding so soon." Rajni had said, cryptically, "It's already written, Janoo. In the stars. Who marries whom."

What did that have to do with anything?

The guava tree shaded them, and in the mottled light, Janavi thought they made a lovely couple. Rajni in her green sari, merging with its leaves like a forest nymph, and the groom with his thick hair and mustache and bright coal-black eyes like one of the satyrs she'd read about in her mythology books from primary school. But then, without warning, Rajni left the garden. The groom remained under the tree for a moment, and then walked to the window. He said, "Would you like to come outside? Or — "

"Where has Rajni gone?"

He looked away, back toward the guava tree, and said, "Your sister says it was planted when you were children. Is that right? It must have been just a sapling."

She stared at him.

"I tried to grow one as a boy. It held on for a year or two, put out a few guavas, all of them eaten by squirrels, and then it died." He laughed nervously and said, "I'm a serial killer of plants. I couldn't grow a cactus in a desert."

A cactus in a desert? Why was he even talking to her? And where was Rajni? And the *guava tree*? Why was he talking to her about the guava tree?

He said, still in a pinched voice, "I don't know your name. What is it? I've only heard them call you Janoo."

"It's Janavi."

He looked at her, and then his face spread with a curious light. He smiled. And it was then that his gaze relaxed, opened; the window in a dark and suffocating room opening onto a sun-dappled river. She felt it again then, with sudden force: the Ganga surging around her, and that moment, years ago, when she'd almost joined Amma, but had, instead, turned back toward life.

He laughed and said, "Janoo! Of course. You're named after the Ganga." And then, growing more serious, he said, "You see, Miss Janavi, your sister — "

Her papa burst through the door. He looked from one to the other and said, "Come, come, Mr. Sagar. The tea is getting cold. Come inside."

Janavi was left at the window, perplexed. A squirrel climbed up the guava tree and disappeared into its branches, and watching it, she couldn't help but smile.

Her papa and Rajni came to the back bedroom, where she was organizing her case files. Janavi jumped up, thinking the wedding details were settled and that she could now meet the groom's family. "When? When will it be?"

Neither spoke, and then her papa said, "They want to marry you."

Janavi nearly laughed. Or maybe she did. "What?"

"It seems the boy likes you better."

The window! Her thoughts roiled, collapsed, and then roiled again. "I don't understand. They want . . . ?"

"Yes, Beti. It seems so."

Janavi said nothing. It was a joke. It *had* to be. But it wasn't, was it? "Papa — I can't. How can I? What about Rajni? What about — "

"I'll be fine, Janoo."

Janavi looked at her sister. "Raju, what are you saying? I don't . . ."

Rajni turned to their papa. She said, "Papa, you should go see if they need anything. I'll bring her out."

Their papa looked from one to the other. Once he'd left, Rajni said, "Janoo, do this for me."

"You? What? But *why*?"

She was half smiling. Or maybe suppressing a full smile. "I've fallen in love. With a colleague. His name's Pavan. He teaches Hindi and Urdu." Here she grew shy and said, "I met him on my first day. He asked to borrow a pen. When I handed it to him, he said, 'Is it too soon to ask for your heart?'" She was practically swooning now, further irritating Janavi. "Isn't that romantic, Janoo? He's going to ask Papa . . . but he can't do that if . . ."

"You've fallen — so? Call this off. Tell them — tell them anything. Tell them you don't like him. Tell them you don't want this match."

"After the families made the promise? All that time ago? It would kill Papa. He'd be humiliated. And you wouldn't ever be able to marry."

"I don't want to marry."

"He's a good man."

Janavi hadn't hit her sister since they'd been children, but she wanted to hit her now. She closed her fist. "Then *you* marry him."

"I'm in love, Janoo." And then, maybe because Janavi seemed unmoved by her plea, she said, "Please don't make me choose."

So Rajni would make *her* choose? Everything — from her job to the promise she'd made to Amma and even the memory of Bulbul — raced through her mind and left behind the fading images of all the children she might've helped, who might've helped her.

"There has to be another way," she said, her voice low and hesitant.

Rajni took her sister's hand, unfisted it, and held it tight. Then she led her out of the room.

The most voluble protests came from Papa. He said, "It's not protocol. For the younger sister to be married first. It's just not done. What will happen to Rajni?" He turned to Rajni. "Rajni? What will happen to you, my dear?"

"I'll be fine. Believe me, Papa. I'll be perfectly fine."

Janavi saw Sagar's parents look from one to the other.

Her papa turned to Sagar. "But — why not Rajni? Why Janavi? How do you know?"

Sagar stammered. "They're both lovely."

"Then *why?*"

"It's better, Papa," Rajni finally said. "I don't want to go to U.S. I want to stay here."

Janavi looked at her, astonished. It was then that she learned that in addition to being married, she was also moving — to America.

Sagar and his parents left, and in the coming days, Janavi, unable to think a single coherent thought, walked through Varanasi in a daze, unable to sleep, unable to comprehend, a cloak of despair, or simply blankness, thrown over her. A week later, a marriage broker contacted Papa and said there was a boy whose parents had been in touch. He was from a good family, based in Patna. His father was a bank manager. The boy had two older sisters, both married and settled with children. They were interested in one of his daughters, either one, and were requesting only the minimum of dowry. Papa asked the broker a few questions, and incredibly, learned that the boy worked at the same junior college as Rajni. Did she know him? Rajni looked at Janavi slyly and said, "I might've seen him, at the faculty meetings. I can't recall."

It was decided soon afterward.

I suppose it all worked out in the end, her papa said.

When she told Ms. Sujata that she was quitting, her boss must've seen the morose look on Janavi's face, because she said, "You could continue, couldn't you? After marriage."

"We're moving. To America."

"I see," she said, and then, obviously trying to cheer Janavi, she grinned and said, "I hear there are children there too."

Janavi nodded miserably.

Just as Janavi was about to leave her office, Ms. Sujata said, "You were right."

"About what?"

She smiled. "You do have a big heart."

On her last day at ChildDefense, Janavi cleaned out her desk and then rode home on the bus, holding a box of her things in her lap — a sweater, a photo of Amma, an old lunch box she'd forgotten in the back of a drawer — and she thought, No, Papa, it hasn't worked out at all.

The two couples were married under the same muhurtham.

Janavi went through the entire ceremony without once meeting Sagar's eyes. At the reception, held at BrijRama Palace (Papa said the cost wasn't so exorbitant, since he was combining what had been saved for both their weddings), they were seated on a stage, on ridiculous-looking fake thrones, with Janavi and Sagar on one side of a low table, and Rajni and Pavan on the other. They were seated close enough together that they could've all spoken, but none of them did. She had nothing to say to Sagar, and for his part, Sagar looked dazed, bewildered, as if he'd been pushed onto a stage in the middle of an unknown play, which she supposed he had. They both had. As for Rajni, she was radiant — wearing a pink-and-silver lehenga, her face glowing with what Janavi could only assume was love, delight, and awe. Why awe? She hardly blinked, gazing at her new husband. They were holding hands and at one point she heard Pavan whisper to Rajni, loud enough for Janavi to hear, "You're all mine now." She saw Rajni smile, blushing. Pavan was dressed in a fitted charcoal suit and a pink tie to match Rajni's lehenga, while Sagar was wearing the same-colored suit with a royal blue tie to match Janavi's lehenga. And yet, even though they were dressed so alike, Pavan exuded a suavity, an ease, and what felt to Janavi a physical prowess, maybe even a gallantry, that Sagar lacked.

It was most obvious as the guests filed past, handing Janavi and Rajni bouquets of flowers and offering their congratulations. Pavan, Janavi noticed, was the most loquacious. He laughed heartily with his friends and complimented the aunties on their jewelry and their saris and shook hands with the uncles as they admired his new bride. He even pinched the cheeks of the babies and passed out toffees to the children. Where did he get toffees? When she looked, Janavi saw that his suit pockets were filled with them. How had he managed to plan such a thing? She looked then at Sagar, staring out at the vast reception hall, lost in his thoughts, an affected smile on his face. He was clearly uncomfortable, and greeted the guests with a shy, distant handshake or namaste. Witnessing his discomfort, and her own, and Rajni's thrall, she saw that Pavan was the luminary, the charismatic one, the masterful one, though, hadn't Rajni been equally masterful, if not more?

Chapter 6

On their wedding night, which, according to custom, was the third night after the wedding ceremony, Sagar entered the marital bedroom and sat down. There was a glass of warm milk on the table. The bed was littered with pink and red rose petals. He waited, and then he waited some more, assuming Janavi would be led into the room at any moment. He was now married, that alone was bewildering, and what was more, it was not at all to the woman he'd thought all his life he'd be married to. And her name was Janavi!

Maybe that was when his mind had turned. Maybe that was when his mind had finally *heard* Rajni's request — when Janavi had told him her name. Of course it was Janavi — one of the Ganga's many names. One of 108, to be exact.

Some of the others? The Ganges, Bhagirathi, Nikita, Jaahnukanya, Sapteshwari, Sureshwari, Bhagvati, Urvijaya, Chitraani, Tridhara, Shubhra, Vaishnavi, Vishnupadi, Bhagvatpadi, Tripathaga, Payoshnika, Mahabhadra, Mandakini, Meghna, Meghal, Gangika, Gange, Gangeshwari, Alaknanda, and then, the Janavi: like Varanasi, yet another beauty that could not be fathomed by one name alone.

He thought, with sudden boyish delight, I've been studying the Ganga for years, and now I'm married to her.

He dozed. After an hour or so, he woke with a start and rubbed his eyes and got up and walked to the window, and that was when he saw her, his river, his wife, on the floor next to the bed, asleep.

The days went on like that: They traveled to Rajahmundry, to his parents' house, and then back up to Varanasi. She helped him pack up his flat. She told him what vegetables to bring home from the market. Sometimes she went to the market herself. She hardly spoke to him. He tried to start conversations, make plans, talk to her about America and Montana and the Cotton River, but she responded in monosyllables, if at all.

She was angry.

He wanted to say, It was *your* sister who wanted this, not me. He once said to Janavi, "I'm not that bad. If you get to know me."

She looked at him as if he were a street vendor hawking a cheap plastic toy.

Another time, he said to her, "It'll be better once we get to America. You'll see."

She said, "Only children believe such things."

She slept on the sofa, or sometimes he would. He considered coming up with some excuse, such as visa issues, and leaving her with her family in Varanasi; letting her continue with her life in India. He knew she'd had a job with a child welfare agency before they'd married. Maybe she could resume her work there. And they could live separately. And then eventually divorce, after a respectable amount of time had passed. But that would bring even more shame to her family, and to his, than if he'd simply rejected Rajni's proposal.

Sometimes he watched her sleeping face, or her back while she was turned away from him, and thought, Women and love. Love and women. I know nothing about one and less about the other.

Jena

Ganges River, 1835

Despite being two hundred thousand square kilometers in size, the Thar Desert, also known as the Great Indian Desert, has only one river: the Luni. Jena never saw the Luni. Her entire life lived in the Thar, twenty-two years (all of them spent in the northwest corner, in what would one day become Pakistan), and she had only ever known water to come from small, murky wells, a few shallow saltwater lakes. Rain, too, she knew very little of. When she'd been a young girl, a lone man had emerged over the sand dunes, in the moonlight, riding a camel. That of course was not unusual, but what *was* unusual was how talkative this man had been. Jena had never known anyone so talkative. And so: Since Jena knew nothing of running water and nothing of talkative men, what *did* she know about? She knew the silence between her mother and father. She knew the greater silence of the desert. Or was the silence between her mother and father greater? She knew the buzzing of flies; she knew the exact contour, the precise dimensions of the quiet they left behind when they died.

That night, the man who'd come out of the moonlight settled himself outside their tent, on the rug, and after dinner had been eaten, and the tobacco was being smoked, he began to tell stories. Strange stories, fantastical stories. Stories that, even at the age of six, Jena was hard-pressed to believe. For instance, the man told of a creature, one of the stealthiest and most dangerous in the forest (What is a forest? Jena asked, for which she was shushed), that was spotted and strong enough to kill a man. Spotted how? Jena's father asked. "Their fur is the color of these sand dunes," the man said, "with black spots. But some of them have white fur, with black spots. But those," he continued, "live in the snow." Snow? Then he told the story of a camel that had died by drowning. Jena of course assumed the camel had drowned in sand, maybe during a sandstorm, but the man said no, it had drowned in water. Jena looked over at the man's camel, drowsing alongside the tent. She tried to imagine it drowning but how could it? How could there be enough water in one place to drown such a big animal? Obviously, the man must be lying. Or exaggerating. Even Jena's father seemed to think so, the way he was taking long, pensive drags of the pipe and nodding into the fire. When she looked at the man's camel again, it had raised its head and was looking straight back at her. It had that smug look on its face that camels have. It seemed to be imagining *her* drowning. And as it did, it seemed to be saying, *Jena, it will have to be you. Or it will have to be me. But one of us, sooner or later, will have to drown.*

Jena, at the age of twenty-two, rarely thought about the man in the moonlight and the spotted creature and the camel drowning. She, like her parents before her and their parents before them, was a nomad. She and her husband had four children, five goats, and two camels. The last time she'd been pregnant, she'd ruptured something during labor and had hemorrhaged so much blood that the midwife had warned her against another pregnancy. Tell your husband, the midwife had said, Tell him to be careful from now on. Jena had looked up at the old woman, through a haze of rank blood and bloated flies and plundering weakness, and had known she never would.

During the fifth month of her next pregnancy, outside of Bikaner, Jena and her husband were joined by a man named Nasir. He and his camel were sitting under a khejri tree and when they passed by him, the man got up, coaxed his camel to its feet, and started to follow them. A hundred or so steps later, Jena's husband stopped. He told Jena to mind the goats and the camels, and then he walked back to talk to the man. When he returned, he didn't say anything, but that night, as Jena was preparing dinner, he told her the man would be joining them. Knowing her husband, Jena said, "What is he giving you in return?"

"Salt," her husband said.

"Doesn't he have a family?" she asked.

"Widower," he replied.

After that, the man stayed with them. He sometimes walked with his camel behind them. At other times, he disappeared into the desert for an hour or two, or for an entire afternoon or evening, though when Jena woke up, she always found him asleep near their tent, wrapped tightly in his blanket against the desert cold. He spoke very little, hardly at all. In fact, she didn't know the sound of his voice until the day — Jena's husband had gone the night before to the market in a nearby village — she walked up the sand dune on which he was sleeping to give him his morning tea and some roti. The sun had not yet fully risen. Only the edges of the sand dunes, and the sky just above them, were beginning to brighten. Pinking, bluing, both at once, as if two birds were squabbling over the nest of sky. Jena set the plate of dry roti and the mug of tea down next to Nasir. She rose to leave. When she'd walked a few steps, she heard the sand shift, ever so slightly, and then she heard a voice say, "What is that tinkling?"

They both held their breath. What tinkling?

"Take a step," he said. When she did, he said, "It's your anklets."

She laughed. She said, "I've gotten so used to them I don't even hear them anymore."

Not once did he look at her face, nor did he look at her ankles. In fact, it seemed to her he was talking to the wind, or the sand. The sky. When she was halfway down the sand dune, she heard him say, "You sound like water."

She paused and then she walked back to the tent, where the children were beginning to stir. She looked at them, their sleeping faces, and thought again of the man who'd told her the stories of the spotted creature and the drowned camel. The memory of that night, when she'd been a girl and had been seated by a fire, listening intently, came back to her with a force so sudden and so fearsome that it nearly crumpled her to her knees. She walked back out of the tent. She looked at the horizon, the sun now risen, an orange ball mocking her life, mocking every one of the years since the man who'd told tales had stepped out of the moonlight. For she'd thought back then, back when she was six, or maybe a little after, that her life would be like that: Out of the wild duned desert there would emerge, on some moonlit nights, glimpses of other worlds — creatures that could not possibly exist, waters treacherously and tantalizingly deep — and that it would be these glimpses, these imagined worlds, that would give meaning to the rest. But it hadn't been so. There had never been another teller of tales; only the days, one after another after another after another. Breathtaking in their monotony. And now here she stood, at the age of twenty-two, pregnant, with a husband, a tent, four children, five goats, two camels, and the same sun, rising and rising, setting and setting. And the same legions of flies crawling over every sweetness: her children's faces, the cups of morning tea, the dreams she had dreamt without even knowing she'd been dreaming them.

In that moment, for some reason she could not understand, she looked down at her ankles. And then she looked up at the sand dune where Nasir was sleeping. But he had already drunk his tea and was gone.

Toward the beginning of her seventh month of pregnancy, Jena woke in the middle of the night and found the blanket beneath her sodden, nearly dripping. It took her only a moment; she knew what the wetness was. She turned to her husband. She was so faint she could hardly say his name loud enough to wake him. When she did, he dressed in the dark and woke the drowsy camel and then he set off for the nearest village to fetch the midwife. As she lay inside the tent, shivering in the soaked blankets, she heard her husband shout something to Nasir and then, a few moments later, she saw Nasir standing at the entrance to the tent. He stood for a long time, longer than she could keep her eyes open, and then he left. He returned, maybe minutes, maybe hours later. She wanted to speak, she wanted to say, I heard them too late. My anklets. I heard them too late and now I'll never hear them again. But she couldn't. The pain came in waves. He bent over her, a candle in his hand, perhaps to see if she was still breathing, and when he did, she felt above her the heat of his breath, his body. The cadence of his concern. So unlike her husband's. So unlike anything she had ever known. And so, after many years, Jena saw it again: a glimpse of other worlds. She blinked. She closed her eyes. The ache that settled inside of her then was greater than the blood that was leaving her, and in the wake of this wasteland, she gathered all the strength she could muster, and she whispered to him, "Water."

Nasir set the candle on the ground and rose to fetch the

waterskin, but she raised her arm to stop him. She said, weakly, "No. Tell me more about water."

He seated himself cross-legged beside her. So close that his leg was touching the side of her arm. And as if they had always been talking, as if he were simply continuing a story he'd always been telling her, he said, "There are two kinds of water. Still and running. Still water I know you've seen. But running? Have you seen running water?"

She shook her head no. But a moment later, despite the excruciating pain and the loss of blood, her eyes brightened. She said, "I've heard it though. My anklets. Do you remember my anklets?"

"Yes, yes, just like your anklets. Naughty, just like they are." He laughed and then he said, "Water runs in different ways. Your anklets are trickling water. There's rushing water, too, which is anything but naughty. It can be dangerous. Like a thousand chinkara, fleeing, stampeding."

"Is it really like that? Could it drown a camel?"

"A camel? Why, it could drown this desert."

They were quiet. The pain a fist, punching through her insides. Jena tried to imagine the desert, drenched now in starlight, gushing with water. All the dunes, with their graceful curves, and all the khejri trees and all the animals and all the insects and all the people and their belongings and all the villages and towns and all the mustard fields with their carpets of yellow flowers spilled on the ground like squandered sunlight. All the anklets. All of them. Underwater. "Have you seen the sea?" she asked.

"No," he said, "but I've seen rivers."

"The Luni?"

"Yes. And the Ravi. And the Ganga. I saw the Ganga in full flood, just after the monsoons. Sweeping away trees like they were matchsticks. Entire villages like playthings. Brown as tea, the water. But deceptive in its power, its beauty. You can't behold such a thing and ever be the same again."

"Why?"

He looked at her then. Into her eyes. "Why," he said. "Why, indeed?" And she looked back into his. And for the briefest moment, there was no pain. For the briefest moment, she thought she might be looking into depths deep enough to drown a camel. Into the depths of a forest teeming with spotted creatures, each of them full of stealth and danger and desire enough to kill a man. She looked away. She wanted to weep. She wanted her body to shun its sorrows. She wanted her baby to not die. A breeze entered the tent; the candle flickered. The children snored lightly. The desert beyond their tent, and the whole of the world beyond the desert, was nothing. Or, if it was not nothing, then it was a wheel, and they were its still and shining center.

With struggling breath, with perhaps the last of it, she said, "I want to see it one day."

"What?"

"The Ganga."

"You will."

She grimaced and then smiled. Or maybe she smiled and then grimaced. She said, "Do I really sound like water?"

"No," he said. "Water sounds like you."

Jena's husband wanted to leave her body to the vultures.

Nasir suggested she be cremated. "Why waste the wood," her husband said, then he looked at him pointedly and said, "Why do you care?"

In the end, Nasir exchanged his camel for her ashes. He traveled on foot to Varanasi. He could've taken her ashes to a place on the Ganga that was closer — Haridwar, for instance — but he'd seen the Ganga for the first time in Varanasi, standing on the steps of Scindia Ghat, and he wanted to stand again on those steps with Jena. He wanted her to see the slowly sinking Shiva temple, its dome petaled like red salvia in the evening light; he wanted her to see the distant sandbank, the damp stone, and the radiance of a river that had no end. He wanted her to feel holiness as he had felt holiness.

When he arrived, the sky hung low with heavy clouds. The stone steps were damp. Puddled. There were only two worshippers, one in the water, hands clasped in prayer, and the other seated on the bottommost step, looking intently toward the river or maybe at the other bather. A couple with their small child shared a packet of yogurt rice and a bit of pickle, using a banana leaf for a plate. A barber, who'd set up a stand at the top of the ghat, was staring listlessly at a goat tied to a nearby post. Both eating something, strangely rhythmic in their chewing. Nasir set his pack down on one of the stone steps. He felt for the urn that held Jena's ashes. He'd felt for it so often, had slept with it in his hands on so many nights, that he could map its surface as he had once mapped the caves and the mountains, the minerals and the monsoons of his wife's body. To be children again, he thought, as he and his wife had once been. To feast before knowing the word *famine*.

He walked down to the bottom step. The seated worshipper eyed him — his dusty clothes, his bare feet, his weathered face, his sunburnt hair — and then turned away. Nasir took out the urn. He placed it on the warm, wet stone. The water, in the turgid, late afternoon light, was gray and swift. He looked at the Shiva temple. More askew than he remembered it, as if it were a sloop in a gusty wind. He'd heard once that the temple was sinking because the stone was too heavy and that eventually it would be completely submerged in the water. He tried to imagine it, the temple, its ornate carvings, slowly becoming sediment. But, of course, he couldn't. Some things are too beautiful to imagine gone. But what he did know was the heaviness of stone. What he knew — he saw his dead wife, he saw Jena — was that each of us carries it within us, this heaviness, this stone.

He untied his dhoti.

He picked up the urn.

He stepped into the river.

He walked until he was waist deep.

He walked until he was chest deep.

He wanted to walk farther still. He felt the river tugging at him, urging him to walk farther still. But he'd too often entered the country of death. For a time, for a little while longer, he wanted to know another country.

He released her. He watched her float away.

She was now the river. Or, as he knew it to be, the river was now she.

Part II

Chapter 7

Sagar's and Janavi's visas finally arrived, and at the beginning of March, they boarded a plane for Delhi. From there, they boarded another plane to Frankfurt. And then another plane to Chicago. They waited in Chicago for eight hours, and then boarded the final plane to Billings, Montana. Sagar had an international driver's license, and he used it to rent a car at the Billings airport. They loaded their suitcases into the trunk and started driving. It was two hours to Mansfield. Once they passed Billings, there were no lights that Janavi could see. The road, flat, endless, seemed as if it would swallow them whole. Maybe it already had. Maybe the world had ended while they'd been on one of those planes and they were on the other side.

She looked out of the window. The quiet. The dark. Not even another car on the road. All of it was an accident, wasn't it? All of it arbitrary. What had brought them here? What, in the waters of the Ganga, had tugged at her? What had let her go? Janavi blinked. Fear shot through her. She was tired, confused. She couldn't understand where they were. Herself and this man who, from what she could see, was leading them deeper and deeper into nothingness.

After an hour of driving, Janavi said, "Pull over."

Sagar stopped the car, and she got out and vomited.

When she climbed back inside, Sagar said, "It's the nausea. From the plane. I feel like I'm still on it, don't you?"

Janavi looked at him. She wanted to answer, Still on the plane? Suspended between earth and sky? Unable to crash down to one or find comfort in the other? "Yes," she said. "Yes, I do."

Her nausea, upon arrival to the Cotton River Valley, persisted.

They were staying at a motel in Mansfield. Double beds. They hadn't yet started looking for an apartment. Sagar went to his first day of work and Janavi was left in the motel room. They'd gone to the store and bought bread and jam and bananas and potato chips and apples. Her first morning alone, she lay in bed and ate a slice of bread with jam. She made the motel coffee and drank two cups. It was the worst coffee she'd ever tasted. She hoped all the coffee in America didn't taste like this.

America.

She'd seen many, many photos, watched programs on television and movies in theaters, but she'd never seen an America that looked like this. She felt as if she were a child, delighted, anticipating the prize inside the closed fist, but when the cruel magician opened his hand? The toy she'd anticipated? Disappeared, and there was nothing there. An empty palm. The empty, open fields.

She was still in shock.

One day she'd been in Varanasi, starting her career, having finally found her calling, walking the crowded streets, and now . . .

There was a chair outside the door to their room.

Janavi sat for hours. Rajni called every now and then, but she didn't pick up. Instead, she watched the cars pulling in and out, people driving by her on the way to their rooms or as they left the motel. Sometimes, a car slowed down as it passed her. Why were they looking at her like that? Once, a child in the back seat stuck his tongue out at her, and Janavi, before she could stop herself, stuck her tongue out too. The mom, seated in front, saw her and gave her a dirty look. Janavi wanted to say, Your kid started it. And then she had to laugh, or maybe not laugh, because looking around her — at the shabby motel, the weeds growing out of the cracks in the concrete, the VACANCY sign that was missing a C, the hours and hours of sitting in a stillness that seemed, at times, to hide yet another greater stillness — there was suddenly nothing to laugh about. She was in an unintended country. She had an unintended husband. And the life she'd intended to have? That was gone, and she knew it was gone forever.

One afternoon, four days after their arrival, she opened a suitcase looking for something. A shawl, a sweater? She couldn't remember. They'd left most of the suitcases unopened. All but the small carry-ons with a few days' worth of clothes and toiletries. But on that day she opened a big suitcase, and as she was rummaging, she came across a long rolled-up piece of paper. What was it? She didn't recall packing it. She took it over to the bed, slid off the rubber bands, and unrolled it on the bedspread.

She looked. And then she looked some more.

It was a nautical chart. Her papa. He must've slipped it into her suitcase.

But a chart of what?

It took her a minute, maybe two, and when she realized what it was a chart of her eyes warmed. It was a nautical chart of the currents around the last island before her namesake emptied into the Bay of Bengal. And its name? The name of this last island?

That is when the tears started. That is when she wept.

Sagar Island.

Chapter 8

The first time Sagar saw the Cotton River dam he wanted to do so alone. He left Janavi at the motel after an early dinner on Sunday and drove out to the dam. It was a few miles south of Mansfield just above the state park and the campgrounds. The Cotton River Road, which ran along the curved end of the horseshoe that Mansfield was tucked inside, led right to the dam. He drove along the river, catching, at times, glimpses of it through the cottonwoods as it wound between the sandstone bluffs. It shimmered green gold in the setting sun and at certain angles, for seconds at a time, seemed to him a solid stretch of bronze. He considered pulling over and wading into it, if only to convince himself that it was, in fact, liquid, but he resisted; it was getting dark.

When he arrived, instead of driving right up to the dam, he parked the rental car a little below it on the side of the road. He approached on foot. It took him less than ten minutes as he followed the river, going slightly uphill, past sedge grass and clumps of sagebrush and even a few wild grape vines. He heard voices, and when he searched the river below, he saw kayakers paddling by. A middle-aged man with a younger man in another kayak, maybe his son.

The middle-aged man waved and shouted, "Ahoy there, landlubber."

Sagar smiled and waved back, feeling the warmth of this welcome.

The sun was nearing the horizon as he approached the dam. When he did, he looked at it. He simply stood and looked at it. He'd seen lots of dams before, of course, and many far larger and more impressive than this one — but this . . . this was his first American dam. He felt a surge of pride as he looked at the water flowing over the spillway and the walking bridge above the dam and the low hills on either side of it and the bluffs that led down to its base and the patches of grass along the river that then flowed on and on to the Yellowstone and then the Missouri and then the Mississippi until draining, finally, into the Gulf of Mexico.

For now, he saw the dam just as it was. Not as a hydraulic engineer or as a civil engineer or as a man who had studied dams and could see their design flaws; he didn't want to contemplate its capacity or its technical aspects or any of the other elements he was trained to consider. What he did instead was to look at it as an object. An object that was beautiful and that had been built by man, maybe hundreds of thousands of times since the fourth century B.C.E., with the first one being the Jawa Dam in Jordan, and that stood, each one, as the epitome of strength and power. That stood in the way all beautiful things stood, without knowing it.

He decided to cross the bridge to the south end of the dam and as he did a strong wind came up out of the west. He stopped in the center of the bridge looking down at the awesome force of water plummeting below him, a hundred feet or more. The reservoir, which was about a mile at its widest point and a little under eight miles in length, was lined with campgrounds and a state park and fishing shacks and fancy homes with private lake access and even a marina, some miles farther downstream. But from where Sagar was standing it was an expanse of darkening water. He turned around and faced upstream. Low hills and bluffs edged the river and then flattened out. Beyond was the vast prairie, and the river, in its midst, seemed utterly tame and slight and alone. He always knew water could be hungry, on the outflow side of dams where it was starved for sediment, but this was the first time, in all the rivers of his life, that he thought, It can also be lonely.

He understood, as he had since the first class he'd taken in hydraulics, that a dam, ultimately, was simply a wall. It was porous, certainly, like all walls, and it separated water instead of people or land, but it was nevertheless simply a wall. And this wall, Sagar thought with pride, looking down at the structure of earth and clay and rock, then down the length of its crest, and then at its downstream and upstream fills, *This* wall I'm going to take down. He'd done so before, or at least assisted in doing so, with the dam on the Majuli, but now he was the lead. The lead! Another surge of pride. He thought then of a clip he'd once seen of Ronald Reagan telling Mikhail Gorbachev, "Tear down this wall," and he wondered how it must have felt when the wall had finally come down between East and West Germany. How had the people felt? In each of the two countries? Free, he thought, they must've felt free. And that is what he said, looking northward into the waters of the Cotton River. He said, "You'll be free."

The following morning, he reported for his first day of work. His boss, Ben Mackey, wasn't onsite. Sagar had interviewed with him, via video call, when he had been in Varanasi, but Mr. Mackey, he realized now, was stationed in Helena, the capital of Montana, which Sagar saw on the map was almost four hundred miles away from Mansfield. Instead, the first person he met was Tim Downing, the project manager on the dam removal project. They shook hands and after a few moments of awkwardness, Sagar asked him when Sir might come to the damsite and Tim Downing — who, along with Sagar, shared the trailer that served as their onsite office — said, "Who the hell is Sir?"

"Our boss, Mr. Mackey."

He said, "You all call your bosses 'Sir' back in India?"

"Well, yes . . . sometimes."

Tim Downing laughed. "You don't need to do none of that out here. In Montana, it's every man for himself. No 'Sirs' around here."

Sagar laughed too, as if he'd gotten the joke, though he didn't understand what Tim Downing meant by "every man for himself." Weren't they on a project together? And wasn't there a hierarchy? According to the organizational chart he'd been given after he'd accepted the job, Mr. Mackey was charged with running the project and Tim Downing, as the project manager, and Sagar, as the lead engineer, reported to him. Beneath Sagar and Tim Downing were a handful of technicians and assistant engineers. There were also consultants (such as riparian ecologists) and construction contractors and subcontractors, and lots of local hourly employees. How, then, could it be every man for himself?

It was simple: Tim hadn't made a joke; he'd been laughing *at* Sagar. For referring to Mr. Mackey as Sir, he supposed, and though he tried not to be, he was reserved around him and self-conscious about misspeaking again. It was a cultural difference, of course, but to be ridiculed in that way reduced Sagar to the bullying of his boyhood. The other people on the dam removal team seemed nice enough — all of them introduced themselves (they had all been working on the project for a month before Sagar had arrived) and were kind, even when Sagar confused their names or their titles. The most mortifying error was when he called the only Native American woman at the damsite, who'd been standing with a group from the construction crew, Jenny, when her actual name was Renny. They'd only met once, and he'd misheard her name. The next time he saw her, she was in the trailer picking up a hard hat. She corrected him, and he apologized profusely, to which Renny, who'd seemed so serious when he'd met her, winked and said, "I'll let it slide this time, since you're Indian."

He wanted to tell Janavi about Tim and Renny and all his colleagues, but he was too embarrassed. What should he say? That he'd been laughed at? That he felt, in the wake of Tim Downing's ridicule, like a schoolboy who'd been picked on? No, he was too shy to tell her. And besides, most nights when he came home, especially during the early days when he stayed late to catch up on work, Janavi was asleep by the time he got back. He sometimes thought she was only pretending to sleep because she found him boring or annoying or that she was giving him the silent treatment out of spite for marrying her and dragging her here. Maybe it was all three.

He buried himself in his work.

He reviewed the specs and other technical documentation for the Cotton River and the Cotton River dam, along with a few internal memoranda that had to do with the discussions and considerations leading up to the decision to remove the dam. From what Sagar read the decision seemed to have been purely an economic one. Maintaining the dam and performing the necessary upgrades to prevent catastrophic failure in case of floods or other unforeseen climate events were deemed too costly compared to simply removing the dam. The removal, from what Sagar learned, was a proactive measure to avoid greater costs later.

Janavi snored lightly. Sagar looked at her, turned away from him, on the other bed. The curls at the nape of her neck, the soft brown of her arm above the blanket, the sediment of her body curving so beautifully. What could he have done differently? It had been a false choice. It had been no choice at all.

When he turned back to his laptop, the numbers swam on the screen. Sagar closed the technical documents. He rubbed his eyes.

He got out of bed and made a cup of the shitty motel coffee and then he went back to his computer and searched online. He read all the articles he could find that had to do with the dam. He scrolled through page after page. He was surprised to discover that there had been community opposition to the dam removal. In India, in his experience, the protests were always over the *building* of a dam, not over its removal. But then again not many dams had been removed in India and even the one he'd worked on, along the Majuli, had only been removed so that a bigger dam could be built upstream.

The opposition to taking down the Cotton River dam was because of the obvious: an object was being removed, and that always created a sense of loss in a community. Beyond that, the draining of the reservoir would eliminate some recreational activities and a few jobs (though in Sagar's estimation, with a running river, many more would become available). In addition, there was a handful of local farmers and ranchers who feared that with the reservoir drained, their water needs would not be met. But Sagar, even with a cursory look at the numbers, knew that even without the reservoir, they would have more than enough water (most of them seemed to have their own wells anyway). What was more, the water they did get would be healthier and more cost-effective.

According to an article in *The Mansfield Register*, the local newspaper, the person who was leading this opposition, or at least its spokesman, was Sam Dooley, the mayor of Mansfield. A grainy photo of him was published with the article. Sagar studied the photo. He was probably in his forties, with deep-set eyes and wearing a cowboy hat. To Sagar he looked like one of the actors in the old Westerns he'd watched as a boy, shown every now and then on Sunday afternoon television. In fact, the shows had become so popular in India that Bollywood had started making its own Westerns, called Curry Westerns. Sam Dooley, in one of the articles, was quoted as saying, "What you have here is a travesty of justice. A rejection of the people's will, plain and simple."

Other articles he found, buried deep in the seventh and eighth and ninth pages of the search, surprised him even more. For instance, he learned that a local tribe, who owned land near the dam and whose reservation was bordered by the Cotton River, had been protesting the dam and advocating for its removal for nearly a decade. When the dam had been built, in 1937, the tribe's long tradition of fishing on the Cotton River had been completely ignored. One of the tribal elders, Marsha Bluestar, was quoted in the article as saying that the fishing of sauger and shovelnose sturgeon and northern pike had been an essential part of the tribe's cultural and spiritual traditions and with the building of the dam, which had compromised the migratory routes of the fish, that tradition had ended. To make matters worse, there had been a massive fish die-off in the 1990s, when the temperature of the water in the reservoir had risen a few degrees. Sagar knew about this phenomenon, where fish languished in waters that were too warm, on the reservoir side of dams, and eventually died from stress and disease.

Sagar looked up into the sparsely furnished motel room, beaming. Once the dam was removed and with the river running again, unobstructed, the habitat for the fish would be restored and the tribe would soon be able to resume fishing on the river. Had he ever before felt such pride?

He scrolled through the rest of the search results. There wasn't much more about the Cotton River.

One article, tucked into the last page of the search results, was about the rivers of eastern Montana — the Cotton, the Missouri (which, much to his amusement, Montanans called "Big Mo"), and the Yellowstone — and of the many bodies that had been found in them. That didn't surprise Sagar — rivers were always a popular place to dispose of bodies — but it got him thinking about the Native American burial site that was adjacent to the Cotton. Situated on a low bluff, this burial site was mentioned in one of the DNRC's memoranda as a factor to be considered, and various protocols for dealing with Native burial mounds were enumerated, but there were no other references to it, while the local tribe's concerns were completely ignored. Why? He dug deeper online and found that the burial site had been revealed when the flow of the river was reduced by the building of the dam in the 1930s. Now that the dam was being removed, all the buried bones and artifacts and whatever else they found had to be excavated and reburied at a different location, or returned to the families to whom the remains could be traced. But who did all of this, Sagar wondered. And how?

He obviously couldn't ask Tim Downing.

Janavi turned in her sleep. Toward him. Sagar glanced at her, got up, and went to the small motel fridge.

He climbed back into bed with leftover chicken nuggets and french fries. He picked at them. He refused to look in Janavi's direction. He turned on the television, muted it, and after a few minutes he switched off the bedside lamp. He sat in the dark, staring at the television screen, eating cold fries, listening to his new wife breathing beside him, his new life developing like a negative in the dark, and he thought, with a keening ache, There are so many kinds of walls . . . and how strange that the ones made of stone and steel are the easiest to take down.

Chapter 9

The town of Mansfield was clustered entirely inside a wide bend of the Cotton River. The river straightened back out south and north of town but the bend, shaped exactly like a horseshoe, contained within it a majority of the town. There was a sprinkling of ranches to the east of the curve, toward Broadus, and a gas station to the north, off the Cotton River Road leading to Miles City, but otherwise, the town, upon reaching the banks of the Cotton River, had seemingly been incapable of figuring out a way to cross it. Their one-bedroom apartment, which Sagar and Janavi moved into two weeks after arriving in Montana, was situated almost exactly in the center of the horseshoe. Main Street, a few blocks from them, was the commercial center and the rest of the town was made up mostly of modest houses with modest yards, radiating out from Main. Their apartment building was an eight-plex, with their unit occupying the second-story northwest corner. Janavi liked the small window over the kitchen sink best — it looked out onto a yard that had a tire swing tied to an elm tree. The family who lived in the house had a little boy and girl and sometimes one or the other of them would come out into the yard, climb into the tire, and swing listlessly. It was never for long, but whenever Janavi saw them, swinging lazily on the tire, looking out toward the chain-link fence that enclosed their yard and then at the row of yards beyond their own and then, she guessed, toward the end of this endless country, she wondered what they were thinking.

What *did* American children think about?

It was probably much the same things that Indian children thought about, though, compared to the street children she'd worked with, the ones here seemed more vulnerable, less cunning, and to bore easily; she wondered if that was true of the adults too.

Once, the little girl saw her. She looked up just as Janavi was looking down at her. She waved but the girl didn't wave back.

During the day Janavi took long walks around the neighborhood. While they'd been at the motel her walks had been around the "historical" downtown, which struck her as not very historical, given that the oldest cornerstone read 1878; in Varanasi, some of the ghats and the temples were over three thousand years old. Such a young country, she'd thought, and had felt charmed by it, as though in the roster of countries, the United States were a child — rambunctious and spirited and full of its own importance. She'd looked in the store windows. There was an Old West store selling boots and cowboy hats and belt buckles and all sorts of frontier-themed trinkets. Another store was more pragmatic and sold ranching and feed supplies. There were two bars, Sweet Molly's and the Longhorn, and a diner called the Copper Penny. To the west of town, according to the signage, was a community college and a public swimming pool, though Janavi hadn't yet seen either.

The downtown was only three blocks long and with Mansfield being the seat of Custer County (Janavi had had to learn how regions within a state were demarcated in America; in India they were called districts), there was a courthouse and municipal building at the end of Main Street. Janavi hardly ever went into the stores. Sometimes, when she'd been walking along the sidewalk or standing at the store windows, people had looked at her for a moment longer than necessary, and from the expression on their faces, she hadn't been able to tell what they'd been thinking. Had they never seen an Indian person before? Under their gaze she'd sometimes felt naked, exposed, and unwelcome, and she'd hurried away.

Now that they were in the apartment, she found that the neighborhood around it was mostly residential. When people saw her here, usually from their cars, they slowed as they passed and then kept going. She didn't always see their faces and for that she was thankful. On one of her walks, a young man rolled down his window as he passed and yelled out, "Fine lookin' Pocahontas, ain't you?" What did that mean? Janavi had no idea.

Rajni had been calling once or twice a week since they'd arrived in Montana, but Janavi still hadn't picked up. Early on, she'd texted her and told her they'd arrived safely, but she didn't want to hear her voice. She did and she didn't. It was hard enough hearing Papa's voice. When she called him on Sunday mornings (evenings for him), he asked after her and after Sagar and then, hearing the listlessness in her voice, she guessed, he usually asked, Can you work yet? She would sigh and tell him, No, not yet. I told you, Papa, not for a few months at least.

Once, her papa said, "It's too bad. Your amma insisted you and Rajni be educated, and yet — "

"She did?"

"It's the only way she'd agree to your sister's betrothal."

Molten lead shot up Janavi's spine. *Your sister's betrothal.* Only Amma could've understood her rage. Only Amma could've — she said a quick goodbye to her papa, her voice trembling, and hung up.

Edwin, their landlord, came over — while Sagar was at work — to fix a leak under the bathroom sink. He was wearing a tool belt and a miner's headlamp. Janavi had never seen either and thought they were ingenious. He tinkered under the sink for a few minutes and then went down to his truck. When he returned, he said, "Past tenants. Used goddamn duct tape. Didn't even wrap it snug." He went back into the bathroom, and she heard the faucet running for some minutes. When he came out again, he seemed even more irritated and said, "Pipe's rusted. I've got to run to the hardware store and buy a new one." He was wiry, with tattoos running up and down his forearms. There was a tan line where a wedding band must've recently been removed. At the door, he turned and said, "Don't try to fix nothing on your own, you understand? Just makes it worse." Janavi nodded. Would he have used that tone if Sagar were here? He returned an hour later, stomped back into the bathroom, and when he emerged this time, he seemed much more relaxed and said, "Now, how do you say your name again? Ja-na-what? Anyway, sorry about earlier. I get cranky. Can't help it. I manage this one and another one over on Custer. And some of these tenants . . . foolish. Just foolish." They were standing in the short hallway leading to the front door. Edwin was nearly at the door when he stopped and turned. He said, "Alright then . . ." but his eyes were looking at Janavi's breasts. She crossed her arms over them. Edwin winked. He said, smiling, "All the gals as pretty as you are? Back home?"

Janavi looked at him.

When she didn't return his smile, Edwin's face hardened. Janavi, who'd been unpacking, had a packet of garam masala in her hand — she and Sagar had brought a few spices, not knowing what would be available in Montana. Edwin pointed to the packet of garam masala and said, "I know about those spices of yours. Had another Indian tenant. Pa-tell. Stunk up the place something awful. Had to leave the windows wide open for a month, middle of winter, before I got the smell out." After issuing this warning he left. Janavi felt the heat in her face, her chest. She felt an impulse to cook up every ounce of every spice she had. She wanted to sprinkle it on the carpet and crush it down with her feet.

When Sagar got home that night, she didn't tell him about Edwin. She didn't know what to say or maybe she didn't know what he would say. Whenever he asked her how her day had been, Janavi resisted screaming. What did she want to scream? Everything. Everything her life had become. She wanted to scream her fury at being jobless and alone and abandoned, first by Rajni in the back garden and then by him every morning when he went off, oblivious, to work. She wanted to scream, Why did you bring me? Why did you marry me? Why am I here at all? She wanted to scream for things no one could give. She wanted to scream, I want my amma. Give her back to me. Only she can make this better, only she can make this make sense. But instead of screaming, she gave him clipped answers, hateful and severe. She said, "I walked for an hour. The other nine hours I thought about the children I can no longer help." Or she said, "My day was fine, fine. Brilliant even. It's amazing the number of ways there are to make a bed." She said these things to him, saw his dejected face, and immediately felt bad. None of it — almost none of it — was his fault, she reminded herself. She tried then to be kind, telling him she saw an orange cat on her walk or that she saw a horse trailer with a horse inside, its large eye peering out at her. She tried but it seemed to her, whether she was being hateful or kind, that she wasn't truly telling him anything.

Just as he wasn't telling her anything, truly. For instance, after his first day of work, she'd asked how it had gone. He'd been vague. He'd told her he'd met everyone and spent most of the day setting up his computer and studying various documents and sending emails. She'd said, "What about your colleagues? Are they nice?"

"Yes, yes," he'd said, almost too quickly. "They're fine."

"Who did you meet?" she'd said.

"I told you, everyone."

"But your boss. You didn't meet him."

He hadn't said anything.

"Where is your office? Is it in a building nearby? Near the dam?"

"No," he'd said. "It's in a trailer. Onsite."

"Is it all your own?"

"What do you mean?"

"The office. Do you share it with anyone?"

He'd turned away and had said, "All these questions. It's only my first day."

She'd been surprised. He was usually so excited to talk about dams, and about the various rivers and projects he'd worked on. Was it something to do with his colleagues? The trailer? But it couldn't be. She tried a few days later. He came home looking tired and said he wanted to take a shower. When he emerged from the bathroom, she saw he'd shaved off his mustache. He seemed to notice her studying his face and said, "No one here has one." Janavi thought, Now his unfamiliar face is even more unfamiliar.

Sagar was usually gone in the mornings when she woke up, but they had dinner together every night. She cooked, though she didn't enjoy cooking. Sometimes he'd call on his way home and ask if she needed anything from the grocery store, though mostly, they did their shopping on the weekends. After dinner, she watched television while Sagar worked on his laptop.

One night, she decided to ask general questions about his work, hoping he'd be more willing to talk. She said, "Tell me about the Cotton River. Does it feel very different? From working on the Ganga?"

He looked up from his laptop. His face, much to her delight, lit up with a smile. He said, "So much is different, Janavi. Almost everything. But . . . after all, they're both rivers, aren't they?" And then he proceeded to tell her about the Cotton River, which he said originated in Wyoming, and he even pulled up a map and showed her (though unlike her papa's, his was on his phone). The river, he said, was a little over 250 miles long—the Ganga, by way of comparison, was 1,560 miles long. And whereas the Ganga was considered the holiest river in the world and hundreds of millions of people visited every year and it provided irrigation and drinking water to one of the most populated regions in the world, which also led to it being one of the most polluted rivers in the world, on the Cotton's course, he told her, it wound through mostly empty prairie and provided water for just a small number of ranching and farming operations, along with a few recreational activities on the reservoir. "Even so," he said, "there was opposition to the dam being removed."

"There was?"

He told her then about how the ranchers and even the mayor had protested it.

Janavi was silent. She wondered if that was why some people gave her curious, maybe even menacing looks when she walked by them. Maybe it wasn't all in her imagination and they were the ones who opposed the dam removal and knew that Sagar (who else's wife could be the new Indian woman in town?) was the engineer leading the project.

She listened and then she said, "Will you take me? To see the dam, the reservoir?"

Some small thing seemed to shift in him, a slight movement of the eyebrows. He said, "Of course. Of course, I'll take you."

She ventured a smile. She looked at him and then at the empty apartment and she felt anew the strangeness of it all — the strangeness of her new husband, the strangeness of finding herself in a new country, in a new life. Why was she here? What should she do now? Where should she begin?

They drove back to Billings to buy furniture for the apartment. They'd bought a used Honda Civic; Sagar had converted his international driver's license to a Montana one, but Janavi still needed to take the driving test. They drove through the south side of town, past the motel in which they'd stayed and the gas stations and the fast-food restaurants along Main Street and then onto Cotton River Road. They passed the last dribble of houses, all of them one-story and all of them with the same white aluminum siding, as if one had been built and had simply reproduced like an amoeba. In less than five minutes they were out of Mansfield. Janavi was amazed. They'd come from a city with a population of nearly two million people to one that was a little over eight thousand. Driving now on Highway 212, through the most barren and unbroken land she had ever known, she thought about those early mapmakers her papa had once told her about. Of how they'd thought the earth was flat and had drawn onto their maps the edges of the known world. She understood that edge now and how they had assumed it and had maybe even wanted it.

Sagar said, "There's an Asian grocery store in Billings. I looked it up. Do you want to go there after the furniture store?"

Janavi thought about the garam masala. She said, "Yes, I do."

On either side of the road were miles upon miles of grassland dimpled here and there with tufts of sagebrush. In the far distance were red sandstone cliffs and low hills and sprawling buttes. Sometimes, if she looked closely, she noticed blue bursts of beardtongue blooms coming up out of the prairie grasses like tiny scraps of fallen sky. Sagar had told her that most of the population of the Cotton River Valley, aside from the local tribe, was made up of the ancestors of those who, in the nineteenth century, and well into the twentieth, had worked the silver and gold and platinum and copper and cobalt mines in Anaconda and Elkhorn and Comet and Granite and Butte. Once most of the mines had been decommissioned, he told her, the miners and their families had drifted eastward. Why eastward? Janavi asked, but Sagar didn't know. She wondered. Why would they come east when, according to Sagar, expansion in America had always been westward?

She looked out of the window. The road was mostly straight and every now and then she saw a dirt path, grown over with weeds, cutting through the prairie and climbing, stubbornly, into the squat hills. Were there ranches up there? Old mining towns? She saw no fences, no cattle. She wanted to ask Sagar to turn onto one of those roads. Not only out of curiosity, the mystery of what lay at their end, not only because of that, but because their solitariness, their abandonment, their tenacity in a landscape so brutal, called to her.

Maybe that's why they, too, had come east. All those miners.

When they got to Billings they first went to R&R Furniture. A sales-man guided them through the vast store. They selected a green sofa and a round dining table with four chairs and a few lamps. The salesman, Frank, as he led them around the various sections of the store, peppered them with questions and quips and jokes that only he seemed to find inordinately funny. He said, "I've been selling furniture for thirty years and didn't see a single Indian couple — your Indian, you understand — for twenty-nine of them and just in the last year seen a dozen of them. A dozen! What is it? A friends and family thing? I know. I know how it is, folks. One of you comes over and then you bring in all your people. Sisters, brothers, cousins, and whatnot. Now don't get me wrong. I got no problem with it . . . can't say I blame you. Great country. Some peo-ple do, but I got no beef with it. None at all. Let 'em in, I say, long as you send them to Frank at R&R for their furniture needs!" He guffawed and slapped Sagar on the back. Neither said a word. He asked how long they'd been married, and when they were in the mattress and bedding section, Frank pointed to a wooden bed frame, which he called a sleigh bed, and said, "A beauty, isn't she? Solid oak. And sturdy." He winked at Sagar and smiled. "Sturdy, my friend."

Sagar glanced at Janavi and then looked away.

She felt in that instant the surrealness of the moment. Arriving as they had to this enormous prairie, under this enormous sky, and now standing in this enormous place, military barracks more than a furni-ture store, amid the acres of furniture — the sofas, the beds, the tables, the chairs — all of which would one day witness every tumult of human life, each of its yearnings and its whimsies and its wanderings. On one of these sofas, Janavi thought, a woman will sit and receive the news of a parent's death, at one of these tables a man will read a pamphlet about the cancer that was growing inside of him, and on one of these beds a couple will sleep, strangers to each other, strangers to a new continent. Each of these things the inanimate furniture and those who sat and

leaned and lay on it would endure, and more. She felt, too, their aloneness: hers and Sagar's and even Frank's. Stripped, as they were, of truly
knowing one another. And the enemy of this knowing? The greatest
had to be, she decided, the casual assumptions, the offhand gestures, the
betrayals that entered no books. The winks. The garam masala. The
sturdy bed. Rajni confiding in Sagar before she'd confided in her own
sister. Sagar leaving her in a moldering motel and then in an empty
apartment while he went to *his* work, to *his* job, and not once saying,
The hours will fill. This country will fill. We will fill them.

They bought a different bed.

At the Asian grocer they bought an assortment of lentils and pickles
and spices and snacks. A young Chinese woman was their cashier and
she held up the bag of Kurkure chips and said, "My favorite."

Janavi smiled and said, "Mine too."

She opened the bag as soon as they got in the car and she and Sagar
finished the chips before the first traffic light. They laughed as they
licked their fingers and Janavi, wiping her hands on her jeans, felt the
sudden ease between them, was disoriented by it, and her dark thoughts
came to a close. She looked at him surreptitiously. The profile of his
face, the line of his nose. She decided that he looked better without a
mustache. Her gaze, instead of focusing on the mustache, was now
drawn to his jawline, his nose, both well angled.

She looked away.

The sun was setting, and they decided to stop for pizza before they
left Billings. "I don't even know what your favorite toppings are," he
said.

She told him onions and capsicum. She said, "What are yours?"

He said, "The same."

Was that true? She didn't know, but that seemed enough. That
seemed enough for today.

Hiram Hicks

Cotton River, 1865

The Cotton River Valley, tucked into the southeastern corner of Montana, was a land of legends. And the least known among them — rarely spoken of, and even then, spoken of in hushed tones — was the legend of the Great Gray Wolf. First around the fires of the Kootenai, the Cree, and the Nez Percé, and then among the trappers who came over from French Canada for the lucrative trade in the pelts of wolves and bobcats and mountain lions and coyotes (buffalo hunters, with their breathtaking bloodthirst, had not yet arrived). Language in the telling of these legends was hardly ever a barrier, because every man, woman, and child on the High Plains knew the language of terror, warning, and wisdom. And so, the legend was passed down selectively, quietly, to only the most deserving, only the most prudent, to only the ones who understood the power of land, the power of wolves.

Which meant, of course, that Hiram Hicks heard nothing of this legend.

At the time, in the mid-1860s, in the early days of what was known as the Montana Territory, Hiram was living in an elegant townhouse in Philadelphia, near Rittenhouse Square, with an ailing mother, three servants, and a dog named Bugsy. He had eight brothers and sisters — most of them married, all of them scattered to the wind. He had no need of work, since his widowed mother's investment in the trade of sugarcane and indigo and slaves kept them in relative comfort, some seasons naturally being a bit more meager than others, given the volatility of Atlantic storms and the vagaries of the financial markets, during which, rather than smoking inferior tobacco, or smoking less of it, or limiting his visits to the brothel run by Madam Mathilda to, say, once a week rather than his usual twice or thrice a week, he instead watered down his mother's nightly port and gave her a smaller portion of meat at dinnertime. Sometimes, he denied her dinner altogether. What did it matter? She was too deep into dementia to even notice. He did on occasion feel a twinge of what could generously be called guilt when, on some nights, he entered her room (the nicest room in the townhouse, he reminded himself, in the southeast corner, overlooking the square) and found her in tears. "Why, Mother dear," he asked, "why are you crying?" And his mother, her eyes brimming and depleted and yet determined, looked at him, and with a biting lucidity, impossible to dismiss, she said, "Because of my nine, you are the one the Lord left me with." Hiram smiled at her as if at a small, unruly child, straightened her bed linens, blew out the candles, and left the room. As for the twinge of guilt, the one he felt when he clicked her door shut, Madam Mathilda and her armada of lovely ladies (girls?), sometimes two of them at a time, helped him to forget, or at least helped him to drive it to the deepest and farthest cave in his impressively cavernous mind.

And the last thing Hiram had? A broken heart.

It was not completely broken though. Not broken in the way a poor sentimentalist's heart would break but broken in the way a rich pragmatist's heart would break — with a certain degree of caution, an awareness of sorrow's transience, and a keen sense of its own importance. And of course, since Hiram Hicks had the fiscal means to indulge in Madam Mathilda's many offerings, this left his rich pragmatist's heart free from any real or lasting suffering. Suffering. And what was the source of this faux, somewhat suffering? Her name was Wilhelmina Powell Granville. Kitty, for short. He never did come to know where the Kitty came from, but that was what her intimates called her — Kitty — and he felt as though he had summitted a great mountain when, one afternoon at the end of tea with her octogenarian Aunt Prudence in the parlor of their mansion on Arch Street, Wilhelmina Granville placed her crumpet neatly on the china plate by her side and said, "Please, Mr. Hicks. Call me Kitty." He smiled. "Well, in that case, you must call me Hiram." Their eyes met and there was, in that meeting, a deep, sweeping search of the other's soul, its intentions, its marriageability, its companionship, and, of course, its compatibility with regard to wealth and social standing, all of which seemed to be well matched and in accord — or so Hiram thought. At the Christmas Ball, in fact, he and Kitty danced twice together — the Slow Waltz *and* the Viennese Waltz — and Hiram smiled to himself, noting that none of the other eligible bachelors were granted neither the pleasure or the privilege. Still, despite all the favorable signs, the reason for his faux broken heart and its faux suffering were that he had sent Kitty's father a note requesting her hand in marriage, along with having a long, grueling chat with him at the Club regarding his prospects (which Hiram thought had gone rather well), but he'd heard from neither Kitty nor her father. That seemed a bad sign. It *was* a bad sign. And what was worse: His mother, consumptive, her pulse barely discernible, and clearly struggling for each meager breath, was nearing death. Though, to be clear, it wasn't her death that worried Hiram, but his awareness of the fact that once she died, his financial means would be abruptly and demor-alizingly reduced. Her investments in sugarcane, indigo, and slaves, along with their requisite proceeds, would have to be split nine ways (according to her will, which Hiram had nearly mem-orized in his obsessive reading of it, as if it were some grand epic poem), between Hiram and his brothers and sisters, and even with the greater portion going to Hiram (for having cared for their mother), it still would not be enough to keep him in the townhouse with three servants, Bugsy, and his current florid life-style.

He pondered and pondered; his heart suffered mildly for Kitty and ached greatly for her money.

But then one February afternoon, all of that changed.

Hiram was to meet a former schoolmate at the Palace Hotel for a drink, before going to the theater and possibly engaging in a bit of debauchery to round out the evening, when, as he passed through the lobby of the hotel toward the bar, he spied Kitty seated with her mother and another older woman in the tea-room. He stopped in his tracks. The tearoom itself was glitter-ingly ornate, almost baroque, with its silvery yellow wallpaper and its profusion of roses and dahlias and lilies of the valley at the center of every table and the gold candlesticks lighted even in midday and the plush rose-colored Oriental carpets and the shining silverware and exquisite plates of blue porcelain all mingling with the scent of Darjeeling teas and cakes, muted by the exotic perfumes of the richest and most beautiful women in Philadelphia. And it was one of them — one of the richest and certainly the most beautiful — who stopped Hiram in his tracks. And who might that be? Kitty, of course. Though he hardly rec-ognized her; in fact, it was as if he were seeing her for the first time. She was wearing a lovely gray silk dress with a simple string of pearls at her neck. Her hair — which he remembered as being of a plain brownish color — today seemed darker, slight but noticeable, and there was one strand that had come loose, curving past her eye and slashing her cheek, which struck Hiram as dangerous in its dark and awful enchantment, like a machete held to a virgin's throat. Still, what intoxicated Hiram most — intoxicated him enough to forget himself, forget that his proposal of marriage was mortifyingly forgotten, or worse, ignored, and probably mildewing in some corner of their vast mansion, intoxicated him enough to forget even his precarious financial situation and his mother's impending death — was Kitty's repose. The way she was reclined in her seat. It was such a simple thing: the act of sitting. He'd never noticed it before. He'd seen hundreds, probably thousands, of people sitting and reclining and sipping tea, but he had never seen anyone do so as beautifully as Kitty. Like a queen upon her throne; no, more than that: like a girl upon a swing. Maybe it was the gray silk dress? Regardless, his mind flooded with all the images, all of them, every last one, that had ever seemed to him, at the time or later, as sublime, as the very burning center of sublimity: the second woman who had opened her legs to him at Madam Mathilda's, when he was fifteen; his first sip of absinthe; his father's face in the moment before his death; the winter wind whipping against his face late one night, so frigid and biting that his lip cracked open and when he raised his hand to it, the fingers came back blood red; twilight on a round, unremarkable hill; the bear that had eyed him and walked away on a hunting trip during his university days, and in its wake, in the middle of the sun-dappled woods, had left an afterglow so palpable that he'd reached out to touch it, and maybe had.

Now he *had* to do something; Kitty had seen him and was waving him over.

He walked toward her in what felt like a dream, bowed and

kissed the hands of the two older women first, and then bent to take Kitty's hand. Slowly, painfully, as gracefully as he could manage. Her fingers, for the slightest moment, curled around his as he kissed them, pressed them lightly, and then, just like that, she let go.

And it was this letting go.

In this letting go, Hiram felt all of life letting go. At least, the life he had been living. He waited for his mother to die, which she did a few weeks later. He waited to hear of Kitty's impending marriage, which arrived in the form of an engagement notice in the newspaper, to an English aristocrat by the name of Hugh Prescott Astley, and then he waited for springtime in Philadelphia to begin. Then his waiting ended. He sold the townhouse. Gave each of his three servants five hundred dollars. And the night before his departure, he took Bugsy to a forested area by the Schuylkill, threw a bone into the woods to distract him, and then he walked away.

The next morning, he left Philadelphia and headed to the Montana Territory.

He arrived at Fort Sarpy, a stockaded trading post surrounded by a handful of adobe-chinked log huts. The trading post was situated on a high bluff overlooking the Yellowstone River, below the mouth of the Big Horn River. Aside from the employees of the American Fur Company, the men living in Fort Sarpy were mostly wolfers and horse thieves. The few women who lived there worked the saloons, knowing that when the men returned from the isolated hills and the shadowed coulees of the prairie, loaded down with fur pelts or blotted horses, they'd made enough at the trading post for a handful of wild nights.

Hiram walked into one of the saloons and realizing his

choice was between legal and illegal trade — hunting wolves or thieving horses — he chose the legal one. He tracked down a man by the name of Irish Joe, and for a small sum, apprenticed under him to learn how to hunt and skin and trade in wolf pelts. Irish Joe was thin, surly, impossible to age, had a scraggly beard and shifty eyes, and in no way looked Irish. He taught Hiram everything he knew about hunting wolves, absolutely everything, but he neglected to tell him the most important thing there was to know: the legend of the Great Gray Wolf. No one in town told Hiram either. They all thought him foolish — a city boy who'd not once skinned a squirrel let alone killed a wolf, wanting now to enter the fur trade, as if it were a thing you entered and not a thing you were born to do — and maybe they were right, maybe he was foolish, but what they didn't know was that Hiram now had what very few of them, if any, had: a heart that was truly and undeniably broken. And that might've made him a fool because the heart does that — makes us fools — but it also gave him courage. The courage that enters through the very canals by which the heart bleeds.

Hiram left Fort Sarpy (fortified with something like knowledge) and traveled east, and then south, and one evening, he found himself and his horse in a sun-drenched valley with distant hills and a nearby river and grass so high and lush and unending he waded through it as if through an inland sea, green and alluring and uncrossable. And he knew immediately, *immediately*, that he was home. His fate was here, in this valley. The Cotton River Valley. He built himself a simple shack under the shade of three cottonwood trees. These cottonwood trees seemed to Hiram as if they'd been waiting for him, and only him (again, the word *fate* occurred to him, and maybe with good reason, given what was to come). He stood under the cottonwoods and when he looked up, their leaves fluttered in the sun and it seemed to Hiram as if they were raining down upon him coins of perfect light. What he didn't notice until much later was that they were positioned precisely in the shape of an isosceles triangle and were growing in the exact cardinal directions of east, west, and south, leaving the north, the holy, heavenly north, wide and windswept and painfully unobstructed. And it was to the north that the door of Hiram's shack opened.

Once his shack was completed, he loaded his six-shooter, made a crude chair out of a few cottonwood branches and a bit of leather, placed it just inside the open door, sat down, and waited.

He thought he'd arrived at the start of spring, but Hiram was wrong. Winter was far from over. In fact, the March and the April and especially the May blizzards nearly killed him. He put on every piece of clothing he owned, wrapped himself in every quilt, and still the wind and cold passed through him; he could feel his blood hardening, halting at the gates to his fingers, his toes. No fire was hot enough. He crouched in his shack and between bouts of snow blindness and uncontrollable shivering, followed by dangerous rushes of warmth and well-being — which even Hiram knew was the delirium just before death — he thought of Kitty. He thought of her garlanded by candlelight, resting on a plush seat of marigold petals and moss. What would it have been like to kiss her? He imagined it would've been like what the explorers wrote of feeling when they entered a new land, an unknown continent, a virgin forest, a hidden cave: Here, the land or the forest or the cave said, in a whisper, Here is the temple built just for you. Here is the altar. Here is the incense. And here. Here is the answer.

Finally, at the end of May, spring arrived. A chinook wind melted a foot of snow in less than a day. Hiram breathed out, and then he breathed in. Neither hurt. The soft, warm wind lulled him to sleep, and so did the sound of the swirling river, but he fought off both the wind and the river. After all, he had been in this shack in the Cotton River Valley since March and hadn't so much as spotted a wolf, let alone aim at or kill one. He would've settled for a coyote. Or a mule deer. Hell, he would've settled for a prairie dog at this point, but he hadn't seen any of those either. He wondered if the snow blindness had actually blinded him; if what he was seeing was simply the memory of what he had seen. But then, just like that, it happened. On a warm June night. He'd just poured himself some whiskey and settled into his chair. He was rocking it back and forth, though it wasn't a rocking chair. The stars were out, twinkling, full and plump and ready to be picked. The night was deceptively soft and sinless. Hiram sighed. He blinked and looked north, his mind empty, in the way that whiskey empties the mind, heats the body, moistens the eyes with gold and mercy. And it was through this lonely emptiness, this tender silence, that Hiram finally saw him: the wolf. And not just any wolf, the Great Gray Wolf. Though how could he know? How could he possibly know? No one had told him. So all Hiram saw — in the distance, against the vast northern sky, walking through the waist-high and whispering silver grass — was a wolf. A wolf like no other. He'd seen them before of course, when he'd gone hunting with Irish Joe, but he'd never seen a wolf like this: so tall that it rose above the high grass, impossibly majestic and graceful, as if it weren't walking at all, but sailing at the helm of an ancient ship, on a calm and ancient sea. And its eyes. Even from a hundred, maybe two hundred feet away, its eyes glowed terribly: They were the drawing out of night; they were the breaking of dawn. Hiram was mesmerized. Struck dumb. He forgot the glass of whiskey in his hand, he forgot the chair, nearly tipped over now, and he certainly forgot the rifle leaning against the door. Then the wolf was gone. Just like that. It turned, stopped, sniffed the air in Hiram's direction, and then it was gone.

Hiram felt nothing for a moment, as if an immense wind had swept through him, but then, in the next, he kicked himself. Why hadn't he shot it? Why? Imagine: If he'd gotten it, he would've been the talk of Montana Territory, the talk of the whole of the West! He brooded, kicking himself, though, in his heart of hearts, in the deepest recesses of his soul, he wasn't kicking himself at all; he was in awe. Of what? A wolf? That's silly, he told himself. I'm a wolf hunter. How can I be in awe of the thing I am meant to kill? *Trained* to kill. But the awe. The awe remained.

A few weeks later, it happened again.

He saw the wolf. This time he was ready: His rifle was loaded; he was not addled by whiskey; his chair rested flat on the ground. Still, the wolf took his breath away. Standing tall and proud on the prow of the prairie. In the moonlight. Shimmering. Hiram picked up the rifle. He pointed. The wolf once again stopped, sniffed the air. Its eyes shone red. Inside Hiram's mind, his body, every cell screamed, Shoot, Shoot. His index finger, curled snug against the trigger, said, Shoot, Shoot. His eyes squinted and they said, What are you waiting for, Hiram? Shoot. Even the high summer night sky and all its votive stars, and the rough-hewn planks of his tiny wooden shack, and the isosceles triangle of the towering cottonwood trees, said, Hiram, my lad. You were born for this. You were born to shoot this wolf. Don't you see? Shoot. Shoot the wolf. For the briefest instant, this commotion of voices, tauntings, urgings, one upon the other, confused Hiram. The moonlight dazzled him. Made him feverish. And in this fever dream, he looked with narrowed eyes at the wolf, its gray shining coat under the chandelier of night, and saw the lobby of the Palace Hotel. Kitty was there. The perfume of flowers and Darjeeling tea. Blue porcelain tinkling as it was caressed by silver. A string of pearls rivaling the moon. And the dress was there. Her gray silk dress, draped over the plush Oriental carpet of rose-yellow grass. Lifting a little in the wind. Falling in folds so lovely, so alive, it was as if the dress itself were an animal, unleashed.

He pulled the trigger.

The wolf stood and stood, then went unsteady, and then it fell.

Hiram stood for a long while. Breathing fast. The gun still raised. The sound of the shot echoed, but against what? There were no hills, no cliffs, no chasms, just open prairie, and yet it echoed. It reached Hiram again and again and clanged so monstrously against his eardrums that he threw the rifle to the ground and closed his ears. Still, it echoed. He braced against the door, and still it echoed. He kicked the chair, and still. Until finally, he dropped to his knees, touched his head to the ground, and only then, only when he was in the posture of a supplicant, did it stop. He got up slowly, took up his rifle again, and walked through the triangle of cottonwood trees and made his way to where he thought the wolf had gone down. There was plenty of light by the moon and the stars, but still, Hiram grew disoriented and wandered for what seemed an eternity through the prairie grass, looking this way and that. Nothing. Where could it have gone? The night deepened, and then the sky began to lighten to the east, and Hiram began to wonder whether he'd dreamed it all. *Had* there been a wolf? Was there a Hiram? After what seemed like endless trekking in ever-widening circles, he tripped. He looked down.

The wolf.

Hiram stared at it, unbelieving. He understood suddenly

what it was to yearn for the divine, to gaze upon the other-worldly. Never in his life had he seen a creature so desperately beautiful and powerful and noble. Even dead. Wait, *was* it dead? He knelt (again). The gunshot wound was in its hind quarter, the bullet lodged in a mangle of splintered bone and guts and gray, gushing organs. The ground and the grass were splattered with blood. Hiram's hand shook as he stretched it toward the wolf's stomach, but he never reached it because, just as he was about to touch the edge of its bloodstained and matted fur, the wolf blinked. *Blinked.* Hiram reeled backward. It was through his peripheral vision that he'd seen the blink, and so he chose not to believe it. He sat on the ground and refused to raise his eyes. Not since he'd been a child had he been so stubborn, so non-sensical. But it was not a child's fear he felt. It was an adult fear. A man's fear. The oldest, most human of fears. *That* is the fear that Hiram felt.

He knew what he had to do.

He rose slowly, picked up the rifle for the last time in his life, and walked around the wolf, clockwise, so that he had to circum-navigate its body to arrive at its eyes. And when he did, he raised the rifle up and then, and only then, did he look into them. What he felt was peace, such peace that tears began to wash over his cheeks, and drip, one by one, like the drops of blood from the dying hairs of the wolf. In fact, they were falling in unison: the tears from Hiram, the blood from the wolf. The wolf's eyes blinked one last time, and it seemed to Hiram that he nodded, ever so slightly. No, not a he, he realized. A she. Hiram gestured that he understood, through his tears, and then he lifted the rifle, pointed it between her eyes, and it was then, just as the sun hit them, that Hiram saw that it was her eyes, and not the sun, that illuminated them all. He pulled the trigger and killed the wolf. Knowing, in that moment, that he'd killed a god.

Chapter 10

Of the five main ways of removing a dam Sagar picked the notch and release method. With this method notches were cut into the top of a dam, one at a time, over the course of many months, and the water and sediment from the reservoir were allowed to drain into the river and reach an equilibrium before the next notch was cut. There were quicker ways: detonation, of course, and the rapid release method, which involved digging a large tunnel at the base of the dam and letting all the water and sediment being held in the reservoir drain out in one go. This method was the cheapest option, but it had its drawbacks, just as detonation did — such a massive and sudden release of water could cause flooding and erosion and could destabilize the river's ecosystem. In one case study that Sagar read, the rapid release approach had discharged such an astounding amount of water that it had broken through substantial levees and flooded an entire village in Ecuador.

He tried to explain his rationale to the mayor, Sam Dooley, and about Ecuador, but he never got the chance.

He was walking back to the trailer late one afternoon, hoping to run some calculations, and was surprised to see the lights still on; he thought Tim Downing had gone home. When he walked in, Tim was at his desk, talking to another man. They broke off abruptly when he entered. The man studied Sagar with fierce gray eyes. Tim barely acknowledged him, but the man extended his large hand and said, "Sam Dooley. Mayor of Mansfield. You must be the Indian they brought over from India."

Sagar, taken aback, nodded awkwardly.

Tim Downing said, "Mayor Dooley has been involved with the dam removal project from the beginning. How long have I known you, Sam?"

"Going on . . . what? Ten years now?"

"That's right, that's right. We met the night Gabe got beat up by that motorcycle gang. You remember that night?"

Sam Dooley chuckled in response.

Sagar thought, *Involved* with the dam removal project? And have they really known each other for ten *years*? And then he thought, Who is Gabe?

He'd seen the grainy photo of Sam Dooley on the internet, but now, standing next to him, it was clear to Sagar that he came from old Montana stock. He was in his early forties, he guessed, with muscled arms and neck, and calloused hands, forged by what could only be decades spent steering cattle and breaking horses and riding in the open wind, brazenly, in winter cold and summer heat alike. He was wearing a workman's vest and a cowboy hat. His face was the leathery reddish ocher of buttes at sunset. Before he even spoke, Sagar saw the dash of frontier arrogance; it was clear that he'd been taught one way to be a man and had become that man.

Sam Dooley said, "I'm not like Timbo here. I'm in touch with my feminine side. And I don't mind telling you it'll break my heart to see it get blown up."

"Blown up?"

"Our dam."

Sagar didn't understand initially. Then his eyes widened. "No, no, it's not going to get blown up. Not at all." And then he explained to him about the notch and release method. Sagar was about to explain the other methods, and why he'd chosen it over detonation, but Sam Dooley stopped him and said, "How many will it take?"

"How many . . . ?"

"To drain it."

Sagar started to explain that tests would have to be conducted after each notch and the results analyzed, but Sam Dooley interrupted him. He said, "You telling me they brought you all the way over from India to punch a couple of holes in the dam? And you can't even tell me how many?" He turned to Tim Downing and said, his voice now cold, "The State of Montana couldn't find someone out here to do the thing?"

They both laughed. When he was done laughing, Sam Dooley said, "Listen here, I don't give a damn what this *method* of yours is, this dam isn't coming down. You understand me?"

Sagar stared at him. And then at Tim Downing. "But the DNRC . . ."

Sam Dooley smiled, in a way that made the hair on the back of Sagar's neck stand on end. "The DNRC, my boy, don't rule this valley. I do."

In the sudden silence, he heard one of the technicians calling to another, and the distant rush of the river. He said, "If you have an issue with the dam removal, I can refer you to my boss, Ben Mackey. He'd be able to — "

"You shittin' me?" Sam Dooley turned to Tim and said, "Is he fucking with me?"

"Sir," Tim Downing said, smirking, "Sir Ben Mackey."

Sagar looked from one to the other, but they were already walking toward the door.

In the quiet of the trailer after they left Sagar paced, enraged. The mayor of Mansfield? A rancher? What did he know about dams? Hydraulics? Infrastructure? It was Sam Dooley's second question that angered him most. Of all the things he wished he'd said, he should've told him that they'd brought him *all the way over from India* because he was good, because he was one of the best hydraulic engineers at the Central Water Commission, which made him one of the best in India. And what was more, he wished he'd told him he was experienced. This dam is nothing, he should've told him, compared to the hydroelectric dams I've worked on, hundreds of feet tall and holding back rivers that make the Cotton River look like a minor stream. And not only that, he should've told him that he'd used the notch and release method before, on the Majuli River, a tributary of the Brahmaputra, in the eastern state of Assam. This *exact* method, he should've said.

But no, he'd said none of it.

During his breaks, or while waiting for tests to run, Sagar researched other aspects of the dam removal, such as the burial site, considered sacred by the local tribe. He read articles about excavations of burial sites and mounds, which said that in Montana the State Historic Preservation Office had to be notified first if any human remains were found at a site. After that, the tribes who were affiliated with the remains had to be informed. The artifacts and remains then had to be protected and returned to the tribes (which was dictated by a federal law called the Native American Graves Protection and Repatriation Act); the tribe decided where and how to rebury them. The actual excavation, he learned, usually involved dividing the burial site into grids, the soil removed carefully, layer by layer, with each artifact that was found cleaned, bagged, recorded, and photographed.

Sagar was amazed. The burial site's excavation seemed to have just as many regulations as the dam removal.

He knew there was a monitor at the site supervising the excavation — since they must have a team, given all the work involved — but who was it? He decided to find out and walked down to the site one afternoon, following the dirt road bordering the western bank of the river, which soon thinned into a narrow, overgrown path; Sagar had to brush aside thick vines and step gingerly around poison ivy to get to a grassy clearing edged with cottonwoods. At the base of one of the cottonwoods was a guy eating his lunch. When Sagar emerged from the bramble, the man held up a stick of celery and said, "Trade you for a Big Mac."

Sagar laughed and said, "Sorry to interrupt your lunch."

"Lunch? Even the rabbits are avoiding me."

His name was Alex Mendoza, and Sagar vaguely recalled meeting him on his first day; he was a technician working under Tim Downing. Sagar asked him how the job was going and Alex Mendoza looked contemptuously at the celery stick and said, "I've had worse bosses, but that's not saying much."

Sam Dooley's threat flashed in Sagar's mind. Should he tell Mr. Mackey about it? And how could he even bring it up? After all, he had yet to meet him in person.

When Sagar told him he was going to the burial site, Alex Mendoza flung the stick of celery over his shoulder and said, "Mind if I join you? Maybe they've dug up some fossilized french fries."

Sagar said, "I thought I should introduce myself to the monitor."

"You met her."

"I did?"

"First day. Renny. Renny Atwood. Standing next to me. An archeologist, from what I understand."

Sagar stopped in his tracks.

"What's wrong?"

"I messed up her name. The last time I saw her."

Alex Mendoza slapped him on the back and chuckled. "Long as it wasn't in bed."

Sagar was amazed. Was this how men spoke to each other in America? So freely? He was taken aback by it but felt instantly warmed by his good humor. They were nearing the burial site when a voice on Alex Mendoza's walkie-talkie summoned him. He rolled his eyes and said, "Never fails." Turning to go, he said, "Downing's such a downer."

Sagar agreed with a smile, feeling even closer to him, and then they said goodbye. As he approached the burial site, he saw Renny and two other people. All three were crouched on the ground, digging. Renny got up when she saw him and waved. The other two he didn't recognize. They were young, maybe students from the community college. Renny said, "Should I be worried? We don't often have fancy engineers visiting us."

Sagar reddened. He said, "Not at all. I was curious. I've only read about the site."

Her arm swept across the cordoned-off section, about a fifth of an acre, and she said, "Here it is, in all its glory."

"How old is it?"

"Don't know yet. We're sending these to the lab," she said, leading him to a plastic table laid out with textile fragments, an arrowhead, and some shards of pottery.

Sagar studied each of them and then he said, "Have there been human bones?"

She smiled. "Everybody wants to know . . ."

He thought she would go on, but she didn't. There was again a playful glimmer in her eyes, the one he'd seen the morning he'd confused her name.

Looking out at the Cotton, she asked, "Do you bury your dead?"

"No, we cremate them. Hindus do." And then, because he couldn't stop himself, he told her about Varanasi and the Ganga and Manikarnika Ghat. He told her of how Hindus believed that to die and be cremated in Varanasi, on the shores of the Ganga, was considered the highest honor. "We achieve Moksha," he said, "which is to reach Nirvana, an end to our cycle of rebirths." And then he told her of how, at Manikarnika Ghat, there were a hundred cremations per day, burning all day and night, year-around. The ashes are released into the river, he said. Then, after a moment, he said, "There is nothing like it, seeing those pyres burning at sunset. You'll never think of life or death or even the soul the same way again. The best thing to do is hire a boat to take you out onto the river. They're quite affordable, you see, and . . ." He stopped. He sounded like a tour guide.

They were silent. He saw her looking at him, searching his face. After a moment, she said, "So is this river."

"What?"

"Holy. The water. The fish. One of our elders, from the Karuk Tribe in California, he said it best. He said, 'The river is our church, the salmon is our cross.' He was talking about the Klamath River, but it's the same with the Cotton."

How strange. He'd never known another people to consider a river a place of worship. A thing *to be* worshipped.

Then she said, "Ours doesn't have any funeral pyres, but it does have the bodies."

"I read about them. In an article online."

Renny looked at him. "Did it mention they are all women? And all Native?"

"No . . ."

He wanted to ask her more about that, but one of the students called to her. Sagar watched as she turned and kneeled to look at something he was holding toward her. He liked the intelligence in her eyes, and the way she moved with such purpose. Whether talking to him, or with the men in the construction crew, as she had been on the day they'd met, she seemed perfectly at ease and determined. Perhaps what also drew him to her, though he was too shy to admit it to himself, was that she and Janavi had similar physiques. Small breasts and oval faces and slim ankles. He caught himself staring at them, Renny's ankles, and turned away abruptly. He was pummeled by a shrill sadness, and then a bitterness that infuriated him. He mumbled a quick goodbye to Renny and trampled back through the bramble, paying no attention to the poison ivy, which, rubbing calamine lotion onto his arms and legs the next day, he came to regret.

Though the dams were the same in many ways, the biggest difference between the dam on the Majuli and the one on the Cotton was their ages. The Cotton River dam was built in 1937 and the Majuli River dam was built fifty years later. And it was this age difference, more than anything else, that Sagar guessed was the reason he'd been hired for the Cotton River job. He was a sediment expert and sediment, in the removal of a dam that was the age of the Cotton River dam, was complicated. One of the first things Ben Mackey said to him was, "Be careful with the sediment analysis. Colstrip is close. Don't want to fuck that up."

Sagar had to laugh. The dams on the Cotton and the Majuli might have been similar but his two bosses on the projects, Mr. Mackey and Mr. Mandal, couldn't be more opposite. Mr. Mandal had been strict and efficient and hierarchical. He'd insisted on daily reports even when Sagar had been in the field, in places like the Majuli damsite, where phone reception was spotty and access to computers nearly impossible. He'd made all his subordinates call him Sir, even calling him Mr. Mandal had not been allowed; Sagar had worked under him for a year before he'd learned his first name. Mr. Mackey, on the other hand, the first time he and Sagar finally met, said, "Mr. Mackey's my dad. Everybody calls me Mack. Ben if you're feeling formal." And then he said, "Mind if I call you Saag?" It was the Hindi word for *spinach* but that was all right. Sagar then asked him if he wanted daily reports, to which Mr. Mackey laughed and said, "How about this, cowboy? How about you let me know if there's a problem."

When Sagar told Janavi about how casual Mr. Mackey — Mack — had been, she told him she'd had a similar experience just that day. They were chatting more, he and Janavi. Sharing what had happened during their day, or some new thing they'd seen or heard. He found himself looking forward to their evenings together.

"Similar how?" he asked.

Janavi told him an elderly neighbor, Charlotte Knudsen, had stopped by earlier in the afternoon. She'd brought over a casserole, which was some sort of baked dish with chicken and cheese. "Where is it?" Sagar asked. Janavi pointed to the refrigerator and then she told him Mrs. Knudsen had said, "Call me Lottie. Only my parents called me Charlotte. Since they died, I hardly ever hear it anymore." When Janavi had asked if she'd like her to call her Charlotte, she'd said, "Oh, I don't think so. It'll only remind me of them. Now say your name again for me, dear. Real slow." When she did, Lottie had said, "That's a mouthful. What did you say you were named after? A river? That's nice. Real nice." And then she'd said, "I'll just call you V. Easier for this old memory of mine."

When Janavi had finished telling him about Lottie, Sagar said, "Didn't your sister call you Janoo?"

"Yes. Why?"

Just as the Ganga has many names, he wanted to say, Now, so do you.

Sagar did not understand immediately what Mack had meant when he'd brought up Colstrip, but it didn't take him long to realize he'd been talking about tailings. They were in Montana after all, and tailings were waste that was left over from mining ore. This waste was mostly ground rock mixed with unrecoverable metals and chemicals and other effluents. And Colstrip, which was a few miles west of the Cotton River, had an open-pit strip mine; it was possible that contaminated tailings from that mine had seeped into the sediment in the Cotton River reservoir. But when Sagar tested the sediment he found no contaminants from tailings and though the salination content was on the high side, it was within range of normal. He was jubilant. He couldn't understand his relief. He'd become so deeply connected to the Cotton River, its health and its future, and in such a short time, that he wondered if it was not that his wife was named after a river but that the river had *become* his wife.

The Cotton River: He told Janavi some of what he knew but not all of it. He knew, for instance, that it was born from snowmelt on the summits of the Bighorn Mountains, in Wyoming, and that it emptied into the Yellowstone River near Miles City. He knew that it flowed for over 250 miles, some of which he'd already driven, most of which he hadn't. He knew a little of its country, its canyons and its breaks and its pine hills, its buttes and its bluffs and its prairie grasslands. He knew the facts of it, this modest river in the southeastern corner of Montana, but growing up Hindu, or maybe growing up Indian, he knew that no structure that was holy — whether a temple or a church or a mosque or a synagogue or even an abandoned hut with a forgotten altar — should be walked into and walked out of without first sitting down. Sitting down and that, too, in silence. It was the only way, he had been told, or perhaps had always known, to know holiness. And rivers, too, and oceans and lakes and streams: It was impossible to know them without stepping into them.

After his conversation with Renny about the holiness of rivers, he wondered if she felt the same.

Sagar, finding himself alone one early morning along the Cotton, took off his shoes and his socks and rolled up his pants and stepped into the water. It was cold, still holding the morning chill, and it was clear. Its flow, the water swirling around his ankles and then his calves, was stronger than he'd guessed. He looked down at the minnows. And then toward the opposite bank where there was a stand of cottonwoods and in their branches, warblers and chats and buntings.

He dug his toes into the sediment.

A river was not a wife, of course he knew that, but what was less clear to him was why, standing now in the Cotton, he should feel a sudden urge to weep. To lie down in the water and let it carry him. The slim ankles. The curve of her hips. He had tried, twice now, to reach out to Janavi in the night. He'd thought, If we come together in darkness, maybe we'll be brought together in light. She had not exactly rejected him so much as not responded in the least, which was worse. His hands had reached out and caressed a body and that body had been indifferent. Standing now in the Cotton, he thought, A river is never that cruel. It is never apathetic. You can touch it and it will touch you back. It was only now, thousands of miles away, that he understood why so many of the rivers in India were named for goddesses. For women. Somewhere, in an ancient time, someone who'd named the rivers of the Indus Valley had understood a small thing: that what is embraced and what will embrace in return are rarely the same.

Chapter 11

What Janavi didn't tell Sagar about Lottie Knudsen's visit was her barrage of questions about their marriage. She was inordinately excited to learn that they were recently married. She said, "Newlyweds? How long did you say?" When Janavi told her, she said, "This is the best time, dear. Enjoy it. Don't let the little things bother you."

Little things?

Lottie was saying, "My husband owned a ranch. Inherited from his father. Worked it for nearly fifty-five years, we did. Died in a snowdrift. Just walked out one winter morning and never came back. That's when I sold it and moved into town. I live right around the corner. In the pink house. Can't miss it."

"Did you grow up here?" Janavi asked.

"Canada. Just north of the border. In a little town called Val Marie." And then she said, "Why don't you have an accent?"

Janavi told her about the call center and then she told her about ChildDefense. "I had to quit. When we got married."

Janavi assumed she would ask how Janavi had met Sagar or tell her how she'd met her husband, but instead Lottie said, "While I was in college, the Canadian government was recruiting for an internship in the Northwest Territories. I said to my mother, 'See? You're wrong. There are uses for my anthropology degree.' I applied and next thing I knew I was on a bus and then a floatplane and then a sled. A sled, can you believe it? I was sent up there to observe an Inuit tribe. A small one living near the Arctic Circle. Their customs, beliefs, all of that of course, but mainly what the government people wanted to understand was why this tribe had the highest suicide rate in Canada. Maybe in the world. They just couldn't make sense of it.

"And so there I was with my notebook and my pencil and my earnestness. Within a day I'd met practically every person in the village. Despite everything they were awfully kind to me. I mean here I was, with my notebook, watching them as if they were zoo animals but they were still kind. When I got there, they were preparing to go on a seal hunt. They took me along. The first seal they killed I thought we would take back to the village and cook, but they started eating it right there. Blood all the way up their arms, all over their faces. They handed me a piece of the meat and at first, I said no, and then it occurred to me that I was being a fool. What did I think I was going to eat?

"Some things I learned quickly, like enjoying the taste of raw seal meat, but other things took time. For instance, I learned that the tribe's numbering system only went up to the number three. That was the highest number they knew. Or wanted to know. And they had no possessions. They had no concept of possession. One day a family would buy a new tool, an axe, let's say, and a few days later someone might need it and so they'd come and get the axe. And then the next person would get it from the person who'd taken it. And so on. When the original family needed the axe, they had to go around searching for it. Didn't bother them one bit. One other thing I learned was that they had no concept of time. No clocks, no watches. Strange, I know. But nothing, no event, no moment, no passing, was marked by time. Or *in* time. It made them . . . I don't know, it seemed to bring them closer. As if without time they were free to truly love. Maybe that's what led to the suicide rate. Love. Without time, maybe they didn't know the pain of it would pass. I couldn't say. I wrote everything down, but I never did figure it out. I don't think the Canadian government did either. Between you and me," she said, looking up with a smile, "they didn't really want to know. They just wanted to *look* like they wanted to know."

Then she explained to Janavi about the casserole. She told her to reheat it in the oven at 350 degrees for twenty minutes. She said a nice side dish with the casserole might be roasted carrots or maybe fresh homemade biscuits with lots of butter. She said, "You know how to make them?" Janavi said no, she'd never made nor eaten homemade biscuits. Lottie nodded and said, "When I got married, didn't know how to boil an egg. But being on a ranch? By the end of the first month, I was cooking for a dozen men. All of twenty-two years old. The first time I saw John he was on a horse, driving cattle. Most any man looks good on a horse but he — he was a rare thing. We were married two weeks later."

Janavi expressed no surprise.

Lottie said, "You all had one of those arranged marriages, didn't you?"

"Yes. In a way."

"What's his name?"

When Janavi told her, she said, "Is he a good man?"

Janavi looked at her. She had no answer.

Lottie said, "As pretty as you are, he better be."

Janavi blushed. She said, "Was your husband?"

"No," she said, without hesitating. "He was an asshole." Her voice had a brittleness to it, Janavi noticed, a dried-up grievance preserved in amber. Then she said, "You know what killed him? Out in that snowdrift?"

Janavi couldn't possibly guess, though Lottie seemed to be waiting for her to answer.

"His own anger."

They were silent.

Janavi's phone rang. Rajni. She turned off the ringer. She saw Lottie watching her, and she said, "Jane Austen wrote that happiness in a marriage is a matter of chance."

"Is that right?" Lottie rose to go. She used the table and the back of her chair to pivot. She said, "She has a point, but she didn't say what the odds are."

"The odds?"

"Sure. Flipping a coin is chance. So is winning the lottery. One is fifty-fifty. And the other? Who knows. One in a million?" Then she said, "Don't forget now. Three-fifty for twenty minutes."

Janavi walked her to the door. She said, "So what is marriage?"

Lottie smiled. "What was it called? The one that was a billion dollars. Just the other day."

Neither knew. Janavi had seen ads for it on television, but she couldn't think of the name. She said, "Mega something?"

Lottie laughed and said, "Yes. That one."

That night, while Janavi was lying on her side, her back to Sagar, she felt his hand on her. Janavi froze.

He had reached for her before, soon after they'd arrived, but she'd thought he might've simply brushed against her in his sleep; this time there was no mistaking it. His hand was caressing her waist. She felt the heat of it through her pajama top. She felt panic, desire, anger, duty, defiance, nothingness — confusion and heat swirled inside of her. She couldn't move. She lay perfectly still, deepening her breathing. Feigning sleep. Did he believe it? Probably not.

In the morning, she noticed, relieved, that Sagar was avoiding her eyes.

After he left for work, Janavi thought about Lottie's question. *Was* Sagar a good man? She had been so wrapped up in her rage, her misery, that she'd never considered the question. She thought about it all afternoon and the only answer she could find was: it depends. Depends on what? Rajni would say that, besides her husband, Sagar was the best of men, if only because he'd given her what she'd asked for. Her father, now that the shock of having his younger daughter marry Sagar rather than the older had worn off, had said as much when they'd last talked. Feeling sentimental, she supposed, he'd said, "Both of my daughters are married to fine men. What more can a father ask for?"

She'd said nothing in return.

Would her amma have thought he was a good man? She remembered how her amma had given Rajni the bigger piece of fish and how she'd told Janavi it was because she had more fight in her. Did her amma equate goodness with grit? If so, she would probably say, I don't know. I don't know yet if he is a good man. As for Sagar's family they would obviously say he was a good man. No one would admit to raising a bad man. But it was more complicated than that. She'd felt it. She'd felt it when she'd gone to stay with her in-laws after the wedding. It was nothing obvious. But sometimes around the dinner table or when she was helping her mother-in-law cook or when she was serving her father-in-law coffee, there seemed in them a coldness, a withholding. Perhaps they were slow to warm to others or maybe they, too, were stunned by a daughter-in-law they had not expected, and Janavi was mistaking that feeling for aloofness, but she wasn't convinced. They had in them a strange and brutal reserve. She sensed it most when his younger brother, Sandeep, was in the room. Almost as if his presence were the lens that magnified their strangeness. She'd noticed, of course, that he wasn't able to fully lift his right arm and though it was certainly an affliction, it didn't, in her mind, warrant the excessive solicitousness of the mother — as if he were a baby bird in a high nest — nor the nonsensical leniency of the father, who seemed perfectly content to have his adult son sit around and do nothing with his life.

She might be undecided as to whether Sagar was a good man but Sandeep, in her opinion, was not. They'd only had a handful of interactions in the three days she'd been in Rajahmundry but that had been enough. On one occasion, she'd passed him in the hall and as was the custom, she'd draped the pallu of her sari over her head. Sandeep, seeing this, had said, "Sister dearest, no need for all that modesty. Didn't Sagar tell you? Aside from the betrothal bit we're a modern family." That might've been true but why say it in that tone? With the slightest sneer. Another time, while they were all seated in the living room, Sagar had gotten up to go to the market. She couldn't remember why. Maybe to buy pakora or bhajji to snack on with their afternoon tea. Sandeep, watching him put on his shoes, had said, "Take her with you. You're newlyweds! It'll be romantic."

Sagar, obviously abashed, had said to Janavi, "Would you like to come along?"

Sandeep had guffawed. "Don't *ask* her. You see that, Amma? Since when does he ask?"

Janavi had looked from one to the other, not understanding any of it.

She wanted to bring it up with Sagar. She almost did when he took her to the dam. More precisely, it was she who took Sagar to the dam; she'd just gotten her driver's license and wanted to practice. At one point, at a curve in the road, Sagar reached over and put his hand over hers, on the steering wheel, to turn the wheel harder. She looked down, suddenly discomfited by the heat and coarse of his skin. Why did she want him to keep it there? Why, at the end of the curve, when he withdrew it, did she want to say, Stay?

When they arrived, he told her to park the car in a gravel lot above the dam and then led her down a slope to its northern edge. Ahead of them and to their left was the reservoir and beyond it were low red hills spotted with pine. He explained to her about the notches and the sediment analysis and how the river's ecosystem would be affected by the removal of the dam. She said, "So the fish can't get through right now?

They're stuck on one side or the other?" He told her the only way to avoid it and keep the dam was to construct fish ladders, which were expensive and not always feasible. He also told her about how he'd worked on the dam removal project in Assam. On the Brahmaputra.

"What was that like? Was it like this?"

"Yes and no," he said. And then he laughed and said, "It was Assam."

She understood what he meant. She'd never been there but she'd seen pictures of the jungles and the mountains, the villages cascading down steep slopes. The state was bordered on one side by the Eastern Himalayas, nothing like these low hills and buttes.

He picked a sprig of sagebrush and handed it to her. Taste it, he said. It tasted bitter and felt cool in her mouth, like camphor, and in a rush every temple she had ever visited came back to her. The burning camphor. She'd heard once that Hindu temples were constructed in the shape of the journey of the soul toward God. Each room narrower than the last until, in the end, the smallest room was only big enough for one person. She looked downstream. On the side of the river on which they were standing was a grove of cottonwood trees from which, she assumed, the Cotton River had gotten its name. She said, "Let's go sit there," and so they walked to the shade of the trees. Sagar sat on the grass, and she sat with her back to one of the trunks. He said, "They release seeds that are carried by a cottony fluff. In the summer." She looked up into their leaves. Silver in the sunlight. She heard the hum of the river; she strained her ears but heard nothing else. She said, "It's such a quiet country." Sagar nodded; he, too, had become a part of the boundless silence. She looked again at the river and felt, in a rush of surprise, the taste of the bites of yogurt rice her amma had fed her, and in its wake, she felt the tug she'd felt standing in the Ganga, at the age of thirteen. She shuddered. Why now? Why again? Would every river call to her? Call to her to drown? She was glad when Sagar interrupted her thoughts. He was pointing downriver. She saw a gentle rise in the distance, to the south.

He said, "That's the burial site. Over there."

"A burial site?" She couldn't believe it. "You've never mentioned a burial site."

Sagar said, surprised, "I haven't?"

"What kind of burial site?"

"Native American. The local tribe," he told her.

"There's a tribe here?"

"Their reservation's just a few miles from here," he said. "They've been advocating for the dam's removal for decades."

She'd had no idea.

The burial site, according to Sagar, was nothing like the buildings in Mansfield, the oldest of which, as she'd seen, was constructed in 1878. This site, he said, was hundreds of years old or maybe even older.

"But — why would the tribe want the dam taken down? And relocate their own burial site?"

"I know it's counterintuitive," he said, "but with the dam taken down, there's going to be so much more *life*. The river will run free. After all this time, nearly a hundred years!"

Janavi thought it over. She said, "But why? Why would they place a burial site so close to the river?"

Sagar laughed. "Well, it probably wasn't. Not back then. Rivers change course, you know. Sometimes by many miles over a very short period. Every river does and back then this site probably seemed far enough removed from the river. It was on a high bluff, you see, but the bluff, too, was washed away. By a long-ago flood, I bet. Anyway, it's being excavated."

"Are you in charge of that too?"

"No, no. Not at all," he said. "There's a tribal monitor who's in charge of the excavation. An archeologist. And she has students from the community college assisting her."

Janavi knew there were Native American tribes in Montana, all over America, really, but she'd had no idea they had burial mounds and fishing traditions and were involved in the very same dam project as Sagar.

She looked at him then, a little shyly, or maybe with something like pride, and thought, What important work he's doing. Ancient and important and challenging and inspiring. Since they'd been married, she'd assumed she'd been the only one doing important work, with Child-Defense, and that it had been ripped away from her, but she saw now, or was beginning to see, that Sagar's work, too, was compelling and necessary in its own way. She said, "Have you met her? The monitor?"

"A few times," he said.

She said, "What's her name?"

"Renny," he said. "Her name is Renny."

Renny. She'd never heard that name before.

Janavi looked again at the river and then the reservoir. How they each held water so differently. She knew rivers could change course but even one so placid? So unassuming? Sagar was sitting with his eyes closed. What was he thinking? Or was he sleeping? She thought of his hand again, on top of hers. What was she supposed to have done? The other night when he'd reached for her? Her anger, even now, while they were talking and laughing, even when she felt pride or kinship, refused to subside. It held like a barnacle. But who was she angry with? Rajni, mostly. Sagar, for letting her talk him into it. Varanasi, for letting her go. Montana, for letting her in. None of it made sense, and yet, seated now under the cottonwoods, she saw, without delight, that Sagar was what she had. The last island. He opened his eyes, and she nodded in the direction of the burial site and said, "What do you think they'll find?"

He said, "In this country? Almost anything they want!"

Janavi looked at him and then into the canopy of cottonwoods. The barnacle held fast. Despite its tenacity, its hardness, she thought, If a river can change course then maybe I can too.

That night, she heated up Lottie's casserole for dinner. It came out of the oven and when they heaped it onto their plates, they saw there were tiny pasta shells in it, along with peas and potatoes and a creamy sauce mixed in with the chicken. There was a golden layer of cheese on top. Janavi took a bite. She'd never tasted anything like it. It reminded her a little bit of a sizzler, without the sizzling part of course. It was the same mishmash of ingredients, almost too many, though this was bland — too bland. Sagar agreed and he got up, rummaged in the kitchen cabinet, and came back with salt and red chili pepper and curry powder. These they added to the casserole and when they took a bite, Sagar said, "Better," and Janavi said, "Way better."

Chapter 12

The morning started like all the others — most everyone arrived at the damsite by 7 a.m., filing into the trailer to fill their coffee mugs and then shuffling back out to start their day. It was sunny in the morning; the thin mist that sometimes hovered above the river had burned off by the time Sagar went out to take calculations of the flow velocity and water depth. As he walked along the Cotton, he caught a glimpse of a white-tailed deer as it disappeared into a grove of trees on the far shore. By midmorning, he noticed a bank of thick clouds rising out of the west. "Storm's coming," Alex Mendoza said as Sagar walked past him. He saw it coming too — as all storms could be seen on the prairie, even when they were hours away — but the strength of this one seemed to catch everyone unawares. The rain came in sheets. Some ran to the trailer, others huddled under the pop-up tent canopy. Sagar, still on the banks of the river, ran toward a tarp that was covering some small machinery and digging equipment being stored in a narrow coulee. Bur oak and Manitoba maple rose in the distance and silhouetted the sky, and by the time Sagar reached the tarp, their branches waved frantically in the wind. Renny and Alex Mendoza were already huddled under it. Sagar wiped at his wet jeans. When he looked up and saw Renny shivering, he took off his jacket and said, "It's not totally drenched." Renny took it with a nod and a small smile, and then she gazed out from under the tarp. She said, "This one's going to last a while." No one disagreed. Alex Mendoza upturned two wooden crates for Renny and Sagar and settled himself on a wobbly cooler. They sat in silence, a little awkwardly, each avoiding the others' eyes, looking out at the storm, listening to the wind. The crack of lightning. Thunder to wake the dead. The clouds heavy and dark. Alex Mendoza broke the spell of the storm and said, "You all have ghost stories over there? Over in India?"

"Of course we do. Everybody tells ghost stories. All over the world."

"Tell me one of yours."

Sagar couldn't think of one, not a single one. He said, "You go first."

"Which state?"

"What do you mean, which state?"

"Every state has its own, of course. Every county practically. You've got to pick carefully."

"Okay then. Montana. Custer County."

Renny laughed and shook her head, as if they were two boys at play.

Alex paid her no attention and said, "Alright, now. That's the ticket. That's the specificity we need. Now, the story I'm about to tell you is true. Every word. Not true like you and I are true, mind you. But true like the wind is true and this here coulee is true. True like the sunset is true and true in the way the grass bends to us but never submits, true like that, like the grass is true. Do you understand?"

Sagar nodded into the storm-dark afternoon, not really understanding.

"Now this happened fairly recently. I would say a hundred and fifty years ago, give or take. By then Custer County, all of Montana really, was full of cowboys. Bursting with them. Not many towns out here but lots and lots of cowboys. Driving cattle up and down the prairie, them cattle munching on the best, the most nutritious, the tastiest grass known to man or beast. Blue grama, it was called. Now, when the cowboys were done with their season's work and the roundup was over, the towns set up carnivals to celebrate. Not like the carnivals you and I know or even the carnivals on the East Coast back then, but Wild West–style carnivals. Gun-toting, mayhem-making, shooting-up-a-saloon kind of carnivals. Nothing like it till then and nothing like it since. You see, with the money they made from the roundup the cowboys bought new clothes and set out for town, and the women, well, it was the one time of year the ladies could put on those big bustling dresses they'd had tailored back east — tight at the waist and lace trimmed, the sleeves all puffed up and pretty, and two or three layers of petticoats to give it a full, beautiful sweep. Utterly wrong for the other three hundred sixty-four days out in Montana Territory but perfect for this one day. Now, these towns would have a traveling fiddler — "

"Fiddler?"

Alex Mendoza said, "Fiddle player." He must've seen the confusion in Sagar's face, because he added, "A violin. Played differently."

He told them the fiddler would come through the towns, play for the night, and keep moving to the next town. They might be accompanied by an organ or a piano, if the town's saloon or hotel had one, but the fiddler was the main act, and Alex told them he'd play all kinds of dance music. And the dancing went on all night — for two reasons, he said. The first was that in cowboy country there was so little entertainment, and the work was so grueling, that they needed all night to work off the frontier steam; and the second reason was that the roads were so bad, and with the wolves and the bears and the mountain lions roaming around, it was best to stay in town through the night. Trying to get home in the pitch-dark, he said, his voice low, could mean you didn't get home.

Sagar felt a shudder go through him. He didn't know if it was the rain or Alex's story.

He said, "Now, this particular town I'm telling about — I can't name it, you understand — this particular town had a famous fiddler who came to play that night. Willie was his name. The best damn fiddle player west of the Mississippi. Hell, maybe even west of the Potomac. He knew all the dance music there was to know: square dancing, circle two-steps, schottisches, Highland waltzes, and all kinds of jigs. French jigs, the minuet, and even some Polish folk dance by way of French Canada called varsovienne. Can you believe it? All that and he was just a traveling fiddler in Montana Territory. The dance floor of every place he played was always packed and the dirt floor of this hotel he was playing in that night was no different. Filled with whirling cowboys and ladies in pretty dresses. Not just because the music was good, not just because of that, but because, back then, if a cowboy asked you to dance, you said yes. You had to. It was an insult to him to say no and that insult could get a lady killed."

Renny said, "Not much changes, does it?"

"Sure doesn't," Alex said. "Women die for saying no and men continue to build countries on top of those noes."

A seriousness entered the conversation, an awkwardness that made Sagar self-conscious. He looked out at the rain and then down at his hands.

Alex cleared his throat. "Like I was saying, there they are, dancing the night away, when, all of a sudden, there's a loud crash. Not a gunshot, as one might expect out on the frontier, but a crash. The music stopped. Everyone looked around. They don't see a thing. And then: another crash. This time they realize it's coming from upstairs, where the rooms are. Next thing you know there is a young woman racing down the stairs, her hair undone, crying, her pretty dress torn to pieces. And right behind her is a rough-looking cowboy, rough even for a cowboy. The young woman is barely in front of him, streaking through the room, and right as the cowboy's about to grab her, Willie meets her eyes, just for an instant. But that instant was everything. She ducks behind him, and the cowboy pulls out his gun, and he says to Willie, in a mean, mean voice, 'Git out of the way. Git.' But Willie, his fiddle still in his hand, doesn't move. He doesn't even think about moving. He can feel the young woman's hand on his back, he can feel her breathing, he can feel all the sagebrush in all the prairie standing still, waiting. 'She's got nothing to do with you,' Willie said. 'Nothing at all. You git.'

"The cowboy laughed. Then he aimed his gun.

"Now, here is the strangest part. Here is the part I can't make sense of. Just as the cowboy was about to pull the trigger, just then, quick as a flash, Willie raised his fiddle bow, reached behind him, as if he had a quiver full of arrows strapped to his back (though how could he?), and let fly a thing that knocked the gun out of the cowboy's hand, sliced open his forearm, and had the cowboy on his knees, howling. Blood spurting all over the dirt floor. All of it executed before the cowboy could *pull the trigger*. I suppose a fiddle bow *is* a bow, right? Though here's the mystery: What did he shoot? And how did he shoot it? No one else was hurt. No one found an arrow. No one knew how Willie did it."

Sagar hardly breathed. From his boyhood days reading about fantastic feats of archery in the Ramayana and other myths, he knew how Willie did it.

Alex Mendoza continued, "Back then, surprisingly, or maybe not so surprisingly, there was a keen sense of right and wrong. Not the religious, moralistic kind — they had to dispense with the Indians, after all — " Here, he stopped, knowing he'd put his foot in it, but Renny's expression remained unchanged. "It was the romantic kind, is what I mean. The chivalric kind. The King Arthur and Lancelot kind. So, after Willie saved the damsel, it was only right and true that he should marry her. And he did. Another great day for our little town out on the frontier. And since Willie couldn't afford much in the way of a wedding present for his new bride, he built her a simple sod house, laid a table with candles and plains phlox, and played the fiddle for her all night. Every song he knew. The music drifting across the hushed prairie. No wind at all. And his hands flying like tiny mirrors over sunlit lakes, reflecting everything. And then, finally, in the early morning hours, he and his young bride, her name was Charlene, by the way, made love.

"It went on like this: their sweet, untroubled life. The sod house. Willie traveling with his fiddle and now also with his bride. And coming home together to the smell of earth and rain and the honey scent of gold-green grass.

"But you know how these things go. No life is untroubled for long.

"One day," he said, "Willie and Charlene came home from a gig, a long ways away, down by Ashland, to find, painted on the door of their little sod house, in white paint, shockingly white paint, not any words but a series of numbers. What numbers, you ask? The numbers 3-7-77. And not just on their door. From that moment forward they started seeing that series of numbers everywhere. Painted onto the trunks of nearby trees. Pebbles at the bottom of the creek were rearranged into that exact sequence. Mice gnawed their conjugal quilt in the pattern of those numerals. Hell, even the stars realigned in the night sky. Willie and Charlene looked up one summer evening and there they were, the first stars; they could trace them, the numbers 3-7-77, silver and shining, as plain as the path of a snail. Of course, they knew what these numbers meant. Everybody did back then. They are the dimensions of a grave. And when you saw these numbers, back in the day, you knew what was coming. You were marked. By death or for death. Either way you knew it was coming. Death. You couldn't run, obviously. And you couldn't outsmart or outmaneuver or outlast that number, that mark. All you could do was wait."

And so, he told them, Willie and Charlene waited.

So helplessly in love that each prayed they would go first, or second, depending on whose eyes were looking into whose. As it turned out, Alex said, Willie died first. Face down in the creek. A willow branch broke off and knocked him in the back of his head, a fatal blow.

Renny shook her head. "That's bullshit."

Alex Mendoza laughed. "Don't believe it? Charlene couldn't either. She lasted another couple of months. Sleeping alone in that sod house. Wondering every night when it would come for her. They found her in bed, her eyes open, a look of terror drilled deep into them. But why terror? Not because she knew death was coming, not only because of that, but because she knew the source, the origin, the map to death led straight back to the cowboy at the hotel. She knew he'd never forgotten. She knew that nothing is forgotten. Not on the prairie. Nothing is forgotten and nothing is forgiven."

A gust of wind swept under the tarp and Sagar and Alex grabbed the ends from blowing away. Alex Mendoza was smiling wide. He said, "You see there? You feel that? That brings us to the ghost part of the ghost story. They are linked now, you understand, for all eternity. Willie and Charlene and the cowboy. They walk together, so to speak, because we will always walk, forever, with those who have changed the course of our lives. And how does a dead man walk? In the wind, of course. Which is why, in Custer County, there are only three kinds of wind. Only three. Listen, and in due time, you'll hear all three. Charlene, wailing and wailing for her beloved, 'Wiiiiilleeeee. Wiiiiiiiiiiiilleeeeeeeee.' Or Willie playing his fiddle, tender and heartbreaking, sweet as syrup, pouring through the high prairie grass, over the creek, and past their sod house. And then there is the cowboy. Howling in pain. Unforgiving. Mad for revenge and driving you mad with his shrieking."

He went quiet. Sagar said, "Who is it right now?"

"Can't you tell?" Alex Mendoza said. "Listen. It's Willie. It's the French jig."

Sagar listened. "But what about when there's no wind? What about then?"

"That's each of the three waiting for the other to speak."

The rain slowed.

"And that series of numbers," Renny said, and though she'd said so little, she spoke now with a strange urgency, "what if it's more than dimensions? What if it's also a date? Like your birth date?"

"Is it?"

Sagar saw their eyes meet.

"Maybe."

Alex Mendoza smiled. He looked at her and said, "Then you're fucked, my friend."

Sagar saw her blanch. *Was* it her birth date? She turned away from them. Sagar, out of some mysterious alchemy or altruism, said, "The thing about dates is, they vary by country."

"How do you mean?" Alex Mendoza said.

"In India, for instance, the day would be written first. It would be 7-3-77. A totally different date. And dimensions."

"Same in Mexico, now that I think of it," Alex Mendoza said.

"And in China," Sagar said, "it would be written 77-3-7."

Renny looked at him, the color now returned to her face. Sagar looked back, struck by, in the storm light, her complexion, like the smooth inside of an almond shell. And there was something else too. In her eyes, maybe in the fall of her shoulders. What was it? He didn't know. And for a moment, an instant, he saw everything: the bison roaming the plains and the veins of copper glistening in the ground and the bodies of the Native women caught in the thrushes at the water's edge. How had they gotten there? he wondered. He had no way of knowing. But he saw them all and then, just as quickly, they all vanished, as if, in this new country, he was living not in time, but as if time were living in him.

Essie

Cotton River, 1868

She appeared out of the morning mist. A young girl, no more than twelve, thirteen. She had long dark hair and a ruddy complexion, and Essie thought maybe she had gotten separated from her family, tribe, whatever those savages called themselves, but Emmett insisted she was mixed and neither side had wanted her, which is why they'd abandoned her at their isolated homestead, though Elijah, their five-year-old son, thought different, and perhaps was closest to the truth. He was convinced she had risen out of the ground, just like that, maybe over there by the triangle of cottonwood trees where he liked to hunt for rabbits and pick bluebells. The thing was: She was the exact color of the ground, which was all the proof Elijah needed. Emmett laughed, smacked Elijah on the back of the head, and said, "Morning mist, my ass. She was hiding out behind the outhouse. And she ain't the color of the ground, my boy, she's the color of shit."

They took her in. Essie, being pregnant, needed the extra help. The chores — the washing, the cleaning, the cooking — were becoming more cumbersome with each passing day. Not that there was much to cook. They'd run out of flour back in

July, so there was no more bread to be baked. Even the barley
and the oats had to be scraped out of the bottom of the sack,
and more and more, Emmett wanted to save them to get the
horses through the winter, and Essie wanted to say to him,
What's worth more to you? Me and Elijah and this baby that's
coming, or those horses? But she knew better than to ask, or
maybe she already knew the answer. The few vegetables she'd
planted in the spring, along with the berries she'd picked, were
mostly gone, though there was a bottle of stewed tomatoes and
a small one of huckleberry jam left. Sometimes, late at night,
when Emmett and Elijah were asleep, Essie slipped over to the
cupboard in the dark (which was all of two steps from the bed),
ran her fingers over the bottles of stewed tomatoes and huckleberry jam, and imagined opening them. The act, in her mind, on
some nights, was so vivid that she could feel the resistance in the
lid as she twisted it and hear the slight sucking sound when she
lifted it off the bottle and smell the aroma that drifted through
their tiny homesteader's shack, the pungent tomato merging
like a river with the sweet sour of the huckleberries. She yearned
to open them — the bottles — in the deepest hours of the night
and taste what was within. It was near winter, the days already
cold and barren, and everything tasted of nothing on her tongue,
and yet, she knew the summers of her girlhood were locked in
those bottles. All she wanted was a taste, a fingertip's worth.
Nothing more. And the rest? The rest she would smear over her
body. The glistening purple and the slippery red. Smothered
together on her breasts and her stomach and her face and her
feet, up the length of her legs, her inner thighs, and into that
dark place only Joseph had ever seen, never Emmett. And then
what? And then she wanted small things — small animals, small
children — to lick it off her body. Elijah, the baby from within,
the little mice that lived in the walls and the hay bed, the prairie

dogs that dotted their miserable, infertile land, and even the
birds — she wanted the birds to land on her, the redpolls and
the siskins and the grosbeaks and the warblers and the sparrows
and the finches and the buntings and the meadowlarks — all of
them she wanted to feed, to nourish. She imagined their licking
tongues (Did birds have tongues?), and she imagined their claws
as they marched up and down her body. The feel of them — a
miniature army, the pelting of hard rain, the promise of flight.

And she wanted the girl. The one who'd appeared out of the
morning mist. She wanted the girl to lick it off too.

What was her name? They never found out her name because she never spoke. Not one word. Emmett decided she was a
deaf-mute, but Essie knew better. So did Elijah. The days wore
on. They got colder. The first snowstorm hit in early October.
They were down to the last of the coffee grounds and an insub-
stantial slab of cured deer meat, from which Essie made a thin
stew that they stretched out for ten days, melting more and
more snow into it with each passing day. Then there were the
two bottles. Emmett tried to get at them, only once. Overcome
by hunger or maybe overcome by his failure to provide for his
family — after moving Essie halfway across a difficult and colossal continent — Emmet pushed her out of the way one frigid
November night and grabbed the bottle of stewed tomatoes. He
felt it immediately. The knife in his back so swift that he thought
she must've been holding it all along. Was she? He turned.
Blanched. Not at the sight of the knife, but at the sight of Essie's
eyes. So vehement, so afire, he wondered who this woman was.
His wife he'd slapped out of the way many times, pushed onto
the bed with just an elbow, but *this* woman? She could burn him
and the shack and the triangle of cottonwood trees and the entire territory of night to the ground. He knew it. She knew it.
And all for a bottle of stewed tomatoes? A smaller one of

huckleberry jam? It made no sense. And yet he put the bottle back.

After that, Emmett went out hunting every morning and came back empty-handed every night. The animals had burrowed for the winter; they knew enough about hunger to hide.

Come spring, the three of them, Essie, Elijah, and Emmett, were so gaunt and weak that they could barely make it the fifty feet to the outhouse. The baby came, and it, too, was an implausibly puny thing. Her own hunger led Essie to produce so little milk she was almost surprised every time the baby let out a cry, whimpered in its sleep, or woke in the mornings. The girl, on the other hand, the girl was downright robust. Essie couldn't understand it. She waited until the girl went to the creek for water one March morning and walked out to the barn — which was empty of livestock, they had all died or had had to be sold in the six years they'd been in the Cotton River Valley. The barn was where the girl had been sleeping since she'd arrived, even through the winter. Essie had wanted to ask her inside once, during a particularly bad storm, but Emmett had said her kind was resilient; he had actually used the word *resilient*. When she'd looked up, astonished, he'd said, "Besides, she'll stink up the house." Stink up the house? It already smelled like horse piss and baby shit and sour milk and moldering hay and bacon fat gone bad. How, Essie wondered, could it smell worse?

When she entered the barn, to her amazement, Essie saw that there was a buffalo hide spread out neatly in a far corner. So that's how she'd kept warm during the winter. But how had it gotten there? She didn't remember her arriving with it. Though, to be honest, she didn't remember anything of her arriving except the morning mist and the girl climbing out of (or made of) that mist. How long did Essie stand in the barn, staring? Something about its closeness compelled her to do so, its coziness maybe, even though it was far bigger than the shack, or maybe it was its smell, which was nothing like the smell of the shack; the smell of the barn evoking not poverty, the thing she had become inured to, but some ageless memory of vast, fecund valleys and sweet grasses and running rivers. Essie couldn't remember the last time she had closed her eyes overcome with pleasure and not sleep, but that was how the girl found her — with her eyes closed. I'm sorry, Essie said, I was just — and here she stopped because the girl was approaching her, her hand outstretched, close enough to Essie that she saw the lines of the girl's palm. Her blood ran cold. And then it ran very, very hot, because the girl then reached for her wrist, raised it to her face, and studied it. Held it, her wrist, *her wrist*, a thing that perhaps no one had ever held before, not like this, so tenderly that Essie thought of the pink of crushed petals, the slow severance after the first kiss. But why hold her wrist at all? Then, just as mysteriously, she let go.

Essie nearly cried out. What was it about lonesomeness? She thought she'd been feeling it for years, but she realized she was feeling it now for the first time.

The girl went to the buffalo hide and came back holding something Essie had never seen before. They looked like flat, brown cakes. She handed one to Essie and motioned for her to eat it. Essie bit into it. What is it? Essie asked.

"Pemmican," the girl replied. Her voice wasn't raspy, as Essie expected, given how long the girl must've been silent, but wonderfully silken and honeyed.

Essie, chewing slowly, looked at her. "So you can talk," she said. "You've been able to talk this whole time?"

The girl nodded.

Essie nodded back, still chewing, looking now at the girl's wrist. How many reasons were there to take hold of another's wrist? One? Maybe two? How was it that such an alluring part of the body, a confluence so haunting, had so few reasons for holding it? When she woke up, Essie was snuggled deep inside the buffalo hide. The girl was nowhere to be seen. She jumped up, ran to the shack, and saw that she'd only been gone for minutes, not hours. How could that be? The next time she saw the girl, she showed no signs of having met Essie in the barn, or of having shared her pemmican, but Essie found the flat, nutritious cakes now and then, stowed there just for her and the children (she could've shared them with Emmett, but she didn't) — under a pot she was sure to lift, at the bottom of the empty milk pail, once under her pillow, and nearly always behind the bottles of stewed tomatoes and huckleberry jam.

When winter finally ended and summer arrived, the drought set in. Emmett muttered, "Goddamn this valley. What's there left to take?"

The dust rose in great clouds and there was nothing to do but watch the sky for rain. But day after day, month after month, it did not come. The girl led Essie and Elijah and the baby to the dry creek one evening and showed Essie where to find the chokecherries. And then, when they'd feasted on those, they lay down in an abandoned sod house by the banks of the creek and went to sleep. When Essie woke up, she was alone with Elijah and the baby, as she knew she would be.

By the end of summer, Emmett had had enough of Montana Territory. He was eyeing places farther west. The Oregon Trail, he said, we can catch the Oregon Trail and be out west by next spring. The baby, Essie said. The baby can't make the trip. Not sure Elijah can either. But really, she was thinking of the girl, and of how Emmett would never agree to take her with them. What worried her even more was that Emmett began to whittle things. She was used to him whittling lots of things — like toy horses for Elijah, or absentmindedly at a stick while she was making supper, but now the whittling became an obsession. There were no chores to speak of — no livestock to milk and feed, no field worthy of plowing, no creek from which to bring up water — and so there were no distractions; he spent hours upon hours whittling. He made a giraffe and a miniature covered wagon and a pipe (though there was no tobacco) and a bird and a little figurine of a girl who looked a lot like the girl who'd come out of the mist. One day he was whittling something Essie couldn't see. After a while he looked up and said to her, "Do you know what *exile* means?"

"No."

"It means this," he said, holding up what she now saw was a figure eight. "It means whittling away at something that gets you nowhere. Except what you're whittling at is your own life."

Essie didn't know what he meant, but the emptiness in his voice frightened her. Or was it the figure eight that frightened her?

Regardless, she was right to be frightened because Emmett did move them out west. And they left in a hurry, though he didn't say why. When Essie went to the barn to say goodbye to the girl, she was gone. "Must've left last night," Emmett said, packing up the wagon. "Must've known we was leaving."

The girl's body was buried at the base of the cottonwood tree that faced south. Why that one? Why not the east-facing tree or the west-facing one? She was starting to show, which was probably the reason she was killed. Though reason, as everyone knows, has nothing to do with death. And as for the bottle of stewed tomatoes and the bottle of huckleberry jam? Essie left them. Right where they'd always been, in the cupboard. Why? What did she hope for, and why did she hope for it? Perhaps not even Essie knew. Hope, too, has nothing to do with reason. Not much later, the bottles were knocked over by a mouse that was scampering past them. They fell to the ground, broke, and all the contents spilled out. The glistening purples, the slippery reds. And in the end Essie got what she'd always wanted: all the small creatures, licking and licking and licking and licking.

Chapter 13

There was a gas station a few blocks away from Janavi and Sagar's apartment, with a convenience store attached. Sometimes Janavi bought herself a Slurpee — cola was her favorite flavor, though her favorite color of Slurpee was blue. The first time she bought one, the cashier, a young woman with hair that was pink at its ends and a piercing on her tongue, a thing Janavi had never seen before, showed her how to use the machine. After that, whenever she went in, if Mandy was working, and the store wasn't busy, she stepped outside with Janavi and smoked a cigarette while Janavi drank her Slurpee. They sat on a low retaining wall that bordered the parking lot of the store. They watched the cars and the trucks driving by. Mandy told her she was born and raised in a town called Baker, near the border with North Dakota. Her parents divorced when she was five and she was an only child, raised by her mother, who'd worked odd jobs to make ends meet — as a waitress and a teacher's aide and a motel maid. She now worked at an RV park. Janavi said, "What's an RV park?"

"Recreational vehicles? People live in them."

Janavi had no idea what she was talking about.

Mandy, whose tongue piercing seemed to give her a slight lisp, said, "Lordy Lordy. Don't they have them over in India?" When Janavi said no, not that she knew of, Mandy explained about them and how some people lived in them all their lives, going from place to place, and once, when they were sitting outside the store, one drove past and Mandy, in the middle of a drag on her cigarette, jumped up and said, "There! There. There's one." After that Janavi seemed to see them everywhere.

Mandy's father, who she said she saw once or twice a year, worked in the oil fields in North Dakota. She told Janavi one afternoon, quite plainly, "I have daddy issues." Janavi wasn't sure exactly what that meant but she could guess. Mandy told her, "I got into some shit in high school. I mean, everybody did, but mine got serious. One morning I woke up and couldn't remember the last three days. Dried puke on the side of my face and a needle in my arm and on the floor of a house I didn't recognize. I walked through the rooms of the house trying to remember and trying to find my phone. House was empty. My phone gone. I stepped into one room, at the back of the house, and my foot went right through the floorboards. I was trying to pull it out when a rat crawled over it. Fucking right over it. I was barefoot, by the way. I screamed. Not that anybody heard me. But I screamed and screamed. And that's when I realized. That's when I knew. That that's what my life would become. Every day of it." She put out her cigarette. "Dropped out. Moved down here. First job I could find." A customer pulled up. Mandy got up to go inside. "When it comes to certain things," she said, "like rats and three days gone, you can't change one thing, you understand. You've gotta change everything." When she came back out, they talked some more and then Mandy said, "You want a shitty job? This place is hiring."

Janavi explained to her that because of her visa she couldn't work, not legally.

"For how long?"

"It says one hundred fifty days online, but it could be more."

Mandy whistled under her breath and Janavi felt again her own loneliness. She was sick of walking. She was sick of having nothing to do and nowhere to go.

"You could work under the table."

"What does that mean?"

"Without papers."

"Where?"

Mandy shrugged. "Beats me . . . the slaughterhouse?"

"What slaughterhouse?"

"The one out on 447. They hire lots of people without papers. Hundreds."

"Hundreds?"

Mandy laughed. "What do you think happens to all those cattle on all them ranches around here?"

Janavi shuddered.

Mandy pulled out a flask from the back pocket of her jeans. Vodka, she told her, and poured enough to refill Janavi's Slurpee cup. Janavi took a sip. It didn't taste much different. She took another. The idea of the slaughterhouse brought to Janavi another thought: She couldn't work a paying job in America, but she could certainly volunteer! There must be some sort of child welfare agency in Mansfield, or at least nearby. The idea thrilled her, kindled in her a warm, orange glow, or was it the vodka? She picked up her phone to search online, but the words swam on the screen.

Mandy took a long swig and started asking Janavi questions. About what India was like and what her family was like. When Janavi told her she had an older sister, Mandy practically swooned. She said, "I wish I had an older sister. Don't care much about having a brother but an older sister would be so cool."

"Why?" Janavi said. "Why a sister and not a brother?"

Mandy smiled. She said, "Because a sister is a mirror. A kind of mirror. Whenever she looks at you, there you are. Don't you think? She's the best kind of mirror."

That afternoon Janavi walked back to the apartment, her fingers sticky from the Slurpee, her gait wobbly. Her mind was buzzing, almost buoyant. In college, she'd had plenty of beers and a whiskey on occasion, but . . . she skipped down the street and giggled when the orange cat darted behind a house. Climbing the stairs proved to be tricky. Once inside, she looked at the empty tire swing and thought of the little girl swinging listlessly, staring into the overgrown yard and the chain-link fence. Did the little girl wish she had a sister too? Instead of a brother? Rajni came to her then with a kind of feverish longing. She wanted to tell her about her volunteering idea. Where was her phone? She looked for it frantically and found it in the pocket of her jacket. She started to dial, but then she stopped. It was the middle of the night in India. She put her phone away. The last time Rajni had texted, asking what she was doing, Janavi had answered, *Trying not to hate u. U?*

Rajni hadn't called or texted since.

A mirror? Next time she calls, she decided firmly, I'll answer.

She ate an entire bag of potato chips.

She lay down on the sofa and texted Sagar. *Bring dinner*. And then, to stop the room from spinning, she closed her eyes and fell asleep.

Her name, the Ganga was calling her name . . . she opened her eyes and Sagar was saying, "Janavi? Janavi, wake up." His hand was on her bare arm. He was leaning over her, close. The room was hot and breathless. His hand. His face so near hers that she felt the heat of his breath. Felt, nearly, the scratchiness of his stubble. What would it feel like? Against her cheeks? Her thighs? He said, "Have you been drinking?" She mumbled something, to which he said, "I brought fried chicken."

She shook her head, closed her eyes.

"Janavi?"

A few minutes (hours?) later, he shook her awake again. He said, "Here. At least eat this."

Eat?

"Take a bite."

She half opened her eyes. "What is it?"

"A biscuit. Have some. It's really good."

"A biscuit?"

He brought it to her mouth, and she thought, A biscuit? Who told me about biscuits? Not the Indian kind, the American kind. And because Sagar wouldn't go away, she raised her head and nibbled on the edge. Then she took a bigger bite. Her eyes widened. She'd never tasted anything so buttery and flaky and delicious. A burfi maybe . . . no, soan papdi! It was like soan papdi, but savory. She smiled and lay back down. She was trailing to sleep when she popped her eyes open. She yelled out, "Lottie."

Sagar looked at her, still holding the biscuit. "Lottie? What about her?"

She waved her arms. "The biscuit, the biscuit."

His eyes narrowed, and he said, "How much did you have to drink?"

He's so frustrating, she thought. Her head collapsed back onto the arm of the sofa, and she whispered, "The American kind," and then she fell asleep again.

Waking in the middle of the night, still on the sofa and with a pounding headache, her tongue so dry she couldn't wet her lips, Janavi decided, No more vodka.

She woke the next morning with a headache. She brewed a pot of strong coffee and sat down at the computer. Custer County, she found, had a Child and Family Services Division, but it was obviously a governmental agency. There were crisis hotlines, but they all seemed to link to CFSD. She scrolled through more pages and finally found a volunteer opportunity with an organization based in Miles City called Impact Youth. She phoned them and left a message. She waited two hours. When they didn't call back, she sent an email telling them she was interested in volunteering and about her work at ChildDefense and that she could start at any time. She waited again.

When Sagar came home, she told him about her plan and he smiled and said, "Of course you should. Why didn't we think of it earlier?"

On the third day after she sent the email, when she still didn't hear back, she looked up their address, dropped Sagar off at work — even though she was still new to driving and was a little frightened of it — and drove to Miles City. She arrived at their office on N. Fourth Street and saw a handwritten sign taped to the door that read BACK IN 5 MINS. On one side of the office was a smoke shop and on the other was an antique store. Only the smoke shop was open. Janavi looked through its window and then into the window of the antique store. She waited half an hour outside the door and then returned to the car. She called her father. When he answered, she said, "I've found a solution, Papa! I'm going to volunteer with a children's organization. Here in Montana. I'm outside their office now."

Her papa said, "I didn't know American children were poor."

"It's not street children, Papa. At least, I don't think it is."

"I was watching a documentary the other day, and — " He went into a coughing fit. It went on for so long that Janavi grew concerned. She said, "Are you sick?"

"No, no, Beti," he insisted, but he said he'd better get off the phone because Kumari (who still worked for him) was calling him to dinner.

Janavi sat in the car for another twenty minutes before she saw a woman approach the office door. She was an older woman and as she walked, she favored her right side. Janavi, relieved that somebody had at long last arrived, jumped out of the car and practically ran to the door. The woman had just gotten it unlocked when Janavi, from a few steps away, said, "Excuse me! Excuse me, madam."

The woman jumped. The door slammed closed again. The woman turned, scowling. "Don't you know better than to run up on somebody like that?"

Janavi stared at her. "I didn't — I'm . . ."

The woman reopened the door and went inside. Janavi stood for a moment, lost, and then followed her.

The woman was seated at a desk closest to the door. Her tight silver curls and coral lipstick were the brightest details in the drab room. There were two other desks, both too bare to have been recently occupied. The woman, when Janavi walked in, didn't look up.

Janavi stood awkwardly and then said, "Excuse me, madam."

"Third time you've said that. You gonna tell me what it is you want?"

"I — well, yes, I am wondering if you have any opportunities. Volunteer opportunities. I've worked with children before. In India, and . . ."

The woman, who was going through her purse, clearly searching for something, said, "Now where did I put that bottle of Advil?" She opened a desk drawer. Closed it. She looked up at Janavi with suspicion, as if Janavi were hiding her Advil. "No. We don't."

Janavi stood as if she'd been struck. "You don't?"

"No."

"I see. But — can I help in any way? With office work? Or answering the crisis line?"

"That's my job."

"Maybe the children . . ."

"You'd need to be trained for that and we don't have the staff to train you. Not right now."

"But I was trained in India, you see. So I wouldn't — "

The woman's coral lips thinned and stretched into a bland smile. "Things are different here. We don't just hand over our kids to someone trained way the heck over there."

Janavi stood, wordless, stupefied, and still.

She got back in her car and drove home without a single thought. Montana. She looked into its agonizing expanse without seeing it, without wanting to, her eyes smarting with tears.

The next time Rajni called Janavi answered. She said, "Janoo," with rare delight, and Janavi, though they were separated by nearly ten thousand

miles, heard the relief in her sister's voice that she'd finally picked up.
She said, "How are you?" and Janavi, for the life of her, could not think
how to answer. She wanted to tell her about the woman at Impact Youth,
and about being so flatly rebuffed, but she was too embarrassed. Instead,
she said, "How's Papa?"

"He's fine. He said you'd called."

"He didn't pick up."

"He's had a cough. It's tiring him out."

"He said it was nothing."

"Probably didn't want you to worry."

"Why didn't you tell me?"

"I tried to call."

"You could've texted."

There was silence, strained. "Would you have texted back?"

Janavi heard the injury in her voice, and then the clatter of something wooden, a timer. "Are you cooking?"

"Puri and chole. They're Pavan's favorite. He — "

She stopped herself. Janavi might've said, Go on, but she wanted her
to suffer in her self-consciousness.

"Meena moved there too."

"Where?"

"Florida. Her husband's in IT."

"I didn't even know she'd gotten married."

"Is it close to you?"

"No." And then she said, "Was it arranged or a love marriage?"

"Love."

"That must be nice."

Neither spoke. The barnacle held.

The conversation ended soon afterward, and Janavi felt a desolation
she had not felt since her first days in Montana. Of all the people in the
world it was Janavi and Rajni — not Amma, not Papa, not their friends,
and not their husbands — who knew each other best. Who'd shared a

common history and all that came with that history: the losses and the glories and the sweetness and the sorrow. And now they could barely have a civil conversation. Rajni, Janavi realized suddenly, with a baffling awe, had been witness to nearly every one of her injuries. Everything from minor paper cuts to splinters to the time she'd needed stitches on her palm when Rajni had knocked against her, and the glass she'd been holding had shattered in her hand. Rajni had cried more than she had. As to crying — it was her, and only her, who knew her crying. Papa used to, when she'd been young, but Rajni was the only one who knew it now. Her adult tears, which, in their way, were more exquisite, more vulnerable than a child's. And yet, even with all that power held in her hand, she'd banished her to another country. Exiled her nearly as completely as killing her. How could she? And how could Janavi forgive her?

Still, what Mandy had said about sisters stayed with her and now, nearly every time Janavi stood at the mirror, she saw more and more how alike she and Rajni looked, especially as they'd grown older. Mandy, of course, had not literally meant a mirror, but of how one sister in some way always reflects the other. And not just Rajni. Janavi stood one morning, after brushing her teeth, gazing into the mirror that covered half of one wall, and was struck suddenly by how much she looked like Amma. Amma as she remembered her, nearly the same age Janavi was now. First Rajni, now Amma. She looked and looked. The more she looked, the more she faded, and Amma appeared. She was almost frightened. Maybe the mirrors in America were too big. Never in India had she known a home to have a mirror this big. Restaurants and hotels, yes, but not a regular house. Was it possible to see too much of oneself?

But the truth was, after that first phone call, Janavi had to admit that it hurt to hear Rajni's voice — artificially elevated, eager, avoidant. Janavi wanted to say, Do you think you're suffering? Because you're not.

The photos she texted didn't hurt as much. They were sometimes selfies, sometimes photos of Varanasi. Usually of something Rajni had found funny or interesting or that she thought might remind her sister of home. Janavi didn't need reminding. Whenever she got a photo from Rajni, especially if it was a panoramic shot, Janavi zoomed in and studied every detail. She didn't at first know what she was looking for but then she realized what it was: She was looking for children, especially street children. (She had told Sagar about what had happened at Impact Youth, and of her humiliation, to which he'd said, "The gifts people can't see are the ones right in front of them." She'd blushed in gratitude.) Once, Rajni sent her a photo of Scindia Ghat. Janavi recognized it immediately — the leaning Shiva temple, the balconied buildings beyond it, the stone steps, the distant sandbar. The ghat was crowded; she didn't know what she was meant to see.

Janavi texted back, *U there now?*

Yes. You see the goat? There was a smile emoji at the end.

Janavi zoomed in and noticed, on one of the steps, a tiny goat chewing on the end of a woman's pallu. The woman was trying to pry it out of the goat's mouth and her struggle, and the goat's stubbornness, did make Janavi smile, but more interesting to her was a boy seated behind them, on a higher step. He was clearly a street child. A tattered shirt, dirty hair, shoeless. He was maybe nine, ten. He was looking out at the water and the expression on his face, through the graininess of the enlarged photo, held a kind of detached curiosity, maybe even boredom, and Janavi recognized the look — it was practiced, poignant, an armor against a world that had abandoned him. He would hold fast to this look, maybe for all his life. Even if Shiva and Parvati stood in front of him, as they were thought to have done at Scindia Ghat at the beginning of time, the boy's expression, she knew, would not change.

She looked some more at the photo, and she thought about the goat's stubbornness and then she thought about the boy's armor and then she thought about barnacles.

Chapter 14

The first notch wouldn't be made for another two to three months, at least, but Sagar was constantly busy. There were tests to run, a slew of permits and bureaucratic red tape to get through, and construction crews and machinery to line up. The excavation work at the burial site also seemed to ramp up. Since the rainstorm, Sagar noticed that he and Renny and Alex Mendoza regarded each other a little differently, with more warmth than they seemed to share with their other coworkers. He had to laugh — it was as if they'd survived some sort of natural disaster together! They waved hello, even when one of them was on the opposite shore; Alex Mendoza once shared his doughnut with Sagar; and Renny, whenever Sagar walked by, paused her work, if only for a minute or two, to explain how the dig was going. It crossed his mind that the reason they'd become friends of sorts was because he was Indian and Renny was Native American and Alex Mendoza's parents were from Mexico. She was the first Native person Sagar had ever met, and Alex Mendoza was the first Hispanic person, while he was the first Indian person *they'd* met. What was more, they were all brown, the only brown people on the dam project. Was that a factor? Was that the whole reason why? He dismissed the idea almost immediately.

But he wondered again when, while discussing scheduling with him,

Tim looked up and said, "Will you look at that." Sagar followed his gaze. Tim Downing seemed to be staring at some point on the western river-bank. All Sagar saw were a few technicians talking and some stray equipment laid out on a folding table. Sagar looked back at him. Tim Downing shook his head. He said, "Won it fair and square, but the ranchers still have to lease it from *them*. They own half the state, I tell you. Crowding us out." And then, when Sagar didn't respond, he said, "But you know all about it, don't you? As chummy as you are with her."

With whom? Was he referring to Renny? And he couldn't be talking about the tribe, could he, owning half the state? He couldn't be, and yet, who else could he be referring to? Sagar looked again at the techni-cians, who'd moved closer to the water, one of them carrying a sonar device, and then at the tall grasses and the forbs at the water's edge, the buff-colored sandstone that rose beyond them, the stretch of prairie and the yellow hills and the dark spots of cattle in the far distance, and he thought of the teeming streets of Varanasi. The alleyways crammed with shops and street vendors. The ghats spilling over with worshippers and bathers. The jostle, everywhere you turned, of every kind of person and animal imaginable, and yet, how funny that a country this vast, with its prairie and its horizon unobstructed, was considered crowded.

When he saw Renny later that day, he said, "Do the Native tribes own half the state?"

She said, "Let me guess. Tim Downing?"

"How did you know?"

Renny laughed. "Some people don't hide it," she said.

He thought it over. "I saw him with the mayor, Sam Dooley. In the trailer. Why would someone opposed to the removal be at the damsite?"

"It's a small town," Renny said, "and Sam Dooley is used to getting his way. I went to high school with him."

"You did?"

"Me, Sam, his wife, Susan, my ex, Gabe, we all went to the same high school."

"Gabe's your ex-husband? They mentioned him."

"They did?"

"Said he'd gotten beat up by a motorcycle gang once."

Renny rolled her eyes. "Sounds about right."

"And all of you . . . you all stayed . . ." Sagar said.

"Each of us for different reasons," she said.

He waited for her to say more but she didn't.

That night, he told Janavi what Tim Downing had said about Montana being crowded. He waited until she stopped laughing. He said, "But I'm wondering . . ."

"What?"

"Maybe that's why Renny and Alex and I are friends. Well, maybe not friends, but . . . maybe . . ."

"I don't understand."

"Nothing," he said. "I'm overthinking it."

They had a dinner of chapati with spinach and potato curry. Everything Janavi made had the taste of a person who didn't like to cook. He didn't mind. He could cook, of course, if it wasn't too late when he got home, but he thought she might be insulted. Besides, he knew how empty her days were; maybe cooking filled them, hardly in the way she wanted, but filled them nonetheless. He sometimes wondered if he'd ever stop feeling guilty for going along with Rajni, and then he'd swing to the other extreme — to a decided guiltlessness. Why should he feel guilty? When he'd only been trying to do the right thing by Janavi's family?

He was washing the dishes, which he did on most nights; when Janavi, dropping a spoon into the sink, said, "Mandy and Lottie are white. They wouldn't agree with Tim Downing."

He smiled at her, gratified that she understood what he'd been trying to say without his saying it. He said, "Are you sure?"

She was quiet for a moment, and then, smiling back, she said, "No."

Sagar and Tim Downing's trailer was where the coffee machine was located, along with a microwave and a small fridge where people stored their lunches. There was a rush in the mornings and sometimes at lunchtime. Tim Downing hated people coming in and out, complaining that they broke his concentration, but Sagar loved it. Even if he was at his desk, focused on sifting through data or studying schematics or filing reports, the bustle and chatter sounded to him like the burbling of a stream. Tim Downing avoided the noon rush, going into town for lunch, but Sagar, if he could, joined the crowd gathered at the microwave. It was while they all waited for one of the crew to heat up his lunch of a leftover steak — it was taking so long that someone joked, "What've you got in there, Doug? The whole fucking cow?" — that someone asked Sagar where he had worked before the Cotton. He told them the Ganga. The Ganges. And then, because there was silence, he explained about where it was in India and its importance hydrologically and for irrigation and ecology, and then, because they were still silent — Renny was there, and three of the male crew — he told them what it meant to Indians, to Hindus. One of the men said, "But why? Why do you all think it's holy?" Sagar, unsure where to start, told them as much as he could remember — about Bhagiratha and his ancestors and how the Goddess Ganga agreed to come down from the heavens, flowing through Shiva's hair. I'm rambling, he thought, and saw that some of them were listening and some were only half listening. But Renny. Renny, he could tell, was listening to every word. When he finished with the Ganga's story, one of the guys laughed and said, "Too bad our rivers don't have stories like that." Renny, turning away from Sagar, said, "Of course they do. You just don't know them." They looked at her, perplexed. And that's when she told them the story. The story of the Cotton River.

Once upon a time, long before Time, there lived two brothers. They were twins, though even in twins, there is always an older and a younger.

These two brothers were born of love, the love of Mother Earth and Father Sky, and for their playground they had all the lands and all the waters and all the heavens. There were no other people, you see. Only the two brothers and the birds and the animals and the bees and the butterflies. Both of them grew up healthy and strong, fed by the fruits and grains of the earth and the waters from the snow mountains. And like all brothers they had their little tumbles and their arguments and their competitions. The younger brother, for instance, could run faster, but the older brother could run farther. The older brother was wiser, but the younger brother was more spirited. The older brother liked to spend his afternoons in green meadows, stretched out in the sunlight, watching the clouds, while the younger brother preferred to wander around the prairie and through the coulees and up and down the hills, chasing this or that antelope or bison or bobcat.

And there was yet another difference between them. This one only visible to those who watched them keenly, studied the two boys over many moments and over many moons. But of course, no one could do that. Older Brother and Younger Brother were the only two people on earth. The difference was this: The older brother loved all things, but the younger brother loved only himself. You would think such a thing would be readily apparent in a person, even obvious, but no, it isn't. Such a thing is often opaque and easily masked. And could take a lifetime to see, whether we love ourselves only or everything equally.

Despite this difference, and all the others, Older Brother and Younger Brother were wonderfully content to play and eat and sleep in the arms of their Mother Earth and wake under the gaze of their Father Sky.

One bright summer morning, Older Brother came out of the tipi and went to the stream to bathe. When he arrived, he found that there was no stream. It had dried up in the night. He went searching for its source, but the source, too, was without water. He continued his search, far and wide, for another stream or creek or even a little pool of water but found none. He had to walk the length of a hundred mountains and cross the length of a hundred valleys before he finally came upon a tiny trickle of water, dribbling noiselessly out of a gap between two rocks. He would've missed it had it not been for the sun glistening just so off the wetness on one of the rock faces. Older Brother looked down at the trickle, closed his eyes, and thanked Mother Earth for the water and thanked Father Sky for revealing it to him. Then he bent down, gathered up some of the cool water in the cup of his hand, and drank. He drank and drank until his thirst was sated. Then he took out his buffalo bladder and filled it with water. He walked all the way back to the tipi — over the hundred mountains and through the hundred valleys.

When he finally arrived one cold night long after he'd set out, he put the buffalo bladder down and explained to Younger Brother about the gap between the two rocks and the tiny trickle of water and then he told him how far away it was. He said, "Be careful with this water. Drink only what is necessary. And when the animals and the birds come, let them drink of it." Younger Brother nodded and agreed but his thoughts were already elsewhere.

Older Brother went to sleep and when he woke up — because of his long journey and because of how arduous it had been — he was ill. His illness lasted for many days and many nights. In the delirium of his fever, he saw many things. One of them was Father Sky bending down to kiss his forehead. Another was Mother Earth swaddling him in the gauzy warmth of blankets made of mist. When he woke up, Older Brother noticed that he was feeling slightly better and that soon he would be healed. He also noticed that the buffalo bladder was gone. As was Younger Brother.

Older Brother cried out. He knew what had happened. And he knew all the creatures would die without that water.

He cried and cried. He was inconsolable.

Day and days, maybe even weeks, went by. Eventually, though he was still weak, he felt well enough to start on his search for Younger Brother. He left the tipi and walked in the direction of the sunrise and slept on the ground facing the sunset. After some time, as he was walking through a barren valley full of rocks and dirt and not much else, he came across Porcupine. Porcupine was sniffing this way and that but with not much enthusiasm. Older Brother said, "Porcupine, what are you doing? And why do you look so glum?"

Porcupine said, "I'm looking for food. But there is no food left in this valley since the water went away."

"Yes, I see," said Older Brother, nodding. They both stood silently, looking out at the red rocks and the dry whirls of dust and the sagebrush that had shriveled up and died. There was not a single thought in Older Brother's head but then, with the clarity of a lightning strike over the plains, Older Brother had an idea. He said, "I know. Why don't you come with me?"

"Where are you going?"

"I am going to look for my younger brother. But I'm not as strong as I once was. Perhaps you can help me."

Porcupine said, "But I am not very strong either. How could I help you?"

Older Brother smiled, looked down at Porcupine, and said, "There are other ways to be strong. Much more important than physical strength."

Porcupine sniffed and seemed somewhat unconvinced, reluctant, but seeing as there was no food in his dry valley home, he agreed to join Older Brother. They began to walk together. The stars rose and set many times during their wanderings. Older Brother began to lose hope. "Perhaps Younger Brother is cleverer than I am. What if we never find him?"

Porcupine, munching on a juicy clover leaf — for they were now in a valley that offered a little bit of food — said, "We'll find him."

That was all he said and then he went back to his clover leaf. Older Brother, in that moment, realized the truth of what he himself had once said: *Strong* is a word that has many meanings.

One night, while Older Brother was making his bed of dried needle-grass and was lying down to sleep, Porcupine wandered off. He had caught a scent in the air (leaves of the cottonwood tree, Porcupine guessed; he'd always found them particularly tasty and though he ate them, he also loved the sound of them rustling in the wind). He waddled off, following the scent. After a long trek he came to it, looked up, and there it was: a cottonwood tree! He was so delighted that he didn't even look this way and that; he simply bounded forward, bumped into something, ignored it, and began to climb.

The leaves were the most tender, delicious, and succulent leaves he had ever tasted. Porcupine gorged himself on cottonwood leaves, one after another.

But what had he bumped into?

It was the buffalo bladder. Though Porcupine hadn't realized it, Younger Brother was sleeping at the base of the cottonwood tree, with the buffalo bladder tucked beside him. And when Porcupine had leapt onto the trunk of the cottonwood tree, not only had he bumped into the buffalo bladder, but one of his quills had punctured it. No one realized it: not Porcupine, not Younger Brother, and certainly not Older Brother, who, like his younger brother, was fast asleep. The next morning, Younger Brother set out again, meandering this way and that, caring for nothing else but himself, and lusting for the water that, unbeknownst to him, was slowly dripping out of the buffalo bladder.

Older Brother said to Porcupine, "Maybe we should change our course. Maybe we should head north instead of east, and sleep facing south instead of west." Porcupine was thinking it over when he noticed a thin trail of water. Again, just as it had been for Older Brother, this trail of water was glistening in the sun. Porcupine said, "Look," and Older Brother looked. They didn't have to say a word to each other; they simply followed the trail of water. In the meantime, not very far away, Younger Brother raised the buffalo bladder to take a drink and found it empty. Empty? He couldn't understand it. He jumped up from where he was seated and started screaming at Father Sky and stomping on Mother Earth because he couldn't understand who else to blame. And that was how Older Brother and Porcupine found him: screaming and stomping.

The Great Gray Wolf, seeing the three of them meet in this way — all of them in such a state of astonishment that they, all three, stood as still as trees, mouths agape, one staring at the other — had a hearty laugh, and She decided to reward them, and so the Great Gray Wolf turned the path of the trickle of water, the one that had dribbled out of the buffalo bladder, into a river. And She turned the three of them into cottonwood trees. Porcupine because he loved the taste of cottonwood leaves and the sound of the wind as it rustled them. Younger Brother because he'd loved only himself and would now have to gaze forever at all he hadn't loved. And Older Brother because he'd loved everything equally and could now gaze forever at all that he had loved.

The river, then, came to be known as the Cotton River.

And the trees? They watch over the Cotton River Valley for all of Time — which, in that moment, began — while the Great Gray Wolf watches over all of them for all of Time, and for all of Beyond Time.

Chapter 15

Janavi changed her walking routes, but it didn't help. It always seemed to be the same houses, with the same cars parked out front. It was monotonous. Or maybe it was her life that was monotonous. Once, a dog behind a chain-link fence started barking at her and lunged so violently against the fence that he bounced backward. The dog sprang up and started barking again. At first, she was frightened, but then she looked at the dog and said, "Are you bored too?" She told Sagar that story, and he said, "Probably the dog sensed your boredom and wanted to play with you. Dogs are good at sensing things."

She said, "They're certainly better than humans."

Sagar looked away miserably, and seeing the misery in his face, *really* seeing it for the first time, especially after he'd been so kind following her visit to Impact Youth, she thought, Enough is enough. She decided to borrow the car on some days; it didn't take more than a glance at a map of Montana for her to realize she couldn't get anywhere without driving, and that for more hours than she'd have in a day. Regardless, she started dropping Sagar off some mornings and running errands in town, if she had any, and then she went out onto the Cotton River Road or to the far end of the reservoir or downstream on the Cotton River.

She even went back to Miles City. But once she got there, she saw that there was not much more activity in the middle of Miles City than there was in Mansfield. She had lunch at one of the fast-food restaurants and then came back home.

Most often, she drove aimlessly. Up and down Cotton River Road or on one of the county roads. She once passed through a town called Epsie — well, it could hardly be called a town since no one seemed to live there — and when she stopped outside the only building in "town," the historical marker read that it had been an operating post office and the postmaster at the time had been found crawling out of his burning house with a gunshot wound. He'd subsequently died, and no one had ever discovered how the house had caught fire or who had shot the postmaster. Another time, she heard the name of a town on the local news and was excited to visit it, thinking it might have some poetic element or be related to Shakespeare's works in some way, but when she got there, she realized, feeling stupid, that it was spelled Sonnette, and had nothing to do with poetry or Shakespeare. All it had was one business, a twenty-four-hour bar and grill; Janavi ordered a cup of coffee, drank it, and left.

One morning, she drove onto a dirt road as it wound up a bluff and when she got to the top, she parked and walked to the edge of the bluff and looked out. It was flat and empty, without end, as far as her eyes could see. She looked some more. No, that wasn't entirely true. There was a spot of blue to her left, maybe a pond for cattle to drink from. There were slight rises here and there, though none higher than the bluff on which she was standing. And maybe the dark spot in the distance was a ranch house or a barn. It was too far away to tell. When she turned around, she saw the dirt road leading back down the bluff and meeting the county road, and beyond the county road, she saw with increasing gloominess, was the same flat prairie that was behind her.

Her phone rang. FaceTime. It was Rajni.

When she picked up, Rajni squealed with delight. She said, "Look at you. Just look at you!"

Janavi held the phone a little away from her face, and Rajni said, "Where *are* you?"

"Twenty minutes from where I live."

"But . . ."

"What is it?"

"It looks nothing like the pictures I've seen of America. I mean, where are the buildings? The people? Where is the coffee shop from *Friends*?"

"I'm looking for them too."

Rajni was quiet, and then she said, "How did you get there?"

"I drove."

"You drive? Since when?"

"I learned when we first got here."

Rajni was amazed. She said, "You've always been the braver."

Was she? Standing on the bluff, in the endless American plains, she didn't know what bravery was. Was bravery Rajni rejecting her fate, or was it Janavi accepting hers? She said, "Have you talked to Papa?"

"I took him to the doctor."

"And?"

"He prescribed cough syrup."

"Cough syrup?"

"With codeine."

When Janavi had talked to him, two days ago, he'd been coughing so much that she, feeling helpless, had said, "Drink tea with ginger, Papa. And lemon. Lemon will help." To Rajni, she said, "When did you last visit him?"

"Yesterday. Why?"

"Maybe it's bronchitis."

Rajni sighed. "I'm doing everything I can."

"Are you?"

She saw the hurt in Rajni's face, or maybe she imagined it. When they were saying goodbye, Rajni said, "Do you remember how we used to buy golgappas on our way home from school? At that stand?"

"The guy always gave you more because he had a crush on you."

Rajni laughed. "Did he?" And then she said, "Do you remember how good they tasted?"

"Yes," Janavi said. "I remember."

She was late to pick up Sagar. Even so, when she got to the damsite and parked in the gravel lot, she got a text from him saying he would be another twenty minutes. The lot was on a slight rise overlooking the dam and the reservoir and from where Janavi was parked, she could see some way down the path leading to the dam. She usually waited in the car, though sometimes she walked to the end of the lot and looked down the slope to see if there was any progress that she could see. There wasn't. Sagar had explained to her that not until the first notch was made would she be able to see any difference, but she was still curious. Today, she waited in the car. A few men walked past. They waved goodbye to each other, though none of them saw her. There was no one for a long while. The sun was low on the horizon, and a feeling of great quiet — windless, the shadows just so — always seemed to Janavi to sweep over the Cotton River Valley at this hour, just before twilight. And it was through this quiet, while she was thinking about Rajni and the golgappas, that Janavi heard it: a clinking sound.

She looked up.

A woman. The first woman she'd seen at the damsite. And she was Native American. This must be Renny, she thought. But what had the sound been? She saw Renny searching the ground. Janavi, from where she was seated, saw a set of keys a few feet from where Renny was looking. Janavi watched her. It was obvious that in the twilight, with the color of the keys and the gravel being nearly the same, Renny couldn't see them. Janavi watched her, perplexed by the expression on her face, which seemed intensely vigilant, maybe even vicious. But why? And then all thoughts of Renny's expression, and Rajni, were swept away. Janavi gasped. A gun! Was it a gun? She held her breath and looked again; a solid black end (barrel? grip?) of a gun was sticking out of the waistband of Renny's jeans. Janavi only caught a glimpse before the flap of her jacket fell back over it, but she was sure of it. Almost sure.

It was nearly dark now.

Should she? The gun frightened her; she'd never seen a civilian carrying one before. She opened the door. The sound of it made Renny turn. In its light, Janavi waved, picked up her keys, and handed them to her. "They were behind you," she said, with a small smile.

Renny thanked her, and then she said, "Are you Sagar's wife?"

"Yes. I came to pick him up."

They traded names. Janavi was trying not to look at the gun. Where it must be tucked. She looked up when Renny said, "He cares. I've never known anyone to care as much as he does."

"Sagar? About what?"

Renny's gaze seemed to be searching again. This time for something beyond her, in the gloaming. She said, "This river, for instance."

Janavi said, "Doesn't everybody who works here?"

"It's a job for most. For him it's a river."

Janavi could hardly make out her features anymore, in the dark, but she warmed to her words. They were kind, thoughtful. Perhaps she understood Sagar better than Janavi did. And though she couldn't be mistaken for somebody from India, Janavi felt a familiarity, a kinship. To recognize care was care in itself. She said, "It's true. All his stories are about rivers. He's loved them since he was a child."

"It's nice, isn't it? To love something that won't leave you."

Janavi understood she was saying two things at once, but she didn't know what the second thing was; her thoughts drifted back to Rajni.

They said goodbye, and Renny drove away in a gray pickup truck. Janavi lingered outside of the car, and after a few minutes, heard footsteps coming up the gravel road. It was Sagar. When they climbed into the car, she told him she'd met Renny. She told him about the keys, and of how they'd talked, but she left out the part about the gun. She didn't know why. Maybe she was being irrational. Why should she be so alarmed at seeing a gun? It had only been a matter of time until she did. In fact, she'd known back in India, since she'd been a child, that everybody in America carried guns. The whole world knew. There was the matter of the constant headlines of mass shootings that made the global news, and there were the American movies that not only glamorized guns but made it clear that they were a part of everyday life here. Still, she was shocked. She'd seen guns before, of course. At military parades or when Indian Army personnel had been marching or providing security at political events. Some policemen also carried guns, at train stations and big sporting events. But they had all been the long, official kind, rifles, she supposed they were called. She'd never seen a handgun, not in real life. And certainly never tucked into a woman's waistband. Anyway, she was being ridiculous. I'd better get used to it, she told herself.

The next day, she declined when Sagar offered her the car. She spent the morning at home. She cleaned the entire apartment first and then she made dal for dinner and then she put coconut oil in her hair. She sat on the sofa and waited for the coconut oil to work. Penetrate each strand of her hair, each pore in her scalp. Had she ever done this in India? Wait like this? For the invisible? For the unseen to do the unknown? It struck her as ludicrous suddenly — waiting. And yet, she realized in that moment that that's all she'd been doing since she'd arrived in America: waiting. But if it didn't have an end, if you weren't waiting *for* something, then what was it called?

She washed out the coconut oil, dressed, and left the house with Lottie's casserole dish and a small Tupperware bowl of dal. She walked to the end of the block and turned a grassy corner and looked for a pink house. Lottie was right: It was unmissable.

Lottie smiled, clearly surprised to see her. When Janavi handed her the dal, she said, "What's this? Pudding?"

Janavi said no, and then she explained that dal was made with lentils and spices. She said, "And on top are fried onions and cilantro, for garnish."

Lottie studied it. She said, "How do I eat it? Straight?"

"You could, but it's better with rice."

She led her inside. They walked through the living room with its flowery cream-colored sofa and upright piano, its top crowded with photo frames, and into the kitchen. Lottie brought over two cups of coffee. She said, "A slice of pie would be nice, wouldn't it? But I take to baking like a cat takes to water."

Janavi asked her about pies.

She said, "You've never had pie? Well, everybody will probably tell you to start with apple, but if you ask me, strawberry rhubarb. That's where you should start. Apple's too cloying."

Her phone rang.

She said into the receiver, "I've got a friend over. I can't . . . what, dear? The church picnic? How the fuck should I know?" When she got off the phone, she laughed and said, "Sometimes this place feels smaller than the Inuit village."

"I've never lived in a small town," Janavi said, secretly pleased that Lottie had called her her friend. Her first American friend.

"The thing about small towns is, once you live in one, you carry it around with you forever."

The scent of crushed marigolds came back to Janavi. The warmth of stones on summer evenings, seated on a ghat. The winter sky above the Ganga, low and gray and unmoving. She said, "Don't you carry around every town?"

"Not like you do a small one," Lottie said. "I've been to Denver,

Minneapolis. They're nice but seems to me no matter how long you live there you're just left with images when you leave. Nice ones, some not so nice. But images. With small towns, you get the whole town. All the characters, their stories, their secrets. You take them with you."

Janavi thought this over. She said, "What kind of secrets?"

Lottie only smiled and took a sip of her coffee.

Janavi said, "I saw a woman with a gun. When I went to pick up Sagar."

Lottie looked at her over the rim of her coffee cup. "Was she brandishing it? Aiming at something?"

"No."

Lottie laughed. She said, "Then you just saw a woman."

Janavi said, "Do you have one?"

"Locked box. Under my bed."

"Why?"

"Protection, I guess."

"From what?"

Lottie smiled. She said, "Remember what I said? About small towns and secrets?"

"Yes."

"Well, dear, sometimes they wash up."

On her walk home, Khalil came to mind. Seemingly out of nowhere, since she hadn't thought of him in some time, though really, she hadn't thought of any of the children she'd worked with at ChildDefense. Why was that? She couldn't know for sure, but she could guess: Her mind was protecting her by keeping all those children at bay so that her sorrow, too, at leaving them, could be kept at bay.

But Khalil. He didn't come out of nowhere, did he?

He spoke to her first. Usually, it was Janavi who approached the street children, but Khalil was the one who looked up at her and said, "A little makeup will help you, Auntie."

Her hand went instinctively to her face. Makeup?

They were at the train station in Varanasi. It was not as crowded as usual — late morning, after the commuters had gone — which was the best time for Janavi to go. The children were generally idle after the breakfast rush and more willing to talk. This boy was on Platform 2 selling trinkets and magazines and biscuits arranged on a wooden tray that hung from his neck. He was wearing a soiled red Chicago Bulls T-shirt, with a rip that looked like a knife slash extending from his left shoulder to the middle of his chest. How had it gotten there?

There was another smaller boy standing next to him.

"Some lipstick, Auntie. Not too bright. It won't suit your face. Something softer. Like this pink." He held up a tube of lipstick that was buried underneath a magazine on his tray. "Try it, Auntie-ji."

"Is that how you get women to buy your lipstick? By insulting them."

"No, no, madam. Keval enhance. Enhance only."

Janavi laughed. He couldn't have been older than ten. She asked him his name and then she asked after the other boy. He was Khalil's little brother, Ayaan. She said, "Who do you work for?" hoping he'd say his father, but the boy said, "Chota Sahib. Bada Sahib died."

"Oh? Is he here?"

Khalil looked at her as if she were crazy. "Of course not. Why would he be here? He's bilkul clever. He runs this city!"

That's what Janavi was afraid of. She bought the lipstick and when she got back to the ChildDefense offices she described Khalil and Ayaan to Ms. Sujata and then asked her if she'd ever heard of Bada Sahib or Chota Sahib. She said she hadn't, and then she said, "They change names. To elude the police. Besides, for all we know the ring could be based in Kanpur or Kolkata or eastern Europe. Anywhere."

It seemed to Janavi that they were fighting a hopeless battle and that every child she helped sprouted a dozen more. But whenever she went to the train station, she wore her lipstick and she looked for Khalil. The first time he saw her wearing the lipstick, he said, "A cinema heroine, Auntie-ji. I told you. You look just like a cinema heroine. I should know," he said, laughing, pointing to the array of film magazines on his tray. When he was there, he was always with Ayaan, but sometimes, when neither was there, Janavi searched up and down the platforms, giving up only when it got dark. One morning she arrived and saw only Ayaan. He was seated next to the Higginbothams; the wooden tray of trinkets was on his lap. She sat down beside him and said, "Where is your brother?"

The boy looked up at her, his eyes large and brown and listless, and said, "Chota Sahib took him."

Janavi, trying to keep the alarm in her voice in check, said, "Oh? When was that?"

"I don't know, Auntie-ji. I don't know my days."

She didn't know a heart could break so quietly or so completely. She said, "Did you see him? Did you see Chota Sahib?"

Ayaan nodded.

Again, she calmed her voice. "What did he look like? What did he say?"

Ayaan told her he'd come one evening to the train station and had told him to watch the tray because he needed to talk to Khalil. He and Khalil had then walked away toward the main part of the station where the tickets were sold. He said he'd tried to look after them, but they'd disappeared into the crowd. Ayaan had watched for his brother to come back out of the ticketing hall, but he never had.

"What else do you remember?" Janavi asked.

"Chota Sahib had a mustache," Ayaan said, looking up at her.

She looked back at him and smiled. That narrowed it down to practically every man in India.

She went back to the ChildDefense offices and looked through the database for the records of every child contacted at the train station and their "employer," if there was one. Boys had disappeared plenty of times, girls had disappeared more than plenty of times, but the names Chota Sahib and Bada Sahib were never mentioned. She returned to the train station and talked to every child she saw but not one knew those names or the whereabouts of Khalil. Ayaan, she saw with a wince, was still seated next to the Higginbothams.

She consulted with the other social workers at ChildDefense and the national and local agencies that connected into the database, spoke to street children in different parts of Varanasi, and considered, within the confines of her obscenely limited budget, what to do and where to go. The police? She laughed out loud. The underground networks? The sex workers, the gambling houses, the drug dens? They might've led somewhere except she was too new at her job to have a network. Nothing else came to mind because children — the ones without papers, the ones without parents, the ones without purchase — they were the easiest to annihilate, make disappear. What difference did one vanished child make in the world? Especially one who was poor and brown, his body unwitnessed and unnamed. The cruelest thing to her was that it was here, in Varanasi, that Khalil had been . . . what? Abducted? Sold? Trafficked? Enslaved? Killed? There was no ghat or river in the world holy enough to explain that.

A month later, maybe more, Ms. Sujata called her into her office. When Janavi was seated in front of her, Ms. Sujata said, "It happens. I want you to know that. It happens all the time. It's not your fault."

Janavi stiffened.

Ms. Sujata paused.

She finally opened a desk drawer and held out a shirt of some sort. Janavi stared at it, perplexed. It was tattered, dirty, scrunched into a ball. Janavi looked at the shirt and then at Ms. Sujata. She said, "Didn't you say the boy, the one at the train station, was wearing a Chicago Bulls T-shirt?"

"Yes, but . . ."

Ms. Sujata laid it on her desk. "It washed up. Rohini brought it in. She read your report and . . . she was by the fish market. Chaukaghat. The one by the station. Said she recognized — "

Janavi grabbed it, the inside of her head screaming, No no no no, but there it was: the knife slash from the shoulder to the chest. Her voice trembled. "Washed up? How could — " The grief in her burst forth. "It's not his. It's not possible. Billions of things wash up, all kinds of . . . it's not his. It's not." Ms. Sujata waited, and something inside of Janavi, in her silence, ceded itself, lost its resolve. She began to sob. "It's not his . . ."

Ms. Sujata reached for her hand and said, "It's not your fault."

Janavi stopped crying, and her voice, spewing lava, said, "Then whose is it?"

Walking home along the streets of Mansfield, Janavi thought of the red Chicago Bulls T-shirt and then she thought about the pink lipstick. She smiled sadly. She wanted to say, Not just small towns, Lottie. Big towns too. Things wash up in big towns too.

Leela & Avni

Ganges River, 1876

Leela didn't like her daughter's new husband from the start. He looked at her daughter, Avni, the same way he looked at the gold pocket watch they gave him as a wedding present — with a drooling sense of possession that reminded Leela of the drawing she'd seen in one of her father's textbooks. It was the year after the establishment of Muhammadan Anglo-Oriental College, where her father was a member of the Faculty of Arts. She'd been only a girl at the time and had been looking on his shelves for picture books. She'd pulled this one down because it was on a low shelf, and was bright red, with gold embossing the color of her doll Piya's hair. She'd flipped to a random page, and there was a sketch of a man and a woman. The man was lifting the woman into the air, but she didn't look very happy about it. Leela tried to read the inscription.

"R-A-P-E. Rapee. Papa, what does rapee mean? And what is this girl's name? The one in this picture."

Her papa, seated at his desk, looked down at her and said, "Bring me the book." She took the book to him. He laid it flat on his desk and looked at it for a long while, and finally he said, "The girl's name is Persephone."

"And rapee?"

"Well — " Her papa stopped. He cleared his throat and then he said, "It means a lot of things. But here, it means seizing or taking away."

"He's taking her away?" Leela asked.

"Yes."

"Where to?"

Watching her new son-in-law lead her daughter away, to the train station and then to their marital home in Kanpur, Leela knew it didn't matter; it was the taking away that mattered, not the where to. A short while later, her daughter had a daughter. And then she had another daughter. That was too many daughters. She, along with the babies, was sent back to her parents' house. Leela and her husband tried to negotiate with their son-in-law. They offered him acreage — a sizable mango orchard — in exchange for taking her back, but he was unmoved. Avni, finding her mother reading in bed, came into the room and lay down next to her. She leaned her head on her mother's shoulder. Leela said, "Did you put the babies to bed?"

Avni nodded. And then she said, "Ma?"

"Yes."

She was quiet. After a moment, she said, "Will you put me to bed?" She spoke in a voice so plaintive that Leela looked up and thought, My girl. What did he do to you?

Sometime later, they found Avni hanging from the rafters of the back room. There was no note. Nothing was left of her except the babies in their cribs. Leela looked down at them. Her granddaughters. She saw their wings, wary and delicate, trapped among their new bones. Early one morning, Leela went to Scindia Ghat. She went alone. She looked up, into the predawn river mist, and saw a boatload of people being rowed across the Ganga. They were dressed in white and chanting. Where were they going? Perhaps to a sand flat, or to another ghat. The mist was too thick to see beyond the boat and the gray water, and to Leela, they looked like they were crossing the River Styx. Entering the underworld.

She could follow them. She could bring her back. And it would be spring.

Chapter 16

They were now a month away, maybe less, from making the first notch. Sagar couldn't contain his excitement. Janavi said to him one night, "You're like a child. The night before his birthday."

Being compared to a child by Janavi seemed to Sagar the highest compliment. He beamed and said, "The crew is ready to go. As soon as we get this last permit approved, we'll make the notch. After that it'll be as if the dam never existed! Not ecologically, of course. That could take years, but . . ."

Janavi, he saw, nodded, asked questions, seemed to follow along with interest. This was their meeting ground — talking about the dam. She'd seemed, when they'd first arrived, resentful and depressed, understandably, that he was getting up and leaving for his job every morning when she had no job to go to. She'd finally stopped lashing out at him, though he worried that her resentment had burrowed to a deeper place. What was more, he was growing afraid that very soon (or had it happened already?) they would settle into a kind of convivial friendship stripped of sex and desire. Lust.

He'd had sex a few times in college, with a classmate. The first time had been after a party, and he and Karishma had both been drinking. They'd taken a taxi back to his room and fumbled through the zippers and the buckles and the clasps, and it was only when she'd been lying back on Sagar's bed, lovely, naked, that he'd been struck by a pang of conscience. He'd said, "I'm sorry — I don't . . . I don't want to mislead you."

Karishma had immediately pulled the blanket over herself. "What do you mean? You have something?"

"Have something . . . ?" It took him a moment. "No, no! It's not that. It's — the thing is, I'm betrothed. To be married. And I didn't — "

"Are you married now?"

"No."

She'd let go of the blanket and smiled. "Then what's the problem?"

They'd met every week or two until they'd graduated, with both of them understanding it was an arrangement of convenience, nothing more. The last he'd heard, Karishma had married and moved to Bengaluru.

Now he, too, was married. And Janavi was the woman he was married to. *Acceptance* seemed a comically unequal word for where he found himself. The previous week, she'd come into the bedroom from the shower, wrapped in a towel, and he'd been instantly aroused. She hadn't expected him to be in the bedroom, rummaging for a pair of socks, and their eyes had met. Who'd looked away first? He couldn't remember, but out of embarrassment or panic, he'd hurriedly left the room. He wished he'd stayed. Should he have stayed? Of course he should've stayed. He should've been a man, and he should've said, You're mine, and he should've stayed. He should have walked over to her and plucked the towel away. But he was being respectful. And yet, he felt meek and helpless and confused and miserable. He felt shame. To be married now, what? Nearly a year, and to not have even truly touched. He wondered, Am I not man enough? How does one know? He was bewildered at times by the oddest things. The smooth inside of her forearm, the wisps of fine hair that came loose when she tied up her hair, the half-moons of shadow under her eyes. All he wanted to do was touch them — the forearm, the hairs, the shadows — and yet, were they even his to touch?

The other person who was confusing him was Renny.

She'd grown distant, reserved. Or was it all in his head?

He couldn't pinpoint exactly when it had happened; he guessed sometime after the conversation they'd had around the microwave. He'd come to value the camaraderie he and Renny and Alex Mendoza had shared, and suddenly it was gone. Now when he walked past her, she seemed preoccupied. She hardly ever said hello anymore, and had not once, since the lunchtime conversation, come into the trailer for a cup of coffee or to heat up her lunch. And, he noticed, if there was any paperwork or tools or instruments to drop off, she sent one of her assistants. He couldn't understand it.

Renny was standing at the water's edge one evening, while he was walking along the shore opposite the burial site. He thought she was looking at him and so he waved. But she didn't wave back. In fact, she was perfectly motionless, looking, he realized, not at him but at the dam. Why was she staring at the dam? Sagar turned away. It was unsettling how mournful she looked. Her posture, at the water's edge, evoked in him the memory of a marble statue he'd once seen in a museum. He remembered its name: *Dreamer Without a Dream*. A slightly bent woman, looking into a distance Sagar had not been able to fathom. He'd read in the catalogue describing the statue and its maker that all sculptors, of some renown, spoke of seeing the finished sculpture in the original rock, well before a chisel or even a hand had touched it. It was as if the medium — the marble or the alabaster or the sandstone or the limestone or the soapstone — already carried the sculpture within itself. Stone, then, he remembered thinking, must be the most patient entity on earth. What else could stand for millions and millions of years, waiting, unmoving, for its maker.

And yet, that's how Renny looked to him.

He decided to bring it up with Alex Mendoza. He got his chance when, a few days later, Alex waved him down while Sagar was walking to his car. He said, "You look like a man in need of a beer." Sagar thought they'd go to a bar in town, but instead Alex went to his truck and brought out a six-pack. He winked and said, "In case of emergency."

They walked down the slope from the parking lot and crossed the bridge to the south end of the dam. They found a patch of sedge grass that overlooked the reservoir. Sagar settled himself against a clump of it. The prairie was behind him, but he could feel it. He could feel it like a presence, not a ghostly presence, but a solid one. Like a boulder.

Alex Mendoza's key chain doubled as a bottle opener. He handed Sagar a beer and said, "First notch is coming up, isn't it?"

Sagar said, "Less than a month, I hope." And then he said, "Have you ever been on a dam removal project before?"

Alex said he hadn't. And then he said, "Best part of being a kid was knocking down the wooden blocks. That's what this feels like."

Sagar chuckled and felt the beer warming him.

They sat for a time in silence. The discharge gates were closed, so there was only the stillness of the reservoir before them, the stillness of the prairie behind them. Sagar, through the quiet, heard the shouts and yips of little boys. Felt the heat of a summer afternoon, the cold waters of the Yeleru. He said, "Have you talked to Renny lately? Noticed anything about her? Anything strange?"

Alex Mendoza shrugged. "No. Why?"

"I walked right past her the other day, and she didn't . . ." It occurred to him in that instant that Alex might think he was interested in Renny, romantically. He was mortified, and suddenly flustered. He said, "It's surprising, that's all. It's not like her . . ."

"Women," Alex Mendoza said. "Who the fuck knows with them."

He finished his first beer and opened another. He said, "Could be Gabe."

"They're divorced, aren't they?"

Alex laughed. "Don't mean shit. They can still make your life miserable."

"Do you know him?"

"Gabe? By sight. I was in middle school when we moved here. He was out of high school by then. But I'd see him. Him and his buddies. Sons of rich ranchers. Guess his family owned a big ranch, too, but they lost it."

"Lost it?"

"Banks."

Sagar nodded in sympathy.

"Don't feel bad. Him and his buddies were assholes."

He heard a bitterness in his voice, a sting.

"This one time, I was sitting right near here. Upstream, on one of the bluffs along the reservoir. Must've been a freshman or sophomore in high school. I used to come out here to smoke. Not much else to do. And that's when I saw some trucks pull up. Right below me. All these guys climbed out, clearly drunk. Gabe was one of 'em, Sam Dooley, bunch of others — "

"The mayor?"

"You didn't know? He and Gabe go way back. Like I said, ranching boys."

Sagar was astonished. Renny had said they'd gone to high school together, but not that they'd been friends.

"They're drinking, smoking, goofing off. Boy stuff, though they were plenty grown by then. Anyway, one of 'em was a guy I knew. He'd come around to our house on a couple of Sunday mornings. Said my mom made the best chilaquiles north of Jalisco. Guess that's where he was from. Don't know why this guy was hanging out with the ranching crew, stood out like a sore thumb. Must've worked as a ranch hand on one of their dads' ranches. So, I'm watching 'em horsing around, laughing, and of course the guns come out. After that, I don't know what happened. I was too far away to hear them. But before I know it, they have the guy from Jalisco on his knees, a gun pointed at him." He stopped. He looked away. He said, "You know what happened next . . ."

Sagar could guess.

"Gabe and Sam weren't the main ones, if you get my meaning, but it didn't matter. They moved like one animal. One machine. All those white boys. I couldn't watch." He fell silent.

Sagar, too, could think of nothing to say.

"Don't matter what brought that about, if anything, but it's not right. It's just not right. Never saw that guy from Jalisco again. The rest? They just went about their business. But you know how it is. Consequences don't come for all of us in the same way. For some, they don't come at all."

They sat in silence again, watching the surface of the reservoir bluing and then deepening into black. They finished the last of the beers — Sagar had two, Alex Mendoza had four — and when they reached the parking lot, as Sagar fished out his keys, Alex said, "It's gotta be tough for Renny. Being the only woman, the only Native, on the project."

"Yes, it must be," Sagar said, and it was as if even the light agreed, because it pulled away from the prairie — in the time it took him to get in his car and turn the ignition — and left it in darkness.

Sagar was shutting down his computer one night, the Friday after he'd had beers with Alex Mendoza, when the door to the trailer opened. Who could be here? Late on a Friday? He thought it might be someone from the cleaning crew that came during the weekends to collect the trash and restock supplies; Tim Downing and most everyone else had gone home. He didn't look up immediately, and then he did. It was Renny.

He rose from his chair. He didn't know what to do after that. They were silent for a moment. Sagar wondered if he was supposed to say something.

Renny rummaged in the fridge and then she looked up and said, "I liked your story. About the Ganges."

"You did?"

"I liked how she's a goddess. How the entire river is a goddess."

He wanted to tell her that his wife was named after the river, the goddess. Instead, he said, "And a powerful one too. That's why she came down to earth through Shiva's hair. Otherwise, her descent would've shattered the earth. As it was, according to the myth, the force of her landing split the river into seven tributaries." He was rambling again.

Renny smiled and said, "Have you always?"

"Always what?"

"Loved rivers?"

"When I was a kid," he said, "I used to dive in the Godavari, the second longest river in India, after the Ganges, looking for sunken Spanish galleons." He laughed. "All I ever found were bottle caps."

She laughed, too, and then her expression changed. Became strangely remote. He thought, inexplicably, of Shiva again. How he held, for all of eternity, the most powerful of poisons in his neck. Swallowing it would destroy him; not swallowing it would've destroyed the universe.

She said, with a sudden seriousness, "You dived?"

"I was convinced I would find them. How Spanish galleons might end up in a South Indian river is something I never quite worked out."

She looked at him then for a long while. He smiled nervously. They stood like that for some time. And then slowly, ever so slowly, he saw something move across her face. What was it? A shadow, a cloud over the prairie. Sagar was perplexed, astonished by the change in her. She turned to go. Just as she reached the door, she swung back around and said, "Did you ever find anything unusual? In the river?"

"Unusual? Like what?"

"Like . . . I don't know. Not a Spanish galleon, of course, but another kind of boat. A car . . ."

"I wish! I would've been the happiest kid in India."

"But . . ." She hesitated. "But if you had found something, a car, let's say, how long before . . ." She seemed to be struggling with something. He couldn't understand what it could be. Finally, she looked out of the small window of the trailer and said, "It's strange, isn't it? How perfect and still it is."

He followed her gaze. She was looking at the reservoir. She said, "I've swum in it all my life."

"I suppose you'll miss it when it's gone."

She smiled sadly. After a moment, she seemed to recover something, a feeling, a conviction, and she said, "Water turns. Spoils. Like milk. And when that happens not even the Wolf can drink from it."

He looked at her. Wolf?

Her eyes suddenly lit up. "The notches. How much is each of them going to drain the reservoir? Which one will drain it completely?"

How odd. Why was Renny asking the exact question Sam Dooley had asked? He said, "Are you worried about the burial site? Don't be. That's why we make one notch at a time. To regulate drainage. We'll take measurements after the first notch, but don't worry, the first one won't flood the burial site."

She nodded absently. It wasn't about the burial site. Something else was bothering her. He was about to ask her what it was, but then, without another word, Renny turned and left.

That night, while they were watching television, Janavi said, "Did you know there's an Inuit tribe in Canada that doesn't have a number greater than three? In their numbering system, I mean. Isn't that interesting?"

"Three? That's it?"

"Lottie worked with them."

He thought it over. "Maybe it's sacred to them."

"Maybe."

"I think it's sacred."

She looked at him, surprise on her face. "Because of Brahma, Vishnu, Shiva?"

"No. Because of water."

"Water?"

"How many atoms are in a molecule of water?"

It took her a moment, and then she smiled.

Chapter 17

For the first time since they'd been in America Janavi picked up the phone and called Rajni. It was Saturday morning; it would be evening for Rajni.

Sagar had gone to work. He'd said, getting out of bed at 6 a.m., "I've got piles of paperwork, Janavi. Tests to run. The first notch is in a matter of days. Why don't you drop me off and keep the car?"

But she'd declined, and now she wished she'd kept the car.

Rajni answered on the first ring, and by the question and concern in her voice, Janavi could tell she was astonished she had called. She was at home, she told Janavi. Janavi heard the television or maybe a radio in the background. Rajni said it was a serial she'd started watching recently. "I can't stop watching," she said, laughing.

"What is it about?" Janavi asked.

"I can't tell you," she said. "It's too silly."

"Tell me."

She launched, excitedly, into a long and meandering story about two babies, both girls, who'd been switched at birth. By accident or by design, no one knew. One of the babies went to the family of rich parents and the other to a family of poor ones — the father worked as a stonemason and the mother as a street sweeper. Both the girls grew up to be beautiful, but the rich one was spoiled and cruel to the servants while the poor girl was the epitome of kindness and grace and intelligence, passing her college exams with the highest marks. Eventually both sets of parents became aware of the switch through the maternity nurse who, following a car accident and as she was dying, confessed to the switch, and the two families, after some turmoil, accepted the way things had turned out. After all, they truly loved their daughters. "But here's the thing, Janoo," Rajni said. "Here's what happens: When the 'father' of the rich girl dies, guess what he does? He leaves his entire fortune to the poor girl—his real daughter. Can you believe it? All of it! And of course, the rich girl is absolutely devastated. And angry. She's terribly angry." That, apparently, was where the serial stood for now. She told Janavi she would tell her more as the story unfolded. She said, "You see? It's silly. I told you it was silly."

"No, I like it," Janavi said. Then she asked about their papa. "He didn't pick up last time I called." Rajni said, "That's because whenever he starts talking, he has a coughing fit." She told her she was taking him to a pulmonary specialist. "Where?" Janavi asked. "Either Heritage or Apex." After a pause, Rajni said, "Everything is okay with you, isn't it?"

Janavi heard the tremulousness in her voice. "What if it isn't?"

"Janoo . . ."

Janavi waited for her to say more, and when she didn't, she said, "For the first time last night, I dreamed a whole dream in English. The entire thing. No Hindi, no Telugu. What do you think that means?"

Rajni didn't know. When they got off the phone, Janavi walked through the living room and looked at the sofa and then the television and then out of the window. She thought about Papa. She thought about the serial. She thought about Rajni seated in her living room, in Varanasi, drinking tea and waiting breathlessly for the next episode. She was there, Janavi was here. They were where they were, and both married. And yet, who had chosen for whom? And choice itself . . . amid the confusion and the constraints and the assumptions and the rarity, if ever, of having all the information that was germane, the choice made was so often wrong. Or unwise. Or hurtful. Maybe what had happened between them, in the moment of the choosing under the guava tree, had not been unique or malicious or all that awful; maybe, Janavi thought, it had simply been life.

She left the house on foot.

When she got to the convenience store, there was a line. Janavi filled her Slurpee cup and when she got to the front of the line, Mandy said, "You go ahead."

Janavi sat on the retaining wall and watched the cars pulling in and out of the gas pumps. It was the busiest she'd ever seen it, but then again, she'd never been here on a Saturday. She was half done with her Slurpee when Mandy came out and lit a cigarette. She said, "You know what just happened? That guy, you see him?" She pointed to a man replacing the fuel pump. "He fucking farted. Right as I was checking him out. Big one too. Didn't apologize, say oops, nothing. Paid, farted, and left. That's it. Can you believe it?"

Janavi laughed and laughed. She watched the man pull away in his truck. She watched the next car pull up. She was baffled suddenly. Why? She didn't know why but what she wanted, intensely, was the smell of cardamom wafting through a night market or the shouts of jasmine sellers on a busy street or the winter sunrise over the Ganga or the sound of Amma calling her name or . . . she stopped. She realized what she wanted was home. But where was home? In all the years she'd studied English, no one had taught her — no one had even once mentioned — that some words, because of what life will do to them, will lose their meaning. And that that meaning will never be regained.

Mandy was saying, "Some nights, I dream of torching this place. If it weren't a gas station, I probably would." And then she smiled and said, "You know what my dream is? My *real* dream? My real dream is to stand in the middle of Times Square and hula-hoop. Right there. Right in the middle. With all the lights and the people and the cars around me. And me just hula-hooping. Right there in the middle. Like I'm the one who's making it all spin."

"Hula-hoop?"

"You all don't hula-hoop? Back in India?"

Janavi told her they might, but she didn't know what it was, so Mandy tried to describe it — the hoop and how to keep it spinning at your waist using your belly and your back. She showed her some videos on her phone. "It's harder than it looks," she said. And then she told her she'd made it to the state championships in middle school and won second place. She said, "I would've come in first but those sausages from the free hotel breakfast didn't sit right."

Sausages from a hotel breakfast?

Janavi thought about how, when she'd gotten up that morning, she'd noticed the bottle of tomato pickle on the dining table. Had Sagar put it there? What could he possibly have had for breakfast that needed tomato pickle? She'd then seen the unwashed bowl of oatmeal. *Oatmeal?* Her face had scrunched up, but as she'd been microwaving her own, she'd thought, Maybe. She'd tried it — instead of adding raisins and honey to her oatmeal, she'd eaten it with tomato pickle. She'd taken one bite and then another, and then she'd smiled and texted him, *You're on to something.*

Mandy was still talking about the sausages and coming in second place. Janavi said that was too bad, about the bad sausages, and Mandy said, "Well, as my mama says, Fate is like a campfire. It can warm you up or it can burn you down, depending on how you handle it."

That seemed to Janavi the wisest thing she'd ever heard said about fate and she told her so.

The next day, she and Sagar decided to go to the Asian store in Billings. They needed groceries, and Sagar told her he wouldn't have another free day for some time, given that the first notch was coming up. When they got to the car, Sagar handed her the keys and said, "You drive."

"Why?"

"Don't you want to practice on the interstate?"

It was true that she'd avoided the interstates; the speed of the cars and the massive semis and all of them changing lanes back and forth scared her. Sagar said, "Stay in the right lane. They'll go around you."

She drove on Highway 212 and then, between Garryowen and Crow Agency, merged onto Interstate 90. It was nerve-racking, even though there wasn't much traffic on a Sunday morning. She only changed lanes once, to go around construction cones in the right lane. Once they reached Billings, getting off at the King Avenue exit was easier than she'd expected. She breathed a sigh of relief when she finally parked in front of the store.

When they were done shopping, Sagar, smiling, said, "You don't want to go straight home, do you?"

She looked at him. "You want to get lunch first?"

"Yes, but let's go eat it by a different river."

"Which one?"

"The Yellowstone. There's a park. Near here."

Of course, she'd *seen* the Yellowstone many times. Every time they'd come to Billings, they'd had to cross it. But they'd never stopped to look.

The park Sagar referred to was less than fifteen minutes from the center of Billings, and yet, when they arrived and settled themselves on a grassy knoll overlooking a red wooden bridge, it felt as though they were in another country. Janavi was charmed. The gentle lapping of the water, the trees reflected on its soft surface, the ducks and the geese gliding by. There was a walking path behind them, and a sprinkling of people, and . . . she stopped. Was that? She looked again. "Isn't that — isn't that Renny?"

Sagar turned to look toward where she was pointing. After a moment, he gasped and said, "Yes, it is!"

They went over to say hello. Renny, too, seemed overjoyed to see them. She said, "What are the odds?" Then turning to the water, she yelled, "Ofee. Not so close."

Janavi saw a little girl playing at the water's edge.

Renny said, "Ophelia. My daughter." And then she seemed to look past her, into the distance, and said, "Wanted to get us out of the valley for the day."

Sagar said, "I didn't know you had a daughter."

Just then, Ophelia ran up to Renny and said, "Look, Mama. Look!" In her tiny cupped hands was a red-and-black beetle. Renny said, "Ooh, that's a pretty one." She studied it some more and said, "See those big antennae? That means it's probably a boy." And then she said, "Let him go now, Fee. I'm sure he has things to do."

Ophelia laid the beetle gently on a blade of grass.

"How old is she?" Janavi asked.

"She just turned four."

Janavi looked back at her. Her plump forearms and her inquisitive eyes and her wisps of hair blowing in the warm breeze. Renny, who must've sensed Janavi's delight, held out a piece of lettuce and said, "She loves ducks."

At the water's edge, a line of ducks was floating by. Janavi, leaning down, said to Ophelia, "You want to go say hi to the ducks?"

Ophelia gazed up and nodded shyly.

Renny laughed and said, "Don't worry. Her shyness won't last more than a minute or two. Then she'll talk your ear off."

Renny and Sagar had already launched into a conversation about work; Janavi held out her hand and Ophelia took it and then they walked down the length of the knoll. Such a little hand. She thought then of Amma holding her hand on the day of the puja, when the boys were being fed before the girls. She was leading Janavi and Rajni out in protest, but she must've felt it too: that when you held a thing as perfect, as fine, and as wondrous as a child's hand, all the world came down to it. To its perfection and its fineness and its wonder.

Ophelia was saying, "Mrs. Nelson doesn't like it when we bring insects inside. She says they like the outdoors better. We have a class guinea pig. His name is Oscar. Oscar has pellets that he likes to eat. Do you like the taste of pellets? I ate one when Mrs. Nelson wasn't looking. But I spit it out. It was gross. Also, the other day . . ."

She went on and on like that. They tore the lettuce leaf into pieces and watched as the ducks gathered around and munched on them. When the lettuce was finished, they remained at the water's edge and Janavi listened as Ophelia told her more about Oscar and Mrs. Nelson and her classmates, especially someone named Lily. Janavi could've listened for hours, days. It occurred to her that, of all the children she'd interacted with at ChildDefense, she'd not once simply sat by the Ganga and chatted with one of them. Why was that? They were usually in distress, that was one reason, and the other, she supposed, was that the adults in the lives of the street children had often betrayed them or abandoned them or exploited them. Why, after such treatment at the hands of adults, would they sit and chat with one, let alone trust them?

What a pleasure it was, then, to be in the sunshine with Ophelia, listening to her chatter. Sagar had told her Renny was divorced (she assumed from Ophelia's father), and Janavi hoped that its tumult hadn't affected Ophelia negatively. Looking now into her eyes, Janavi decided, No. This girl is unharmed.

And then she thought, A child unharmed. What a rare thing. What a thing worthy of protecting.

Chapter 18

The day arrived — the day of the first notch.

Sagar got up early. He showered and made coffee. He shaved and combed his hair with great care and put on his best shirt and newly washed jeans. When he was leaving, Janavi said, excitedly, "Call me. Call me as soon as you can. Will you?" He assured her he would, and then he thought, How have I never noticed? That her voice is like water. The previous night, she'd pointed to a faint scar on her right palm. He'd always thought it was a palm line, but she told him it was from a piece of broken glass. He'd smiled. These minor intimacies, the slight discernments — each one was a small, twinkling jewel.

Driving to work, it felt to Sagar as if he'd been waiting all his life for this moment. Building toward it. Even as a child, when he'd jumped from one puddle to the next in the rain, this moment had been inevitable. When he got to the damsite though, everyone, even as they smiled and said good morning, didn't seem all that excited. If a dam was being built, Sagar thought, and the ground was being broken today, there would've been such celebration. Champagne would've been popped. When ground was broken on dam projects in India there was always a ribbon-cutting ceremony and a clay statue of Lord Ganesha, the remover of obstacles, was released into the river. Here, there was only the shouts of the foreman, yelling to one of his crew, "What's taking them so goddamn long? At this rate, we'll be here till Christmas."

Midmorning, he and Tim Downing stood on the edge of the dam. Tim had his clipboard and a walkie-talkie, Sagar had the blueprints and another walkie-talkie, and they waited for the heavy machinery — the barge-mounted hydraulic jackhammer, the sledgehammer — and the trucks and the construction crew to make their way to the dam. Tim Downing said something into his walkie-talkie that Sagar couldn't make out. He was mumbling, or maybe the wind carried away his words. After that he looked at Sagar and said, "I hate this part."

"What part?" Sagar said.

"Waiting."

It seemed to Sagar construction projects were mostly time spent waiting but he didn't say so.

"Oh, hey," Tim said then, grinning widely, "I gotta joke for you." Sagar turned to him. He nodded toward the burial site, which was cleared of workers for safety reasons. He said, "If you and Renny had a baby it'd be half Indian and half Indian. Get it?" He snickered. "Get it? Half Indian and half Indian? Do you get it?"

Sagar said, "Yeah. I get it."

After he was done laughing, they waited some more, and then Tim said, "That's all bullshit, you know."

"What is?"

"It's just some broken pots and an arrowhead or two, and we've got to invest all this time and money just to rebury 'em somewhere else. Waste of time, is what I think."

"It was a burial ground."

"I know *that*. Don't you think I know that? All I'm saying is, dig it up and let's be done with it. No need for the monitors and the archeologists and the BLM and the BIA and the whatnot. The tribe makes everything into a federal case. Rebury them and let's take this puppy down. Don't you think?"

Sagar didn't know what to say so he didn't say anything. By then the hydraulic jackhammer hove into view, coming up the river, and Tim hurried away.

By the end of the day — five months after he and Janavi had arrived in the Cotton River Valley and two months after Sagar had submitted the final engineering design plan to the Water Resources Division at the DNRC — the first notch was cut into the dam. Ben Mackey couldn't be there, but everyone on the project, along with Alex Mendoza and Renny and her burial site crew, was there. They clapped and hurrahed when the first chunk of the dam broke free. Sagar, beaming, watched the water that had been held back for nearly a hundred years gush through the notch and rejoin its river. The water came within a few dozen feet of the burial ground, but a man-made levee of red clay topped with sedge grass, constructed decades ago, steered the water away. Sagar's plan called for four notches in all, but it wouldn't take that many before the burial site would be submerged. Maybe the second notch would do it or the third.

But none of them would see the second notch for a long time to come, and Renny? Renny would never see it. Because two days later, on a cloudless Saturday afternoon, she was drawn through the first notch and found dead, hours later, at the base of the Cotton River dam.

Caroline

Cotton River, 1899

Caroline was tied to a tree. She had come to the Cotton River Valley on one of the wagon trains along the Bozeman Trail, or maybe she was one of the ones lost in the freak storm that had blown in last June. But she couldn't have tied *herself* to the tree. No one knew that she had been a music teacher — piano, violin — back in Platteville, Wisconsin. Not that anyone bothered to look at her hands or her nails. If they had, they would've seen how shredded they were, the nails, the nail beds, the tongue too.

Caroline woke one morning in Platteville — twenty-three years old, an old maid, really, with not much more than a small income teaching five of the local schoolchildren. She also had a locket of her dead brother's hair that her mother had passed down to her — and she realized, while drinking her morning tea, that dreaming every night of graves with no names on them, no dates, just plain, granite stones that were gray and grim and pointless, were not the dreams she wanted to dream. That very morning, she went to the general mercantile and picked up the previous month's Milwaukee paper. She turned to the classifieds and ran her finger down the column for "Brides Wanted." There were about a dozen listings. She glanced at each one, just as she had when, as a girl of eight, she'd picked out a puppy from the litter of a neighbor dog: knowing she'd know it when she saw it. And so she did. The classified was from a lumberjack in Washington state. He was thirty-five, widowed, and wanted companionship. *Hard life*, he said of being a lumberjack's wife, and then the classified read: *Emphatic sense of self*. She didn't know if that meant *he* had an emphatic sense of self, or if he wanted a bride with an emphatic sense of self. It didn't matter. She knew the puppy when she saw it.

They began a correspondence and soon thereafter, Caroline began her journey to Aberdeen, Washington.

While packing her entire life into two small valises, she wondered, as she had many times before, why her mother had given her the locket of her brother's hair. It seemed the final assault in a lifetime of assaults. The wrong child, her mother sometimes said, if she said anything at all. When her brother died — scarlet fever, age five — Caroline realized very quickly that her mother had gone with him. Not in body, but the body is rarely needed; there are other ways to die. She understood that the locket was a family heirloom and of course it would be passed down to her, but all she wanted to do was crush it under her heel, throw it into a river. She'd always kept it in a box, but instead of putting the box in one of her valises, she took out the locket and sewed it into the hem of her blouse. Why? she wondered. Why am I doing this? What an odd thing to do. But when the stagecoach she was traveling on was robbed, it made all the sense in the world. They took everything else: the two valises, the life of the stagecoach driver, her virginity, all the mail and cargo, and the horses, but they didn't take the locket. They then shot the two male passengers and tied the three female ones to trees. Cottonwood trees. The temperature that night dropped precipitously, and the other two women died almost instantly. Caroline, by the fifth day of being tied to the tree, was also near death. She thought of Odysseus and felt as if she were tied to the mast of a ship. Were those Sirens she heard in the distance? And why tie them to trees? Just so they would die slowly, she understood — there could be no other reason. She had been eating the snow stuck to the tree for the first two days, but on the afternoon of the third, the snow melted. So, this is how I will die, she thought: of thirst.

On the fourth day, she realized there were thin shards of ice stuck deep in the bark of the tree trunk, still frozen. She used her tongue to wedge between the ridges of the bark and scrape out the shards. The droplets of water that she sucked out with the tip of her tongue kept her alive for a fourth day. On the fifth day, even the shards of ice were gone, and Caroline looked down at the ground of the Cotton River Valley, under the triangle of cottonwood trees, and saw the gray and grim and pointless tombstones from her dreams and realized that that's what she'd always been standing on, not just now but for her entire life — the tomb of her brother. She scraped the hem of her tattered blouse against the tree bark until the locket fell, broke open, and the hair flew out to where it belonged, onto the tomb that had been all her life, and only then did Caroline die.

Part III

Chapter 19

The morning after they learned of Renny's death, Janavi was on her phone. When Sagar walked past her, pacing, as he had been all morning, she turned to him and said, "Look at this."

It was an article in *The Mansfield Register*, published online the previous night. The headline was LOCAL WOMAN FOUND DEAD, COTTON RIVER DAM REMOVAL TO BLAME?

They both read, huddled over the phone.

Authorities report that a local woman was found dead at the base of the Cotton River dam. After being alerted by kayakers, a rescue team found the woman, Renata Atwood, on Saturday evening at 9:08. She was pronounced dead at the scene. Though she appears to have drowned, the cause of death has not yet been confirmed. The Cotton River Reservoir was in the process of being drained in order to remove the dam. The Custer County sheriff, Brian Oswald, said the woman was a consultant on the dam removal project but he did not indicate in what capacity. "A horrific incident," Sheriff Oswald said, "just horrific. One that impacts all of us in the community."

The removal of the Cotton River Dam, which has faced opposition, was begun only months ago. The Department of Natural Resources and Conservation, the state agency responsible for the dam removal, said in a written statement, "Safety is our highest priority. Our thoughts and prayers are with the friends and family of the victim. The department will be conducting a full investigation of this tragic incident." Tim Downing, the lead project manager on the dam removal project, said, "We do the best we can. Most of us do. It's just a sad, sad thing."

Sam Dooley, the mayor of Mansfield, the town closest to the dam, released a statement immediately following the gruesome discovery. "We are concerned about the children of our community, and the well-being of our town. The safety of this project has always been my concern. The question is whether this project should've been undertaken at all. In my capacity as the mayor, I will be forming a committee ex officio to investigate exactly what happened here." Mayor Dooley led the fight to keep the dam from being removed.

Sheriff Oswald's office has also launched an investigation. The sheriff said, "We won't stop until we figure out how this senseless death could've occurred. Custer County doesn't back down."

The victim's family could not be reached for comment.

Janavi looked up at Sagar's face and thought she'd never seen an expression of such misery. Unthinkingly, she said, "I wonder why they didn't talk to you," and immediately regretted it. The anguish in his face, which had seemed so immense only a moment ago, deepened further, like dusk.

He took the phone from her and stared at the screen. "Renny? At the dam? Why? Why was she there?" And then he said, "Something isn't right."

"What isn't right?"

Sagar only shook his head.

She asked again, but still he said nothing. Instead, he handed the phone back to her and wandered into the kitchen.

For Janavi, the days after Amma's death returned. She remembered that when Papa had come back from Amma's cremation he had smelled of woodsmoke, and she remembered the old neighbor lady who'd smelled of Zandu Balm, and she remembered sitting at her table, a plate of rice and kadhi in front of her, waiting for Amma to come out of death and feed her. Everything kept returning, and she wanted to tell Sagar — about the woodsmoke and the old lady and the waiting — over lunch, but just as she was about to, Sagar's phone rang.

They both jumped.

They'd become unused to sound.

He got up from the table and went into the bedroom, where his phone was. She heard Sagar's voice but not what he was saying. When he came back, he walked past her to the fridge and took out a beer. Before he could open it, she said, "You already have one."

"What?"

She pointed to the open bottle of beer on the table. He replaced the beer in the fridge and wandered aimlessly back to the table. "Who was it?"

"Alex Mendoza."

"What did he say?"

He sat drinking his beer, staring at the wall behind her, and then he said, "Her funeral is tomorrow."

Janavi nodded or thought she nodded. Ophelia. Where was she? Was she safe? Was she cared for? She heard the creak of the swing, and she thought, It's the wind, not the little girl. I haven't seen her in so long. In college, while she'd still been an English major, she'd had to read parts of *The Inferno*. The word *Phlegethon* popped into her head. Phlegethon. The river of boiling blood. The seventh circle. Violence against one's neighbors. Oneself. God. "Are we — "

"Yes," he said. "We're going."

The day of Renny's funeral, Janavi was rummaging in the closet when Sagar walked into the bedroom after his shower. She looked up. Gasped. He'd shaved his head. Now the memory of not just woodsmoke but also her papa's gulab jamun head came back. How, without hair, his face had changed utterly, just as Sagar's did. Death remakes us, she understood them to be saying, And so here we are — remade.

She tried to find words, something lighthearted, but all she could manage was a nod and a small smile.

They arrived at the Catholic church at the corner of Custer and Main just as Mass was starting. Janavi wore her chiffon shalwar kameez, the only outfit she had that was mostly black. They sat on the aisle of a pew in the back. As soon as they sat down, Janavi scanned each row, looking for Ophelia. Her gaze reached the front . . . the casket. Janavi's eyes held. Warmed. The casket was closed, decked in flowers. She swallowed painfully, and then she looked down. There was a tiny stool by her feet. There was a Bible and a hymnbook slipped into slats affixed to the pew in front. Janavi closed her eyes. When she opened them, she forced herself to look again in the direction of the coffin. Above it was the crucifix, suspended from the ceiling, holding the most emaciated Jesus Janavi had ever seen; his ribs protruded horribly. The veins in his hands and legs were clearly defined, even from where they were seated.

The priest was talking about eternal life.

Sagar nudged her and pointed to a man a few rows in front. He leaned over and whispered, "That's the mayor." Janavi saw only a broad back and thinning hair. And then he nodded toward a man two rows away, across the aisle, and said, "Alex."

Janavi studied him. His skin color nearly matched hers, and his lush hair made her think of the cool, pillared shadows of a temple she'd once visited in Araku Valley. His cheeks were chubby like a little boy's. "Do you want to move next to him?"

Sagar shook his head no. When he turned back to the priest, she looked, surreptitiously, at Sagar's head. Its brown was lighter than the brown of his face. There was a shallow depression in his scalp behind his left ear; she wondered if there was a matching one on his right. She hadn't known Renny had meant that much to him — to mourn her so visibly — but maybe she should have. He'd spoken of her often enough. What startled her, though, was his depth of feeling for someone he'd so recently met, and she thought again of Lottie's question. Yes, she answered her, he is a good man.

After Mass, they went in a procession to the cemetery adjoining the church. The pallbearers, the pause at the door for the final blessing, and then outside, the enormity of light, the chirping of birds. Janavi had passed the cemetery before, on her walks, when they'd first moved to Mansfield, but today, as she approached it, she saw it anew — the way its emerald stretch of grass, in the leaf light, looked like a sari sequined with white stones. Rustling, a little, in the wind. If I could gather its folds, she thought, pleat them by hand, and pin them over my shoulder, I could bring them back: Amma, Renny.

They stopped short of the gravesite. It was clear that it was only for close family and friends; most everyone seemed to be part of the tribe. She still didn't see Ophelia. She looked behind her. She said, "I think Alex Mendoza left."

Sagar turned.

"Should we leave too?"

Sagar didn't answer. He was watching the committal with great attention, as if it were all a giant jigsaw puzzle and he only had to stare at the pieces long enough to understand how to put them together.

The priest uttered incantations, a few homilies, and then the casket was lowered slowly into the ground. Some threw fistfuls of dirt onto it. Others wiped their eyes. She searched again for Ophelia. She's only four, Janavi reminded herself. She tasted salt in the back of her throat. Anger rose. Ophelia's amma was in the ground. And Janavi's amma was in the Ganga. Land and water. Water and land. These, in the end, were the only two places that received us, the only two places of rest.

After the burial, a few people lingered. Janavi saw a man near Renny's grave tie something onto the low branch of a nearby tree. It looked like a small packet or satchel. She saw Sagar watching him, too, and said, "What is that?"

"Let's go see."

Janavi grabbed his arm. "It might be something private."

"On a tree?"

But she was adamant that they give the man privacy.

Before they left, Janavi went back into the church to use the bathroom. She passed the nave, empty now save for a man and a woman who seemed to be straightening the pews, or maybe they were straightening the little stools and the books. She turned to the left. The bathrooms were down a short hallway. The door of the men's room was propped open, but the women's room, beyond it, had a closed door. Janavi reached for the door handle, but then stopped. She heard voices. Clear through the wooden door. She hesitated. One woman was saying, ". . . picked it up at Irene's this morning."

"I hope it was cold."

"Who would leave potato salad out? Anyway, like I was saying, it doesn't make sense. And her girl with her."

"You don't buy it?"

"Norma sure as shit doesn't."

The faucet squeaked on, and Janavi opened the door and walked in.

As soon as she did, the conversation stopped. They looked at her — one woman was at the sink, and another leaned next to the paper towel dispenser. Both Native. Janavi said hello, and the woman by the sink, who was wearing a beaded blouse and large iridescent dragonfly earrings, half smiled in response. She turned off the faucet, smoothed her hair back, and said to no one in particular, "Rusty's probably ripped the couch to shreds by now." The woman by the paper towel dispenser smirked and said, "Just the couch, you think?" The mention of Rusty seemed to release the tension in the air. Soon after, they nodded toward Janavi and left.

When Janavi went back outside, she looked for Sagar. He wasn't where they'd been standing. She wanted to tell him about the conversation she'd overhead between the two women, but what was there to tell? She found him under the tree to which the man had tied something. It was a small pouch, made of rough cotton. "What's in it?" she said.

Sagar raised himself onto his tiptoes, his nose just under the pouch. He breathed in, closed his eyes. "Sage," he said.

Chapter 20

After Renny's death the dam removal was halted, and Sagar was placed on administrative leave.

The shock he'd felt when he'd gotten the phone call at Reynolds did not wear off. It traveled with him through the days, through Renny's funeral (it was in this state of shock that he'd picked up his electric shaver, run it over his scalp, and then looked down at the mound of hair in the sink, and that had been the end of it; what more was there to grief?), and even into his sleep. He woke every night — not out of a nightmare, but out of nothing — and lay for hours listening to Janavi breathing. During the days, he walked listlessly around the apartment or stood at the living room window or stared at his cup of coffee until it grew cold. Janavi said things to him, and he said things back, but none of them made sense. Not her words, not the figure of this woman moving through the rooms of their apartment. All he saw, whether his eyes were open or closed, was Renny at the burial site. She'd been there monitoring — digging, bagging, cataloguing — watching all the holes grow bigger and bigger, when really, he thought, what she'd been watching being dug was her own grave.

He left the apartment and drove aimlessly, turning west on Main so that he wouldn't have to cross the Cotton River. He drove deeper into the prairie. He looked at the sky and felt nothing. After an hour or two, he stopped the car on the side of the road and climbed out. All was quiet. He looked at the stretch of prairie and then he walked a few steps into it. He looked down. Blue grama. The kind of grass Alex Mendoza had told him about. Native grass. Indigenous grass. He closed his eyes. Before him was a herd of bison. Not reintroduced bison, as most on the Great Plains were now, but the ones from the time before. Before the Great Slaughter. Sagar smelled them; he heard them bellow. He saw them as Renny's people must've seen them, hundreds, thousands of years ago. And he saw that though the bison, undeniably, were beacons of light, beacons of a wild and untamed country, they would soon be extinguished. Their magisterial brown bodies would be massacred. And in a moment, in two, their skulls would be piled high like fruits in a market, their skins stacked, one on top of the other, like Persian rugs, in that same market.

When he opened his eyes, there was no herd. No bison. There was only the vastness, the quiet of the emptied prairie.

And now that vastness, its quiet, was inside of him.

Following the funeral, a town hall meeting was being held to discuss the dam accident. Sagar had not heard of such a thing. In India there were of course public meetings, but they were generally conducted after the close of any investigations; meetings early in an investigation were usually only for the press. But he understood that the Cotton River dam and the reservoir, surrounded by homes and a recreation area and of course the burial site, were an important part of Mansfield and the Cotton River Valley. Not just for the fishing and boating and other activities afforded by the reservoir, and the spiritual and cultural importance of the burial site, but because the dam had been on the Cotton River for nearly a hundred years and anything, even if it has outlived its use, could take on the patina of nostalgia and necessity and tradition. Still, it was because of Renny that he most wanted to attend the town hall meeting. Her death probably had the residents of Mansfield confused, or worse, panicked.

Aside from the article they'd read, no further information had been released — nothing official, and there was nothing more online except remembrances and condolences. Sagar read and reread the article in *The Mansfield Register*. What had they meant, Sam Dooley and Sheriff Oswald, when they'd said, *Safety has always been a concern? Shouldn't have been undertaken at all?* And *Custer County doesn't back down?* From what? And why, as Janavi had wondered, hadn't the newspaper called him? Maybe they'd thought that as the lead engineer he couldn't speak to Renny's death because his role was too technical. Or maybe the DNRC hadn't provided his name to the press. Or maybe they hadn't been able to get his contact information. But how had they gotten Tim Downing's?

More than anything, he couldn't understand *how* Renny had died. Why had she gone anywhere near the dam? Had she gone to check on the burial site and somehow fallen in? But if so, the river's current would've carried her away from the base of the dam, not toward it. He tried calling Mack and Tim Downing and left multiple messages with the DNRC headquarters in Helena, and with the regional office in Billings, but none of his calls were returned. Their silence was perplexing, especially because he might've been able to help in some way. And even more worrying: He'd never known Mack not to return his calls within the hour.

The town hall meeting was held at the Elks Lodge event hall, off Main Street, on Gallatin Road. Sagar didn't think Janavi would want to come but when he asked, she said yes immediately. The event hall was not very big, as Sagar had imagined it would be. There were not more than fifty or so chairs set up. The front row was full, the second row was being saved, and the middle and back rows had a sprinkling of people. Janavi pointed to two seats near the back. As they made their way toward their seats a woman leapt in front of them. Her heavily made-up eyes widened and she said, "Who might you be? You look familiar . . ."

Sagar and Janavi introduced themselves.

"Of course! The couple from India. You're the engineer they brought over."

Sagar looked at her. She was smiling widely, the corners of her mouth glopped with pink lipstick. "I'm Susan Dooley. Sam's wife." Her expression then grew serious, and she said, "That poor, poor woman. *I* know it wasn't your fault, but that dam removal was reckless from the start. It was a perfectly good dam. I told Sam, I told him, 'Something's going to happen. I can feel it. I can feel it in my bones.' I'm never wrong about these things, you know. The best thing to do is stop this nonsense, before something worse happens."

Worse? Sagar had the sense she was trying to scare him, much like Sam Dooley had been trying to do when he'd spoken to him in the trailer. But why?

Her smile returned. "How long have you two lovebirds been married?"

Janavi turned to him. She said, "A year, almost."

Susan Dooley squealed with delight. "Now isn't that precious. Sam and I were high school sweethearts, you know." She paused. Sagar turned his gaze toward where she was looking. A group of Native Americans had entered the room and were making their way to the seats that had been saved. Susan Dooley leaned toward Sagar and Janavi and said conspiratorially, "They all live on the reservation. Every one of them. They're not like your kind. You all get your degrees, do so well out here. But they — "

A man was at the podium. Susan Dooley hurried off to one of the front seats.

The meeting opened with remarks from a representative of the

DNRC whom Sagar had never met — Ray Wilson, a spokesperson from the public relations department. He told the room about the DNRC's commitment to safety (once again stating it was their highest priority), and said the department was always on the side of the community and its needs. Someone in the second row, whose face Sagar couldn't see, but who introduced herself as a member of the tribe, asked, without any preamble, exactly how Renny had died. Hers was the question Sagar assumed everybody in the room wanted the answer to, but the spokesman seemed taken aback by it and instead of answering he said the matter was still under active investigation and for that reason he could say no more about it. He then passed the microphone to Sam Dooley.

Sam Dooley began his speech with a prayer. Sagar had never been to a public meeting in America, but was this how they all began? He looked around. Everyone bent their heads and it felt like church when they all said "Amen." Sagar supposed Sam Dooley had that quality: of a pastor. When he'd been in third class, Sagar had gone with a Christian classmate, Joseph, to Easter services at his family's church in Rajahmundry. Sagar had never been to a church before, and he'd been mesmerized by the altar and the sermon and the clothes and the incense — all so different from a Hindu temple. Even the pews; everyone had been seated on benches instead of on a stone floor. Afterward there had been an Easter egg hunt, and Sagar, after finding his first egg, had plopped down right where he'd found it, under a jacaranda tree on the grounds of the church, and had started to eat it. By the time Joseph had found him he'd been licking the powdery yolk from his fingers. Joseph had said, "The point is not to eat them, doofus. It's to find them." Sagar had looked down at his hands, feeling like a clod.

He realized now that the reason Sam Dooley must remind him of a pastor was because he so resembled the pastor at Joseph's church. His sermon had been about the meaning of Easter and the Resurrection and even at the age of eight, Sagar had been captivated. To die and come back to life? He'd decided he'd try it out with the next slug or caterpillar that he found. And of course, the moth that he'd tried it out with had stayed dead. But he understood that whether it had been Joseph's pastor or Sam Dooley, and whether they were talking about Jesus's death or Renny's death, both men had a somberness and a stateliness about them, edged with a kind of secret mirth, as if they knew some great truth no one else did.

After Sam Dooley led the prayer, he cleared his throat, looked penetratingly into the room, and talked about himself, and in an obtuse way, about the dam removal. It was clear to Sagar, not just from when they'd met but even now, barely into Dooley's speech, that he had been vehemently opposed to it. He said, "It's always been a safety issue, folks. All that water and silt. Held back by the dam — not a thing wrong with it, mind you — getting released like that. Something was bound to happen." Sagar stared, stunned. Dooley was wrong. Everything had been calculated, controlled for. *Sagar* had calculated and controlled for everything. By the time his shock had passed, Sam Dooley had moved on and was relating a memory from when he was a boy. He told the audience that he'd gone with his father to the reservoir, long ago, when he'd been no taller than a half-pint of milk and his father had taught him how to fish. They'd sat in the boat, drifting.

"My pop, as you all know," he said, "was a ranching man. Tough as they come. Tough on me too. But he was gentle with me that day. Sittin' on that lake. He took out two worms for baiting them fishhooks. One of the worms was real, you see, squirming and all, and the other was just a curled-up piece of twine. Wouldn't fool a horse in a haystack. My pop leaned down to me and said, 'Now, watch this.' He baited one of the hooks with the real worm and one with the twine. He said, 'Which do you want, son?' Well, folks, I'm embarrassed to say I picked the twine worm. That real bugger, twisting and turning on the end of that hook, scared the daylights outta me!"

The room burst into laughter.

"We waited. Had my first sip of beer waiting on the Cotton River reservoir with my pops. Eventually we got a bite. Just one of us, you understand. You want to take a guess, folks? On which one of us got the bite?"

There was some chuckling, and then someone called out, "Half-pint!"

"That's right. That's right. That ding-dong carp got ahold of my no-good piece of twine and hung on to it for dear life. My pop helped me reel it in and wouldn't you know it, as soon as it flopped out of the water, my pops burst out laughing. Laughed and laughed. It was such a little thing. Hardly worth the trouble. But it was my first fish. Just before he tossed it back into the water, my pops said, 'We'll let it grow up a tad. Sound good to you? Until then, how about we call him Gary? Whaddya think of that?'

"I said that was fine by me. That's when my pops said, 'Gary the Gullible, that's what we'll call him. You know what gullible means?' I said I didn't. He said, 'Could've gone for the real thing, the live worm, but Gary here chose the twine. Not the smartest, is he?'" Sam Dooley paused here, and Sagar thought it might be the end of the story, but then he said, "Became a joke between my pops and me. We'd see somebody who was weak or chose badly or was just downright stupid, and we'd just look at each other and smile and say, 'Gary. Two o'clock.' It might've been one of the last things he ever said to me, my pops. At the old folks' home. One of those foo-foo male nurses walked past his room and my pops said, 'You see him? Another Gary. Can't get away. World's full of 'em,' and we had a good laugh. Died a week later, my pops did."

Sagar heard someone sniffle, and a few coughs. Sam's voice grew serious then, and he said, "God gave us this country, folks. This land. These rivers. Now, this dam removal fiasco has been cursed from the get-go. Safety failures from the start. And now a life lost." After a moment, with a surge of feeling, he added, "Which is why, as mayor of this great town, I am forming a committee to investigate exactly what happened here.

And if necessary, we will petition the state to grant an injunction. Stop
the dam removal. This is about your safety, folks. The safety of you and
your families."

The room erupted into applause.

Once it died down, a woman from the tribe, the same one who'd
spoken earlier, said, "Who is on this committee?"

She and the mayor must've known each other because Sam Dooley
said, "Jumping the gun, as always, aren't you, Norma?"

"No one in the tribe's been asked."

"Is that right? I'll have Jeanie call first thing."

"Will you," she said, sarcasm evident in her tone, and then she said,
"You can speak her name, Sam. It's Renny. Renny Atwood." There were
murmurs in the audience. "We're here because we want a place on that
committee."

"Of course you will. You're part of our community. I'll make sure of
it. Jeanie, you here?" Sam Dooley scanned the room. "I don't see her,
but I'll have her call you. First thing. That's a promise."

"Those have certainly worked out for us in the past," she said, rising.

The other tribal members stood up in unison and walked toward the
exit. They were silent as they moved through the room. A few people in
the back jeered and hissed as they passed. Sam Dooley didn't seem to
notice them in the least. He continued with his speech, which ended
soon afterward.

As they were leaving, Sagar thought, The speech was for him. It was
so that he – and no one else – could tell the story, *any* story.

When they were outside, Janavi said, "An injunction? Do you think
he'll get it?"

Sagar didn't answer. His mind was still elsewhere, thinking now
about the moth, which, no matter how much he'd willed it to, had not
come back to life.

———

Sagar called the DNRC again. The receptionist, Abby, was clearly getting impatient with him and so he stopped calling. Instead, Sheriff Oswald from the Mansfield Police Department, the one who'd been quoted in the article, called him. He asked if Sagar wouldn't mind coming to the station. "Nothing to worry about. Just tying up a few odds and ends," he said. What did that mean? A few odds and ends? Ends he could guess, but odds? Sagar realized he was perplexed not by the phrasing but by the sudden jolt of fear he felt. It was natural, of course, to be nervous about talking to the police, but all this time Sagar had *wanted* to help and now he was being called to do so, so why feel alarm, as if he'd done something wrong?

Janavi said, "Who was that?"

"The police. The sheriff from the article."

She was in the bedroom folding clothes.

"He asked me to come in." When he saw the look on her face, he said, "It's nothing. They're just tying up a few odds and ends."

She looked at him for a moment longer, sudden concern in her expression, too, and then went back to folding without a word.

He picked up a pair of pants. He watched as Janavi sorted the socks, how she stood, the fall of her blouse down her back, the rise of her hips. Her face in profile. When they'd first moved here, she'd pulled her curls into a ponytail or braid, but now she'd started wearing her hair down more often. He liked it.

They finished folding, and she said, "Do you want me to come with you?"

Did he?

"No," he said, "you'll just be in the waiting room. It might take some time. Hours. Who knows?"

Janavi said nothing for a moment, and then she said, "She had a gun."

He looked up. "Who had a gun?"

"Renny."

Sagar's eyes widened. "*A gun?*"

"That time we met. When I came to pick you up."

Janavi then explained that she hadn't thought of it much since or maybe hadn't wanted to think about it. She told him how she'd seen it, tucked into her waistband when she'd bent down to look for her keys. But why had she had a gun? Was it for a reason? Or was it simply that Montana was an open carry state and lots of people had guns? The questions and the doubts swirled in his mind. He went into the bathroom, took a shower, combed his hair, dressed, walked into the living room, sat down on the sofa, and when he looked up, he had no idea how he'd gotten there. Where, he wondered, am I?

Sheriff Oswald led him into a small room and asked him if he wanted water or coffee. Sagar said he was fine. The sheriff had a high voice and a deeply lined face, though he couldn't have been older than forty or so. The first thing he did was open a manila folder and flip through some pages. Then he closed it, picked up a pencil, and started tapping it on the table. It was a silly gesture, as if he were copying something he'd seen a detective do on television, but also nerve-racking. He asked how long Sagar had been in America. Sagar guessed he asked because of his accent. He told him almost six months. Then Sheriff Oswald asked a strange thing. He asked, "Do you know why you're here?"

Sagar looked at him. "Well . . . yes. Isn't it because of Renny? Because — "

Sheriff Oswald said nothing. He made a show of checking his notes again. He finally looked up and said, "Why did you make that divot?"

"Divot?"

"In the dam. The hole. Why did you make it?"

"You mean the notch?"

"Yes, yes. The notch. Why did you make it?"

The way Sheriff Oswald was looking at him, the tone of his voice, gave Sagar pause. Was there a wrong answer? "It's the most common way of removing a dam," he began, and then he explained to him about the notch and release method and the rapid release approach. He described the pros and cons of each and then he explained about sediment and endangered species and riparian ecology and about how they each affected the method chosen for a dam removal. Sheriff Oswald had clearly stopped paying attention. Sagar could tell by the way he had, in the beginning of his explanation, held his pencil steady, aloft, but had now begun to twirl it between his fingers.

He said, "Seems odd though, doesn't it? That a woman who was from here, who was familiar with the area, the terrain, the lake, would drown like that?"

"It's been . . . confirmed? Drowning?"

"What do you think? She got sucked through. Right through that notch of *yours*." Now the fear that Sagar had felt when he'd first gotten the call came back. His notch? He felt the insinuation in the air. And because it was so misguided and accusatory, Sagar thought suddenly of what Janavi had told him, about the gun. He blurted out, "She had a gun. Renny. My wife saw her with it."

"Doing what?"

"In the parking lot. Walking to her car."

"Doing what with the gun?"

"With the . . . ? Nothing."

Sheriff Oswald said, "So she was walking? Across the lot?"

"Yes."

He looked at him as if Sagar were an idiot. He said, "You do realize you're in Montana, don't you?"

In his desperation, Sagar said, "Why was she even in the water?"

"Swimming, apparently."

Swimming?

Sheriff Oswald, looking directly at him, said, "What exactly was the nature of your relationship with Ms. Atwood?"

Sagar stared at him, confused, rattled. "The nature . . . ? No. We just . . . she was a colleague."

"Colleague? You're working on the dam. She's on the burial site. Not really colleagues." When Sagar didn't respond, Sheriff Oswald said, "Anyway, luckily the daughter survived."

"Ophelia was *with* her?"

"Didn't I say? They were on a picnic. Mother got sucked through this notch of yours, the kid didn't. Hell of a time finding her though. Dark as it was. Thought at first she might've drowned too."

His callousness enraged Sagar. He steadied his voice. "Where? Where was she found?"

"In the mom's pickup. Must've been sittin' there for hours. Scrunched down on the floor with her ball. Couldn't get her to let go of the darn thing."

Sagar said, "That doesn't make sense. Why would Renny leave her like that? To go swimming?"

Sheriff Oswald shrugged. "She'd had a few."

"A few what?"

"Beers."

"*Beers?* How many beers — "

"Enough to make a decision she shouldn't have," he said, looking straight at him.

Sagar looked back. He thought of Susan Dooley. He thought, Their minds are made up. And then he thought of Ophelia at the park in Billings. Carefree, full of laughter. Cupping a beetle in her palms to show her mother.

Her mother.

He felt sick. Feverish. He heard Sandeep laughing. Or maybe it was his father. Maybe it was both. What had he meant? When Janavi had asked him what he thought they might find in the burial site, and he'd said, Almost anything they want, what had he meant? He wondered now. He must've been thinking only of Montana and its mines. All that had been discovered and dug up and profiteered in over the centuries. The gold and the silver and the copper and the coal. The lead and the zinc and the manganese and the molybdenum. He'd been thinking of the platinum and the palladium. The garnets and the gravel and the bentonite and the covellite. The lime, the clay, the stone. The list of metals and minerals and gemstones that had been mined in Montana, continued to be mined to this day, was endless. And buried, too, were the bones — the bison and the wolves and the coyotes and the bobcats and the beavers. All of them slaughtered for their pelts. And the other kinds of bones, the ones Renny had been digging for: the remains of her ancestors and the things they had once held dear, tools and pipes and pottery and jewelry. Thousands of years. Death after death, the mining of mineral after mineral, and now, with a hole he'd made . . .

He wanted to leave this room, leave Montana. And never come back.

There was a knock on the door.

A uniformed police officer came in and told Sheriff Oswald he was needed. Sheriff Oswald turned to Sagar, annoyed at the officer or Sagar or both, and said he'd be back in a minute. He left his folder on the table. Even through his misery Sagar knew enough to know that the window that looked out into the hallway was a two-way mirror. He didn't dare open the folder, but the tab had something written on it. He arched his neck. As he could've guessed it was Renny's full name, Renata Atwood, and below it was her date of birth.

Sagar's blood ran cold.

When Alex Mendoza had told them the story of Willie and Charlene and the cowboy, Renny had recoiled in what had seemed to Sagar physical pain. He'd guessed it then, though he'd never thought of it again, but maybe he should have. The dimensions of a grave, 3-7-77: they were her birth date.

Chapter 21

Janavi's mind raced. Renny, her death. Ophelia. She wanted to call and ask after her, maybe even see if she could visit, but she had no idea who to call. How cruel life was — how indecent. Less than a month ago, they'd been sitting together and feeding the ducks, and now, all the horror of losing a mother, at an even younger age than Janavi had been when she'd lost her amma, was raining down upon her. Harm was a hunter, she understood, the most merciless of them all. If she could just see her, if she could just hold her hand again — beneath Janavi's frantic thoughts of Ophelia was yet another thought: of when she'd seen Renny in the parking lot. Janavi couldn't pinpoint what it was, precisely, that her mind kept returning to, but it wasn't the gun. At least it was not only the gun.

She called Rajni, but she didn't pick up. She texted her, *Call me when u get this.*

She turned on the television and then she turned it off. Sagar had said the meeting with Sheriff Oswald could take hours.

It was only now, while Sagar was at the police station, that Janavi, in recalling the moment in the parking lot and the expression on Renny's face, thought, inexplicably, of the little girl with the piglet. But why am I thinking of her, Janavi wondered. It made no sense. A woman in Montana bending to pick up her keys and a girl in Varanasi cradling a piglet? What could they possibly have in common? Not a single thing that she could think of. So why did her brain link the two?

She left the apartment. She went first to Lottie's house, but she wasn't home, and then she went to the convenience store, but Mandy wasn't working. Across the street was the Copper Penny. She sat in a booth by the window. She and Sagar had been here before. It had always been busy, but today it was empty except for two men who were sitting at the counter. It was after the lunch rush, and Janavi figured that's why some of the tables hadn't been cleared. The waitress brought her a menu, and Janavi ordered coffee and then she remembered what Lottie had said so she asked the waitress if they had pie.

"All we got is peach," she said.

Lottie hadn't said anything about peach pie, but Janavi got a slice anyway.

"You want it à la mode?"

"À la mode?"

"With ice cream."

Lottie hadn't said anything about ice cream either. "Yes, à la mode, please."

"You want that warmed up?"

Another question she didn't know the answer to. "Yes," she said again.

The waitress, whose name tag read Allison, left with the menu. Janavi studied the backs of the men at the counter. Ranchers. They were wearing baseball hats and scuffed boots and flannel shirts stretched across broad backs. They had glanced at her when she'd walked in and then looked away. Janavi tried to hear what they were saying, but their voices were low, and she only heard stray words — *bucket calves* and *colostrum* and *knuckling*. She didn't know what they meant, but they all had the hard *c* sound, and she wondered if that made them easier for the human ear to hear.

Allison came back with a pot of coffee and a mug and after filling it, she walked away and returned with a slice of pie and vanilla ice cream. The ice cream had begun to pool. One of the slices of peach had slipped out of the triangle of pie and this Janavi ate first. Her next bite included a piece of the crust, along with ice cream and peach, and that was when Janavi started to like it. While she was chewing, Allison walked past her and said, "You need anything else?"

Janavi smiled awkwardly, still chewing, and shook her head. She thought Allison would leave, but instead she said, "Mind if I take a load off?" By the time Janavi had swallowed her bite, Allison was already seated across from her. They were about the same age, she guessed, but Allison was wearing too much makeup and there was a vague grayness in her skin that couldn't be concealed. Maybe it was only tiredness. Janavi said, "The pie is good."

Allison didn't seem much interested in what she thought of the pie. She said, "This is my third shift in a row." And then she said, "Have I seen you in here before?"

"Maybe. I've come a few times with my husband."

Husband. It never sounded right.

The waitress shrugged. "Friday lunch shift is the worst," she said, and then after a silence, she said, "Sunday after church is pretty bad too."

Janavi ate another bite, thinking of what to say.

Allison looked at her. She said, "I like your eyebrows."

Janavi reached up to them instinctively. "They're too thick."

"No, I think they're just right."

One of the men motioned to her, and she got up and poured them more coffee. When she came back, she said, "Had to bail my sister out. That's why the extra shifts."

Janavi wasn't sure she understood. "Bail her out?"

"From jail." She must've seen the alarm in Janavi's face because she said, "Shot at her husband. He had it comin' though. Should've aimed better. Broke my nephew's arm. That's what did it. Don't know how many bones he's broken of hers."

Janavi put down her fork. She thought of Renny. Why? Why had she reminded her of the girl in Varanasi?

"*Her* they arrest. Isn't that something?"

Janavi said, "How is your nephew?"

"Arm's in a cast. He'll be okay."

Janavi used her spoon for the last of the melted ice cream and peach syrup. The men got up to leave. Allison went over to get them change. This time, when she came back, she sat down and looked out of the window. After a moment, she turned and picked up a wooden coffee stirrer. She spun it in her hand as if it were a flower. She said, "She made her own wedding dress. Took her ages. I said to her, I said, 'You know you can go online and get one for under a hundred bucks, don't you?' She just smiled and kept on sewing." The stirrer twirled and twirled in her hand. Janavi thought of Renny. And then Ophelia. And then the girl with the piglet . . . she heard a snap. When she looked at Allison, the wooden stirrer was in her hands, broken in half. Her eyes were gazing at something beyond Janavi, and she said, "The thing is, it's what nobody sees, isn't it? You hear it break, you see it break, but it's what nobody sees. Nobody sees all the pressure it took to break it."

Janavi walked home. She passed a swing set and then she passed a sycamore tree and then she passed a car propped up on cinder blocks. It would be late for him, but she wanted to hear his voice, so she called Papa. He picked up on the first ring. She didn't even have a chance to ask after his cough before he said, "What's wrong?"

"Nothing. Nothing at all."

"You said it twice."

She smiled. She wished they were sitting on the floor together, poring over a nautical chart. "How's your cough?"

"Better."

"Rajni said that — "

And as if she'd brought it about, her papa went into a fit of coughing. It was a dry cough, wheezy, worrisome. When the cough died down, he said, "Nothing to worry about, Beti. A little tickle in my throat is all. Nothing to concern yourself with."

"Now you've said it twice."

He laughed, and though Janavi wanted to tell him everything, everything of what was happening, she didn't have the heart to upset him. They got off the phone soon afterward.

Janavi kept walking. A right and then a left.

In one yard was a trampoline. Janavi had never been on a trampoline. She'd seen children jumping on one on television, squealing with laughter as they bounced in and out of contorted positions. On this one a few leaves had drifted down from an ash tree at the edge of the yard. Janavi stood and looked at the trampoline. And then she looked at the house whose yard it was in. Then she looked at the neighboring houses. All was quiet. No cars drove by. There was not a single movement or animal or sound. All the windows were empty or closed or curtained. What could it hurt?

She walked noiselessly into the yard and climbed onto the trampoline. She tried to stand, fell, got up again, and flipped face-forward. She giggled. She finally managed to stand and started to bounce. At first tentatively and then higher and higher. She faced the ash tree. If she bounced a little higher, she could reach the very tip of one of its branches. If not with her hand, then with her hair, which, in the wind and with her bouncing, flew like black wings toward the tree. She closed her eyes.

"Hey!" A man's voice. "Hey, you."

She stopped. Dropped to her knees. Scrambled off the trampoline.

He was holding a plate of food, waving his free arm at her. "What're you doing? Hey. You. Yeah you."

"I . . . uh," she stammered, stopped. Her thoughts froze. She stared, paling, a rush of cold. He'd lifted his plate. On the underside of the plate was a gun.

"What do you think you're doing?"

She shook her head. Looked away. Stumbled toward the driveway.

He followed her. "What's your name? Hey!" The plate of food was lowered, now that it was clear she'd seen the gun. "Do you understand English? Do you? What's your name?"

She hurried down the drive.

"Hey!"

Janavi reached the end of the sidewalk and started running. She ran and ran. She ran, not paying attention to where. When she was a few blocks away she slowed and turned, afraid the man might be following her. He wasn't, not that she could see. She noticed now, when her hand went to her face, that she was crying. And noticing herself crying made her cry harder. A gun. A gun under a plate.

She was still shaking when she got home. She splashed cold water on her face, and then she pulled down a bottle of whiskey from the cupboard and took a shot. She closed her eyes and willed her hands to stop trembling. Stop, she told herself, Stop it, and gripped one hand with the other. She opened her eyes and looked down at her hands, finally stilled. It wasn't true that America had no official language, was it? It had one: Guns.

She took another shot and that's when she had it. Just like that — out of the blue. It had been their expressions. The expression on Renny's face had been the exact same as the expression on the face of the little girl with the piglet. And what was that expression? It took her a moment, but it had been right there, on both occasions, for her to see — ferocity. A wild look, searching, scanning, protecting a precious thing. A thing more precious than even themselves. In the girl's case it had obviously been the piglet. And in Renny's? Had it been Ophelia? But why? All she'd done was drop her keys.

Chapter 22

Sagar told Janavi what he knew: that Renny and Ophelia had been picnicking, and that Renny had gone for a swim and had somehow drowned, but he didn't tell her about Renny's birth date. It seemed absurd, its coincidence with the dimensions of a grave unbelievable, and he couldn't bring himself to mention something that spooked even him.

Janavi was grief-stricken. She said, "She was there? When Renny died? Ophelia was there?"

"Yes. She was."

They sat in silence, and he saw her looking at his hands resting on the table. They were shaking. When he made a move to hide them, she reached out and steadied them. Closed her hand over his. He was surprised by the gesture, by her touch, and made bashful by it.

She said, "Where is Ophelia? Who is she with?"

He shook his head. "Oswald wouldn't tell me. But I'm guessing with her ex, Gabe. If he's the father. But . . ."

"What?"

"From what Alex Mendoza told me, he's not the most upstanding guy."

"How so?"

He saw the alarm in her face and said vaguely, "Pulling pranks. High school stuff."

Janavi, with a surge of frustration, said, "What was Renny doing in the water? Why would she leave Ophelia? Just leave her like that?"

He told her he wondered the same thing, but again, he kept from her what Oswald had said in response. He then got on his computer. He searched — as he had many times over the years, first in preparation for the dam removal on the Majuli River and then again on the Cotton River — if there were any documented cases of people being injured or killed due to a notch. He didn't believe Sheriff Oswald — when he'd suggested the notch had been the culprit in Renny's death — and so he analyzed again the safety studies on the notch and release method, and read through the anecdotal evidence of their superiority to other methods of dam removal.

He researched for hours, late into the night.

Neither of them was hungry for dinner so Janavi suggested they take a drive. They sometimes took drives through the Cotton River Valley. Through small towns with names like Woods Place and Jimtown and Lame Deer and Muddy and Busby and Dunmore and Hardin and Toluca and Indian Arrow, the roads curving and coiling through the buffalo grass and the scrub pine and the sagebrush. Sagar, on these drives, felt each time as though he were entering a greater and greater mystery. In every direction was the prairie, beckoning him deeper. Stands of Russian olive and tamarisk trees marked the landscape. Cottonwoods lined the dry creek beds. He looked down the length of the road or in the rearview mirror, or downstream or upstream at the Cotton River, and wondered if he'd entered a dream. Not a modern dream, if there was such a thing, but a dream that must've always been dreamt. By the earliest man, by the tiniest creature. A dream of sweetness that seemed as endless as the prairie.

But on this evening as he drove, Janavi quiet beside him, the only mystery seemed to him the depth of his own failure. But what failure could that possibly be? After hours of research, he'd found, as he knew he would, that the notch and release method was the safest, most common way of taking down a dam. Indeed, he found no evidence that a death or even an injury had occurred due to this method. So, why had Renny, who knew her way around the damsite, been in the water at all? And so close to the notch? Leaving her daughter alone? And why hadn't he left Sandeep alone? By that other river? Why?

He headed west in the direction of Billings, toward the mountains. He didn't know their name; maybe they were the Absaroka Range or the Big Belt Mountains or the Little Belt Mountains or maybe, with their distant snow-covered peaks and sharp, gray slopes, the Rockies. He didn't know their name, but they called to him, they called to him as the sea calls to sailors. No mountains in India had ever called to him in this way. He'd read that some sailors out at sea had once seen an island being born. Just like that, out of a flat blue sea the island had risen. And that's what it seemed to Sagar he was witnessing when he saw the mountains rise in the west out of the flat grass prairie: that he was seeing an island, as wide and high as a continent, being born. And he, a wanderer, was shipwrecked on its shores.

Janavi halted his thoughts. She said, "What's that?"

"What?"

"Right there. Under the wiper."

There was a piece of paper tucked low under the windshield wiper, on the driver's side. A ticket? He pulled the car over. Not a ticket, a note. It was dark; he had to bend low to read it in the headlights. GET OUT GO HOME. He stared at it. It was scrawled, but in all caps and clear. A tingle went up his spine.

"What is it?"

He crumpled it up. "Nothing."

"Let me see it."

She came around to his side and took the note from his hand. "Who wrote this?" Her voice was strained, a whisper.

They looked at each other, knowing there was no answer, though it seemed ominous, in the way Renny's birth date had seemed ominous. He took it back, crumpled it again, and threw it into the dark of the prairie. "Get in," he said.

Late the next morning, Mack called him on his cell phone and said, "We need you to come in, Saag." The tone of his voice confused Sagar because it sounded like both an apology and a demand. He thought he meant for him to come to Helena, which was over five hours away. Sagar said, "Of course, but I won't get there until evening." Mack said no, they wanted him to come to the DNRC's regional office in Billings and not until the next day. He told him the DNRC was interviewing everyone who had been onsite for the dam removal. They were also talking to a handful of contract workers and technicians who'd been onsite intermittently. "Just routine is all. Nothing to worry about."

The rest of the day was the longest Sagar had ever known. The hours dragged on. Janavi suggested another drive, but he said no. "Like he said, it's probably just routine," she said.

"Routine . . ." he repeated. He didn't tell her that all he could see, whether his eyes were open or closed, was Renny's body floating at the base of the dam. And every number, everywhere he looked, was the dimensions of a grave.

It was a two-hour drive to Billings and Mack had told him 2 p.m. The DNRC sign out front, on a sloping green lawn that led to the low office set back from the street, was bordered by thick, wooden logs. He knew it was meant to be rustic and to evoke log cabins and frontier days, but, more than anything, it reminded him of a Japanese torii. When he went inside, there was no one at the reception desk, but Mack, within seconds, emerged down the hallway. They shook hands and Mack, understandably, was far more tense than the previous times they'd met. Sagar thought bitterly of what he'd said: *How about this, cowboy? How about you let me know if there's a problem*, and never had he imagined, in the worst of his nightmares, that the problem would be this.

He was led to a room at the end of the hallway looking out onto the parking lot. He was introduced to the others. The tables and chairs in the room were laid out in the style of a reverse classroom — a wide table with four chairs at the front and one lone chair facing them; Sagar, had he thought about it, would've assumed they would be in a conference room of sorts but this room, with its layout, made it seem more like he'd been called here for an interrogation or a parole hearing, and he was so overcome with nervousness that he hardly caught the names of the two men and one woman Mack introduced him to. He did catch one man's last name, Headley, who was the director of the Water Resources Division for the entire state of Montana. And the other, whose name might've been Ethan or Ian or Evan or Aiden, was somebody from the legal side. The woman, Shelly Moore or More or Morse, was from the human resources department. It took Sagar only one glance at each of their faces and their tight smiles to realize that Mack had been lying; this was in no way routine. If they were here to discuss Renny's death and a plan for how to proceed with the removal, then why was there a lawyer here? And somebody from human resources?

Mack said, "Like I said, Saag, we've talked to everybody. Tim Downing was here. Spoke to the contractors on the phone. It's tragic. Just tragic. All the way around."

Sagar looked at him. His mind was in a rush of confusion. They'd already talked to Tim? And all the others? And he was the last one?

"Can't remember the last time we had a casualty on a worksite," Headley said, leaning back in his chair. "Not under my watch, I can guarantee you that. This is the first. Never had to suspend a project midstream."

There was silence. Was Sagar supposed to say something to that? He thought, Midstream. That's funny. And did Headley mean the dam removal was suspended permanently? He was about to ask when Mack said, "Look, I'm going to jump right into it. Save us some time. The thing is, we have some questions about the notch, Saag."

Sagar turned to him. He'd been looking at some indistinct point on the blank wall between Headley and the HR woman. "The notch?"

Mack said nothing. The human resources woman, who had an open laptop in front of her, typed something into it. What did she type?

"What about the notch?"

He flipped through some papers. Pulled one out of the stack in front of him. "The size."

"The size?"

"According to my calculations, you could've made the notch smaller, by almost six inches. Now, those inches could've . . ."

The lawyer cleared his throat.

Mack looked at him, and then he riffled through more pages. "It says here the medical examiner determined the cause of death to be accidental drowning — "

"Which," the lawyer said, "the DNRC does not dispute."

"But there's still the matter of the oversized notch."

Sagar looked at him. "Oversized? But — you approved the notch size. If you recall, the flow rate of a smaller notch wouldn't have been enough to meet the drainage requirements. The reservoir's capacity, the sediment — "

"You made it bigger than the standard, Saag."

"There is no standard. The size of the notches depends on the size of the dam. I can show you my calculations. If I could just access one of the computers — "

There was silence in the room. Sagar heard a car pull into the parking lot.

Mack said, "No need. We've made our decision. We, the committee, that is, has decided the best thing is to let you go."

"Let me go?"

"Evan?"

"Unsatisfactory job performance," the lawyer said. "Termination for cause. It's in your contract. We can get you a copy — "

"Unsatisfactory? But you approved the plans. We — "

Mack placed one of the loose pages in front of Sagar. "It says right here, in the DNRC's Rules and Regulations, which were sent to you with your offer: Creating an unsafe work environment may terminate an employment contract."

Sagar ignored it. "What did the others say? The engineers? Tim Downing?"

"That's confidential."

"If I could just access my email, it has the calculations, the measurements . . ."

"Your email account has been disabled."

Sagar studied Mack's face. Was he joking? No, no he wasn't. Sagar started laughing then, laughing with total abandon, as a child might. But he also wanted to cry. In the midst of these four, in the midst of afternoon light that was becoming unbearably bright, he felt small and brown and gutted.

"I see you're not taking any of this very seriously," Headley said, meeting his eyes once he'd stopped laughing.

Sagar had not heard a condemnation this fierce, or this final, in years — not since Sandeep had said, *He pushed me, Papa. He pushed me.*

The lawyer said, "If you could sign here. The letter of termination, effective immediately. We will be notifying Homeland Security, as required by law. We are also obligated, per federal regulations, to reimburse you for reasonable transportation costs back to your home country. You have sixty days to — "

Sagar didn't hear the rest. He was in a windless cave. He was looking at the walls, damp with his defeat. The lawyer handed him the piece of paper and a pen and pointed to where he needed to sign. Then he asked him to sign another piece of paper. What was he signing? The words on the papers swam before him. Blurred as if underwater. They asked for his key to the trailer. As he handed it to them, Sagar thought of the Ganga in the early mornings, when the river mist floated just above the water. Thick as porridge but once touched by the sun it was nothing, nothing at all. Mack shook his hand, told him he wished him luck, and then he said, "It's a bad business, Saag. A bad business all around."

What was a bad business? The notch size? Renny's death? Removing a dam? Being railroaded out of a job?

He drove out of Billings on Interstate 90 and then onto Highway 212. He entered the Cotton River Valley. The sun was low on the horizon, behind him, and the canyons and the sandstone glowed red in the late afternoon light. This red was the red of Andhra dirt and he knew it had formed forty, fifty million years ago, when it had been a subtropical jungle, with rains so heavy that this region, this valley, had been a swamp. Averaging 120 inches of rainfall per year. What was it now? Ten, twenty? Dying vegetation had layered the silty soil with peat beds and then it had compressed over the millions of years that had followed. That was what had made the coal seams. They'd ignited, maybe from prairie fires, and had burned so hot that the soil had turned red. He drove and drove into that red and shadowed valley; the longer he drove the better he understood the compression of something flammable. The spark that set it burning. The fire that raged just beneath its skin.

Sagar drove to Sweet Molly's. It was a few doors down from the Copper Penny, on Main. There was another bar down the street, the Longhorn, but it was closed for repairs after a kitchen fire. It was Irish night at Sweet Molly's. What was Irish about it? Not much. There was a special on Guinness and Tullamore Dew whiskey and a yellowed banner hanging on the wall with a pattern of four-leaf clovers on it. That was it. He'd been to a more convincing Irish bar in Guwahati, Assam. The jukebox was playing country music and a noose hung from the ceiling. Sagar wanted to believe the noose was for roping cattle, but he wasn't so sure. He drank two whiskeys, one after another, and when his head started throbbing, he ate the entire bowl of peanuts that had been set in front of him and then he asked the bartender — young, maybe a ranch hand working a second job — for a third whiskey. A couple sat staring at their phones at one end of the bar and two men played pool at the rear of the bar. His headache worsened; every time one of the men took a shot it felt like his head would split in two. He looked up and noticed the mirror behind the line of bottles. The mirror had gold veins running through it, like rivers, and when he saw his face reflected in it, it was shattered.

Someone from the direction of the pool table yelled out, "Hey Jakey, come over here and take a shot."

Sagar didn't know if they meant a shot in the billiards game or a drink. He still didn't know when the bartender yelled back, "Not falling for that again, Mace."

Sagar stared into his whiskey.

Guwahati, Assam.

He saw it again: the mountains nestling the city, the planetarium, the red of the Kamakhya Temple, the green of the river islands, the Brahmaputra, Mr. Das. Mr. Das was the one who'd taken him to the Irish bar in Guwahati. By the end of the night Sagar was the most drunk he had ever been.

Mr. Das was the administrator of the Central Water Commission's Guwahati office and was the local river management liaison for the dam project Sagar would be working on upriver, closer to Jorhat. He'd met Sagar at the train station. When Sagar had texted him and asked how he might recognize him, he'd texted back, *I'll be the one with one leg.* Sagar had spotted him immediately and Mr. Das seemed to recognize him, too, though they'd never met before. He'd extended his hand, anchoring a crutch on his right side with his underarm. Mr. Das, who was maybe in his late forties or early fifties, had then dropped him off at the guesthouse so that Sagar could shower and change after the long train ride. Since he would be traveling to Jorhat the next day, Mr. Das insisted on treating him to dinner.

They met at Mr. Das's favorite restaurant, an Indo-Chinese place in Paltan Bazaar. Sagar thought he might be early but when he got there Mr. Das was already seated, drinking a beer. He insisted on ordering: Gobi Manchurian and fried rice and Szechuan chicken tikka and egg rolls. Sagar ordered a beer too. When the food arrived, Mr. Das served Sagar and then himself. He began to eat with great relish. After a few bites Sagar had to admit it was the best Indo-Chinese he'd ever tasted. He wondered, given Guwahati's proximity to China, if the cook was Chinese. Even Mr. Das's features seemed more Chinese than Indian.

After dinner Mr. Das took him first to one bar, where they drank whiskey and beer, and then to the Irish pub. When they sat down with their drinks at the pub Mr. Das told Sagar his wife had left him. "She went back to her village in the mountains," he said. And then his eyes grew distant, and he said, "A mountain girl . . ." The dim orange lights of the bar and the hushed whispers made Sagar think of an opium den, though he'd never been to one.

Mr. Das said, "Do you know who Oscar Wilde is?"

"No."

"He's a writer. He said, 'Women are meant to be loved, not understood.'" Sagar was too embarrassed to tell him that he was betrothed and had never truly loved a woman. "He was Irish," Mr. Das said, and then they both lapsed into silence. The waitress came around. Mr. Das ordered another round (was it the fifth? sixth?), and Sagar was too drunk to protest. When the drinks arrived, Mr. Das said, "A boy ran onto the road. I was on a motorcycle and swerved to avoid him. That's how I lost my leg." And then he chuckled and said, "That's it. That's the story. Some things are not very complicated, are they? When I was in the hospital, he came to visit me. The boy. I don't know how he found out my name, where I was, what hospital, but he did. He was a street boy, illiterate, and yet he found me. Eleven years old. He snuck in a cigarette for me. I got up for the first time to smoke that cigarette. Until then I'd been too depressed to get out of bed. I refused. They'd amputated the leg right after the accident and I woke to find it gone. But the boy. He stood next to me and held out the cigarette and the only way to smoke it was to get out of bed.

"After I was released from the hospital, I checked on him every now and then. Gave him money. He was clever. I'd give him twenty rupees and he'd turn it into a hundred. Gambling, probably. I asked him if he wanted to come and live with me. This was after my wife had left. He agreed. I bought him clothes, enrolled him in school. After a few weeks I came home from work and all the money in the house was gone. He'd taken the television too. But Guwahati is not so big. I saw him again. He apologized. I took him back in. A few months later the same thing. This happened a couple of more times and I kept taking him back. After the third or fourth time he said to me, 'You're a fool, you know that?' When I asked him why he thought so, he said, 'Nobody but a fool would keep taking in a person who was stealing from them.' I just smiled and asked him what he wanted for dinner.

"After that it never happened again." He looked at the drink in his hand. He said, "Now he's a doctor. In Shillong. With a wife and a baby on the way." He finished his drink. By now Sagar, when he got up to go to the bathroom, could barely steady himself. "My house is a block away," Mr. Das said, when Sagar came back swaying. Sagar remembered nothing of the walk to Mr. Das's house and collapsed in a chair when they got there. Mr. Das, clearly better able to hold his alcohol, brought him a glass of water and asked if he wanted to watch television. Sagar shook his head. "I prefer this anyway," Mr. Das said, and put on a record of old Hindi film songs. Sagar had never known anyone with a record player before and so Mr. Das explained how to place the record onto the platter and how to lift the tone arm and how to lower the stylus. Sagar listened, though the room was spinning. He laughed. Spinning! When the needle touched the record and made a slight crackling sound, Mr. Das said, "That's my favorite part." After they'd heard the second side as well (the B-side, Mr. Das told him it was called), they listened to a few more — American bands that Sagar had never heard of. In the middle of one song, a slow, syrupy ballad that Mr. Das told him was called the blues, Sagar said, "I have a brother. Sandeep."

Mr. Das, whose eyes had been closed, opened them.

Sagar said nothing more. He wanted to. He wanted to tell him about that afternoon at Pinjari Konda, on the Yeleru River. He wanted to tell him about the heat of that afternoon. The cool of the water. The laughter of little boys. He wanted to tell him that that afternoon his boyhood had ended. And that perhaps he had never loved his brother more than he had on that afternoon.

The record stopped. Into the quiet that entered the room, Mr. Das said, "When I step into a river, I can still sometimes feel the water swirling around my lost leg." And then he said, "It's enough to make a man weep."

Yes, Sagar wanted to say, It is enough to make a man weep.

The next morning on the train to Jorhat Sagar was so hungover that he couldn't keep water down. He ran to the lavatory every few minutes to throw up, mostly bile. And the swaying and lurching of the train didn't help in the least.

He tried to summon the bartender to pay his tab. The bartender, talking to the couple at the other end of the bar, didn't see him or maybe he did. Sagar waited. The men playing pool cheered. The couple on their phones looked up. A man walked up next to Sagar. Sagar saw him first in the mirror of rivers. The man looked over and nodded. Sagar nodded back. The man was Native, old, with oily silver hair and a nose twisted by what Sagar guessed could only be multiple falls or multiple fights or both. His right forearm, resting on the bar, had a huge tattoo of a trident running along its length. The man saw him looking and said, "Merchant mariner. Vietnam." And then he said, "You waitin' on a drink?"

"No. Waiting to pay."

The old man looked at the bartender, who'd now taken out his own phone. He said, "Warm them young folks like a fire, don't they? Them contraptions." Then he said, "Jake's not headed over here anytime soon. Come out for a cigarette."

Sagar didn't see any reason not to. He headed for the front door, but the old man pointed with his trident arm, said, "This way," and led him to the back of the bar. A single bulb lit some dented trash cans, along with a pile of rusting parts to what, Sagar could not guess. They were standing on a patch of gravel but beyond, under the darkening sky, was a vast tract of prairie. It must be owned by somebody, being in town, but Sagar could see no fences nor even that the field was tended in any way. It ran wild and brazen toward the horizon.

The man lit Sagar's cigarette, and the smoke burned his lungs and he coughed, but nothing about it was awful. The man said, "You one of them dot Indians?"

Sagar blew out smoke. Sure. Okay. "Yes," he said.

"What're you doing way the hell out here?"

Way the hell out here. A fine question. Sagar looked again into the prairie. Wind rustled the waist-high grasses, standing thick and monastic in the darkness beyond Sweet Molly's circle of light. And it occurred to him that all of this would one day perish: the grass, the gravel patch on which they were standing, the point. The point of what? He felt wobbly; he thought at first it was from the cigarette, but no, his dizziness was from something he could not understand, something in the old man's eyes, his silver hair, the silver of the immense and unparalleled prairie. He wasn't going to tell him, he was going to make up some lie, but he was tired and drunk and really, what did it matter? So, he told him about being on the dam removal project and then about

Renny and then about Ophelia and then about meeting with Sheriff Oswald and then about how he'd been fired. He found, much to his bewilderment but also to his relief, that he couldn't stop talking.

When he finally paused to take the last drag of his cigarette, the old man, who was already on his second, said, "So you're the man they picked."

"Picked to what?"

"It makes sense, don't it? An outsider is easiest."

Sagar looked at the old man. His mind emptied. Willie the Wind blew through it.

The old man, his voice softer, said, "I've known Renata since she was born."

Sagar stared at him, his trident. He felt a fool. Obviously, he knew her; they were in the same tribe.

He and the old man stood in silence. The bulb above them flickered. Sagar said, "What was she like as a kid?"

"Just as she was at the end," he said. Sagar thought he'd say more about her, but instead he said, "She told me about you."

"*She did?*"

"Said you liked stories."

Stories? Sagar blinked; his heart flooded with sweetness for his lost friend.

"I got one for you," the old man said, reaching into his pocket. "Here, take this." He put something in Sagar's palm. What was it? "You know what that is?"

"No."

"Finger bone. Human."

Sagar nearly dropped it. It was hardly anything. A half-smoked cigarette.

"Renata found it."

Sagar examined it more closely, transfixed by how slight, how puny it was — the color and weightlessness of white chalk. Who had it belonged to? How many hundreds (thousands?) of years ago had they lived? "I asked her how old she thought the burial site — "

"This here didn't come from the burial site."

Sagar looked up at him.

"It came from upriver. On the other side."

Sagar understood. Renny had too. They'd even spoken about the dead bodies in the river.

"But — why did Renny give it to you? Why didn't she take it to the police?"

The old man laughed. He took the finger bone from Sagar's palm.

Sagar said, "Do you know who it belongs to?"

"I know in my heart who it belongs to. Renata knew for certain. Don't know how, but she knew."

"Who?"

"Wouldn't tell me. Too dangerous, she said."

"But you know . . ."

The old man put out his cigarette, and then he put the finger bone back in his pocket. "That's not the right way. You hand somebody a hammer, and everything starts lookin' like a nail."

What did that mean? The old man said, "You've got to go about this the right way. You can't be partial."

Sagar looked at him, perplexed. Partial about what?

"Renata's dead. Nothing we can do about that. But what're you going to do about the rest?"

What was *he* . . . ? "About what?"

"You believe it?" the old man asked. "That she went for a swim?"

"No."

"Then how did she end up drowned?"

"It was an accident . . . something must've . . ."

"Or someone."

Sagar stared at him. The old man, against the dark prairie, looked like Poseidon standing in the middle of a swirling sea.

"Riddle me this then: Why did they fire you? Why do they need a scapegoat if it was an accident?"

"A scapegoat?"

"You, my friend."

Sagar's thoughts stilled, and then they shot out of him as if a starting gun had been fired. "Even if it wasn't an accident, what can I do? I have to leave. My visa expires. My wife's. In sixty days. Besides, I talked to the police. I talked — "

The man laughed again. "I don't know about your visa, but I do know talkin' don't get you shit."

"But where would I even start? How would I even — "

"I saw you. At the funeral. Shaved head. You did it for Renata, didn't you? We cut off our hair too."

Sagar fell silent. He asked him for another cigarette. The glow of its tip was a star, not distant like the others, and still alive.

"You know what else she told me? About you? She told me you loved rivers."

Sagar closed his eyes. He opened them. "Whose is it? The finger bone?"

The old man was staring into the dark prairie. "One of three," he said.

One of three? What did that mean? Sagar followed his gaze into the murky gloom of the prairie. GET OUT GO HOME. Who'd written it? And home. Where in the world was home? He turned back to the old man. An idea came to him. "You said Renny knew who it belonged to. Someone in the reservoir. And maybe she even knew who'd done it. And maybe — and maybe she was blackmailing the person. And when the person — "

The old man shook his head. "That's all wrong, my boy. All wrong."

"But that's what they say. They always say, Follow the money."

The old man put out his cigarette and looked at Sagar. He said, "When it comes to women, you don't follow no money. You follow the fear."

Nell & Teddy

Cotton River, 1928

No one settled under the cottonwood trees for many years, until, in 1928, Nell and Teddy arrived. Lovers, so much in love that they slept holding hands. They called to each other in their dreams. One night, Teddy got up in the dark of their six-room town house in Copley Square and found Nell weeping. "Why, my sweet," he said, kneeling, holding the lantern high so that it would illuminate her lovely, tearstained face, "why are you crying?"

Nell raised her face to his and shook her head, clearly unable to articulate her sorrow.

"Are you ill? Are you in pain?"

She shook her head again, and then she nodded slowly.

"My dear," he said, setting the lantern down, taking her in his arms. "My poor dear. What is it? Why are you crying?"

Nell sniffled and she said, "It's silly. You'll think I'm silly."

"Of course you're silly," he said, smiling. "You're silly for not telling me."

She smiled, too, just slightly, in the way she thought made her look the most beguiling to him. It was the same way she'd smiled at him the first time they'd met, at a dinner party at her parents' home in Cambridge.

Teddy was her father's student. Philosophy, graduating with the highest honors. Her father, in fact, had been delighted to give his daughter's hand in marriage to such a promising young man. He bought them the town house as a wedding present, and gifted Teddy with an ornate hourglass that had purportedly once belonged to Kierkegaard. After the wedding, everyone, especially his father-in-law, expected Teddy to pursue a certain established, scholarly path, not particularly innovative, but that had a roseate, poetic, almost plaintive quality, despite being time-worn: an extended honeymoon in Europe, perhaps followed (rather conveniently) by an academic year or two in one of the old European universities, thinking great thoughts in the coffee-houses of Vienna or Prague or Paris, and then a return to Boston for a professorship that would eventually lead to the deanship, which post his father-in-law would've happily vacated for the most gifted of his former students.

But Teddy didn't oblige.

He didn't want old Europe, with its musty ideas and thoughts and cakes and coffees; he wanted space. Wide, open space. One of the first photographs he saw of the West was taken in some unidentified location, and had wild horses galloping over a lush and impossibly beautiful valley, with mountains so majestic and mighty in the background that Teddy, usually so serious, imagined, with a kind of childlike glee, that the gods lived on top of those mountains. Not the old gods — Zeus and Hera and all the others — but the new ones. The god of promise and the god of possibility and the god of infinity and the god of beginnings and the god of glacial waters and the god of green valleys.

Nell was not so easy to convince. When he showed her the photograph, she looked at it and said, "What's that there, Teddy?"

"Where?"

She pointed to a discoloration at the base of one of the mountains. He said, "That? That's just a smudge." He lifted the photo closer to the lamp. "Yes. A smudge."

"I think it's one of those horrid little things they live in. What are they called? Tepees. That's what I think it is. A tepee."

"Why, Nell. What if it is a tepee? That would make the photograph even grander, don't you think? More authentic. Besides, I think they've all moved away by now. They're certainly not living in tepees any longer."

"When was the photograph taken?"

Teddy looked at her. He had no idea. He was surprised by her resistance to the obvious charms of the image, and he was even more surprised that she'd asked him a question for which he had no answer. Still, it didn't take long for him to convince her to move to Montana. He showed her more photographs of thriving fields of winter wheat and white-tailed deer grazing in riverine meadows and one of a humble but lovingly cared for homesteader's cabin, with potted flowers in the windows and white lace curtains and a vaguely alpine freshness to the slope of its roof — which was unsurprising as the photograph was of a house situated nowhere near Montana (as indicated in the caption), but in the lower French Alps, outside of Les Houches. Nell's one protestation was when she said, "But, Teddy, you don't know anything about farming or wheat. Or anything at all about this ranching business. Papa said it's a foolish idea and that you're a fool and that I should refuse to go. That's what he said," and then she lowered her voice and said, "But don't tell him I told you so. You know how he is about keeping confidences."

Teddy was furious with his father-in-law, and yet his daughter, dressed this evening in a pale lavender gown, was so pretty and ethereal and naiad-like, he could hardly believe she belonged to him. He swallowed his rancor, took her hand in his, and said, "I've been reading, Nell. All about farming and soil and crops and I've been in touch with a broker."

"A broker?"

"They help locate good land. Out west. There's so much of it, you see. How would people like us know which is best? All we have to do is tell him how much acreage we want, and he'll find us a place with lots of water and fertile soil and maybe even a cottage, already built."

"What if it's not already built?"

He smiled. "I've been reading about that too."

Her eyes gleamed, to have a husband so clever and so adventurous and above all so fearless. They embraced, and the decision was made.

They were — in that moment, and for the last time — young.

The dust collected everywhere: in their ears, in the backs of their throats, in their genitalia, in a thick layer on their pillows every morning when they woke. And the wind. The wind howled and howled, screamed through their shack as if it meant to blow it down. And if the wind wasn't howling, it was eerily, awfully, idiotically still. Those were its only two moods: shrieking with rage or still with sorrow. Nell was obsessed with the wind, and with the thought that they were breathing in the dust it blew in, all night, all day. "Dust," she muttered. "Our lungs are coated in dust. Just like everything outside of us, everything inside of us is also coated in dust. Teddy? Did you hear me? Everything. Everything is coated in dust."

It was 1931, the driest year ever recorded in the Cotton River Valley. The earth dried up, the Cotton River dried up, and Teddy and Nell's plot of land, under and around the cottonwood trees, dried up. By late spring, it was already baked and cracked and split open like a watermelon. *Watermelon.* That's the word Teddy used to describe the land because all he could ever think about were watermelons. He hadn't been particularly fond of them back in Boston, but now he felt like there was nothing in the world more delectable or more fascinating or more beautifully articulated than watermelon. And all that water. Sweet and so achingly trapped in the ruby red insides.

He thought he might try growing them once the drought ended.

Nell laughed. "You couldn't make a weed grow on this land, Teddy. What makes you think you can grow watermelons? Or anything at all? And do you see this house? All this dust? Who knew the earth was made of dust? Only dust. Honestly, Teddy, I think it's inside my head. I can feel it. It's just — *there*. Coating everything. It'll get in the crevices soon. All those crevices. So many crevices. So many places for the dust." Her head was tilted, and she was hitting the side of it.

"In your brain? You think there's dust in your brain?"

"On. *On* my brain. For now. It's trying to get inside. It will. It will get inside."

He hated when she got like this. He would occasionally engage her, but that was becoming less and less frequent. Mostly he ignored her. She continued hitting the side of her head, while he sat at their table (admittedly coated with dust) and played with Kierkegaard's hourglass, turning it over and over and over. He looked up when he couldn't stand it any longer and said, "Stop it. Stop doing that. Dust can't get inside your head, Nell. It cannot. Don't be an idiot."

"Then how did it get inside there?" she asked.

He looked at the hourglass. "Inside here? What do you

mean? It was made that way. Probably they leave one end open and pour it in and then seal it. Besides, it's not dust. It's sand."

"Sand," she repeated, spitting out the word as if it were a curse. "It's just a different kind of dust." And then, after a moment, she said, "I don't think that's how they make it."

"No? How then?"

She wouldn't say. But she glared at the hourglass (or was it at him?) with a look that unsettled him.

As the drought wore on, Nell began to change. Well, not change. *Change* was not the right word. What she did was surrender. She surrendered to the dust. She stopped wiping down the table or airing out the pillows or closing the windows and door. She stopped sweeping. She in fact stopped cleaning altogether; she stopped eating the few things that remained in the larder; she stopped even the most basic grooming, like combing her hair or brushing away the sleep from her eyes. Instead, she began, in earnest, to do what children do in dust: She began drawing. She drew simple things at first, like houses and trees and hills and sometimes a smiling face. But then the drawings became odd, fantastical, disturbing. One was of a branch of a cottonwood tree reaching down to the ground, all the way down to the earth, and the mouth of the earth opening in horror and agony and unimaginable despair. Another was of a pleasant mountainscape with sheep. The sheep were clearly descending into a valley, but the valley was studded with row after row of mouths — mouths like tiny, murderous mountains — waiting to gnash the unsuspecting sheep. In fact, there were mouths in many of her drawings. Mouths in the act of copulating or in the act of slaughtering or in the act of suffering or in the act of self-damaging or in the act of dying. Mouths in every position and permutation imaginable. Mouths that worshipped a god and mouths that worshipped a demon. Mouths that stood like phal-

luses and mouths that opened like orchids. Mouths that did everything, absolutely everything, except eat. *Eat* is the one thing
they never did. "Why don't they ever eat?" he asked her once.
He was seated in front of her, turning the hourglass over and
over. Watching the sand pour through the pinched glass. The
little grains like nameless planets, racing to their graves. There
was nothing else to do but watch them.

She looked up at him from a drawing she was making, her
finger still poised in the dust. She blinked. "Why don't what
eat?"

"The mouths. They do everything, but they never eat."

She blinked again. And then she laughed maniacally. She
said, "They aren't mouths, Teddy. They're you and me."

Teddy sat stunned. The wind howled. The dust blew into the
shack, through the wide cracks between the slats of wood. He'd
built it — the shack. He'd built it, imperfect as it was, with his
own hands. But he saw now that he hadn't built it for his wife or
for himself or for their shelter or for their future; he'd built it for
the dust. He looked down at the hourglass in his hand, picked it
up, and threw it across the room. It shattered. And all the dust
inside joined the dust outside. Is that what was meant, Teddy
wondered, by dust to dust?

After that, it was hard to know which of their declines was
more precipitous.

Teddy was examining a line of ants when Nell ran out of the
shack and said, "Look, look, look, Teddy. Come inside and look.
You have to look." And she dragged him inside even though
Teddy was greatly fixated on the ants — their military coordina-
tion, their compact bodies, their ceaseless march toward the
killing fields. She pulled him to the table, smiled wide, and said,
"Look. Look." She was pointing to the table on which, in the
dust, she'd drawn a large oval. "What is it?" he asked. "What do

you think? A watermelon, of course. I grew it just for you, Teddy. Go ahead. Go ahead. Have a slice." He saw that she was no longer smiling and was waiting, truly waiting, for him to eat a slice. He looked back down at the oval — such a simple shape — and knew it was the most grotesque thing she had ever drawn. And that the drought may one day end, but what had begun with this simple oval would never end.

That night, he woke to no wind, to its sad and sinister silence, and he held a pillow over Nell's face. Kierkegaard's hourglass was broken, so time no longer existed. And now Nell was dead. It was when he was holding the pillow over her, and the first of his teardrops landed, that he saw all the bodies. All the ones that had come before and all the ones that would come after. He saw the harmony that had been lost. And he saw, just for a moment — with a dense and impenetrable forest behind her and emerging through the mists that veiled her — the Wolf.

As for what Nell said? On that long ago night in Copley Square? When he lifted the lantern to her lovely, tearstained face? It was nothing. Not really. It was what all young lovers say to their young beloveds. She said, "Please, Teddy. Please don't die before me. I couldn't bear it. Please. Please let me be the first to die."

Chapter 23

She smelled the alcohol on Sagar the minute he stepped through the door. She'd never known him to drink to excess — not even at their wedding reception. She wanted to ask what had happened in Billings, but something told her that whatever was coming had already arrived. She said, "Do you want dinner? I made roti with — "

"They fired me."

She froze. Halfway out of the kitchen. "Fired you? *Why?*"

He didn't respond. He instead threw his car keys on the kitchen counter and slumped down on the sofa. Janavi walked over and sat down carefully, noiselessly, in the chair next to him. His face was impassive in its inebriation, as if made of stone. She wanted words but none came; she saw only his face. She'd seen the pristine white of the Birla Mandir in Hyderabad and its impeccable beauty but what she preferred was the ancient, dilapidated temples of Varanasi — the color of their original stone lost to the centuries and most of them now simply a dusty, ageless brown. She'd always thought that that must be the true face of God, not the fancy polished white of quarried marble but the brown of everyday dust.

He said, "This guy, at the bar, he . . ." and then he stopped.

Janavi waited. What guy? She couldn't guess his thoughts but the one that underlay whatever he was thinking must be the same as what she was thinking: His firing meant they would soon be out of status and had sixty days to leave the country. She wondered, though she felt guilty even considering it, whether she was happy he'd been fired. This meant they would have to go back to India. She could probably get her old job back at ChildDefense and they could rent a flat near Papa and she could resume her life exactly where she had left it. It would be so easy. As if Montana had never happened.

"Did they say anything about the visa?"

"Why would they?"

He closed his eyes. Rested his head against the back of the sofa. She didn't — not until just this moment — realize how much she loved the arched neck of a man. Bent back, shadowed with new hair. The strength and the sinew of it, even in a posture of defeat or despair, bewildered her. She thought, No, it would not be so easy.

She saw a crumpled piece of paper on the coffee table.

"What's that?"

"What?" He opened one eye, closed it again, and said, "The termination letter."

She picked it up, smoothed it in her lap, and started to read. She read nearly to the end, stopped, and then read it again. She sat with the letter in her lap. After a moment, she said, "Why did they fire you?"

"Some bullshit."

"Like what?"

He opened his eyes, kept his gaze on the ceiling. "It didn't make any sense. They had to fire somebody for Renny's death. The new guy. The foreign guy. How stupid do they think I am?"

"Wasn't it an accident?"

"I don't think it was. The guy at the bar doesn't think so either."

"What guy?"

"Renny knew something. She had to. She found a finger bone. In the river, not the burial site. The guy from the bar . . . he thinks Renny was murdered. I don't know if I believe him, but I think we need to find Gabe. I think — " He seemed to change his mind. His burst of excitement collapsed.

Janavi wanted to comfort him but who was this man he kept mentioning? And a finger bone? And Renny *murdered*? All of it seemed implausible, enormous. Finally, she said, "Do you want to go?"

"Go?"

"Back to India. Our visas — I'm sure the Central Water Commission will give you your job back."

"No," he said, his answer so abrupt, so pained, that she immediately regretted asking. And there was something in his face — something of what she'd seen when they'd been at his parents' house in Rajahmundry. A vulnerability, as if some protective armor had been pierced and he was looking at the blood or the arrow or the opponent who had pierced it. Or maybe all three. And it occurred to her, out of some hollow place of her own need, her own ache, that her husband was no different from the street children she'd worked with. They had no place to go either, just as he clearly didn't. They, too, had been discarded, just as he had. Her husband. *My husband.* The words repeated, echoed off the cliffs of her consciousness. And then, miserably, he added, "But I guess we have to. They said they'd pay for the tickets."

Did they have to go? What was the first thing they'd taught her in the training course? Was repeated at every meeting? Was the motto for ChildDefense?

Give a child your hand, and you give them the world.

"It says here we have sixty days."

"They told me."

"No, not just to leave. To appeal."

"Appeal what?"

"The termination."

He reached for the letter and read it. She followed the movement of his eyes and realized this must be the first time he was reading it all the way through. He put it down again, deflated. "Based on what though? What some guy at Sweet Molly's told me? Calculations they won't even look at? A finger bone?"

. . . you give them the world.

She met his eyes. She saw him standing under the guava tree, faced with an impossible choice. And here he was again. Except this time, they were facing it together. She said, "Let's find out."

Let's find out.

Janavi knew where those words had come from. She knew where they would lead.

After the Chicago Bulls T-shirt washed up at the fish market, Janavi had no idea where to turn. She refused to assume the worst and continued to make inquiries. Her tenacity paid off, she thought, when an older woman who worked at a different agency called her and said, with a weary voice, "Are you the one searching for a boy named Khalil?"

"Yes, yes. Do you know where he is?"

"No, I don't. But I have Ayaan here."

Ayaan?

Janavi went to the woman's office right away. Ayaan was seated on a wooden bench; the tray was next to him. The woman, Ms. Padmini, told her the boy was being led away by a man at the train station when one of her colleagues had spotted something odd. "What was it?" Janavi asked.

"The man leading him away was wearing an expensive watch. Gold, apparently. She only saw it because he was yanking on the boy's arm."

Her colleague had stopped them and started asking questions. The man had quickly become belligerent, insisting that Ayaan was his nephew. When the colleague had turned, only for a moment, to summon the police constable at the other end of the ticketing room, the man had disappeared.

Janavi could hardly believe it. She said, "Was it Chota Sahib? Was it the same man who took Khalil? Did Ayaan say?"

"Poor boy is so frightened he says he doesn't know. I'm not even sure he got a good look."

Janavi, deflated, said, "But — was it?"

Ms. Padmini looked at her and said the same words to her that she would say to Sagar. She said, "Let's find out."

Ms. Padmini's colleague had helped a sketch artist render a portrait of the man. They had then emailed the drawing to the other agencies in the city. What was more, Ms. Padmini, who'd been working in the field for decades, did have connections in the underworld and she'd passed the drawing around to some of her contacts. In the end a woman in the red-light district, a young sex worker, had told someone she knew who told someone she knew that the man was her pimp. A flurry of activity had followed but not much had come of it; he had not been Chota Sahib. His name was Toofan and he'd been running a prostitution ring with dozens of young women and children. He'd been detained by the police but through a bribe or a connection or both he'd been out again in no time. Ayaan was safe for now, Janavi remembered thinking. As for Khalil?

She looked at Sagar, seated on the sofa looking back at her.

It still hurt to remember Ayaan, just as it hurt to remember Khalil. But the words *Let's find out*, they had given her hope like nothing else had. And that's what she wanted to give Sagar: hope.

And though it was true that Khalil was never found, at least not during Janavi's time at ChildDefense, working with the next child or the one after that or maybe the one after that, she'd decided, not knowing she'd been deciding it, that despair in one world did not mean despair in every other.

Chapter 24

Sagar couldn't tell her. He couldn't tell Janavi why he refused to return to India. What was he supposed to say? That it was because of Sandeep's arm? Or his father's ridicule? That to have failed in America and go back to India — a place where, in their eyes, he was already a failure and had been since the age of twelve — would be humiliating, unthinkably shameful. And what would he to say to them? How was he supposed to face them? Pride. He sometimes thought of the fact that he'd never apologized to Sandeep. In the rush and the clamor and the string of surgeries that had followed their visit to Pinjari Konda, and in the inattention of childhood, it had never occurred to him to apologize. But as an adult he sometimes wondered if he should say those simple words, I'm sorry, and if that would make any difference. Maybe not to Sandeep but maybe it would make a difference to him, in the way he walked through the world. Would it? He wondered again now. Sandeep was only a phone call away; it would be so easy.

But he didn't.

Sagar tried to think of ways to find Gabe and came up empty-handed. He didn't even know his last name. Stupid, stupid, he thought, not to have asked the old man. Frustrated, he reverted to what he'd been doing since he'd first learned of Renny's death: furiously reading and downloading articles on the safety of the notch and release method, running and rerunning his calculations on its dimensions, based on what he'd saved to his hard drive, and putting together a dossier of dam removals from around the world, test results run by hydraulic engineers, and studies published in the *International Journal of Hydraulic Engineering*.

When he looked up, Janavi had gotten a notebook and was making a list of all the things they knew about Renny. Her reasoning was that if they could learn more about her then maybe they could find out something about Gabe, or at least find somebody who knew something.

"Her full name?" she asked.

He told her, "Renata Atwood. I don't know if she has a middle name." He heard the scratching of the pen. He closed his laptop.

"How old is she?"

"I don't —" A chill ran through him. "Actually, I know her birth date."

"How?"

"I saw it. At the police station." He told her: 3-7-77.

She wrote it down and said, "What else do we know? We know about Ophelia, but is Gabe her father? We're assuming he is, but . . ."

Silence. Out of this silence, she said, "She had a gun."

"Yes," he said, "she had a gun."

She wrote. "Where did she live? On the reservation or in town?"

He thought it over. "Must've been the reservation. She had to have worked out of the tribal administration office if they hired her to monitor the excavation."

She started writing furiously. Now they were getting somewhere. He could see the delight in her face. And there was something else. Something he couldn't name but that held steady in her face, her posture, the pen in her hand, even in the fall of her curls. Something deeper and more enduring than delight. Something more daring. Was it curiosity?

The thrill of pursuit? He couldn't decipher it. He said, "She told me a story once."

"Who? Renny?"

"Not *me*. A bunch of us. We were taking a break. Early on. Soon after I'd started."

"What was the story?"

Sagar told her the story of Older Brother and Younger Brother and Porcupine, and when he finished, she said, "Do you think it's true? About the cottonwood trees? Do you think they're still there?"

Sagar shook his head and said, "I don't know. I didn't ask."

Janavi looked down at the notebook in her lap. He could see that, aside from the legend of the Cotton River, which didn't help them, there was not much there. She must've seen it, too, because she said, "What do we do? All we have is a legend and her name." Neither said a word. He heard the trill of a bird. He'd been in Ooty once, on a group trip, late in college. He and his friends had been drinking and playing games all night and at one point, he'd walked out of the cottage they had rented and had stood at the edge of its garden. The moon had been rising and the mountains had been darker than the dark of the sky. He'd stood there, on the edge of the garden, on what had felt like a precipice, with his life before him. His future on the edge of sunrise. What had happened to it? To that promise? It was strange but it was only now, on *this* precipice, that he felt not the promise but the presence, in the moonlit dark, of someone beside him. This person whose proximity, he sensed, was more important than the promise had ever been. He said, "There is no way Renny went swimming. Leaving Ophelia? No. No way."

"What then . . ."

They sat in shadows now. And in the silence, he heard the wind. Who was it? He listened. Nearly smiled. It was Charlene calling out for her Willie. Was it true? About the dimensions of a grave? And the three cottonwoods? What was true and what wasn't — this land, these waters would never offer it up. He didn't have to be in Montana for long to know that much. "I think we should go to the tribal office. First thing." She looked up at him with a smile. It was a half smile, but he took it as a yes.

Sagar woke before Janavi and made coffee. He sat at the dining table. The morning was cloudy. Maybe there would be rain later. The mug he was drinking from was a DNRC mug. They'd given it to him when he'd first started. He studied the logo: the curving river, pine trees on one side, prairie on the other, snowcapped mountains above the lettering with the sun rising behind them. It was idyllic in the way a logo should be. Sagar stared at it with such intensity it was as if he wanted to enter that arcadian scene, live in that perpetual dream of Montana. He hadn't yet told his parents about his job. He'd had stilted conversations with his mother a couple of times a month since they'd arrived, but he'd let the last call from her go to voicemail. He looked at the clock. Seven. The tribal office opened at ten. He didn't know if Janavi heard it, but he'd started hearing it the moment he'd lost his job — the ticking of the passing hours. Each hour nearer to the end of their sixty days.

Janavi came out of the bedroom.

He liked her this way, in the mornings. Walking sluggishly to the kitchen. Pouring herself coffee. Her eyes and lips puffy from sleep. He was watching her now, the way the tendon on the inside of her wrist surfaced and hardened into a line when she lifted her coffee cup. A coffee cup. Such small things required such unfathomable strength. She sat down across from him. He could see that she hadn't slept well. Neither had he.

He looked again at his mug; the white ceramic, the white of the finger bone.

They started after breakfast. The headquarters of the tribe was in a town called Loomis, a little over an hour's drive from Mansfield, off

Highway 212. As they drove the land evened out, the sky cleared. The bluffs and the coulees flattened, with the low hills pushed to the edge of the horizon. All around them were the grasses, blue grama and Idaho fescue and western wheatgrass. The wind was blustery, and he felt the car leaning into the gusts, as easily as a branch bending. They were early, so at one point, Sagar pulled onto a dirt road. They got out of the car, into the sunlight and the wind, and scanned the prairie and the road cutting through it. Empty. There was a cattle guard a few yards away, but he didn't see any cattle. As far as he could see the road led nowhere, only deeper into the gold of the prairie grasses, the squat hills in the distance shining like tiny loaves of bread not yet fully risen. They walked for what seemed like hours, but it was only ten or fifteen minutes before they came to a tuft of tall grass, flattened by wind or maybe the invisible cattle. They stood, studying first the ground and then the sun, as if, in a new country, they too were unfamiliar, and needed surveying. When Sagar turned to walk back to the car, Janavi pointed to the sky and said, "Look," and when Sagar looked up, he saw a hawk swooping low and then plunging into the grasses. Out it came holding something in its beak. "A field mouse," Sagar guessed, and watched as the hawk and its catch sailed northward.

They arrived a few minutes before ten. The tribal administrative office, a squat, blue building off the highway, had a few double-wides sprinkled around it along with a small combination grocery store and post office next door. A handful of dogs loitered. Sagar knocked but there was no answer. They milled around the entrance until a dusty red pickup pulled up. A woman got out of the truck. She looked at them, expressionless, and then walked past them to the front door of the office. Janavi nudged him and whispered, "From the meeting." She was right: This was the same woman who'd spoken up at the Elks Lodge meeting.

He and Janavi followed behind her like obedient children. Once they were inside the woman put some bags down behind a desk, went into the back, and when she came out and saw that Sagar was looking at a topographical map of the reservation on the wall, she said, "You tourists? Car break down?" Her gray hair was pulled back in a ponytail, and she was wearing jeans and a sweatshirt. Her skin was a little lighter brown than his own, her features more precise.

"No. No, we're . . ." He looked at Janavi. He saw her again: Her face raised to the sky, watching with astonishment as the hawk rose out of the grass and into the air. She nodded, just once, as if to urge him to continue, though he felt in the simple nod, in its elegance, a deeper affirmation. Sagar turned back to the woman. He told her he'd been the lead engineer on the dam removal project and that he'd been fired from the job after Renny's death. At the mention of Renny's name he saw the woman stiffen, her face tightening in some way that was not entirely visible, but he continued. He said, "It doesn't make sense. That Renny would go into the water, right by the notch. She knew it was unsafe. She had to. She was from here. She knew the river better than anyone."

The woman said, "So? What about it?"

"Where is Gabe? The ex-husband. Do you know? He's the key to this. He has to be."

"And Ophelia," Janavi said. "How is she? Is she alright?"

The woman, her expression implacable, said, "This is to get your job back? Ennit?" Sagar was stumped. Then she said, "Seems like you about have the run of it."

She stood silently, waiting for them to leave, he assumed. "No. Not just that. There was this guy at Sweet Molly's. He said . . ." He thought of telling her about the finger bone, but he didn't yet know if this woman could be trusted, or if she would trust him.

"A guy at Sweet Molly's?" She shook her head. "I've got a map if you need it. Otherwise — "

"Wait. Just — was there an autopsy? And where is Gabe?" *Follow the fear,* he'd said. "Where is he? The police don't seem to be looking for him. Not really. Not that I can tell."

"How do you know?" she said.

He didn't know. "There's — there's been some injustice. That's all, and . . ."

The woman chuckled. "Injustice? Just this one, you reckon?"

Maybe it was the chuckle or maybe it was his babbling, regardless, a kind of affability entered the room. She told them her name was Norma, which they already knew from the Elks Lodge meeting, and then she said, "You all from India?"

Janavi said, "Yes, we've been here almost six months."

She said, "Already you've asked me more questions than the police have. That Gabe is a bad egg is all I can tell you. But everybody from here to Fort Peck knows that."

"What is his last name?" Janavi asked. She'd brought her notebook with her.

"Bowman. Gabriel Bowman. His people used to own a ranch around here. Lost it to the banks. Dad moved away, someplace in Ohio. Mom ran off when Gabe was just a kid. Messed him up, I guess. Always been a menace. Fights in school. Hard drinking. When he and Renny got together we thought he'd straighten up. And maybe he did for a while. Then you started hearing stories . . ." Sagar thought she might not continue but she said, "Ugly ones. I heard once he loaded up all her shoes in his car. Drove off to work. Just so she couldn't leave the house. Loaded them right up in his truck that he's so fucking proud of and drove off. They lived off the county road, you see. Gravel. She couldn't go anywhere without shoes. Other times she'd be out with bruises on the side of her face. She finally got out. Never know if a girl can but she did. Divorce just went through. Should've seen her smile. Brought in cupcakes to celebrate."

Sagar felt a keen pain in his stomach. In its keenness he felt a convergence, a rage that must've seeded at the meeting in Billings, and having fought off numbness and despair and downfall, now reached the white heat of a different question. "How do we find him?"

"Don't know. No one's seen him since Renny died."

"Who's looking?"

Norma smirked. "Anybody's guess. Probably nobody. They *say* they are. The sheriff's office, tribal police, BIA. But are they? I'd love to know. All of us would."

Sagar thought about Tim Downing. About how he'd been complaining about the BLM and the BIA, too, and now, listening to Norma, he thought, all these acronyms are their own kind of failure.

"You'd know though," Norma said. "You'd know if you saw him."

"How?"

"That truck of his, it's an F-150 Raptor. And he's got a huge raptor's claw painted on the hood. Foolish, if you ask me, but that's Gabe for you."

Janavi made a notation in her book and then she said, "What about Ophelia?"

"She's in shock. Losing her mother like this."

"She's not with Gabe?"

"No. He knows better. I get a whiff of him, and I've got a shotgun locked and loaded."

"Where is she then?"

She looked from one to the other. "Better if I don't say."

Sagar said, "Has she said anything? About what happened?"

Norma shook her head. "Hasn't said a word since . . . what's it been now? Two weeks nearly?"

"Not a word?"

"No."

They were silent.

"Renny's the most recent in a long line," Norma said. "Our girls are found dead, go missing all the time." She smiled bitterly. "Sometimes it's three at once. Hardly ever solved. It's so bad it's considered an epidemic. Here. Canada. Has a name too. MMIW. Missing and Murdered Indigenous Women."

Another acronym.

"Ophelia needs a psychologist," Janavi said. "A child psychologist. Someone — someone who understands what she's been through."

Norma said nothing. Sagar feared that she'd been offended by Janavi's suggestion. Or by the way she'd said it. But when they turned to leave, he and Norma exchanged phone numbers, in case either had any news. In the car, Sagar was quiet, thinking, more convinced than ever that Gabe was the key to Renny's death.

When they got home, Sagar did an online search and found over twenty Gabriel Bowmans, none of them living anywhere near Montana. Janavi searched on her phone and didn't come up with anything either. Neither felt like making dinner. Just before they went to bed Sagar's phone beeped. It was Norma. He looked at the text message and then he held it out for Janavi to see. She'd sent them a photo of the three of them — Renny and Gabe and Ophelia — smiling, standing in front of a black truck that he assumed was Gabe's. It seemed to Sagar an act of great trust that Norma had sent it. In the photo, Renny looked much happier than Sagar remembered her. Gabe was wearing a plaid shirt and holding Ophelia in his arms, her feathery hair covering half of her round face, while a chubby arm reached for something beyond the camera. When he looked up from the phone at Janavi, her eyes were filled with tears.

"What is it?" he said in a near whisper.

"We're going to find him. Forget the police. *We're* going to do it."

Her voice, when she stopped, seemed to him as if it had been all the sound in the world. He said nothing and then he started laughing. He didn't mean to, but he couldn't stop himself. She said, clearly irritated, "What?"

He sniffled when he finished, and then he said, "We have nothing so far. We can't get beyond Renny's birth date, not even Norma can help us, and you think we're going to find a guy who's disappeared? Who the police or the BIA or God knows who else can't find? Who's probably three states away by now?"

"Why not?"

"Before our visas expire?"

"Yes."

He raised his eyebrows. He was entertained, maybe even curious. "So do we buy airline tickets or not?"

"No. We wait."

Another silence. "Have you always been this decisive?"

"Only when there's a child involved."

He looked at her. And it was then, out of nowhere, seemingly out of nothing, that he kissed her.

Chapter 25

The next morning Janavi vacuumed the entire apartment, even though there was no need. After breakfast Sagar had gotten up from the table and said he was going out.

"Going where?" she'd asked.

He hadn't said. Only that he would be back soon. "Don't wait on me for lunch," he'd said, just before closing the door behind him.

Where did he go?

There had been nothing more than the kiss, warm and surprising and the salt of seawater. It had ended and each of them had looked away. Made shy, a little. Janavi had wondered what would happen when they went to bed but there had only been the kiss. She'd been kissed once before when she'd been in college. She and some classmates had been studying for exams and afterward, one of them, Hemant, had offered to walk her home. On the way they'd stopped for beer and though Janavi didn't particularly like beer, she liked the masala cashews they served with it. The music in the bar had been loud and Hemant had been talking and Janavi had said, "What? I can't hear you," and that's when he'd leaned in and kissed her. Some of her friends had thought Hemant might've been gay and maybe that was why Janavi had been more taken aback than she should've been. Still, he'd tried to kiss her again when they'd gotten to her house, but she'd turned her cheek to him. It had been awkward the next time or two she'd seen him but that had been the end of it.

She understood, with Sagar, that when they hadn't had sex, as was the custom, on the third night after their wedding, that a ritual moment had passed. She'd never subscribed to the primitive ideas of virginal purity or saving oneself, but she couldn't deny that not following that tradition had altered some thread in the tapestry of their lives. Maybe not a dramatic one, maybe not even a painful one, but one she now saw with the plainness of a brick wall in which just one red brick had been replaced with a white brick. It wasn't a lesser wall, it might even be a more beautiful wall, but the alteration gave her pause.

But would she have slept with him if he *had* tried? Was that a decision one made? Or did the heart just know? Or was it the body that knew? Once, after dropping Sagar off at work, she'd driven out onto a county road and stopped the car and stood looking into the distance. What had she been looking at? Even she hadn't been sure. Some point on the horizon. Some distant point where the grasslands, after bending and bending in obeisance, finally met the sky. Or maybe a clump of trees that, among the buttes and the canyons and the dry coulees, signaled water, sometimes the slightest trickle, an oasis in the never-ending plains. She hadn't known what she'd been looking for. Perhaps it had only been to feel the wind or the lack of it. The Great Gray Wolf, she thought now, had gotten it right. With the three cottonwood trees. Here, the Wolf had declared, Here is where you will stand for all of time. Here in this place and nowhere else. Wasn't that love? Declaring, *Here*, though the horizon may draw me, though the oases may seduce me, here I will remain. With you. And nowhere else. Was it a decision then, whether made by the body or the mind? Or was it more romantic? Or was it what Rajni had said? That it was already written in the stars, who marries whom, and love (except in *her* case) had nothing to do with it.

These questions swirled in Janavi's mind. For lunch, for lack of a better idea, she made herself a simple omelet of cheese and onions. She wondered again, as she did every few minutes, where Sagar had gone. She looked at her phone. She thought of texting him. Then she thought of calling him. She put the phone down. She wanted to give him privacy, but she couldn't help but worry. It was this worry that churned in her mind, as did the memory of the kiss, and the question of what she would've done (would do?) if he'd reached for her. But in the center of all these questions and these thoughts there was a stillness and in the center of this stillness? There was Ophelia.

She'd asked Sagar to forward the photo that Norma had sent him of Renny, Gabe, and Ophelia. She pulled it up on her phone. She looked at Ophelia. The round face, the baby hair falling across her face, the sweetness of the raised arm. What could she have been reaching for? How old was she in the photo? Where was she? And then Janavi thought of sitting with her in the park. The sunlight. The water. The river of her words now stilled.

Her words.

Janavi had met lots of street children who'd stopped speaking. It was impossible to know, of course, whether their hearing and speech were impaired or whether something had caused them to stop speaking. Only once, in her time at ChildDefense, had she been witness to a child *start* speaking. The little girl's name was Kushboo. She had been part of a group of street children, ranging from six to eleven, who worked the traffic circle at Girja Ghar Crossing. Every hour, hundreds, if not thousands of cars and lorries and bicycles and scooters and people and animals crossed the intersection of five roads, just east of the Ganga. Each of the children was armed with rags and the older ones with bottles of water and when a car stopped, or even slowed, they ran to it and leapt at the windows, cleaning them furiously. The drivers, unless they were seasoned in the ways of street children, stood no chance of declining their cleaning services. It was unclear, in Janavi's estimation, if they improved the windows in any way, given how dirty the rags and the water were, but they seemed to earn enough to keep their gang of half a dozen or so children more or less fed.

Kushboo was one of the younger children. Seven, at the outside. When Janavi first saw her, she was sitting under a banyan tree to the side of the crossing. There was a patch of dead grass leading to a church behind the tree. The children, Janavi could see, had built a sort of housing complex for themselves under the wide branches of the banyan using rusting sheets of corrugated tin and distended cardboard and burlap sacking. The leaning tent structures were sophisticated for children who were of such a young age, but Janavi was no longer surprised by the ingenuity of determined and desperate children.

Kushboo was sitting alone.

What was she doing? When Janavi drew closer, she saw that she was picking lice out of her own hair. How did one do that? Janavi felt a presence behind her, hovering. When she turned, she saw that it was one of the other children, a boy a little older than Kushboo.

"What do you want?" he said.

"I'm with an agency," she said.

"Which agency?"

When she told him, he said, "Are you here to give us money?"

"No. Not money."

"Do you have a car?"

"No. Why?"

He held up a rag, a flag raised to her stupidity. She said, "I'm not here to give you money. But we have resources. Resources that — " When he stared at her, a blank look on his face, she said, "Do you know what the word *resources* means?"

"Yes," the boy said, moving closer to Kushboo. "It's the thing you give us when you're too cheap to give us money but still want to feel good about yourselves."

Janavi blinked. She blinked again. She said, "I'm going to bring her some shampoo for the lice." The boy sat down next to Kushboo, clearly protective of her. "Alright with you if I ask her if she needs anything else?"

The boy smiled, revealing a row of dazzling white teeth. "She doesn't talk."

"Doesn't? Or can't?"

"Doesn't."

"Why?"

The boy shrugged. She looked at Kushboo. She said, "For how long?"

"Since I've known her."

"Then how do you know she even can?"

He said, "I just do."

"What's your name?" Janavi asked.

"Gokul."

"Hers?"

Gokul and Kushboo. She wrote the names down in her notebook and then looked at Kushboo. Their eyes met. Janavi smiled but the girl didn't smile back.

She returned to work and, using her own money (it was easier than navigating the maze of ChildDefense's requisition process), bought a bottle of lice treatment shampoo and went back to Girja Ghar Crossing. The tents under the banyan tree were empty. She looked from one road to the next and finally, at the last one, in a tangle of cars and bicycles and scooters on Godowlia Road, she saw them. Gokul was wiping energetically at the windshield of a Maruti Suzuki while Kushboo was at the driver's side window, her palms cupped, pleading wordlessly for a tip. When the driver pulled away, Janavi called out her name. Kushboo turned, her eyes brightening, or so Janavi thought. She waved and Kushboo waved back and then she started walking toward her. She had almost reached Janavi, waiting under the banyan tree, when some small thing — perhaps an instinct, a breeze, a shift in some inaudible realm — made her stop. A bicycle swerved. A car honked. And in the instant that Kushboo turned, Janavi, too, saw it: the lorry heading straight for Gokul. His back was to it and he, on the course in which he was moving toward another car, would almost certainly be struck. Janavi, in her peripheral vision, saw Kushboo's body stiffen, her arm went up and then, to her amazement, she heard it.

Kushboo's voice. "Watch out!"

Gokul did, too, he must have, because he took a step back, swiveled, and as he did, was sideswiped by the lorry and flung across the road.

Kushboo reached him first and then Janavi. Was he dead? A crowd was gathering. Cars were slowing. Swerving. And in Janavi's head the swirl of traffic and horns and lights and brakes and blood, her own, reached a fever pitch, pounding against her temples. She fumbled for her phone. The right side of Gokul's body had hit the ground, and she was afraid to move him. She dialed 112. It was ringing, ringing, and then, before it answered, miraculously, Gokul opened his eyes. Janavi's hand, the one holding the phone, dropped to her side. He turned his face toward them. Bruised but alive. Janavi cried. Kushboo cried. And Gokul looked at Kushboo, smiled, and said, "You can talk."

Sitting now in the emptiness of the apartment, Janavi felt again how soft, how insignificant our animal bodies. She thought of Kushboo, silent for years, and she thought of Ophelia, silent for who knows how many years to come. She felt as if she were an ambassador to a nation of girls who'd lost their mothers before they could fully understand what a mother was — and she, a veteran standing at its border, looking at the photo of Ophelia, welcoming its newest member.

Her phone rang. Rajni.

Janavi said, "I was just thinking of Amma."

"What about her?"

"Just — do you think about her?"

"Of course I do. But I was older when she died."

What did that mean? She wanted to ask, but the barnacle, with a tenacity that disoriented Janavi, still clung. She said, "Did you take Papa to the specialist?"

"They're running tests."

"What kind of tests?"

"They said —" Janavi heard a gasp, and then Rajni said, "Janoo, I have to go —"

"What? Wait . . ." But she'd already hung up. Janavi stared at the phone. *Had* she hung up? What were the sounds? Still coming through the phone? She brought it back to her ear. She listened. Voices. A man's, Pavan's she assumed, and Rajni's. There were other sounds — scratching, a dull thud, scraping, as if furniture were being moved, but what was most distinct was Pavan's voice. Not so much what he was saying, but how he was saying it. His voice harsh, demanding. But it couldn't be Pavan. Maybe he was talking to another man. Maybe it was the television. She listened and heard Rajni's hushed voice in response. And then the man, or Pavan, said, coldly, "Come here," and then the phone went dead.

Janavi sat, unmoving, on the sofa. She sat until her motionlessness became too much and then she left the apartment.

She called Sagar on the way to Lottie's house. Maybe he'd have an explanation for what she'd heard. But it went to voicemail. When she arrived, Lottie's car wasn't in the driveway and the curtains were drawn. She knocked, and since there was no answer, Janavi sat down on one of the steps leading to the front door. She could've gone home but she knew she would only turn around and come back within minutes. She'd never gotten Lottie's phone number.

She looked up and down the street. It was quiet. The houses were all about the same size, each with a detached garage. The house across the street from Lottie's, for instance, was a one-story with a narrow front porch and aluminum siding and a red asphalt roof. It, too, had a detached garage that was stacked with firewood along its side. A riding lawn mower stood at an angle as if it had been deserted mid-mow, next to the firewood. The windows of the houses were small to keep out the cold. The street had no sidewalks; the lawns came right up to the curb. There were hardly any cars parked on the street. No one got in or out of any of them, and no one came or went into any of the houses. In fact, she thought, this would be an ideal location to film a scene of an abandoned city. Or an abandoned planet. She was looking at the house across the street, no longer studying it, but simply looking in its direction, when she thought she saw a curtain move. Ever so slightly. It could've been the wind, though when she focused her gaze again, she saw that the window was not open. It was a flat, dark-colored curtain, and nothing was visible between the slim gap at its center. She looked and looked, waiting for it to move again. And then it did. A woman parted the curtain and was looking right at Janavi. The paleness of her face, its remoteness and hostility, startled her. She felt like a bad child. What had she done? What was Rajni doing? Janavi looked down at her hands, repentant, and when she looked up again the woman was gone.

She didn't see the car until it was nearly in the driveway. Lottie's car. She waved and Janavi waved back. Lottie got out of the car and said, "Well, look what the cat dragged in."

Janavi stared at her.

"It's a saying." She was wearing a belted yellow dress with blue flowers and low heels. When Janavi told her she looked lovely, she laughed and said, "I own two dresses. For church. Any more and I'd feel too much like a lady. Want some coffee?" When she was seated at the kitchen table, Janavi said, "Who lives across the street from you?"

"Young couple. Moved down here from Malta. The husband's got himself a job at the auto repair shop. The one on Comstock. Right off Main. Lars, I think his name is. Don't know about the wife."

Janavi said, "Do you go to church every Sunday?"

"Only if I get the sign."

Janavi looked at her. "What sign?"

Lottie told her that she had a ritual every Saturday evening. She made a cup of tea, just before bed, and when she finished it, she read the tea leaves and let them tell her whether she should go to church the next morning. She said her mother had taught her. "The sides of the teacup," she told her, "tell you the near future. The bottom is for the distant future and the rim is the present." And then she said, "*Heathen* is probably the word they'd use down at that church, but I've lived here a long time and every last one of them lives in a glass house, if you know what I mean." Janavi didn't know what she meant but she didn't say so. Lottie went into a back bedroom to change and when she returned, she sat down at the table and said, "Why were you sitting on my stoop, anyway?"

When Janavi said, "No reason," Lottie said, "If I had a dime for every time a woman sat in that chair you're sitting in, and said that exact thing, I'd be a wealthy woman." Janavi looked at her, perplexed. Lottie said, "Never mind. Another saying."

What could she tell her? She herself didn't know why she'd been sitting on her stoop. Maybe only to say goodbye. She and Sagar would be gone in less than two months; Montana and the Cotton River Valley would be nothing more than a short interlude, a remembered feast that had ended badly.

Lottie got up and said, "I'm making a sandwich. Want one?"

"What kind?"

"Peanut butter and huckleberry jam."

"Isn't it usually made with grape jelly?"

"My husband got me on to huckleberry. He was from Idaho."

Janavi didn't know what Idaho had to do with it, but she said yes, she'd have one and got up to pour the coffees. She brought them to the table while Lottie was turned away, making the sandwiches. Lottie set the plates down and settled back into her chair and took a bite of her sandwich. She said, "Best thing he left me." Then she said, "Is this about the girl?"

How did she know? "Yes."

"What's her name?"

"Ophelia."

"*Hamlet*."

Janavi hadn't thought of it until now, but she shuddered, recalling that in the play, Ophelia had died from drowning. "She was with her mother. When she died."

"That's what they're saying. Poor child."

She studied the kitchen table. It was wooden and scarred here and there by what must've been knives. Probably simply from past meals but the scars looked ominous. Janavi knew this ominousness. Just after Amma had died, every child in her class and every tree on her way home had seemed poised to attack her. Reduce her to the ash her amma had become. Even the sky was a tarpaulin of menace. Menace. Surely that couldn't have been Pavan speaking to Rajni like that.

She finally told Lottie about Sagar losing his job and about the visas and of how they would soon be out of status. She said, "My husband thinks he's being scapegoated."

Lottie let out a guffaw. "Well, of course he is!"

Janavi was astonished. She said, "How do you know?"

"Listen, V. You had to have come over on the goddamn Lewis and Clark Expedition to be considered *from* here. Do you understand? And from here are the only ones that matter." After a moment, she said, "So what about the girl?"

"She's so small. Where is she? Who's taking care of her? She's lost her mother, Lottie. And Norma, from the reservation, said she's stopped talking. Where *is* she?"

Lottie said nothing.

Janavi looked at her. She said, "Did you ever go swimming in the reservoir?"

"Few times."

"Close to the dam?"

"Not particularly."

"Did anyone you know?"

"No one with sense."

"Then why would Renny?"

Lottie took a sip of her coffee. "All these questions."

"It's just — where is Ophelia? Is she even safe?"

Lottie was quiet. And then she said, "I can tell you where she is today."

Janavi looked at her. "Where?"

"A gal at my church owns a ranch. Out by Birney. On Hanging Woman Creek Road. Isn't that a name? She works at the daycare. Said the kids were coming down this afternoon to pet the horses. Couple of baby goats. Said Renny's girl would be there."

"Are you sure?"

Lottie said, "Greta, that's her name, told me herself. Been planned for a while, she said, but it's a little hush-hush. Given that father of hers. No telling . . ."

"No telling what?"

Lottie didn't say.

"What do you know about him? About Gabe."

"Why?"

"He's violent, isn't he?"

"One of those lost boys, is all. Montana's full of 'em."

"Not really a boy."

Lottie looked at her. "What're you getting at?"

What *was* she getting at?

Janavi finished her sandwich and stared abstractedly at the wall. She thought of the woman who'd been watching her from the window. What had she been thinking? And why was Lottie so reluctant to answer questions about Gabe? Just as she was about to ask, Lottie said, "Not just talking. Says the little thing has stopped eating too."

Janavi turned to her. Her body stiffened.

"That's what Greta says. Must be nibbling something now and then but — "

Not just stiffened; something inside of her galvanized. It clenched her heart, its throbbing growing louder and louder. "Stopped eating?"

"Kids are tough though. I remember this — "

"I know why she's stopped eating."

Lottie looked at her.

"She's waiting. She's waiting for her amma to feed her."

"Her what?"

Janavi got up from the table. She made for the door. Lottie, surprise in her voice, said, "You're going?"

"Where's Birney?"

"South of here. Why?"

"Could I walk?"

Lottie's eyes narrowed. "You're not thinking of — no, that's a bad idea, V. Don't — "

But Janavi didn't hear the rest.

Radhika

Ganges River, 1930

Radhika lived less than a kilometer from the Ganga. The Salt March had just taken place, but Radhika knew nothing about it. She was seven years old; she had a baby brother who baffled her with his constant drooling and crying and sleeping; and she had a mother who was dying.

She asked her father why her amma was sick.

After a long while, he said, "She has a disease of the blood."

"Blood?"

"It's rare. It's a rare thing, and yet — " Here her father stopped, inexplicably.

Radhika smiled. "Amma said I was a rare thing too."

Her father looked at her and then he looked away.

Soon after that conversation with her father, the dog started following Radhika to school. Well, not following, *chasing*. The dog started chasing her to school. Every morning, the dog ran at full speed out of a narrow alleyway, two blocks from Radhika's school, and chased her until she was through the school gates. The dog then stood at the gates, head tilted, tongue out, and watched until she disappeared through the front doors of the school.

Radhika went to Hindi class and then she went to English class and then she went to music class and then she went to math class and through all these classes, she thought about the dog. She was afraid of it of course (who wouldn't be?), but even though it was a street dog, Radhika saw, in the way that arrows and children can see through wildness and into the true and trembling heart of a thing, that the dog wanted to be her friend. She thought it over and decided the best thing to do was talk to it. So, the next morning, when the dog shot out of the alleyway, Radhika stood perfectly still. The dog raced toward her and stopped. He looked at her curiously, and then he leapt and yipped and barked and wagged his tail and then, without warning, he lunged at her skirt and caught it in his mouth and ripped a chunk from it. And then he started to run again. Radhika called after him and said, "Come back here. You see what you did to my skirt? That's no way to make a friend."

The dog ambled back.

She placed her bookbag on the ground and knelt beside him. The dog sniffed her arm. She pointed to the rip in her skirt and said, "You see? You see what you did? Bad dog. What will I tell Teacher? And Papa?" The dog lowered its eyes. He scratched the back of his ear. Radhika supposed that meant he was sorry. She said, "The first thing you need is a name. Do you have a name? I didn't think so. I am going to name you Chintoo. Do you like it? It suits you."

The dog seemed pleased with his name.

The next morning, when Radhika walked past the alleyway, Chintoo ran out again, and again tried to coax her to run after him. But Radhika shouted, "Stop that. Papa said we can't run to school anymore. He was mad about the skirt, and that's what he said. He said we can walk to school nicely together, but that we can't run." Chintoo hung his head and walked back to her. When she patted his head, he looked up and seemed to understand that they would now be walking to school. No more chasing and running.

After that, instead of dashing out of the alleyway, Chintoo waited patiently for her every morning, and as they walked, Radhika fed him scraps from her breakfast and shared stories about her baby brother. She laughed and told Chintoo all the things he'd spit up the previous evening, or about his bald spot, or about how he couldn't even hold up his own head. Once or twice, she stopped laughing, and added, "And then Papa picked him up. He just picked him up and held him. He wasn't crying or anything. Can you believe it? He's squishy, like a pillow. I guess that's why he gets picked up for no reason. He's a pillow. A crying and pooping pillow."

One of her classmates, Nikhil, saw her walking with Chintoo one morning and asked her, "Is that your dog?"

"Yes."

Nikhil looked him over. "He looks like a street dog."

"So? He likes the freedom of the streets. But he's still mine."

Nikhil sneered. And then he said, "Watch out. He'll bite you if you're not careful."

Nikhil, of course, was too stupid to understand.

The following week, Teacher took them to Scindia Ghat for a class trip. All the children sat in a row on the steps. Nikhil sat next to Radhika. Radhika looked up and down the ghat to see if maybe Chintoo was there, but he wasn't. Radhika then turned to the river. She watched the pilgrims bathing. Their arms coming up out of the water and then their heads and then their torsos. And then back into the water they'd go. "What do you think they're doing?" she asked Nikhil.

"You don't know?"

"No."

"My papa told me long ago. I thought everybody knew."

"What?"

"You go into the water, like they're doing, three times — count them, three times — and then, when you come up the third time, you give up the thing you love the most."

Radhika grew alarmed. "Why would you do *that*?"

"That's just how it is. It's what the Goddess Ganga wants, I guess."

"And what does she give you in return?"

"One wish."

"*Really?*"

"That's what my papa said."

"Anything?"

"She's a goddess after all."

Radhika gave it some thought. "What did you wish for?"

"I haven't yet."

"How come?"

Nikhil shrugged and said nothing.

Radhika had clearly underestimated Nikhil. He was far more knowledgeable about life than she was. "What if you love two things the most? Both the exact same amount? What do you do then?"

"Your mama and papa?"

"No."

Nikhil was silent. He seemed to see her in a new light too. He said, "You have to pick one."

"What if — what if one of them is sick, and what if what you want to wish for is for them to get better? Then how can you give them up?"

She could tell he was getting exasperated because he started poking another classmate — a boy named Rahul, who was sitting on his other side — with a stick. "What do you do then?" she said.

"Look. How should I know? I don't have all the answers."

Teacher said it was time to go.

As they walked back to school, Nikhil said, "Then I guess you have to give up the second thing. And your wish can be to make the first thing better."

Radhika lay awake that night and gave the matter some thought. Nikhil was right, of course, but the thought of what she must do made her sad. She sniffled into her pillow. She wiped away the tears with the sleeve of her nightgown. She tried and tried to find another way, but she couldn't. And so, deep in the night, when even the river was sleeping, she came to a decision: If she wanted Amma to get better, then she would have to give up Chintoo. There was no way around it.

The very next morning, she fed him two entire idlis that she'd secreted away when her papa wasn't looking, and then she took his chin in her hands and said, "Now listen, Chintoo. I have to do something today. After school. I'm going to give the Goddess Ganga the thing I love the most. Do you understand? Do you?" And here she teared up again. Chintoo was watching her avidly. His eyes fixed on hers. "After that, we can't be friends anymore. I'm sorry. It's so my amma will get better. You understand, don't you? But I'll always remember you. And I was thinking last night that just because you give something up doesn't mean you don't love it anymore. Don't you think?"

When she let go of his chin, Chintoo walked with her to school, matching her stride, just as he always did. When they arrived at the gates, Radhika hugged him for as long as Chintoo let her, and then when he squirmed out of her arms, she turned and ran through the front doors. She didn't look back.

After school, Radhika walked back to Scindia Ghat. She placed her bookbag on the step just above the waterline. Then she took off her shoes and her socks and her skirt and her shirt.

She left her underwear on. She looked at the river and was a little worried by how swiftly it was moving. But there were other people praying in the water, so she dipped her big toe in first, then her entire right foot. Someone behind her yelled, "Go ahead, little girl. I won't let anything happen to you." Was that the voice of God? Radhika turned to look, but none of the people on the ghat was paying her any attention.

Maybe it was God.

She stepped into the river, gingerly, up to her small, shivering chest, and then she looked into the water. Green gray, and the pink of roses. Thick with debris. She looked for fish but saw none. Three times, she told herself, and then you give him up. She felt like crying and so she did it quickly. Once, twice, thrice. On the final plunge, she said to the Ganga, "I'll give you Chintoo. I'll give him to you, and you give me this." The rest she spoke only to herself and to the river. And that was it. She opened her eyes. She looked around her. She looked at the other worshippers, bobbing in and out of the river, slick like otters; she looked at the half-submerged temple; she looked at the distant sandbank. All of them were exactly as they had been. How could it be? Why hadn't the sky broken in two? Radhika came up out of the water, her underwear soaked, and she put on her clothes, pushing back tears. And then she walked home, heavier and lighter, both at once.

She found a different route to school. This route avoided Chintoo's alleyway. Sometimes, in Hindi class or English class or music class or math class, Radhika pricked up her ears, thinking she heard Chintoo's bark. One night, she saw Chintoo sitting in the corner of her room. He was watching her, his gaze doleful, and she said to him, "You're brave. You're braver than a wolf."

A month went by. Two.

Her amma was the same, but Teacher, when Radhika's mustard seeds didn't sprout and all the other kids' did, said, "Some things take time," and so that's what Radhika told herself when she was saddest: Some things take time.

Maybe it was this — that her amma's health remained stubbornly unchanged — that made Radhika do the unthinkable. Or maybe it was simply that she missed him too much. Either way, Radhika decided to walk past the alleyway one morning. She just wanted to see Chintoo one more time; a glimpse would do. She started from her house earlier than usual, with a phulka from breakfast in her hand. Did he still live in the alleyway? Would she have to coax him out? Would he even remember her?

She skipped all the way. When she neared the alleyway, she stopped and stood at one end, where Chintoo usually met her. Nothing. The alleyway was narrow, and the sun hadn't yet reached it and it curved so that Radhika couldn't see beyond a furlong or two. She waited, the phulka stiff in her hand. She thought she might call out his name, but a man was walking down the alley now, toward her. What should she do? While she was considering, just like that, out of the alleyway, came Chintoo. Racing past the man and straight to Radhika. She squealed with delight, knelt to him, but — but it was wrong. What was wrong? What was it? Chintoo. It was him, *he* was wrong, but why?

She backed away.

The man was out of the alley. He stopped. He looked at Chintoo and then at Radhika and then he said to her, very sternly, "Don't move. You hear me? Don't move."

Radhika didn't move. She *couldn't* move. She stood paralyzed and watched as the man picked up a broken pipe that was lying there, just lying there along the thin gutter of the thin alley, and he raised it above his head and he brought it down. He brought it down on Chintoo. Hard.

Radhika screamed. She screamed and screamed, even after

his legs stopped twitching. And his head lolled to the side. And his fevered blood began to draw the first flies. The man said, "You got lucky. Did you see? He was staggering. Foaming at the mouth. You know what that means? He's rabid. Rabies. No saving him. He would've gotten you, little girl. He would've bit you. You would've died. Even a little dog like that. Nothing to do but kill them. You're lucky I was here."

She was crying now. The man was patting her head. He was saying, "Don't cry. You're perfectly safe now. You're on your way to school? Is it the primary school? Just up the road? Should I walk with you? No? Stop all that crying. You're safe now. The dog is dead."

The dog is dead.

All through Hindi class and English class and music class and math class, Radhika's little body shook. She saw Chintoo dying. She saw him being struck, and then dying. She held back tears. It was her fault. She'd tried to cheat. That's why Chintoo had died. She'd cheated by *saying* she was giving him up, but not really doing it. And as Teacher said, Cheaters always get caught.

Radhika looked down at her hands, clasped in her lap. She felt empty. She felt a thing for which she had no name; even a child can yearn for childhood.

That night, she said, "Papa? What do you think happened to him? To Chintoo."

"What do you mean?"

"Will he still be there? Tomorrow?"

Her papa said, "No. They probably came and took him away."

"Who?"

"The people who take away animals when they die."

Radhika, deep in thought, waited until he came to tuck her

into bed that night. When he rose to turn off the light, she said, "Will they put his ashes into the Ganga?"

Her papa's face grew sad. Sadder than she'd ever seen it. And he said, "Of course they will. Everything that's good, that dies far too soon, goes into the Ganga."

Chapter 26

When Sagar left the apartment on Sunday morning, he had no idea where he was headed, and though he couldn't say he'd been *led* here, certainly not by anything resembling an external force, within a minute or two of leaving Mansfield and driving onto the Cotton River Road — which more or less followed the course of the Cotton River — he knew where he was going. He settled himself on a flattish part of a boulder that was situated on a bluff overlooking the river. He was hidden from the road by more boulders behind him and the incline of the bluff. Before him was the river, twenty-some miles upstream from the site of the dam removal, so that Sagar saw nothing of the notch or the dam or the reservoir. This part of the river was untouched, flowing past with innocence, with immaculate disregard, and with the kind of unchecked power that he'd always loved in rivers. What river had he first loved? Was it the Godavari, flowing through Rajahmundry? Or was it the Yeleru, the one that had taken something of Sandeep's arm? Was that why he was here? Because the boulders and the bluff reminded him of that afternoon?

Of course he had wanted to, after the kiss, but the kiss had been so perfect, so spontaneous, he had wanted to leave it as it was: complete.

Would she have said yes? He wasn't sure yet.

He looked toward the opposite side of the river. Wild orache and asparagus lined the bank. Downstream he saw box elders and tamarisks and cottonwoods. One canopy of cottonwoods (so extensive they couldn't be just one tree) towered over the line of the other trees. So tall that he wondered, as a child would, whether those were the three trees from the legend Renny had told him.

He'd read once about a therapy or a hypnosis in which the patient was led back to a traumatic incident or a moment of great agony and asked to relive it, so that they might undo the trauma, or at least remake the memory, and in a case like his, make a different decision. It was obvious: If he could remake a thing, an event, it would be to undo Renny's death. He thought it over. In the case of Sandeep, it was easy: He would not have pushed him off the boulder but in Renny's? Would he have not made the notch — which his research showed was the preferred, and indeed the safest, way of removing a dam? Would he have not made it the size it was — which all his calculations, down to the millimeter, had indicated was necessary? Would he have not come to Montana — which, the moment he'd ripped the *International Journal of Hydraulic Engineering* out of the cow's mouth and read the advertisement for the Cotton River dam removal, he'd felt inextricably drawn to? Destined for? How could he have changed any of that? And would he even if he could? What was more, professional pride kept him from utterly dismantling any of his actions or decisions. Sagar had considered them all — the results of the sediment analysis, the effects of its release and transport, all the potential nutrient and mineral shifts, the ecology of the riparian system, the water quality, the infrastructure, and the budgetary limitations, staying, almost to the dime, within the constraints. Every one of these considerations and calculations had, down to the minutiae, been weighed and deliberated in considering the notch and its size.

And still, they'd fired him. And still Renny was dead. And no amount of hypnosis would bring her back or heal Sandeep's arm or . . . or what? Gain his father's love.

Sagar was at Raithu Bazaar with him. He was six or seven. He couldn't remember why exactly they were at the market — for what vegetable or spice his mother had needed. Did his father drive or was Gopi, their driver, waiting for them in the car? That, too, he could no longer remember. They were walking together (though not hand in hand; Sagar couldn't recall his father ever holding his hand), with his father stopping now and then to make a purchase. While his father was bargaining with a shopkeeper, Sagar turned to look at a bright-red motorcycle that was driving by. The driver was wearing black jeans and a black helmet. Both the driver and the motorcycle looked as if they'd come right out of one of the video games Sagar had started playing. He watched the motorcycle until it got to the end of the street and rounded a corner. When Sagar turned back around his father was gone.

Sagar recalled looking this way and that. He couldn't find him. He started walking. He was too shy to tell any of the adults that he was lost so he walked around and around the market, looking up into the faces of each of the men he passed. Even if Gopi had driven them and was waiting in the car, he had no idea how to find him either. On his tenth or eleventh circuit around the market one of the vegetable sellers stopped him. The man was old, and he said, "Arré, abbai. What are you doing? Are you picchi? Alright in the head?"

Sagar looked at him, a little scared. "Yes, I'm alright."

"Then what are you doing? I've seen you walk by a dozen times. Lose your dog?"

Sagar shook his head.

"Are *you* lost?"

Sagar looked down at his shoes. He could've lied and told the old man he was just taking some exercise. Or maybe running an errand for his mother. But he was tired. He wanted to go home. He said, "How did you know?"

The man smiled a toothless smile.

Sagar explained to the old man about the red motorcycle and the man in the black jeans and the black helmet; he told him that at the time, he and his father might've been standing outside of an electronics shop or a shoe store or a dry goods store, he couldn't remember, and of how, when he'd looked up, his father had been gone. Then he said, "Thathaiya, can you help me?" The old man laughed, more heartily than Sagar had ever heard anyone laugh, and said, "You call me Grandpa, and I'll do anything." Sagar looked at his leathery neck, his tattered shirt, stained with the dirt that the vegetables he was selling had probably been wiped clean of that very morning. His hands, Sagar noticed with some alarm, were gnarled, like those of one of the demons he'd read about in his *Chandamama* comics.

The man, who told him his name was Bali, said, "You know the best way of being found?"

"No, I don't, Thathaiya. What is it?"

"Look around you. What does everyone here, every single creature in this market, have in common?"

Sagar looked around. "I don't know."

"Look. *Think.*"

It took a moment. Maybe two. A man on a scooter honked his horn and sped by. A dog sniffed at Sagar's leg and moved on. Two women walked past, chatting. The evening's first lights were on, a radio was blaring Telugu cinema songs, the colors of the market swirled and then, for the briefest instant, in mid-pirouette, they stood still. It was then that Sagar smiled as if he'd made a great discovery — dug up the most amazing fossil or found the key to a secret vault — and shouted, "They're all moving."

Bali laughed, patted the space next to where he was sitting, and said, "And if they're all moving, do you know the best way for one of them to find you?"

Sagar ran over, plopped down next to him, and said, "By staying still!"

In Sagar's memory it hadn't taken more than a few minutes but maybe that was because Bali had been regaling him with his tales and adventures of growing up in Sitanagaram and hiding from his mother in the watermelon patches and skipping fieldwork to take the bus to Kakinada to swim in the Bay of Bengal, but before he knew it, his father was standing in front of them. Sagar jumped up, delighted to see him. He'd assumed he'd get chided a bit, lectured for not paying attention, but instead, his father was apocalyptic. He pulled Sagar by the ear and when he finished yelling at him, he yelled at Bali. Sagar couldn't understand it. Why was he yelling at Thathaiya? He didn't recall what his father said but he did remember standing beside his father and feeling embarrassed. Why? Because he'd gotten himself lost? Because his father had had to waste hours trying to find him? No. He was embarrassed for his father, not for himself. Here was his father: a young man, certainly younger than Thathaiya, the owner of orchards that, even with the mealybug infestation, put him in the upper-middle echelons of Rajahmundry society, and with a driver who was waiting to drive him home, a wife who would have a hot, freshly prepared meal for him when he got home, and who mostly led a life of leisure. And then there was Thathaiya: an old man, clearly a poor one, who'd probably picked the vegetables he was selling from a meager plot of land that he didn't even own, whose fingers were so gnarled that he couldn't have gotten one of the many rings his father was wearing onto them, even if he'd wanted to, and who, from what Sagar could tell, didn't have a rupee to his name, let alone a golden ring. So, why was his father yelling at *him*? Sagar didn't understand it, though what he did understand, or maybe simply sensed, even at the age of six or seven, was that he had a choice. It was not a complicated choice, but it was nevertheless a crucial one. And the choice was this: Either he could be like his father or he could be like Bali.

No matter what happened in his life — whether he inherited his family's money or it was all lost overnight in a bad business deal, whether he had an army of servants when he grew up or found himself working the fields for another man, whether he walked the marketplaces of the world buying them up or was one of the ones who waited, hungrily, for the fat pocketbook to emerge — it did not matter. He still had a choice. Every man did. And on that day perhaps Sagar had made his choice, and maybe that, and not any of the events that came after, was why he had soured on his father.

Sitting now on the banks of the Cotton River, what did any of that mean? The choice Sagar had made. The choice of Bali and his stillness. Should he rage instead? Should he go back to the DNRC office in Billings, put all the evidence, all the calculations, in front of them, and demand to be reinstated? Demand a true explanation and not the bullshit they had handed him? That's what his father would've done.

He looked around. At the river flowing past, at a cottontail rabbit that was sniffing at something in the sedge grass, at the prairie that went as far as his eyes could see. And at the sky, the greatest dome of sky he had ever known. What would his father say about him? If he could see him now? That he was a failure? A quitter? Or would he agree? That though he could've chosen many ways of being a man, he had chosen a way that was one of the best of them.

He got up from the boulder.

Something wasn't right. He was missing something. The rabbit hopped away. What was he missing? The sky from the west was clouding over and the leaves of the box elders and the tamarisks shimmered in the wind.

The air around him cooled. A storm was coming.

Therapy. In which one reentered the trauma.

What is it he should do before the storm came?

The rabbit. The clouds. The cottonwoods. There was so much that time told and so much that time took away.

What was he missing?

His thoughts turned to Renny. Usually, when he thought of Renny, he recalled the conversations they'd had, or he heard her laughter, or he worried about Ophelia, and then, invariably, the image of her body floating at the base of the dam muscled its way into his mind, and he settled, miserably, back into his anguish and onto his phone or his computer, frantically redoing his calculations and searching through the dossier he'd compiled, trying desperately to find an explanation for how she could've died. But this time was different. This time, he thought about her body. He remembered her ankles, which he'd sheepishly admired. And her small breasts, so like Janavi's. And her waist, slim, with a slight swell at the belly. She was petite — maybe five three or five four, at the outside. And she had a small build. She couldn't have been more than 120 or 130 pounds. He thought of all this unabashedly, brazenly, allowing himself to drift.

He sat back on the boulder. Closed his eyes.

Yes, someone of her size could easily get sucked through the notch, though given the flow rate on the second day after the notch was cut, it wasn't obvious *how* — which was the source of his frustration. Especially if the picnic site . . . the picnic site!

He ran to the car. He put it in drive and squealed onto the road. He was there in less than an hour: the exact spot where Renny and Ophelia had been picnicking. He knew it by the bright yellow police tape blowing in the wind, one end tied to the trunk of a tree. How had he not thought to visit the picnic site until now? He had accepted, from what Mack and Sheriff Oswald had said, that it was dangerously close to the notch, but that wasn't true. It was nearly five hundred feet from the notch.

He walked gingerly, disbelievingly. They had been picnicking on the western shore of the reservoir. He looked first upstream and then downstream. He walked to the water's edge. It didn't make sense. Prairie silt gathered downriver but here the water was clear and green. He turned his back to the reservoir. The silt also gathered along the shore, onto the red clay soil. Here and there were clumps of sedge grass and in the center was a patch that was clear of grasses. This must've been where Renny had spread out a blanket. The silt was disturbed. Sagar looked down at it. It was impossible. What was impossible? He wouldn't articulate it, not even in his own mind. Not yet. Don't make assumptions too quickly, he told himself. But that didn't matter, because it was obvious: Given the distance to the dam, the flow rate on the second day, and the rough volume and mass of Renny's body, there was no way she could've been swept through the notch. Not unless she was swimming *toward* it, which was ludicrous, or — it was too gruesome, and the idea annulled itself. His heart ached.

Not only was water hungry, he decided, but it was also cruel. He started back toward the car. He refused to turn around and look at the notch. Or the dam. Or the reservoir. Or the river. Those he was done with.

He thought of the story Renny had told him about Porcupine. What was it he'd said to Older Brother? He couldn't remember; his heart sank further.

Going to Sheriff Oswald and explaining this to him would get him nowhere. He understood by now that, in America, an immigrant brown man's theories about the death of a Native brown woman were of no concern to a powerful white man. What about Mack? He could show him the location of the picnic site, its distance to the notch, and his dossier, and he would see that Renny couldn't have been carried by the current. She had to have been *taken* to the notch. Or to the base of the dam. Her body dumped. There — he'd thought it. His mind had articulated the awfulness. But Mack wouldn't take his call. He knew that much. Norma? Alex Mendoza? What could they do?

He called Janavi; she didn't answer.

He pulled up the photo of Renny and Gabe and Ophelia. What was the little girl reaching for? Nothing, he saw now. She wasn't reaching for anything. She was pointing. At him. All this time, since Renny's death, he'd been lost in his numbers and his research and his reconstructions, without once stepping into the world, coming to the picnic site, and seeing that it couldn't have happened in the way they were saying it happened. He stared some more at Gabe's face — fights in school, hard drinking. After talking to Norma, he and Janavi had said they'd look for him, but beyond the online searches, they'd never discussed how. How did you find a person in a county the size of Custer County and in a state the size of Montana (assuming he was even here)? And how did you find a little boy in a market the size of Raithu Bazaar? Thathaiya's words came back to him. He smiled. Could the reverse of those words be true? Could you *find* somebody by standing still?

He had no answer, but he remembered. Porcupine had said, "We'll find him."

Chapter 27

Janavi called Sagar. It rang and then went to voicemail. She texted him and waited. It was early afternoon and Birney was an hour's drive from Mansfield. She needed a car. Where *was* Sagar? When she left Lottie's, she walked in the opposite direction from home, aimlessly, waiting for Sagar to call back. A child's bicycle on its side, a yellow patch of grass in a sea of green, a porch swing creaking in the breeze. She studied each of them as though they were signposts; she thought of Ophelia. She thought of herself in the days and weeks after Amma's death. Girls not eating, not speaking. Hunger and wordlessness and violence. Was that all there was? She had to see her. She had to. When she'd left Lottie's, she'd thought she would wait for Sagar. But no, she couldn't wait.

She looked around her. Where was she? The house with the green shutters, the deer ornament on the lawn of another; she'd been here before. Her mind raced. It landed two blocks away. Mandy.

She ran again. When she got there, Mandy looked up, smiled, and said, "Haven't seen you in a — what's wrong?"

"Can I borrow your car?"

"It's my mom's . . ."

"When do you get off work?"

"An hour. Why?"

"Can you leave now?"

"No. I mean I guess I could call Aaron and see if he can — why?"

"It's an emergency. Please."

Mandy, who'd been restocking cigarettes, paused, and said, "Are you hurt? What's wrong?"

"It's not me. It's a child. Hurry."

Mandy seemed unconvinced. She said, "He's not gonna be happy. He covered for me last week."

Janavi waited while she called him. She told him she had bad cramps and then she winked and gave Janavi a thumbs-up sign. Janavi went back outside and sat down on the low wall. She checked her phone, but Sagar hadn't called. She thought she should text and tell him she was going to Birney, and why, but then she decided against it. It was too hard to explain. And besides, what if Sagar, like Lottie, tried to talk her out of it? She put her phone away. She looked at the lone car at the gas pump. She watched a man wearing jeans and a dazzling silver buckle the size and shape of a tea saucer replace the nozzle and drive away. And then for the first time, she thought, What will I do once I see her?

A young man drove up. He glanced at Janavi and then went inside. Mandy came out. She said, "Only reason he covers for me is because he thinks it'll get him laid." And then she said, "Where we going?" When Janavi told her, she said, "Fucking Birney? What's down there?"

"Hanging Woman Creek Road. It's off Cotton River Road."

Mandy started driving. She played with her tongue piercing. After a few minutes, she said again, "What's down there?"

Janavi looked straight ahead at the black road unspooling. She said, "Did it hurt? The piercing?"

Mandy sped up. She said, "Tell it to me from the beginning."

The beginning? Where was the beginning?

She looked out of the window. The prairie stretched in all directions. And the river wound through it. Nothing broke the taste of the last bite Amma had fed her, and the knowledge that she and Ophelia would spend the rest of their lives waiting for another. She said, "The woman who died at the dam, Renny, we're going to see her daughter. She's in Birney."

Mandy turned to her. "*That* lady's kid?"

"What about her?"

"Wasn't she drunk or high or something? When she drowned?"

"Who told you that?"

Mandy shrugged. "People talk. Gas station, around town."

Janavi looked away.

Twenty minutes later, they came to Hanging Woman Creek Road. At the T-junction Mandy turned left. More prairie, their backs now to the river. Janavi scanned both sides of the road. She had no address but that didn't matter. They drove for a few more minutes. They came to a dirt road with a ranch gate at its entrance. Beyond was a barn and a house and some low outbuildings. "Here," Janavi said. They drove onto the dirt road and as they neared the structures Janavi saw that the land behind the house and barn was broken up into fenced-in pastures. A van was parked around the side of the house. She told Mandy to park behind the barn so that the car couldn't be seen from the house or the fields beyond the house.

"Why can't they see it?"

Janavi didn't know. She said, "Just in case."

"In case what?"

She told Mandy to stay in the car.

Mandy said, "Wait. Why? Are we even supposed to be here?"

Janavi closed the car door gently. She heard voices. She knew they were in one of the pastures behind the house. She darted from the barn to one of the smaller outbuildings and then to the house. She crouched alongside the van and snuck to the rear of the house.

There they were: a group of six children and an older woman who was probably Greta and an older man who Janavi assumed drove the van. The pasture they were standing in had three horses and a foal. An adjoining pasture had a few goats. Greta was holding a bag of carrots. The children were clustered around her. One or two of them ventured closer to the horses. Janavi looked from child to child. Their backs were to her, mostly, but the fifth child — the fifth child was Ophelia. Janavi smiled and held herself from running to her. Ophelia was holding a carrot. Greta said something to her, or to all the children, and Ophelia raised her head and took a tiny step forward. The horses were munching on the grasses, ignoring the children and the carrots. As Janavi watched her, she turned her face up toward Greta, and it was only then that Janavi saw the full roundness of it, the dark of her eyes, the small of her hands. Her aloneness. Janavi's eyes warmed.

After some minutes they all moved out of the pasture and toward the house. Janavi hadn't noticed but a low table was set up with snacks and juice boxes. She was anxious, waiting to see if Ophelia would eat any of the chips or the cookies. She couldn't make out the other items on the table. The children crowded around and though Ophelia joined them, Janavi saw that she was not eating. The other children jostled each other and yet she, in their midst, stood apart. The others grabbed fistfuls of chips, a cookie in each little hand. Janavi tried to catch Ophelia's attention but couldn't. After a few moments, Greta and the driver, along with the other children, drifted away toward the goats, but Ophelia, miraculously, hung back. This was her chance! "Ophelia," she whispered.

Nothing.

"Ophelia." A little louder. The girl's face turned to her. Janavi smiled, waving her over.

She took a step, tentatively, toward Janavi. Just when she was about to take another a door slammed behind Janavi. She turned and saw the old man coming from the direction of the goat pens. He yelled, "You there. What are you doing? Who are you?"

Janavi straightened up, taking a step backward.

He was in front of her in no time. Her back was flush against the wall. "I said, what are you doing here? I know you?"

She said, "Ophelia . . ."

"What about her? What do you have to do with her? You with that Gabe fella?"

"No! No, I'm from India."

"India?"

The door slammed again. A woman's voice said, "Jerry, what's — *you?*"

Janavi looked in her direction. Norma. She was so relieved she nearly ran into her arms. Norma looked from Janavi to Jerry and then back to Janavi. She said, "I know her, Jerry. It's fine." The man stepped back, reluctantly.

Norma said, "I got one guess for what you're doing here, and I better be wrong."

"I was worried. About Ophelia. I've worked with children. In India. And I thought — "

"You thought what?"

Janavi looked down. How could she explain? I want to feed her, she wanted to say, I want her to know she will be fed again.

Norma took a step toward her. Jerry moved away, but Norma didn't move any closer. She said, "You're confused. You know what you're confused about? You're confused about what kind of Indian you are." She looked at Janavi for a long while. Under her gaze, Janavi felt remorse for all the injuries she'd ever committed, starting with the poor ants she'd snipped in two.

A goat bleated. Mandy appeared. She said, "What's going on here?"

Everyone looked at her, but no one said a word.

Chapter 28

Sagar was back in Mansfield and seated at Sweet Molly's in less than twenty minutes. He ordered a beer and sat at a table next to the jukebox, facing the door. This was the best place he could think of to wait for Gabe. Or for somebody who knew where he was. Practically every man in Custer County seemed to pass through here over the course of a week, but today there was no one. It was just Sagar and Jake, the bartender. The jukebox was silent. The pool cues stood like sentries. He was hoping the old man would be here or Alex Mendoza or, hell, he'd take Tim Downing at this point.

He went up to the bar with his empty bottle. Jake said, "You want another?"

Sagar took out his phone. He showed him the photo of Renny and Gabe and Ophelia. He said, "Have you ever seen this guy?"

He studied the photo. "Who wants to know?"

Sagar could see it in his eyes. "He's been here, hasn't he? When? When was the last time?"

"You know how many people come through here?"

Sagar looked over his shoulder at the empty bar.

"Not this very instant, bud. I'm not talking about right this fuckin' minute."

"When?"

Jake seemed to consider or pretended to consider. "Couple of weeks maybe."

"Couple of — how did he look? What did he say? Did he say anything?"

"Same shit as ever — his stupid truck. Bitching about the banks. Who knows? People talk about the same shit over and over."

"But *that* day. When he was last here."

He shrugged, said nothing.

Sagar, more solemnly than he meant to, said, "Renny was my friend. She was my first friend in this country."

Jake looked at him and then back at the phone. The silence that followed was greater than the silence had been. Sagar, embarrassed, took out his wallet to pay for the beer. He placed a ten on the bar.

Jake paid no attention to it. Avoiding Sagar's gaze, he said, "Something about the reservoir. He was drunk. Wasn't making any sense. But he kept saying reservoir. I remember that."

"Reservoir? What was — "

The phone rang. Janavi, probably. Jake turned it toward him, said, "You want to get it?"

Sagar glanced at the screen, already shaking his head no. But then he stopped. He took the phone from him. He said, "*Norma?*"

He and Janavi were on the Cotton River Road. Sagar hadn't spoken a word to her since they'd left the ranch. He'd gotten nothing more from Jake, but maybe he could have if Norma hadn't called. She'd explained everything on the phone and Sagar was so angry with Janavi that he focused all his attention on breathing evenly. In and out, in and out. She was saying, "I just wanted to check on her. What's so wrong with that? At ChildDefense, I — "

He broke his silence. The words came out cold, withering on their vine. "You're not at ChildDefense anymore."

He felt her slump in her seat.

"She didn't have to call you," Janavi said. "Mandy could've driven me back. I don't know why she called you."

"Mandy. Was she the chain-smoking, pink-haired one?"

Janavi said nothing.

He said, "She probably called me to talk some sense into you. What possessed you to — "

"She's not eating. And I thought if I could just feed her, just one bite . . ."

A car passed them, going in the other direction. And then a truck.

Silence, heavy as lead. The first raindrops hit the windshield.

"This isn't India, Janavi. You can't go around luring children — "

"*Luring* them?" she yelled. "You're right, this isn't. This isn't India." She started sobbing, continuing to yell, "I never wanted to come here in the first place. It's because of you — "

The rain strengthened. Dark clouds moved overhead.

"Me?" He was shouting now too. "Me? You're the one who wanted to stay for the sixty days. I was ready to leave, but no, you . . ."

He stopped. He looked at her. She gasped and looked back at him. He slammed on the brakes. They both turned to look.

Was it?

Lightning flashed. Then a deafening peal of thunder.

Yes, it was. He saw it, she saw it.

The truck that had just passed them. Yes, it was. Receding now into the distance: a black F-150, a raptor's claw painted on its hood.

Agatha

Ganges River, 1941

Agatha traveled overland at first. A Gentile friend, a former lover, dropped her off at the border, at Ostritz. They both understood the risk they were taking; they hardly spoke in the car, as if by not speaking, as if by breathing very deliberately, in and out, in and out, and by sheer force of will, they could keep from getting caught. How childish, Agatha thought, as she looked out at the lights of distant farmhouses, how naïve. How foolishly optimistic. Maybe that was why men waged war, she thought, so they could play with rubble as they'd once played with wooden blocks. On the drive, which was in the middle of the night, Agatha wondered if they'd come this way before, she and Erich. It was entirely possible. They had been lovers over twenty years ago, during their last year at university, when she'd been studying economics and he philosophy, and they had lain in bed for hours, arguing passionately over what was the greater determinant in an individual life: one's economic status or the status of one's soul. They had lost a whole year that way, arguing and making love and drinking wine and arguing some more. How laughable it was to her now, as they raced toward the German-Polish border in the dark of night — she fleeing, he abetting — that *that* had been their paramount concern.

For most of the drive, she avoided looking at him. She thought, We may have come this way before, we may have. Perhaps during summer holidays to visit the Kloster St. Marienthal or the Berzdorfer See, though why they would do such a thing, something so plebeian, she could not imagine. Maybe it was with a different boyfriend? Regardless, when they reached the border, Agatha wanted to ask Erich to make love to her. In a field. In the car. At the abbey. It didn't matter. Nothing mattered. The entirety of her forty-five years was in her bag: one scarf, one identity card, one thousand reichsmarks, and one pair of nylon stockings, but what she really wanted to take into the emptiness that awaited her was one act of love. And with only Erich (who was now married and had two children). What Agatha wanted was for hands that had once traveled over her body and knitted it into womanhood, to travel once more, all these years and wars and slaughters later, and unravel her womanhood and make her virgin again. Make her a child again. Make her brave again.

When they reached the border, Erich did nothing more than glance at her, and then, speaking more formally than she had ever heard him speak before, he said, "Auf Wiedersehen, liebe Agatha."

She gripped his hand, and then, since he neither rejected nor returned the gesture, she let go.

She traveled east through Poland, mostly on foot. Sometimes a farmer gave her a ride on his horse cart. She once stole a bicycle that was leaning against the entrance to a two-story stone house. Was it in Lublin? She couldn't remember. The journey became a blur. Exhaustion and hunger and desolation were the only trinity. She took trains and carts across the Soviet

Union. Somewhere in the steppes, she slept with a man for a loaf of bread. One morning, waking, she heard flute music, streaming from an upstairs window in a town along the Angara River, and she closed her eyes in relief, convinced that she had died in the night. In Ulaanbaatar, she met a woman who told her that India was taking Jewish refugees. "India," Agatha repeated, as if it were a country she'd never heard of. Though, really, what *did* she know about it? Beyond the fact that it had the Taj Mahal, the British for the past three hundred years, and an alarmingly large number of pagan gods?

She instead traveled to Mandalay and loved it so much — the warmth, the lushness of the trees, the ruined palaces — that she decided to stay. But then the Japanese invaded Burma and the first ship on which Agatha could get passage was bound for India, and so Agatha went to India. She disembarked in Calcutta. Within hours of entering the city she was so overwhelmed by the surge of people and color and sound and plenitude and poverty and the absolute bedlam of it all that she walked up to the nearest tea stall, ordered a cup of tea, and when the vendor handed it to her, saying, "Here is your tea, madam," Agatha looked from the cup of tea to him and then back at the cup of tea, and she thought, What do I want to drink more? The brown of this tea or the brown of his skin? And then she thought, This is exile.

Her second year in India she decided to leave Calcutta. She'd overheard someone speak of the Ganga, and how the river was born high in the Himalayas, in a place called Gangotri, and so that is where Agatha decided to go. How will I get there? she wondered aloud, and an Indian friend, whom she'd met while walking in the Maidan, laughed, pointed to the Hooghly, and said, "Follow this river and you'll reach the source of the other." On the train to Varanasi — where she'd have to transfer to a train to New Delhi, and then somehow make her way from the sprawling capital to the far-flung pilgrimage site — one of her berth mates, a young man who'd just returned from his studies at Oxford and was wearing homespun, as was the rage in those days, said, "Why stop at Gangotri? Why not go to the Ganga's true source?"

"Where is that?" Agatha asked.

"In Gomukh."

"Gomukh? But where is that?"

"Twenty miles from Gangotri. Twenty miles *straight up* from Gangotri. It's an ice cave. That is where the Ganga truly originates." Then the young man smiled and said, "Few reach it, as you can imagine."

Yes, Agatha agreed. She knew all about the places few can reach.

When she arrived in Varanasi, the train to New Delhi was delayed due to signal failure, and so, instead of two hours to spare, she had twelve. She hired a rickshaw outside the train station and asked the driver to take her to the Ganga. Which ghat, he asked. What is a ghat? Agatha said. He shook his head and dropped her off near the Hanuman Temple. Agatha paid him, but first she looked at the driver and said, But where is the river? The driver nodded toward the east and said, That way. Agatha walked and walked, through the thick constellation of alleyways, thinking the rickshaw driver had stiffed her, but then, just as she was about to turn around to try to retrace her steps, she emerged from the web of narrow lanes and onto the ghat, as easily as one would step out of a forest and into a clearing. The warm stone was beneath her and the river was before her. Agatha blinked. Then she blinked again, because though she had seen many rivers in her life, in every permutation of light, she had never seen one in such a state of sensual and languorous repose. As if the river were a lover, sleeping, in a room shadowed and curtained in blue. She felt hollow, excavated — perhaps by memory, though in truth, she had no memory of rivers, she had no memory of any of the ground on which she'd walked, or slept, or eaten, or lain on, or been laid down upon, so no, it was not memory.

Memory, she understood now, was a jackal, too cowardly to kill, feeding on what time had already killed.

No, what laid Agatha bare was her sudden awareness that she had never been meant to stand as she stood now: a girl born and raised in Leipzig, who'd gone to university in Dresden, and who had imagined she would marry and have children and stand only by rivers she knew, and only on land she loved. But what is known and what is loved . . . they are nothing, she realized, as easily taken away as the thin mist that trembled just above the water's surface. Was that a reason to love them less? She thought then of Erich's hand on the gear shift. It had curled so beautifully. Like a seashell around the delicate, beating thing within.

The delicate, beating thing within.

How easily it could be silenced.

Agatha sat down on the warm stones. She closed her eyes and she wept.

Part IV

Chapter 29

On one of her trips to Miles City, soon after she'd started dropping Sagar off and taking the car on drives around the Cotton River Valley, Janavi was walking along Bridge Street when she passed a large plate glass window. She stopped and found that she was in front of an old-time bar. There was a taxidermy animal standing on a raised platform behind the window of the bar. The platform was shaped like a rock and around the rock were a few miniature trees. The intended effect, she realized, was to make it look as if the animal was walking through one of the many forests that blanketed Montana, mostly in the western part of the state. The animal looked to Janavi like a chinkara, though it couldn't be because its horns were curled backward instead of sticking straight up. Besides, she didn't think there were any chinkara in the Americas. Still, she stood for a long while and looked into its eyes. Its eyes looked back at her. She couldn't believe, given how lifelike it looked, that in the next second or the second after that, the animal wouldn't blink or charge at her or simply turn and walk away. She asked it, "What is greater? Your stillness? Or mine?"

She searched its eyes some more.

But then, just as it seemed the chinkara-like animal was going to answer her, she noticed one of the patrons, seated closest to the window, watching her, and so she turned to leave. That's when she spotted the plaque embedded in the sidewalk. She'd of course seen plenty of plaques on buildings and various monuments and even on signs along the highway, but she'd never seen one inserted into a sidewalk. It read, AT THIS EXACT LOCATION, ON JUNE 18, 1887, NOTHING WHATSOEVER HAPPENED. What a strange thing to put on a plaque! She walked away and realized, after some thought, that it was meant to be funny. And it was, in its way. On the drive home, she considered the plaque some more. She rounded a bend on the Cotton River Road, glimpsing the river through the thrushes and the wild orache, and maybe it was the sparkle of the river or the way the water was rippling just so — as if seducing the chinkara in the window to come and take a long drink — nevertheless she decided, in that moment, that the plaque was wrong. Something *had* happened in that exact location, on that exact day, June 18, 1887. What was it that had happened? Janavi had no way of knowing. How could she? And probably no one alive had any way of knowing. But something knew. Something always did. She thought of her amma dying all alone, by the side of Lahartara Road. She thought of Bulbul dying, on that same road. And then she thought of herself, wanting to die, standing in the Ganga and longing to be swept away. No one had engraved plaques to these things, and yet they had happened, hadn't they?

She looked at the prairie on one side of her.

And then she looked at the river on the other.

And it was then that she knew. It was then that she understood what held all memory.

And now, she thought it again, as she and Sagar watched the truck drive away.

They had managed, after a treacherous combination of speeding to catch up to the F-150 and then blinking their headlights and waving frantically out of the window, to get the driver to pull over. The storm had mostly passed, leaving a steady rain. They approached the truck, and as they did, Janavi felt a sudden surge of fear. Guns. She said, "Wait," but Sagar went on ahead to the driver's side. She followed him. He waved awkwardly and took a tentative step forward when the driver raised a hand in return. Through the rain-splattered window, Janavi saw two women, both young. The radio was turned up, and neither made a move to turn it down. Sagar signaled for the driver to roll down her window, but she and her friend looked at each other and laughed and then she shook her head. Through the spattering of rain against the windows, Sagar yelled, "Do you know someone named Gabe?"

The driver stared at him.

"Gabe. Do you know Gabriel Bowman?" Louder this time.

The woman shrugged. They waited.

"She doesn't," Janavi said.

Sagar looked at her, desperately, and then back at the driver. Janavi nudged him. It wasn't a raptor's claw painted on the hood of the truck; it was flames. The truck pulled away. She and Sagar were drenched, and they stood like that, in the rain, for a long while saying nothing.

"What if it had been Gabe?" she asked.

"It wasn't," he said.

The rain dripped down her face. She wanted to say, It doesn't matter, but she knew that it did. Gabe and the F-150 Raptor were the only leads they'd had. Seeing Sagar, his head bent low, with the road and the prairie beyond him darkened by rain, she saw for the first time that it was not only her need, and Ophelia's, but Sagar's. He needed to understand Renny's death. And she saw, too, that it was not merely to get his job back, or to keep from returning to India, but that there was a deeper, more primal reason. What could it be? Had he been in love with Renny? The thought came with such a rush of sorrow that she had to steady herself. The rain fell and fell. It was like a monsoon rain — warm but not comforting, a deluge without end. She told herself, looking at the sky, her eyes open against the rain, No, I don't believe that. But they shared this now. Along with leaving India, they shared this now: standing alone in America.

Sagar's voice, thin, as if reaching her from a long way away, said, "Let's go."

And it was then that Janavi looked at him, at his crestfallen face, and thought, On this day, in this exact location, nothing whatsoever happened.

The seasons were changing. They'd arrived at the beginning of spring, and now autumn was approaching. The heat and the summer storms and the humidity made way, in the early mornings and in the evenings, for a chill in the air. Janavi looked out at the prairie from the car window and was reminded of the cold that hung over Varanasi on winter mornings, and everyone crouched, wrapped in woolen dupattas, and the small fires kindled in the alleyways. Even the little goats and stray dogs came sniffing toward the warmth of the fires.

They bought their tickets back to India. Billings to New York to London to Mumbai to Varanasi. It seemed the best thing to do. Even so, Janavi started looking for jobs. Not Impact Youth, and maybe not in Montana, but there had to be child welfare agencies all over the country — one of them might be willing to hire her and sponsor their visas. She didn't tell Sagar. Not yet. She found a listing for an agency in Kansas City that looked promising. They specifically stated that international applicants would be accepted. But when she submitted her résumé, within an hour she got an automated email stating the position had been filled.

She filled out more applications. She dragged the suitcases from the back of the hall closet and dusted them off.

She thought about telling Papa that Sagar had lost his job, and that she was looking for one. But his voice, when she called, sounded tired. He said he was taking some new medication whose side effect was fatigue. Then he said, "I wish you could visit, Beti."

"Maybe I can," she said. "Sooner than you think."

When he asked what she meant, she said, "Nothing. I'm just worried about you."

She was also worried about Sagar. He'd stopped reading articles, he'd stopped researching and analyzing, he'd stopped staying up till dawn trying to find an explanation; he'd even abandoned the computer model he'd been building. Instead, he went to Sweet Molly's every night. When he left that night, Janavi drove to the convenience store. Mandy wasn't working and the cashier, a young woman she'd never seen before, said she didn't even know Mandy. Maybe their shifts didn't overlap? "Do you know Aaron?" Janavi said.

The girl looked at her, clearly irritated. "What's your deal, lady? You gonna buy something or what?"

Janavi bought a Slurpee and sat in the car in the store's parking lot. After a long while, a man pulled in beside Janavi's car, bought a pack of cigarettes and some kind of soda, and then he left. The cashier, who Janavi saw clearly through the lighted windows, took out her phone and stared at it. She didn't move. Her sudden cessation of movement, and the utter lack of nighttime noises, even of cars passing or the scurrying of nocturnal animals, and the dazzling white of the store's lights made Janavi feel as if she were inside an aquarium, looking out into a world that was familiar only as a dimensionless screen, and not one through which she'd always traveled.

She tried Rajni again. She'd called and texted many times since the false hang-up, but Rajni had texted back only once, writing, *Will call later*. Janavi didn't expect her to pick up this time either, since she would probably be at the college, given that it was morning for her, but she tried her anyway. When she picked up immediately, Janavi said, surprised, "Aren't you at work?"

There was a pause. Janavi heard noises in the background. She listened for Pavan's voice.

"I quit," she said.

"You quit? But . . . why?"

Another pause. A thought crossed Janavi's mind; she could hardly contain her excitement. "Are you pregnant?"

"No," Rajni said. Her denial was so swift and certain that it sounded like a rebuke.

"Then why?"

She said, "Pavan asked me to."

"He asked you to? Why on earth would he do that?"

There was rustling. A car horn. Janavi strained her ears, trying to understand something of her sister's silence. Finally, she said, "It was becoming too much for me."

"The class load?"

"I suppose so," she said vaguely.

"Did they give you more classes? More students?"

"No."

"Was it your colleagues?"

"Sort of. Most of them are men, you see, and, well, you know how it is."

Janavi guessed at what she was saying. "There're laws, Rajni. Against harassment. You should talk to the principal. Let her know. You should file a complaint."

"It's not like that, Janoo."

"Then . . ."

"Pavan . . . well, he was uncomfortable."

Pavan? What was she talking about? "Are you saying he asked you to quit? Because of your male colleagues?"

Silence. "I wouldn't say *because* of them."

"What would you say?"

Rajni didn't answer. "Papa's tests came back."

Janavi thought of her ChildDefense training. You didn't ask the children questions; you waited for them to offer answers. She said, "Did they find anything?"

"Not yet."

"It's been months!"

"Could be asthma. The air is so smoky here." Her voice was forlorn.

Janavi said, "It's not just the open fires. It's also the diesel smoke and the — "

Rajni interrupted her. "Is it hard for you?"

"Is what hard for me?"

"Marriage."

Hard? She wanted to tell her everything — about Renny and Ophelia and Sagar and the dam and . . . but she knew that's not what she was asking. "Yes," she said, "at times. A lot of times. But I'm sure it is for everybody."

She could almost see her sister nodding absently, thinking of other things.

After they got off the phone, Janavi finished her Slurpee and gazed some more at the inside of the store. The cashier was still on her phone. She looked at the displays, at what she could see of them, and then she looked at the Slurpee machine and the coffee machine and the hot dog machine — she focused on the pink hot dogs, spinning and spinning with the slowness and patience of monks. Then she thought about Pavan seated on the throne at the wedding reception. How regal and charming he'd seemed.

But none of it was true, was it?

Beneath the charisma and the gregariousness was a small, jealous man. Why else would he ask Rajni to quit her job? Because some of her colleagues were men? It was absurd, petty, and possessive. And how dare he speak to Raju in the way that he had? She sat fuming. She had half a mind to call Pavan and tell him off, but she remembered about Ravi, and of how her meddling had left Rajni weeping, and so she refrained. She wished Mandy were here.

When she got home, Sagar still wasn't back. She lay on the sofa, her eyelids heavy, listening to the last of the summer winds howling through the branches of the elm tree. She fell asleep, dreaming of a little girl on a tire swing. Her back was to Janavi, and though she wanted her to, and kept wishing she would, the girl never once turned.

Janavi was going to the grocery store in Mansfield to buy milk and pasta and chicken and vegetables. Before she left, she said, "Do you want to go to the Asian grocers in Billings instead? We could get Indian vegetables." And then, smiling, she added, "And Kurkure." But Sagar said no, he didn't.

When she got back, they ate dinner and then they watched television. The football season had started, and Sagar wanted to watch the Monday night game. Neither of them knew how the game was played. The teams that were playing were called the Kansas City Chiefs and the Detroit Lions. Janavi watched for the first few minutes, her mind wandering, but then she noticed Sagar. He was leaning forward, his hands clasped, and so absorbed in the game that she wondered if he'd bet on it. What was he doing? Trying to work out how the game was played, obviously, but there seemed to be an added intention, an intensity. At a commercial break, she said, "What do you think of it?"

He said, "Did you see? When that one player dropped the ball, and the other team got it, did you see the look on his face?"

"No. Why?"

Sagar was silent. The night air hung heavy. Janavi looked out of the window. Not a single leaf fluttered. There were no stars. She thought, This is how it will be. This day, and all the days to come. No wind, no heavenly light. Watching a game neither of us understands. GET OUT GO HOME. The words came floating back as if they'd always been there, just at the edge of her vision. Finally, Sagar said, "Did you know that when a notch is made, the jackhammer is mounted on a barge, and that's how it reaches the dam? No one ever thinks of that. That's the only way for a jackhammer to get to the middle of a river. I tell them, and people are always surprised. It makes sense, of course, but no one ever thinks of it."

"I didn't either."

"Not the only way. Aerial might work . . ." His voice faded, even and uninterested.

Janavi wanted to ask a question, keep him talking, but none came to mind.

They were still watching the commercials at halftime when Janavi got up to get a glass of water. She was at the sink when Sagar's phone rang. It rang and rang. When she came back into the living room, she said, "Who was that?"

Sagar didn't look up from the television. He said, "I don't know. My phone is in the bedroom."

She went to find it. It was on his side of the bed, still plugged in from the morning. She looked at the missed call on the screen and brought it to the living room. He said, "Who was it?"

Janavi held out the phone and said, "That's strange."

Sagar looked up from the television.

"You haven't heard from him since Renny's funeral, have you?"

"Who?"

She handed it to him. "Alex Mendoza," she said.

And in what felt like the first time in months, Sagar smiled.

Chapter 30

They met at Sweet Molly's.

Sagar couldn't express his relief, his gratitude, at seeing Alex Mendoza walk through the door, meeting his eyes, shaking his hand with such open emotion it was if they were two brothers separated by war. When they sat down, at one of the tables in the back, all he could think to say was "I've come here every night this week."

Alex Mendoza chuckled and said, "Don't be fooled, Saag. Alcoholism's only fun for the first decade."

Sagar laughed, and after so long a time — he couldn't remember the last time — the sound of it was unfamiliar. They drank beers and Alex told him about a new job he was on — a conservation project on the Yellowstone. "Fish habitats," he said, and then, when he asked whether Sagar was working, he told him about his visa running out.

"I could try to find another sponsor for our visas, but I haven't looked. The demand for hydraulic engineers, especially the overseas kind, isn't great."

Alex Mendoza was astonished; he'd had no idea about the visa constraints. "Sixty days? What the hell can you do in sixty days?"

Sagar said nothing.

"My parents came over from Mexico," Alex Mendoza said. "Crossed over illegally. Reagan gave 'em amnesty. They picked lemons in California. Santa Paula. That's where I was born. Don't know how the hell they ended up in Montana, but they did. They live up in Glasgow now. My dad's a professional wasps' nest remover."

"Wasps' nests? Really? I didn't know they were such a problem."

"Especially in summer. They love grasshoppers. Every time I go up there in the summer, soon as I pull up the wasps swarm my tires. They feed on the dead grasshoppers stuck in the treads."

Sagar wrinkled his nose. "How did he get into that business?"

"Runs in the family," Alex Mendoza said, "from back in Mexico."

"It's a family business? Knocking down wasps' nests?"

"You could say that," he said. It was a common profession in many parts of the world, he told Sagar. And then he said, "Renny had a wasp problem at her house too. Funny . . . it was one of the last things she told me."

They both grew quiet at the mention of Renny.

The jukebox played a country song, and a group of men laughed at something one of them said and a dog at their feet looked up and sniffed the air and then laid its head back down. Jake wasn't there, and Sagar didn't know the name of the bartender. "It's bullshit," Sagar said, suddenly frustrated. "Nobody gives a shit. She goes on a picnic and . . . and that's it. She dies and nobody gives a shit. I went out there and no way. No way she was swept through the notch."

Alex Mendoza looked at him and then at his empty bottle of beer. He went to the bar and came back with two more. He said, "We're building fish ladders. On the Yellowstone's diversion dam. You should see those fish go. Uphill all the way. But they keep at it." He took a sip of his beer and met Sagar's eyes. He said, "They get there. They get there eventually."

Sagar also took a sip.

They talked for a while longer. Then Alex Mendoza said, "I didn't call you to tell you about no wasps' nests and fish ladders, Saag."

Sagar waited. Alex looked around the bar, a quick sweep with his eyes, and said, his voice lowered, "Sam Dooley called me. Little bit before the notch. He wanted me to do some odd jobs for him."

"Like what?"

"Testing around his family's property, mostly. Water quality, salination, that kind of thing."

"Where's the family property?"

"On the reservoir. Didn't you know? Been in the family for a couple of generations. One of the fancy ones."

Sagar froze. His thoughts ground to a halt.

"The thing is, he needed a diver. Underwater equipment."

"He has a house? On the reservoir?"

"Wanted photos too."

"A diver? And photos? You don't need a diver and photos to — "

"Exactly." Alex Mendoza looked straight at him. "Might be good if someone looked into that, don't you think?" And then he said, "You remember what I told you? About the guy from Jalisco?"

"Yes."

"The thing is, those guys, and Sam was one, they were so cocky none of 'em even turned to see if anyone was watching. If anyone might see them. Not one. That's what the rich, the powerful, have over us, Saag. They don't have to turn to look."

Sagar nodded, understanding without understanding.

When Sagar got home, he told Janavi everything he and Alex Mendoza had talked about. When he finished, Janavi said, "We have them in India."

"What?"

"Professional wasps' nests removers. I once saw a wasps' nest as big as a jackfruit." And then she said, "Did he say anything more about Renny? Did he know where Gabe might be?"

Sagar shook his head.

When they went to bed that night, he watched her braid her hair, as she did every night. She gathered the curls, pulled them back. He wanted to say, Let me, but he didn't know how to braid hair. And maybe she'd laugh at him if he told her he only wanted to touch it. To feel the plaits in his hands. He wanted to bury his face in it, not to weep, as he'd seen men do in the movies, and not to inhale its scent, which he'd also seen them do, but to reach the coolest and deepest part of it. The darkest of its waters. She took no notice of him and turned off the lamp on her side of the bed. He did, too, though he lay awake for a long while. Had they come any distance at all? Since he'd lain next to her on the motel bed after his first day of work? A diver. Why had Sam Dooley needed a diver? And a family home on the reservoir. How had Sagar not known that Sam Dooley owned property along the reservoir? And did this have anything to do with Gabe telling Jake about the reservoir?

Janavi's breathing evened.

It was after 2 a.m. He got up and went to the kitchen for a glass of water. He stood at the window looking into the shadowed branches of the elm tree.

A diver. Sam Dooley had wanted a diver.

Maybe he shouldn't be looking for Gabe. Maybe he should be looking for something else.

The branches of the elm tree swung in the wind. "Is that you, Charlene?" he asked. He listened some more and then, just as he was about to turn away and go back to bed, an idea came to him. A small one, a wobbly one, but an idea, nonetheless. No, he thought, that makes no sense. But the idea wouldn't let go. It held.

Chapter 31

There was a thick layer of mist on the water. Janavi was seated on the bank of the river watching as it burned away, disappearing so slowly, so imperceptibly that she wondered if it were she and not the mist that was dissolving. She'd been to the Ganga one early morning on a festival day long ago, when she'd been a girl, but she couldn't recall whether there had been such a thick mist on its waters. There had been so many people gathered on the ghat and in the water, and so many worshippers bathing, that perhaps the mist couldn't form. Is that how it worked? I should ask Sagar, she thought.

He was already in the water. He'd said, climbing out of the car, "Dive with me," and she'd laughed and said, "I don't even know how to swim."

He'd looked at her, astonished, and said, "But you were born and raised next to the largest river in India!"

She'd watched as he'd taken off his shoes and his shirt and his pants. He was wearing swimming trunks underneath. He was determined. He'd woken her up, just after 5 a.m., and said, "We've got to go. I know it's early."

"Where?"

"The reservoir," he'd said.

They'd driven in the half-light, and then crept along the gravel driveways on the fancy side of the reservoir. The south-facing side. On the others were mostly fishing shacks and empty lots. "How do you know their name will be on the mailbox?" she'd asked.

"I don't," he'd said.

He'd brought a flashlight, and from the passenger seat, she'd pointed it into the darkness. There was a place that rented kayaks and paddleboards. After that were only houses. She'd scanned the end of the driveways. A few houses in, she'd said, "I don't see any mailboxes."

"What do you mean?"

"None of them have mailboxes."

He'd stopped the car and gotten out. He'd looked up and down the road. "Dammit," he'd said, climbing back in.

"What?"

"P.O. boxes. I should've known. There's no mail delivery here."

They'd sat in the car, the sound of the engine the only sound, the sun rising. Its pool of spreading light only increasing their misery. "Let's keep going," she'd said. "Maybe — maybe we'll find something."

Sagar hadn't protested.

They'd driven another twenty minutes or so, and that's when she'd seen it. "Stop, stop. Look," she'd said.

And there, at the entrance to a driveway, was a wooden sign carved with a last name.

Sagar had stopped the car and leaned over. DOOLEY. He'd smiled so wide she thought she could see something of the boy he'd been. He'd taken her hand, squeezed it, and said, "You're a genius." He'd then driven a few houses farther, to an open lot, and they'd followed a rough path through cottonwoods and tamarisks to the water. At its edge she'd sat down, leaned against a tree trunk, and watched as Sagar, with the confidence that only strong swimmers had, approached the reservoir. She'd watched his slender back, his tufts of hair like black foam, the muscles of his calves tightening, releasing. He'd walked into the water without a moment's hesitation, and then, after a few steps, he'd slid beneath it, silently, so that none of the occupants of the houses would be woken, though not many seemed to be here; they were mostly second homes, he'd told her. The water had received him. Hardly a ripple and he'd been gone. She sat, in the sudden aloneness, and was struck with a kind of terror. It seemed like an afterlife — the still, indigo-dark water, the far, unattainable shore, the light not yet reaching, maybe never reaching the forest floor. He was gone for what felt like hours. "Come up, come up, come up," she whispered bravely, but with a rising panic.

And then he did.

He looked toward her and shook his head and went back in again.

She felt better now that she'd seen him. And the world became familiar again. The mist was nearly burnt off, and the edges of the houses and the trees grew clearer. Would he find anything? His theory was that there might be something in the reservoir — if Gabe had spoken of it, and Sam Dooley had wanted a diver — but what? He came up again and again, took a lungful of air, and then dove back down. Finally, with the sun just below the treetops, he swam toward her and then walked out of the reservoir. As he came up, the water slid off his body, and she thought of seals, river otters. Slick and solitary and half water. She wondered . . . she wondered what it would be like . . .

He said, "I'm a fool. Should've known it would be too murky." She saw the disappointment in his face, his frustrated glance backward. "I could go in again," he said, "with more light. Equipment."

"Someone might see you," she said. There were NO TRESPASSING signs everywhere. And behind the NO TRESPASSING signs, she knew, were guns. "Besides, you told me the reservoir was eight miles long."

Sagar toweled off and said nothing.

When they got home, he took a shower and said he was taking a nap. He said, "Don't wake me up for lunch. I'm not hungry."

She was listless. She tiptoed around the apartment, not wanting to wake Sagar. She wasn't all that hungry either, and after eating leftover macaroni and cheese that had been spiced with jalapeños, she left Sagar a note and went to Lottie's house. When she got there, Lottie was taking grocery bags out of the car. Janavi helped her carry them in. Lottie held up a six-pack and said, "Have a beer with me."

Janavi laughed and said, "I just had lunch."

"Good," Lottie said. "Only a rookie drinks on an empty stomach."

She opened a bottle of beer and handed it to Janavi, and then she opened a bottle for herself. "You don't want a glass, do you? No? That's what I say. Drink it out of the bottle like a ranching woman."

Janavi hadn't planned to, but before she was halfway through her beer, she began telling Lottie of how she and Sagar had gone to the reservoir and of how Sam Dooley had asked Alex Mendoza for a diver and of how Sagar suspected there might be something in the waters around the Dooleys' lake house. Something Sam Dooley had wanted to dredge up.

Lottie said, "Did he find anything?"

"No."

Lottie looked at her. "I wouldn't go poking around the Dooley house if I were you."

"Because it's private property? I know. We were careful."

"They're powerful, V. Around here, at least. Big fish in a small pond."

"Then whatever Mayor Dooley was trying to dredge up should be easy to find."

By the look on Lottie's face, Janavi sensed that that's not what she had meant.

"They're rich. And respected. They've funded the 4-H kids, helped with building the community center, and not one of them misses a single Sunday church service. Even helped the tribe out. I remember one time, this was years ago, the father, Sam Dooley's, deeded a couple of rental houses over to the tribe. Just like that. Nice ones too."

"Why did he do that?"

"Long story. Felt bad for 'em, I guess. You see, their daughters had run off. Sixteen, seventeen. Probably with their boyfriends. You know how girls that age can be. Nobody ever heard from them again. I guess Fred, the father, felt bad for their families. The girls' parents were renting from him, and he just up and signed over the deeds to them. Native, like I said. Didn't owe them a thing."

Janavi thought it over. "Nobody's that nice."

Lottie laughed. "You sound like me."

"I met them," Janavi said. "At the town hall meeting. Not both of them, just Susan Dooley."

"What'd you think of her?"

"She seemed nice . . ."

"I gave her piano lessons. When she was a girl."

"You did?"

"Her mama brought her out to the ranch and there she'd be, banging on the keys for an hour."

"Was she any good?"

"Oh god no! But she stuck with it. She got a little better, but not by much. Didn't practice a whit. She was spunky though. Strange in a way, but maybe every child is strange in some way. I remember this one time, after a lesson, she was waiting for her mother to come pick her up. I had enough to do without having to babysit her after her lesson, so I let her wander around the house. When her mother gets there, we couldn't find Susie anywhere. Called her name all over the house, went out to the barn, the pond, nothing. Finally, I open the door to the basement and yell down her name and there's no response, but just as I was about to close the door, I smelled smoke. I go downstairs and poke around and there she is, just sitting under the stairs. Must've heard her name being called, but she was paying no attention. She was turned away from me. And when I crept up behind her to see what she was doing, I see that she's cutting out paper doll chains. You know what they are? You all make them over in India? You do? Well, this girl was so absorbed in making those chains, so meticulous in how she cut them out, I couldn't believe it. Absolutely perfect edges and extra details added on, like little curls at the ends of the doll's hair. You'd think she was about to put them up in a museum, they were so perfectly done." Lottie sat back in her chair. She said, "And you know what she did then? After she cut them out?"

Janavi shook her head.

"She burned 'em. Set those doll chains on fire."

"Burned them?"

"I mean, lots of kids play with matches. But why not just burn the paper? Why spend all that time cutting them out just to burn them?"

Janavi didn't know either.

Lottie said, "You better believe she got a spanking. From both me and her mama. Could've burned the damn house down." She was quiet, and then she said, "Stayed with me though, her all hunched over and focused and then setting the thing she'd made on fire."

Janavi didn't say anything to Lottie, but she could relate. She thought of herself after Amma's death, and of how she'd hit her classmates without cause and snipped the ants crawling past her in two. Only destruction had made any sense. "She told us she and Sam Dooley were high school sweethearts. Is that common here?"

"Suppose so, but we all could've guessed."

"Why?"

"Two of the richest families in the valley? And the two kids growing up together, couple of years apart? Might as well have been arranged."

Janavi smiled. "Are they that rich? Both families?"

"Put it this way," Lottie said. "The Stowells, that's Susan's maiden name, gift every baby that's born into the family with a horse, the minute they're born. Every single one of them is an equestrian. As for the Dooleys, they might be even richer. Houses, boats. One time, one of their cars got stolen. Right off their driveway, the one along the reservoir. A seventy-four Camaro, I believe, a rare model of some sort. Couldn't be bothered to report it. Didn't want to take the time. Filing a police report was too much trouble, I guess. Can you believe that?"

Horses for every baby? Stolen rare cars that went unreported? No, she couldn't.

Janavi left soon afterward.

On the walk home she thought about Camaros and wondered what they looked like, and then she thought about paper doll chains.

Her phone rang.

Was it Rajni? It couldn't be. It was the middle of the night in India.

She looked at the screen. Norma. How had she gotten her number? She was about to ask, but as soon as she answered, Norma said, "Can you come down to the reservation?"

"Why?"

"She knows you. And didn't you say you'd worked with children in India? You're probably the best one to watch her."

"Watch who?"

"Ophelia," she said.

Beatrice

Cotton River, 1963

Beatrice wanted to be like fire.

She knew the course of fire was the reverse of the course of water. Water spread out like a fan. Into valleys, floodplains, seabeds. Into wide basins, plateaus, and mesas. But fire was the opposite. Fire sought out the narrow gorges between rock faces and box canyons. It hurtled down the deep and tapered rifts, gaps, and coulees of the Cotton River Valley. Fire, Beatrice knew, harnessed the power of wind and rock — all three tightened, gathered and relentless.

At the bar, Johnny was trying to talk to a woman with dyed blonde hair Beatrice had never seen before. Older than Beatrice, and probably older than Johnny, too, though not by much. Just enough, Beatrice thought, to teach him a thing or two. That's what Johnny would be thinking too: that the woman was older, and that if he could get her in bed, she'd most likely be feisty, as older women were, and could probably teach him a couple of tricks. That might be true. But what Beatrice was thinking (watching the way the woman barely regarded Johnny, and completely disregarded his charms) was that the best thing she could do was show him something about being a man, by pointing out (in you, Johnny) the boy.

It was after one o'clock in the morning, and Beatrice had to pick up her daughter, Leah, at Leah's dad's at eight. It was a two-hour ride back to get her car and then a one-hour ride to Leah's dad's.

When she tapped Johnny on the shoulder and mentioned this — that the earliest they could get back was three in the morning, and she had to pick up Leah at eight — he smiled sweetly at the blonde woman, who was drinking her whiskey and soda and not even looking in Johnny's direction, and pushed Beatrice toward the back wall and hissed, "Leah? You think I give a shit about when you have to pick up Leah? Can't you see I've got a good thing going here?" Then, maybe because he saw the look on her face, his voice softened, and he bent down to her ear. "She's loaded, B. Loaded, I tell you. Let me do this. Let me do this for us."

She knew that voice and she knew those words, and so, after downing the rest of her beer, Beatrice left the bar. She started walking, and then she started whistling. Her dad had once told her, "Whistling is what gauchos do," and so that's what Beatrice did. The dark didn't scare her, nor did the desolate roads. What *did* scare her? Not picking up Leah on time; Leah forgetting who she was; Leah feeling, ever in her life, a single day of unhappiness; wasps; the thought of their hives and all those openings and how they were constantly crawling in and out of them; Leah dying. When a truck pulled up and offered her a ride, Beatrice looked up and down the road, and into the tall of the moonlit trees, and climbed in. The man asked her name. She usually didn't tell people her real name when she was hitching, but tonight she told him the truth. "Beatrice," she said.

"After Dante's — "

"Yes," she said, cutting him off, "after her." That's why she didn't tell people her real name; they liked to show off.

A few hours before she was murdered, while she was seated in the passenger seat, her hair blowing in the wind — cool and sweet and scarlet, greater than the prophets, the undying kings — Beatrice decided she would make pancakes for Leah in the morning. In animal shapes, the kind the mothers in movies made: a bear and an elephant and maybe even a whale. Leah would like that. I, Beatrice decided, won't be like the ones who killed themselves, the ones who poured themselves into whatever valley would have them. She would be methodical, disciplined. She would be like fire. She would travel the narrow gorges, the ones millions of years had made smooth, and that had one entrance, one exit. One way through.

Chapter 32

Janavi had come home from visiting Lottie and had said, "Get up. Get up. We have to go."

"Where," he'd said, rubbing his eyes.

He'd slept a little during his nap, but mostly he'd lain awake. Drifting, still, in the waters of the reservoir. He hadn't found anything, but what had he been looking for? The cold of the water, its silken hands — he'd barely felt them when he'd been underwater, he'd been so focused on discovering whatever it was that Sam Dooley might've wanted to find. But he felt them now and felt, too, his stupidity. He knew the depth of the reservoir. He should've known it would be too obscure, algae-ridden, to see much below the surface. It was farcical to think he could — searching a mucky reservoir that was eight miles in length and a mile wide at times for a thing he couldn't even name. But the water. The last time he'd swum in this way had been on a work trip to Rishikesh. He'd forgotten how silent and soft and dark — not a lightless dark, but a tremulous one — the world beneath the water could be. The eroticism of it. The taking in of one body by another. Once, when he'd come up for air, he'd seen Janavi sitting on the shore, against the cottonwood tree, and she'd seemed so distant, so unreachable, that he'd despaired, but then, just as he was about to dive back under, she'd begun to wave, frantically, like a child, delighting him, and he'd thought, This is what it must feel like to sight land after a long time at sea.

She was saying, "Hurry. Get dressed. We have to go."

"Where?"

"To Norma's house. She needs us to watch Ophelia."

He'd never seen her so excited. She was packing a bag of snacks and a Noddy and Big-Ears book she'd had since she was a girl — *Noddy Has an Adventure* — and then she looked anxiously around the apartment and said, "Maybe we should go buy some toys."

He'd laughed and said, "Where? Billings?"

When they got to Norma's house, she told them Ophelia was just waking up from a nap, and then she said, "Wouldn't have called you, except . . . she likes you."

Janavi, beaming, said, "How can you tell?"

Norma said, "She watched you leave. Back at the ranch. She waved."

Janavi only smiled, but Sagar said, "You couldn't have called anyone better."

Norma went in the back and brought Ophelia out by the hand. Janavi knelt to say hello. Ophelia, rubbing her eyes, gazed at Janavi, and Sagar saw how easily Ophelia's hand was guided from Norma's into Janavi's. He was charmed by it, and seeing Janavi smile as she did, the way her posture suddenly lightened, as if she were about to dive into a warm, blue sea (but she can't swim, he reminded himself), he thought, in a way that he never had before, What a beautiful woman she is!

Norma left, saying she had some urgent business to take care of.

Sagar looked around. Neither he nor Janavi had been to her house before. Janavi and Ophelia sat on the sofa in the living room, and Janavi showed her *Noddy Has an Adventure*, and asked if she wanted to read it. Ophelia looked from her to the book and then back at Janavi. She nodded. Sagar listened as Janavi read, and he studied Ophelia's face, looking for Renny. Their mouths were the same, and the little girl's expression, curious, attentive, slightly bemused, was the same expression he'd seen on Renny's face.

"You think she might want a snack?"

Janavi paused in her reading and said, "We could try . . ."

He took the bag of food they had brought into the kitchen. He looked in the refrigerator and poured out a glass of orange juice. From the bag he dug out bread and peanut butter and jelly and cookies and then, at the very bottom, he saw a half-full bag of Kurkure, and he added them to the plates. When he came back to the living room, Ophelia had moved closer to Janavi. They were nearly snuggling, peering at the pictures together. He set the plates on the coffee table. Janavi put the book down and said to Ophelia, "All this reading is making me hungry. Aren't you?"

Ophelia, of course, said nothing.

They waited. Sagar had prepared the exact same plates of food for himself and Janavi. He and Janavi ate them with great relish as Ophelia looked at them, wide-eyed. She was still seated on the sofa, her little legs sticking straight out toward Sagar. Janavi held up a Kurkure and said, "Do you know what these are? They're called Kurkure, and they're an Indian snack. Indian from India." She put one in her mouth and closed her eyes and chewed with an expression of immense bliss. Sagar wondered whether the bliss was real or put on for Ophelia. When she opened her eyes again, she said, "My sister and I used to eat them when we were little. My sister, her name is Rajni, would eat them right then and there, handful after handful. But I would take them to our bedroom and crawl under the bed and lie on my tummy and eat them one at a time. That's really the best way to enjoy them. On your tummy."

Ophelia looked at her and then she looked at the plate.

Sagar and Janavi took their empty plates and went to the kitchen. Janavi said, "We've got to give her time to think it over."

They stayed in the kitchen for a long while. Putting away the food.

Washing and drying the plates. Wiping down the counters. When they could think of nothing else to do, Janavi signaled for Sagar to be quiet and tiptoed down the hall. There they hung back, and then, after Janavi shushed him with a finger to her lips, they peeked around the corner into the living room. Sagar saw that Ophelia was now standing, scrutinizing the plate of food. She didn't touch anything, but simply stared at it. He saw Renny most clearly now — in her daughter's suspicion, in the way her gaze so perfectly swept the surface, hungered for what was beneath. After a time, one chubby arm reached out and she picked up a Kurkure chip. Janavi turned to Sagar and smiled. They looked back again, and he thought she would take a bite, but instead, she climbed back onto the sofa, lay down on her tummy, and only then did she take a bite. Janavi, gleeful, swung around and threw her arms around his shoulders, and the softness of her breasts against his chest, and the scent of her hair rushing into his lungs was so sudden, and he so surprised, that before he could form a single thought, she swept out of his embrace and was looking at Ophelia again. She was eating the Kurkure now, slowly, and Janavi whispered, "I think she likes it," and it was true: She ate another.

They put Ophelia to bed at eight o'clock. He and Janavi then watched television. He said, "What do you want to watch?" Janavi, still jubilant from Ophelia eating the Kurkure, said, "You pick." He flipped through channels and eventually gave up and handed the remote control to Janavi.

Did he doze off?

He must have because he was jerked awake by loud voices. He and Janavi looked at each other.

They were coming from outside.

He and Janavi crept to the window. Norma was there, and a man he didn't recognize. Janavi whispered, "That's Gabe. The photo." Sagar looked again. And it was.

He was shouting, "Where is she? She in there? Let me have her."

Norma had her arm stretched toward him.

Sagar sprang toward the door, but Janavi held him back. "Wait," she said. "Wait to see what he says."

"She's safe, Gabe," Norma said. "I'm telling you she's safe. Won't let nothing happen to her."

"Where is she? She with them?"

"That's a promise."

"She's *my* daughter."

Norma, her voice even, said, "And Renny was like mine."

Gabe, who'd been waving his arms frantically, dropped them to his side.

"He knows we're here," Sagar said and stepped outside. Janavi was behind him. Gabe and Norma turned to them.

"*You . . .*" he sneered. "I know you. Both of you."

He was lankier than he had seemed in the photograph. A thin face, unkempt. He was wearing a cowboy hat and boots. Though he was probably ten years older than Sagar, he looked to him like a boy. A boy who believed dressing like a cowboy would turn him into one.

"From who?"

"None of your fucking business."

"Renny?"

Gabe didn't answer. He was standing in the shadows, at the edge of a rectangle of light that stretched across the grass.

Sagar took another guess. "Was it Dooley? Sam Dooley?"

He saw Gabe stiffen.

Norma said, "Thick as thieves in high school, from what I recall."

Ignoring her, Gabe looked at Janavi and said, "I heard you've been chasing my kid around. Stay the fuck away. You hear me? What business you got with her?"

Janavi said, "My mom died too. When I was a child."

Gabe said nothing; all four stood looking at one another. The night was still; the grass held its breath. A far-off coyote, somewhere to the west, Sagar guessed, howled. Out of this silence, Norma said, "You kill her, Gabe? You kill Renny?"

"Kill Ren — no!"

"But you know who did."

Gabe stared at Norma. He said, "No . . ." and by the sorrow in his voice, Sagar knew that he'd cared for Renny, had maybe even loved her.

"She didn't go swimming, Gabe," Sagar said. "That we know for sure."

He looked away.

Norma said, "You know how many of our girls have died? Been taken from us. I know you do." Gabe seemed pulled back to Norma's gaze, unwillingly, as if by the gravitational power of a planet. "Why was she in that reservoir, Gabe? What's in it? What's in that reservoir?"

Norma's questions, bleak and direct, sent a bolt of savagery up Sagar's spine, and he added, "I will drain it. I will drain the whole thing if I have to."

At those words, terror seemed to take hold of Gabe. His eyes darted from one to the other. A frightened animal. The block of light from the house reached the tip of his boots. Gabe looked down. He wants it to swallow him, Sagar thought. He wants it to drown him. "We was drunk," he said, his voice breaking. "We was drunk, driving around. Kids. We was just kids. I told her. I told Renny. Not everything, but she put it together though, you know how she was. And that's — that's . . ." He was quiet so long Sagar wondered if he would say more. Sagar saw him wobble, as if he'd been pushed, and then came a feral sound. Wild and desolate. He was sobbing. He said, "One of 'em . . . one of 'em might not have been all the way dead."

"One of who?" Norma asked.

But Gabe was already running. Into the dark. And as his truck pulled away, Sagar saw it on the hood, blazing through the shadows: a raptor's claw.

Chapter 33

The next morning, Sagar said, "I'm calling Sheriff Oswald." Janavi agreed. He picked up his phone, but he put it back down again and said, "No, I'm going to go see him."

He left after breakfast.

Janavi looked out of the kitchen window. The tire swing was empty. There was a dog in the yard she hadn't seen before. She wondered if the family who lived there had adopted the dog. And then she thought, I haven't seen the little girl or her brother in ages. Did they move? She hoped they hadn't. Why? She couldn't understand her kinship with the girl. To the listlessness and the boredom and the cadence of her days. It was as if she and the girl were connected by an invisible thread, and her swinging in the tire plucked at something in Janavi's heart. They were the same: both gazing through the chain-link fences, looking into the distance, watching the light bend toward the western sky, beseeching it to come back.

Janavi turned away from the window.

She walked through the living room and into the bedroom. The bed was still unmade. She lay down on it and stared at the ceiling. She thought of Ophelia's tiny hand on hers as they'd turned the pages of *Noddy Has an Adventure*. She saw again how spellbound she'd been looking at the drawings of Toyland and the red noses of Noddy and Big-Ears and their red-and-yellow car and the panicked policeman and the gray dog. At one point, Ophelia had swiveled her head and peered up at Janavi, as she'd been explaining to her what a gnome was, and the look in her eyes had been so trusting, so alive with beguilement and innocence, that Janavi thought how undeserving she was, how undeserving all adults were, with their betrayals and their deceptions and their avarice and the acid in their hearts.

Why had Gabe come? Obviously to find his daughter, but what had he meant when he'd said one of them might not have been all the way dead? And who, along with Gabe, had been drunk? Who had been a kid? And Renny — had she been killed because she'd known the answers to these questions?

It was the prairie. It was the prairie in its slyness and in its monotony that fooled you. Made it seem as if everything was knowable, visible, when really, the greatest mysteries were the ones that it hid.

She got out of bed abruptly and went back into the living room for her phone.

She called Rajni.

Rajni picked up, and the moment Janavi heard her voice, she was pierced with an aching need to see her. She said, "Hold on. I'm turning this into a video call."

Immediately, Rajni blurted out, "No!"

"What? Why not?"

"I'm not — it's been a long day. I look terrible."

Janavi laughed. She said, "I've seen you in the mornings. I've seen you blubbering, with snot running down your face. Hold on."

"No — "

When it switched to video, the screen was pointed away from Rajni, at a room with a wardrobe and a portion of a window that Janavi assumed was their bedroom. She said, "Come on, Raju. Who cares what you look like?"

The screen swiveled and when she saw Rajni's face, the hairs on the back of Janavi's neck stood up. There was a deep shadow across the left side of it. Janavi looked closer. No, it couldn't be. Rajni immediately placed a hand under her chin and over her cheek.

Janavi steadied her voice. "Why are you holding your face like that?"

"I told you. I'm tired. I was just about to fall asleep — "

"Why?"

Rajni looked away.

Don't provoke her, Janavi told herself; children and cornered animals didn't respond well to being provoked. "What did the doctor say? About Papa. Is it asthma?"

"Probably. They gave him an inhaler."

"I talked to him. His cough doesn't seem better."

"What do you expect? We live in a city with fires burning nonstop."

It was no use pretending.

"Did he hit you? Did he fucking hit you?"

"No! Of course not."

Janavi focused on her breathing. "Rajni. What happened?"

"It was nothing. We had an argument and it . . . well, it got out of control. You know how it is."

Janavi waited.

"He was waving his arms around. And . . . well — "

Rajni stopped. She looked directly into the phone.

Neither blinked. Neither said a word. The fury in Janavi was so pure, so crystalline, she could've reached through the glass of the screen and across the ten thousand miles between them and around the curve that was half the earth and taken Pavan by the throat. "I'm going to kill him," she said. "I'm going to fucking kill him."

"It was an accident, Janoo. I told you he was waving his hands around. I was too. And his arm sort of, you know, sort of . . ." And then she was crying. Sobbing. Janavi saw the tears, fat and full of sorrow, tumbling down her cheeks.

Don't worry, Amma. I'll take care of her.

"I'm coming," Janavi said. "I'll move my ticket up. Give me a day. One day, and I'll be in Varanasi. And Pavan — "

"No." Her voice was adamant. "You can't. I don't want you to."

"Why not? I could — "

"Janoo, no."

"But — "

"What will you do? Set his batting pads on fire?"

Janavi said nothing.

"Move what ticket up? To India?"

Janavi explained a little of what had happened, but not all of it. She left out the parts about the finger bone and Gabe and Ophelia. She left out the Elks Lodge meeting and all the opposition to the dam removal. She left out so much that she wasn't sure it made any sense. She said, "Raju, please, please go stay with Papa. And leave him. Leave the asshole . . ."

Rajni said, a little sadly, "It's not so easy, Janoo."

They got off the phone soon afterward, but only after Janavi made Rajni promise to call the next day.

Janavi stared at the phone in her hand, and then she crumpled to the floor and wept. She was still weeping when Sagar came home. He looked at her, alarmed, and said, "What is it? What's happened?"

"I'm going to kill him. I swear, I'm . . . Pavan . . ." She spit the name out as if it were venom in her mouth.

"What about him?"

"He . . . he . . ."

She collapsed against Sagar's chest. Her wailing filled the apartment, pummeled the walls. She felt a thing beating against her like a fist, and she knew it was Sagar's heart, but it reached her as the shriek of a thousand birds, wounded in a thousand ways. He tilted her face toward his, looked into her eyes, and said, "Tell me what's happened."

What was a man, but this? Fragile and heroic and helpless?

It was then that she kissed him, deeply, and she tasted such hunger that she didn't know if it was his or her own.

When the kiss ended, he nudged her away from him and said, "What's wrong, Janavi? What's happened?"

It wasn't words she wanted.

They were seated on the sofa, and with the next kiss she slid herself off it and pulled him down with her. Her foot pushed away the coffee table. Her hands fumbled with the buttons of his shirt. She kissed his neck, bit his ear, felt him harden against her hips. He said, "Janavi, no, wait, are you . . ." He gripped her face in his hands, hardly an inch from his own. He searched her eyes. What did he mean to find there? He said, "Are you sure?"

She nodded. Her face still stained by tears.

He took her hand and lifted her up off the floor and led her into the bedroom. He tried to unbutton her blouse, fumbled, and said, "How do these things work again?" She smiled and undid hers and then his and then, when they were lying together on the bed, his face trailing over her body with an incurable sweetness, she closed her eyes and the graininess of the sheet against her back was the prairie grasses, and she thought — his tongue at the bend of her waist — when did they become mine? This country, this unfamiliar earth, this body above me. His head was now between her legs. There is a matching depression behind his right ear too, she was thinking, as the gold of the afternoon raced to the tips of her toes and the wind whipped the stalks until they sang and sang, and when their voices could go no higher, she found herself co-cooned in a sudden silence, as if at the bottom of the sea. Or the inside of an empty cathedral.

She wanted to weep again, but this time with sorrow of a different kind.

Afterward, he went to the bathroom and came back with a towel and wiped her clean. He said, "You should go pee."

"I should?"

"Yes."

She came back into the bedroom and lay down on the bed, and she said, "That was way better than a Slurpee." Sagar burst out laughing, and it was this laughter, floating up out of the golden grasses, out of the late summer silence, that spilled like honey over the brim of the world.

Chapter 34

Sheriff Oswald listened to him, and then he narrowed his eyes and said, "You wouldn't be conducting your own investigation, would you?"

"I was there. I talked to him. If you're looking for Gabe — "

"Already spoke to him."

Sagar stared at him. "Did he tell you? That Renny knew something. Something that got her killed . . ."

Sheriff Oswald took out a piece of paper from his file and placed it in front of Sagar. "This is the autopsy report. 'Death by misadventure.' See that? That means drowning."

Sagar scanned it. "And what about this? Right here. The trauma to the head."

"She could've hit the side of the notch."

"She didn't swim *toward* the notch. Don't you see that? She didn't swim at all!"

Sheriff Oswald looked at him, unmoved.

"Was she wearing a swimsuit?"

Silence.

Sagar said, "There's a finger bone. It came from the reservoir. Renny found it. Or was given it — I don't — "

"Why didn't you bring it to the police?"

Sagar was stumped. And then annoyed. "From what I understand, the police aren't all that *enthusiastic* about investigating crimes against the tribe. Especially the ones against their women."

He was practically thrown out of the office.

He went home and found Janavi weeping, and then . . .

A chill set in. They woke to frost; the forecast called for snow flurries. None came, but Sagar walked again and again past the window, imagining he saw a flake or two falling.

They discussed for hours what could be done about Rajni. They could leave now; only Janavi could go; or they could both stay. She was on the phone for hours with her father — who was grief-stricken: "How did I not know, Beti? How could I not see?" he lamented — and with Rajni, who only defended Pavan; she even called her old boss, Ms. Sujata, to ask her advice.

After she got off the phone with her, she said to Sagar, "Should I call the police in Varanasi?"

He told her, "Probably Rajni has to do that. At least, she has to cooperate. Will she?"

Janavi said nothing and looked away.

Never, as he'd lain in bed beside her after sex, had he felt so exhausted and yet so undiminished. Her body had been more exquisite than he'd envisioned, and sometime in the night she had taken his hand, or maybe he'd taken hers, and they'd woken in the morning still holding each other's hands. He'd once read — somewhere, long ago — that leaves spin and flutter in the wind in summertime to keep their cells from drying out. Dying out. And he thought of it now, looking at Janavi seated on the sofa, quiet, pensive. And of how, holding her in his arms, naked, he'd felt something like those leaves, careening in too much light, such heat.

He wished it would snow so she'd be distracted from her worry.

Four weeks remained before their visas expired. Maybe it was for the best. Janavi could go back and care for Rajni. And there were so many dam projects in India he could probably easily find a job, even without Mack's recommendation.

He dreamt that night. He had no idea what the dream had been, but it woke him. He lay in bed listening to the sound of the wind howling past the eaves, and then he got up soundlessly and moved to the sofa. Maybe it was the wind that had woken him and not the dream. He listened. It was the Cowboy. Screeching for his revenge. He thought of Willie and Charlene and of Alex Mendoza and Renny and of that stormy afternoon under the tarp, and then he thought about all that had come after.

Suddenly, in what felt as if a blaring radio had been switched off, the wind went silent. Ceased completely. What was it Alex Mendoza had said? That this silence was each of the three, waiting for the other to speak.

Each of the three.

His thoughts wandered through the dark of the room, darted here and there, but didn't descend. Didn't catch. He'd been told as a child to count out the seconds between the lightning and the thunder, and he wondered, Is it the same with the wind? Why not? He started to count: one . . . two . . . three . . . and there it was again, the wind, rising in some cold northern place and hitting the Rockies and then sweeping down into the Cotton River Valley. Surging and then falling. Everything a pattern — the wind, the weather.

What was it though? About the number three?

He didn't mean in a numerological sense, or a religious one, but something more obvious. But if it was so obvious, why couldn't he think of it?

He turned on the television. A Western. He muted it. From what he could gather, it was about a group of men herding cattle. Where were they coming from and where were they going? He grew so intrigued that he unmuted the television and turned the volume to low. He moved from the sofa and sat on the floor, closer to the television. It soon became clear that they were in Texas. A couple of the characters were former Texas Rangers, and they were in a town along the Rio Grande. He realized then that he was at the beginning of the movie. It also soon became clear that the place they were herding the cattle to was Montana. Apparently, Texas had gotten too crowded, and they were going to Montana because it was pristine and untouched and would provide lots of grazing ground for the cattle. Sagar looked out of the window and thought, In a way, it still is all of those things. He got lost in the movie again, and he gasped when one of the characters, fording a river, was killed by snakes. The snakes were called water moccasins, and the man, caught in the middle of the river, was attacked by them. A young boy, also on the herding trip, turned his horse around, on the opposite bank, to see the man's hand come up out of the river clutching the writhing snakes. He screamed out, "Water moccasins," and that was it: A snake came out of the water, opened its mouth wide, and locked onto the man's cheek.

The episode ended on that breathless scene.

Sagar couldn't wait for the next installment, the following night.

He turned off the television and went back to the sofa. He lay on it and thought about the movie. It had ended, at least this segment, with another death. On another river.

People always underestimated the power of water, its strength, and even the strength of the creatures living within it, but Renny would've never done that. Of that he was certain. In fact, he remembered how the look in her eyes had changed, warmed, when he'd told her about diving in the Godavari, and of how he'd always loved rivers, since he was a boy. Since he was a boy . . .

He rubbed his eyes.

He went to the window and even in the dark, even in town, from their small apartment window, he saw why Montana was called Big Sky Country. It was obvious, driving anywhere, looking in any direction, that the sky, stretched high overhead, vast and arrogant and stubbornly unreachable, was the biggest and widest he'd ever seen. He wondered, Is it only here? Where else would the sky be this big? Certainly, nowhere he'd ever been in India. Maybe it could only be so in flat and sparsely populated places. Antarctica, he thought. Maybe the Serengeti. Siberia. Or the wilds of northern Canada. Then he thought of what Janavi had told him about the Inuit tribe. And of how they didn't have a numbering system past three.

Three, again.

How was it possible? he wondered. To not count past three? How did they count the birds, the stars? The number of years they had been alive? And then he thought, Maybe, instead of counting them, they simply see them. Though there was nothing simple about it, was there? To see a thing, to actually *see* it, was the most complicated effort in the world. It required a grace and a devotion and a stillness that eluded most men.

Of all the people he had ever met, the old man, at Sweet Molly's, he thought, would understand the necessary grace and devotion and stillness. Maybe he even had them in him. What was it that he had said? About the finger bone? Sagar had hardly been listening at the time, but it had stayed with him. What was it?

One of three, he'd said.

And then — patterns, memory — something Norma had said also came back to him. *Sometimes it's three at once.*

What a strange coincidence.

He went back to the sofa. He hadn't been imagining it . . . there *was* something with the threes. Maybe everywhere in the world, given the Trinity and the Trimurti and even his affection for the molecular formula for water — who knew how many other sacred variations of the number three there were in the world. But here, in the Cotton River Valley, it meant something very specific. It meant something very immediate and very precise, but what was it? He lurched off the sofa. He started to pace.

One of 'em . . . one of 'em might not have been all the way dead.

The elm tree. The three cottonwoods.

One of three.

Three at once.

The old man had been talking about who the finger bone had belonged to. And Norma had been talking about Native girls who'd gone missing. But who had Gabe been talking about? Were they all talking about the same three girls? Were they? And what if . . .

The thing is: If you wanted to drown something, in a reservoir, let's say, then why would you drown it in the waters adjacent to your family home? You wouldn't, of course. You'd drown it in the place farthest from your family home. And how would you drown it? You'd dump it from a boat or fling it from the shore. There were other ways, but these seemed the most likely. Sagar thought it over. What was it Gabe had said? He'd said they'd been drunk, and that they'd been driving. So, if you were driving, you'd use a gravel road, that way the tire tracks wouldn't be noticeable on any flattened patches of grass. And what was more, you'd do it in a place with very few people, so that the risk of being seen would be low. Where then, along the reservoir, far from the Dooley family home, were there gravel roads and not many people?

It was obvious. And no, unlike what he'd told Gabe, he couldn't drain the entire reservoir. But he could do the next best thing.

He left a note for Janavi. This time, he was going alone.

Miranda & Raja

Ganges River, 1968

Miranda walked out of her marriage of eleven years by leaving a note that read "Going to pick up eggs. Back soon!" She drove from her house in Rockford, Illinois, to Chicago, and then took a train from Chicago to New York. When she arrived in New York, she checked into a hotel room for the night, near Penn Station, and in the morning, she took a taxi to the airport and boarded a Pan Am flight to Delhi, with stops in Frankfurt and Karachi. Once she arrived in Delhi, she took a long pull of its winter air — woodsmoke and diesel fuel and frangipani and desert dust — and decided to spend a few nights in a hostel near Chandni Chowk. It was here that she met Raja, and it was Raja who led her to Varanasi.

The marriage that Miranda abandoned could be considered a classic American love story: She and Sam met in high school, in freshman algebra, and at prom their senior year Sam asked her to marry him. Miranda said yes for three reasons. The first was that she had no idea what she wanted to do after high school and marriage seemed like the least demanding and most grown-up of the various options (the others included being a secretary, a teacher, or a waitress). The second was that her mother was determined to sew her a wedding gown, and Miranda decided that the best way to avoid the fate of an ugly, homemade dress was to marry Sam the week after graduation (which would be far too short a time for her mother to sew one). What was more, if they married that week, they could honeymoon for free in Albuquerque, where Sam was scheduled to attend a sales conference before starting work at his dad's wholesale bathroom fixtures business. The third reason was simply that Miranda was too young and stupid to know any better.

The marriage proceeded briskly, and with the usual flourishes. Sam and Miranda bought a starter home (the down payment was Sam's parents' wedding gift to them). After suffering two miscarriages, they continued to try half-heartedly and then they stopped, without discussing it, because discussing it would've acknowledged, in a way neither of them wanted to acknowledge, that beauty and youth and rectitude were not enough; that they, too, could be punished by something as trivial and tacky as fate. In the fifth year of their marriage, Sam had an affair with his secretary; in the sixth, he had a one-night stand with the woman at the tailor's who was measuring him for a suit; in the eighth year, he had another affair — this one quite serious, with Sam contemplating divorce — with a woman who was the purchasing agent for a hotel chain and had contacted Sam regarding buying bathroom fixtures for a hotel that was being renovated. Miranda suspected all three affairs but had hard evidence for only one. When she, crying, confronted him with it, Sam said, "So what? You might want to try it. Might make you less of a hard ass."

In the eleventh year, the year Miranda left the marriage, nothing happened. Not really.

While listening to the radio, Miranda heard the story of a man who had only one leg (he had lost the other when he'd fallen while rock climbing), and yet, he had climbed to the summit of

Kilimanjaro. The following week, she and Sam were watching
the news and they saw a five-second clip of Ravi Shankar teaching George Harrison how to play the sitar. Behind George was a
blue river, the bluest Miranda had ever seen, and the lone tree
beside him was perfect, it was everything a tree should be, and
the Indian man, too, seemed so happy, the happiest man Miranda had ever seen. Sometime after that, sitting at the kitchen
table, Miranda noticed the mailman. She'd seen him many times
before, of course, but she'd never once talked to him, she'd
hardly paid attention to him, but she watched him now with
keen interest — the way his bag of letters was slung over his shoulder, the way he opened the mailbox, rooted the letters out of the
bag, inserted them into the box, closed it, and then moved on to
the next house. After he was gone, she thought of how he did
this with great dedication or great resignation or maybe great
monasticism, but he did it day after day after day. She wondered:
Is that what he'd meant to do with his life? Go on foot in a
never-ending circle?

The next morning, she left Sam the note and headed for
India.

Raja, the man she met at the hostel in Chandni Chowk, had
arrived from Dehradun, after graduate studies, and was on his
way to start a new job in Jhansi. He'd stopped in Delhi to visit its
Jantar Mantar, as he'd always been a hobbyist in astronomy, and
had dreamed of visiting it since childhood. He first noticed Miranda at the reception desk when she was checking in. He
walked past her, heard her American accent, and thought, How
strange. She has hardly any luggage for having come such a long
way. The second time he saw her, she was standing on the landing of the hostel's stairwell, crying. He saw her bent back, her
head in her hands, the cheap cotton of a purple skirt that she
most certainly overpaid for at one of the street stalls in Chandni

Chowk. Probably one of the stalls alongside the hostel. Raja, at that point, thought he might simply turn around and go back down the stairs, but something about her — maybe the way she was trying to stifle her sobs, with such touching effort, though she could not have known anyone was there to hear her, or maybe it was the fine blonde hairs on her arms, lit by the small grimy window above her. Even through the filthy light, the hairs shone like burning filaments on a just-born planet. In the end, he climbed one step closer to her, held his arm out, just a little, not enough to frighten her, and, though they were about the same age, he said, "Madam? What is it that is troubling you?"

Miranda froze.

She wiped her nose on her sleeve and dried her tears and adjusted her blouse and only then did she turn and say, "Oh, nothing. Nothing at all. Thank you."

"I see. But — perhaps I can help you with something?"

Miranda shook her head. "You're very kind, but no, thank you."

Raja climbed to the landing where she was standing. He was just about to pass her when he turned, looked at her, and said, "I've always wondered . . . why is it that you Americans say 'thank you' at the end of every sentence?"

Miranda stared at him. "Do we?"

"Every sentence."

"I don't . . . I didn't know that we did. Do we? Thank you for pointing that out."

He looked at her and she looked at him and then they both burst out laughing. When she laughed, her face took on the uncorruptible look of a child, and so he said, "There is a very good sweets shop near here. Would you like to have some ice cream?"

"Yes," Miranda said. "That would be nice."

And so, ten minutes after they met, he was eating pista ice

cream and she was eating vanilla ice cream, and they were talking about their shared love of comic books and trains and kites. "When was the last time you flew one?" he asked.

She smiled sadly. "I don't remember."

They looked out of the darkened sweets shop into the teeming street. The heat of summer pushed against the windows, and Miranda was homesick, but not for anyplace she could name.

Raja said, "I have two weeks before I have to start my job."

"Oh?"

"Would you like to go to Varanasi with me?"

"What's that?"

"It's a city. Along the Ganga. The Ganges."

"I've heard of the Ganges."

"Would you like to go?"

"But why?"

"I was thinking it would be a nice train ride. I could buy you *Betty and Veronica* comics at the Higginbothams, at the station. And we could fly a kite. Along the Ganga."

Miranda laughed. "Alright. But — where is it?"

"By train? Fifteen hours from here. Maybe a little more."

"Fifteen hours!"

"The truth is," Raja said, "I promised my mother I would try to go. Before starting my job. To take darshan."

"What does that mean?"

"To get the Ganga's blessings. Roughly. But literally darshan means to *see* a thing. A holy thing."

"Darshan," Miranda repeated, and wondered whether it was the Ganga that George Harrison and the Indian man had been seated by. The next morning, she and Raja were on an express train to Varanasi. As he'd promised, Raja bought her a half dozen *Betty and Veronica* comics and she read them — cracking open peanut after peanut (also bought at the train station) — with a joy she had not felt since girlhood. When the wind through the train's windows whipped past her, lifting her hair, coaxing her skin to feel as if for the first time, she thought of a racehorse she'd once seen. He had grown too old to race, and after years of maltreatment had been brought to a farm near her parents' house. When he'd walked out of the trailer for the first time and been released into the lush meadow in which he would live, Miranda thought he might run, gallop to its ends and back to celebrate his freedom, but instead, the horse stood still. He found the shade of a tree, with a carpet of clover beneath it, and stood still. The wind had lifted his mane, and that is what Miranda remembered on the train to Varanasi: the wind lifting the horse's mane. Perhaps that was the essence of freedom, she thought, to not have to run to feel the wind, but to be able to feel it standing perfectly still.

On their second night in Varanasi, she and Raja had sex. Miranda had never had sex with anyone but Sam, and certainly not with an Indian man. It started inauspiciously, with him embracing her awkwardly, and then trying to kiss her in such a savage way that she felt she was being stabbed by a wet, slimy snail. But then he laid her down, more gently than she thought possible, and then, much to her surprise, he didn't enter her. He didn't. He simply laid his head next to hers and sniffed her hair, took in its scent as one would incense in a temple, and then he tugged at a curl, over and over, watching it spring back into place as if all the world depended on its springing back. She said, "What are you doing?" And he said, "Taking darshan." She smiled. She cradled his head. This man, this man. All the years had led to this man. She thought then of the two pregnancies she had lost. Where were they now, those two runaway sprites? Wandering a forest? Wandering the desert in which she, too, had wandered for so long? And why didn't I name them? she wondered. Why?

The next day was breezy. They hired a boatman and had him row them out to a long stretch of sandbar across from Scindia Ghat. When they pulled ashore, Raja bowed and held his hand out to her in such a gallant gesture that Miranda laughed. She thought, I'm entering a ballroom, and perhaps she was. The kite flew high and swooped and sailed and leapt like a mighty dragon. The sky rang with their laughter. The same boatman came back for them in the evening, and as he rowed them across the Ganga, Miranda leaned back in the stern, closed her eyes, and dozed in the river's swaying, and in her dozing, the flutter of waterbirds, the voices of the praying, the shouts of children, the bleating of goats, the waves lapping against the hull — they all quieted, just for a moment — the cessation of a symphony. And into this quiet, in the fearlessness of sleep, Miranda thought (or dreamed) that they were both girls. Of course they were girls. And though she had not named them then, she would name them now.

Raja, seeing her smiling, said, "What is it? What are you smiling about?"

And Miranda, without opening her eyes, said, "Betty and Veronica."

She and Raja were walking along Lahartara Road one evening after dinner. They had been in Varanasi for a week. Neither spoke of leaving. As they were crossing, Miranda looked in the wrong direction, stepped onto the road, and was struck by a lorry. She died instantly. The ambulance took her away and Raja watched it leave. He couldn't understand it; this woman whom he had known for eight days. Who was she? Why had she come to India? Why had they met? What was he meant to do now? How could he now go to Jhansi? How? How could eight days break a heart?

He went back to Scindia Ghat and sat on the steps. The priest, the one who'd conducted the crematory rites, had said, "What a blessing. To have died in Varanasi. It's every Hindu's dream."

Raja had said nothing.

Seeing the look on his face, the priest had added, "My lad, she's attained Moksha. She's broken the cycle of rebirth. Don't you see? She's found salvation in death."

Raja looked toward the sandbar on which they'd flown their kite. The sandbar on which a weightless scrap of flimsy paper had blotted out the sun. Blotted out, for an instant, every one of its flaming pavilions. You're wrong, he thought. In life. In life is where we found it.

Chapter 35

When Janavi woke to find Sagar gone, she sat at the dining table, a cup of lukewarm coffee in front of her, and thought of all the ways she could hurt Pavan. She could call the college where he worked, Adarsh Inter College, and tell them what he had done to Rajni. But she realized that if she did that, and he ended up losing his job, Rajni, too, would lose her livelihood. She could call some of her male friends and have them beat him up. Or better yet, through one of these friends, she could hire a goonda to beat him up! Each one of these ideas came to her and then they floated away, impractical. Ms. Sujata, when she'd called to ask her advice, had told her to be patient. She'd said, "It takes an average of seven times for a woman to leave an abusive relationship. And from what you're telling me, your sister hasn't yet left the first time."

Janavi looked wretchedly into her cup of coffee.

Sagar's note read, *Don't worry. Back soon.*

She waited all morning, and then, instead of eating lunch at home, she decided to visit Mandy (whom she hadn't seen in weeks, and who hadn't been working the last time she was at the convenience store) and buy a Slurpee and maybe try one of those hot dogs that spun and spun on the heated rack. Maybe she could even learn a little something about patience from them.

But when she got to the convenience store, it was the young man, Aaron, who was working. She waved to him, but he either didn't recognize her or pretended not to. She got a Slurpee and a hot dog; she squeezed a thick helping of mustard and another of ketchup onto the hot dog. She'd never eaten one before, but she'd seen other people do the same. She peered into the container of relish and spooned it on top. When she got to the counter, she said, "What days does Mandy work?"

Aaron rang up her Slurpee and the hot dog and said, "She doesn't."

Janavi looked at him.

"Quit, I guess. Stopped showing up."

"Stopped? But why?"

Aaron shrugged. "How should I know? Ask her."

Janavi paid. She said, "I don't have her phone number. Do you?"

"No."

"You do. I remember. She called you."

"I might," Aaron said. "Can't just give it to you though."

"What if something's happened to her? Why would she just stop showing up?"

"Nothing's happened. Probably some guy. One started coming around here, you know. Saw him pick her up once or twice."

"But why would she stop coming to work?"

"Why wouldn't she?"

Janavi heard the hostility in his voice. The stubbornness. "Please," she said desperately. "What if something's wrong?"

"It isn't."

She said, "Do you have a sister?"

"Yeah. So?"

Janavi looked him in the eyes and said, "I do too."

After a moment, Aaron looked away, took out his phone, and gave her Mandy's number.

She dialed it seated on the low wall. It rang and rang. The voicemail message said the mailbox was full. She tried again. She realized then that Mandy wouldn't recognize her number, so she texted her and waited. She took one bite of the hot dog and then another and then she threw it in the trash. Nothing she'd ever eaten had tasted like that, and she wasn't sure food was meant to have its texture. She waited ten minutes for Mandy to respond to her text, then she dialed her again. This time, Mandy picked up. Or someone she assumed was Mandy because there was only silence on the other end of the line.

Janavi, confused, said, "Can I speak to Mandy?"

"Who is this?" A man's voice.

"Janavi. I'm a friend of — "

"A friend? What friend?"

"From Mansfield. From the store."

"Oh. That shithole." There was a pause. "What do you want?"

"Is she there? Can I talk to her?"

There was silence, and she wondered if he'd hung up. But then came a rustling sound followed by Mandy's voice. It was unrecognizable. Without the verve or the lilt, without any of the pleasure or warmth of a girl who dreamed of hula-hooping in the middle of Times Square. Janavi heard a clicking and an inhale. "Where are you?" she said.

"Back in Baker."

"Why?"

"You think I was going to work that shit job for the rest of my life?"

"But — you never said goodbye."

"How was I supposed to find you?"

"Aaron said you just stopped coming. And another cashier didn't even know who you were. And . . ." There was silence. "Are you there?"

Mandy said, "No, not really." And before Janavi could ask her what she meant, she said, "I fucked up."

Janavi felt it again, anger. Rajni. And now Mandy. "It's that guy, isn't it? The one who answered your phone. He — "

"No. *I* fucked up."

What did she mean? Janavi looked at the gas pumps, at the store, at her fingers sticky with ketchup. She'd never felt so lost, so without a compass, so without words in all her life. Fate. The campfire. You tended it with the utmost vigilance, scrutinized every spark, and then, from fatigue or monotony or from life and its false assurances, you looked away, just for a second, and . . .

"What will you do?"

"Get clean. Go somewhere. I've always wanted to see the ocean."

"Will you call me?"

"No." Janavi was startled. But then Mandy said, "Not until I'm standing on a beach. That's when I'll call you."

"Or in Times Square."

"Or in Times Square."

Janavi could almost see her putting out the cigarette, looking up from the ashtray, staring at whatever dirty and peeling and colossal wall she was facing. When they got off the phone, she waved goodbye to Aaron, who didn't wave back, and then she walked home. The orange cat stopped to watch her, and she thought it would dart away when she got closer, but it didn't. She leaned down and petted it and nearly sobbed to feel its body, so soft and warm and trusting.

Chapter 36

It was dark when he got to the trailer. He cut the headlights.

The door was locked, as he knew it would be. He'd brought a stepladder, and this he positioned under a south window. It opened. He flung his duffel bag inside. Then he lifted himself and shimmied through, scraping his shoulders, his torso. Drawing blood. He searched the interior with his flashlight — everything was covered in a thick layer of dust, files were left open, abandoned mid-read; the hard drives were gone, and the laptops, but not the monitors or any of the other equipment. That's what he'd counted on.

They had taken his key for the front door, but not the smaller one to the secure cabinet.

What he came for, the side-scan sonar device, was tucked into the third shelf. He gathered the components, loaded them into his bag, unbolted the door, and walked out.

He drove to the reservoir, to the kayak rental place. All was quiet, motionless. No wind. The sun a good two hours from rising.

He slit the cord holding the last kayak in a chaotic line of them. He climbed in. He turned on the sonar device and adjusted the settings. He paddled to the opposite side of the reservoir and then downriver, toward the fishing shacks. He passed them and paddled some more. The reservoir was bound in fog, and it felt to Sagar as if he were on the River Styx, drifting into the underworld. How had he ever thought — given water pressure, temperature, and the limitations of human vision — that he could've seen something by simply diving? Unaided? With the naked eye, humans couldn't see more than fifteen or twenty feet below the surface, but the side-scan sonar, depending on its frequency, could detect hundreds of feet on either side.

Nothing so far.

He stayed on the side opposite the Dooley home.

There were three possibilities on this side, three gravel roads. Three, Sagar thought, of course there were three. There were other roads, but they were much farther downstream, and he wouldn't have time to reach them before the sun came up.

The end of the first road yielded nothing. Natural sediment rises and falls, but nothing else.

Same with the second.

He paddled to the third. The sky lightened at the edge of a far embankment. He paddled harder, determined to reach the third gravel road before the sun cleared the embankment. And it was then, just past the second road and through his peripheral vision, that he saw it.

He stopped paddling. He stared at the screen.

The outline of a car could not have been clearer.

Chapter 37

She had been home only for a few minutes, eating a bowl of cereal, when Sagar burst through the door. Janavi came out of the kitchen, bracing herself for more bad news, but his face was jubilant. He said, "We have to go. Right now."

"Where?"

"Norma's."

She noticed then that his jeans and T-shirt were wet, his skin damp. He raced into the bedroom, came back out wearing dry clothes, and then he started loading his laptop into a duffel bag, out of which spilled various instruments she'd never seen. He looked at the bowl of cereal in her hand and said, "Bring it with you."

When they got onto Highway 212, she said, "What's all this about? Why all the rush?"

He looked at her for a long moment, and then he turned back to the steering wheel and said, "I can't say."

"Why not?"

"I don't know what it means. And I don't want to involve you. Not yet."

"Is it dangerous?" She was half joking, but Sagar looked at her and said, "Maybe."

They drove without speaking the rest of the way. When they got to Norma's, she and Ophelia were watching an episode of *Dora the Explorer*. Sagar said to Janavi, "Would you mind watching her?"

Norma looked from him to Janavi.

He took out his laptop. "Could we go out back?"

There was a patio they'd seen from the kitchen window, and Sagar followed as Norma led him down the hallway. He turned his head, nodded once at Janavi, and then they disappeared through the back door.

Janavi sat down on the sofa and looked at Ophelia. She was so absorbed in the show that Janavi wondered if she knew Norma had left. She watched the show for a few minutes, as Dora and Diego and Boots traveled back to the time of dinosaurs to bring back their friend Baby Jaguar. Baby Jaguar had made a wish to see a real dinosaur before blowing out the candles on his dinosaur-themed birthday cake and had promptly disappeared. Janavi liked that the characters often spoke in Spanish, and how they routinely turned to the camera, presumably toward the kids who were watching, and asked them questions. The kids were expected to shout them out, Janavi guessed, but Ophelia only sat and watched in silence.

What were Sagar and Norma talking about? And where had Sagar gone this morning? He'd never said, but she guessed the reservoir again. But why?

Janavi, lost in her thoughts, noticed a stack of mail on the coffee table. On the bottom of the stack was the latest edition of *The Mansfield Register*. She hadn't even known there was a paper version. She slipped it out from under the stack and looked at the front page. There was a photo of Sam Dooley, with the headline MAYOR OF MANSFIELD, CITY COUNCIL, FILE LAWSUIT TO HALT DAM REMOVAL. It had been expected of course, after his announcement at the Elks Lodge meeting, but her heart still sank. She read the article all the way through, and then she looked at the photo again. It wasn't that he looked smug so much as a person unused to losing, whether by design or determination she couldn't tell. She flipped through the other pages of the paper, and on the fourth page, she started reading an article about "rooster hot spots." These were apparently places where the concentration of roosters exceeded Montana's five chickens per acre law. What was more, according to the article, the rooster-to-hen ratio was so high that some officials suspected a cockfighting ring in the area. And cockfighting, stated the article, was linked to gambling, drugs, and alcohol abuse. Janavi was deep into the article, wondering about the rooster hot spots, when there was a commercial break in the *Dora the Explorer* episode.

She lowered the newspaper.

To her astonishment, Ophelia wasn't looking at the television screen, but directly at Janavi. She said, "What is it?" not really expecting a response. Ophelia looked back at her, the round lamp of her face strangely unsettled — a candle, Janavi thought, with a flickering flame. They looked at each other. After a moment, the girl's gaze left Janavi and shifted to the newspaper. The television went quiet. Janavi didn't register this quiet, not until later, nor did she register the unusually long pause between the commercial break and the show resuming. In fact, out of that pause, out of its preternatural silence, came one of the most extraordinary moments in Janavi's life. So extraordinary that, years later, Janavi would think, Did that happen? Could it have been so clear? And yet it was.

Out of that silence came Ophelia's voice. She was pointing to the newspaper. Her tiny finger was raised to its front page. And she said, "He pushed Mama."

Paulie

Cotton River, 2003

Paulina, or Paulie, as everyone called her, was eleven before she could read the time. Until the age of eleven, she would look up at the clock, lift her finger to her mouth, deep in contemplation, and if the small hand was on the one and the big hand was on the six, Paulie would say, "Mama. The time is one o' six o'clock." If the small hand was on the eight and the big hand was on the twelve, Paulie would say, "It's eight o' twelve o'clock, Mama." If the small hand was on the twelve *and* the big hand was on the twelve, Paulie would say, "Look! Look, Mama. They're standing straight up. Both of them. Look. It's twelve o' twelve o'clock." But when her mother died — in the *exact* moment she died, in fact, a Tuesday in October, when Paulie was eleven years old — she looked up at the clock outside of her mother's hospital room, and she read it perfectly. Perfectly. "The time, Mama," she said, speaking out loud to her mama for the last time, "is three forty-seven on a Tuesday afternoon."

Three forty-seven. On a Tuesday afternoon in October.

Funny how time fell into place, or out of place, in the exact moment her mother died.

After that, Paulie was sent to live with her grandmother

in Kalispell, though she soon became too much for her grandmother — truancies at school piled up and she was failing every class except for math, which she seemed to understand with a staggering intuition that surprised the teacher, scared Paulie, and confused her classmates so much that they didn't know whether to beat her up before or after they stole her homework. The final straw was when the janitor caught her smoking weed inside a storage shed in the middle of fifth period. After that, Paulie was sent to stay with an aunt who lived southeast of Kalispell. Paulie got off the bus in Bozeman with a backpack, a brown paper sack that still had the sandwich with a slice of bologna and the apple her grandmother had packed for her, and with hair much shorter than when she'd started the trip. Her aunt glanced at her when she got into the car and said, "Who cut your hair?"

"I did."

"That explains it."

"Explains what?"

Her aunt didn't say anything, so Paulie pulled the visor down and looked in the mirror. There was not much to see; hair that five hours ago had been down to her waist was now just above her ears. Paulie showed her aunt the straight-edged knife she'd used to cut it. "Where is it?" her aunt asked.

"Where's what?"

"The hair."

"On the floor of the bus."

Her aunt nodded, her eyes fixed on the road. She said, "Why they sent you way the fuck out here is beyond me. You don't need to be taken care of."

The child inside Paulie, the one who was still on the wrong side (presumably) of time, cried out, Yes, I do. The Paulie who was on the right side (presumably) of time, said, "I told them. I told everybody. The school, Grandma, the protective services people. No one listened."

Her aunt looked over at her and said, "Get used to it."

Paulie turned her head and sat silently gazing out of her window with a serious expression on her face, mimicking the kind of expression she'd seen on the faces of adults when they looked out of car windows — in movies, on television — just before they said something beautiful and heartbreaking. But, of course, she could think of nothing beautiful or heartbreaking to say, though she did wonder when it would be a good time to ask her aunt to pull over so she could pee.

At her new school, Paulie killed even the part of her that was good at math. Her exceptional skill scared her, and so she killed it. Or silenced it. Or put it under a blanket and smothered it, or, as with all the other things that scared her, she looked at the clock, looked at it long and hard and bitterly, and said, "Take it." After that, what was left was her body. She liked the thought of it; the thought of her body, full of galloping blood going nowhere, just around and around, all of it nothing more than a hamster wheel and a few organs — most of them no bigger than a fist — and a handful of muscles. That was the sum total of a body, and all that one person ever really offered another. How paltry, Paulie thought. How small and inconsequential a thing to give. The first boy she gave it to barely got his pants off, and certainly not hers, before he was finished. The second boy was eating crackers afterward, and he laughed and said, "Polly want a cracker?" and Paulie said, "I'm not that kind of Polly, you asshole." The third guy, named Kurt, who she met outside the schoolyard, flicked his cigarette out of the car window and said, "You could make money, you know. Lots of it. Doing what you and I just did."

Paulie was silent for a moment, watching the glow of the cigarette butt on the ground, and then she said, "How much?"

"Like I said, lots."

True to her word, her aunt didn't much take care of her. Sometimes, she left a plate for Paulie warming in the oven before she went to her night shift, but most often, Paulie was left alone after school and all through the night. And even if her aunt was home, she couldn't make any noise — no television, no radio, not even a phone call — because her aunt was a light sleeper, and only got four hours of it between her three jobs. Paulie thought about her aunt, and then she thought about the pile of her hair on the floor of the bus. Nothing before and nothing since could compare to that pile of black hair — coiled like snakes. No, coiled like the universe, all the galaxies and stars and asteroids and solar systems trapped inside. With all their light, lusting to get out. She said to Kurt, "What do I need to do?"

In the dark of the car, she saw the smallest flicker of a smile, smaller than even the flicker of the cigarette butt had been in the vast of the night. Kurt said nothing, not until just before he dropped her off, when he said, "I'll let you know."

At the end of the month, he told her to pack a small bag and be ready. He would pick her up on Sunday night. They would go to a safe place — his mother's basement, where he lived — and they would wait for the signal. What signal, she said. Stop asking so many goddamn questions, he said. He was not as kind as he used to be, but that was true of all the boys. That was true of all the days. Then he said, "Don't say goodbye. Not to your aunt. Not to no one. Don't give any sign that you're leaving. In fact, leave your toothbrush. I'll buy you a new one." So Paulie left her toothbrush and packed her backpack — the same one she'd brought with her, except this time, at fifteen, she added a packet of tampons.

Kurt arrived promptly, just after her aunt left for her night shift. They drove an hour, maybe more, and when they reached his mom's house, he didn't introduce her to his mother, even though Paulie could see that the lights were on, and that she must've been home, but instead he told her to be quiet and ushered her into the basement, which had its own entrance in the back. How long was she there? In the damp basement with the blackout curtains? She couldn't say. Maybe three days? Four? Kurt wouldn't let her leave, he wouldn't let her turn on the television, and he wouldn't let her flush the toilet unless he was home. The food he snuck down to her was never a warm meal, but bags of chips or strips of beef jerky or a slice of cheese and once a hard-boiled egg. When she asked him why he locked the door behind him when he left, he told her to shut the fuck up. At the end of the three or four days, he said it was time to go. She packed up her things again and it was dark again, but this time, Kurt took her on a much longer drive. She was asleep when they pulled up to a low ranch house in the middle of a flat little town. Kurt said, "Wait here," and went around to the back of the house. She thought he would take her to another basement, but instead, Kurt came out of the front door of the house with another man, and he said, "Come on out. Get your bag. You're going with him."

"Who's he?"

"I'll tell you what you need to know. Hurry up."

The other man was now pulling out of the driveway in a pickup truck. He hadn't yet turned on his headlights, but when he did, right as Paulie was looking at them, they were so bright, so ruthless, they burned in her like charcoal, and Paulie turned to Kurt and said, "I don't know. I'm not so sure anymore." He yanked her out of the car, threw her backpack on the ground, and slammed the door shut. The pickup truck with the strange man was idling next to his car. Kurt said, "It's a done deal, sweet-heart." Deal? What deal? And then he said, "He'll take care of you. You'll be right as rain."

Right as rain. Paulie had never heard that expression before. She didn't know exactly what it meant, but she knew it was a lie. No rain, not in her lifetime, had ever been right.

Kurt pulled away, and the man didn't even look at Paulie when she climbed into his truck. He lit a cigarette, rolled down his window an inch or two, and started driving. She had dozed in Kurt's car, but now she was wide awake. She was thinking. She was thinking about her mother for what must've been the first time in months. A year? And she was thinking a precise thought. She was thinking, Why didn't she correct me when I was wrong? About the time? Why didn't she say, It's not one o' six o'clock, Paulie. It's one-thirty. Or say, It's not twelve o' twelve o'clock. It's noon. She had never corrected her, and Paulie had never won-dered why. Maybe she hadn't corrected her because Paulie was right. Just as the actual time was also right. They were both right. Or maybe they were both wrong. Just as Kurt and this man were both wrong. It was suddenly obvious: how wrong both were. How wrong time could be.

Paulie looked out of the window. There was a clump of trees ahead. Far ahead, in the distance. And as she had never known anything in her life, Paulie knew that all was lost once they passed that clump of trees. That she would never find her way back — not to her aunt or to her grandmother or to anything that resembled the mystery of a girl's life. She had killed all else, and only her body was left, and she knew it too would soon go missing.

"Mister, I have to go to the bathroom."

"We're almost there," he said.

"Bad."

"Hold it."

"Really bad. I might pee myself."

"Go ahead."

He never once looked at Paulie. If only he would look at me, she thought, he would see: that the gates are closing, that he is taking me to a war for which I have no weapons. But he never did. He never looked at her. When they passed the clump of trees, she saw that it was three trees, and it seemed to her their branches were bent low, as if — though, how could it be? — as if they were weeping.

Chapter 38

Norma led Sagar to a patio table with three chairs. Beyond them was the prairie. A house in the distance stood on a low rise and a chain-link fence ran like a seam across the yellow grass. There were more hills, even farther away, patched with the blue green of sagebrush. Norma said, "I have coffee and iced tea."

But Sagar was already logging on to his computer. His thoughts were racing, but he forced himself to calm them. Nothing would make sense unless he stilled them. He took a breath. He said, "There's a car. In the reservoir. On the side with the fishing shacks."

Norma, who was at the screen door, stopped.

"I saw it."

He turned his laptop toward her. He'd pulled up a map of the reservoir. "Right here," he said, pointing to a spot between the two gravel roads. "Current must've carried it. Wasn't even that far in. None of the fishing shacks are close."

Norma sat down. Stared at the screen. She said, "You sure?"

He nodded. "It was a car. No question. And . . ."

"How long has it been down there?"

"No telling."

"What kind of car?"

"Sonar can't — but that's where the finger bone came from. The old man — "

Norma stared at him. "An old man? What old man?"

"I met him at Sweet Molly's. Renny gave him the finger bone. Said she knew who it belonged to. And after what Gabe told us . . ."

"What did he look like?"

"Old. Silver hair. Had a tattoo of a trident on his arm."

Norma smiled. "Clyde."

Sagar breathed out.

"Makes all the sense in the world that Renny would trust him with it. He's an elder. An old-timer. It's sacred, that finger bone. And our elders — they're custodians of our sacred relics."

Sagar wanted to say, We need to go to the sheriff. Right now. They have to dredge the river, but he held back; the conversation took on a reverence, a gravity that had nothing to do with dredging the reservoir.

Norma's gaze grew distant. "They're in there. I know they are."

Sagar said nothing.

"They were coming home after their shifts, I'd guess. The three girls we lost. At the slaughterhouse. Walking home on the county road." She was looking now toward the far hills. "Gabe said it. Spelled it out practically. I was too stupid to put it together."

"I wouldn't — "

"They always said they'd run off. The police, people in town. Drugs or some man, they said. And here, all they were doing was walking home from work. I know how they think. They think, Why should the lives of a couple of white boys be ruined because of some dead Indian girls?" She wiped at her eyes, and then she sat up straight in her seat. "And one of them might've only been injured. Remember? That's what he said. Remember? That finger bone is evidence — that's the other reason Renny gave it to Clyde. For safekeeping." Sagar saw her face solidify with rage, turn to rock. "Who was it? Who was driving that car? Wasn't Gabe," she said, looking steadily into Sagar's eyes, "so, who the fuck was it?"

Neither spoke. Sagar thought again, We have to go to the police. We have to. We can't figure out anything sitting here. And that's when Janavi threw open the screen door. She was holding up a newspaper, a look of shock on her face. She said, "Guess what Ophelia just said."

"Sam? Sam Dooley?"

Sagar and Norma were in Sheriff Oswald's office. Oswald started to laugh. "So let me get this straight. You're telling me some four-year-old kid told you the mayor was involved? *Recognized* him from a newspaper photo. And what? I'm supposed to go out and arrest him? Based on the kid's ID? Hold up in court, you think? Oh now, wait. Wait. We've also got that pissant father of hers. Saying what? That he was in a car with somebody who might've done something. And that he was drunk at the time. Irrefutable, if I do say so myself. His word is definitely bond, don't you think?" He laughed again.

"There's the car," Sagar said. "In the reservoir."

The sheriff, his annoyance incandescent, turned to him. "Right. The car." His face grew serious, as if the joke had ended. "You know how much junk is in that lake? How many cars? You sure it wasn't a refrigerator? An old washing machine?"

Sagar refused to look away. "I'm sure."

"You know the worst part of my job," he said with disgust. "You goddamn amateurs."

Norma's expression was stone. Sagar said, "I can come with you. I can show you where it is."

"I guess you've got time," the sheriff said. And then he added, "Though, from what I understand, you've got some packing to do."

Fire shot up Sagar's spine. Punching him would most certainly get Sagar and Janavi deported faster. "There's the finger bone."

"What finger bone?"

Sagar explained to him how he'd come to see it, and how Renny probably found it washed up on the shore. "That's why she was killed. She knew about the car," he said. "She wasn't swimming. She was pushed into the reservoir. Into the notch."

"So, the mayor of Mansfield does all this? A man as upstanding as him?"

"Upstanding?" Norma said, speaking for the first time.

"He might not have done it," Sagar said. "But he was there."

"And the kid? They just up and left the kid?"

"I guess . . ."

Sheriff Oswald looked at them, bristling. He said, "And the old man? Who is he?"

"I met him at Sweet Molly's."

"An old man at Sweet Molly's, you say? That don't — "

Norma stopped him short. "Clyde," she said.

Sheriff Oswald looked at her. He quieted, the name seeming to command respect even from him.

All three sat in silence.

A wall clock, above the sheriff's head, clicked forward a minute. Then another.

Out of this quiescence, Norma said, "The other Dooley, the father, handed over the deeds to a couple of rental houses to the parents of the girls who went missing. No questions asked. Now, what makes a man do something like that?"

Sheriff Oswald said nothing.

"Guilt, that's what. And that car's a Camaro. I'd put my money on it. I remember it. A real pretty maroon. You'd see it every now and then. When it was running, I'm guessing. But right around then, now that I think of it, up and stopped seeing it. Right around the time our girls disappeared. You understand what I'm saying?" Norma said, looking straight at the sheriff. "Do you?" And then, into the quiet of the room, she said, "Are you going to dredge that goddamn lake, or do I have to do it for you?"

Chapter 39

Janavi and Sagar waited.

A few days after their meeting with Sheriff Oswald, after hearing nothing about plans for the dredging, Sagar called him. The sheriff was short with him; told him there was paperwork to be filled out, equipment to be ordered. He said, "I'll call you."

Janavi went to visit Lottie one afternoon. Over coffee, Lottie said, "The Dooleys won't let this go."

"Why not? We don't even know what's down there."

Lottie said it didn't matter. "They're powerful, V."

"What can they do? Throw us out of the country? If we do nothing, we'll have to leave anyway."

Lottie wasn't convinced.

"You think Susan Dooley knows?"

Lottie waited a long time to answer, and then she said, "She knows."

Janavi asked how she could be so certain, but Lottie wouldn't say.

She and Sagar waited some more.

They stopped by Norma's. Ophelia was playing in the yard with a puppy they had adopted. Norma said, "Last thing I need is a puppy, but it's probably the first thing she needs."

Janavi thought of the little girl and her piglet. She thought of what

Renny had said. *It's nice, isn't it? To love something that won't leave you.* Janavi looked out of the window at Ophelia, laughing as she tumbled in the grass with the puppy.

While they were at Norma's, Rajni called and told Janavi, "Papa is feeling better. His cough is almost gone."

Janavi, after a moment, said, "Raju, all you have to say is, Come. And I'll come."

"I know."

There was silence.

"Whatever happened? In that serial about the two girls who were switched at birth?"

"Oh, that? All the money was lost. A long-lost relative of the dead father showed up and stole it all."

Another silence.

Rajni then added, "But it brought the two girls together and they ended up with something even better than the inheritance."

"What's that?"

"A sister," Rajni said.

Chapter 40

I t took another ten days.

Mack was there. Sagar had called him and told him about the car, and the rest of it. When he'd arrived, he'd patted Sagar on the back and said, "It's a bad business, Saag," and this time, Sagar had said, "Yes. Yes, it is." Alex Mendoza was there. Sagar had called him too. They shook hands. Sagar said, "It was after we talked. That's when I started putting it together."

Standing on the banks of the reservoir, at the end of the gravel road, the group waited for the divers to come back up. They had used sonar again to locate the car. Sagar had offered to dive to connect the cables, but Mack had said, "It's got to be official. If we're to appeal the termination."

Sagar liked that he'd said *we*.

Alex Mendoza, with a sadness Sagar had never known in him, said, "What do you think they'll find?"

He didn't answer; there was no answer, or the answer was too gruesome to speak.

It was cold. The first truly cold morning. Everyone was bundled up. Jackets, mittens. He breathed out and saw white smoke. It was suspended for a moment, in midair, and he thought of winter mornings seated on a ghat, watching the waters of the Ganga flow past him. He looked at the waters of the Cotton. Here at last, being hooked up to a tow truck, was his Spanish galleon. And like so much in life, it was nothing like he'd imagined. It was not gold, and it was not a ship, and it was not treasure. And he supposed he understood now what he had not understood as a boy: how deeply linked treasure is to tragedy.

He would tell Sandeep he was sorry. Of course, he would. But would Sandeep forgive him? Could Sagar forgive himself? Forgiveness. He wondered what made them who they were, he and Sandeep. One carrying the fire of grievance like a torch to the gods, while the other was drawn to water, purifying, cleansing, yearning again and again to put out the flame, and yet never knowing how.

He searched the crowd for Janavi. She was standing a little distance away, with Norma. They were both solemn, standing together and waiting for the divers. He caught Janavi's gaze and held it in his own. She was wearing a bright red woolen hat, and her cheeks were crimson from the cold, and he saw then what she must've looked like as a child. They'd both been children, standing under the guava tree. She began to move toward him when the divers reemerged and gave the thumbs-up. By the time the cables tightened, and the tow truck had started pulling, Janavi was next to him. She took his hand. And her body — like a blade of grass in wind, which, no matter how many blades surround it, or how vast the prairie its home, is still, when it is yours, the most beautiful, the one that matters most — leaned into his.

Chapter 41

It was a false start.

The rear bumper ripped off, and the divers had to go under again and reattach the cables.

It wasn't until late in the morning that the surface of the water finally began to bubble and quiver as the car dislodged from the sediment. The tow truck made a creaking noise as it crawled, inch by inch, up the embankment.

Janavi looked at Sagar. He was watching the water with such attentiveness, such intensity, that she thought, It's not the tow truck, it's him. He's pulling the car out. By sheer will. The back end of the Camaro, its tapered end, emerged. Its rusted maroon. She squeezed Sagar's hand tighter. What was it? It wasn't marriage, no. What was it? The thing that woke in our breasts every morning and decided to love?

The back window, mud and sediment spilling from it, came slowly out of the water. She didn't want to see. She wanted to look away, but that wasn't right. To look away. To look away was to deny whoever was inside, once again, the life they might've lived.

She shivered.

Sagar let go of her hand and wrapped his arm around her shoulder and pulled her close. She leaned her head into the curve of his neck.

There was no answer. Or, if there was an answer, it was what her papa's nautical map had shown her long ago: the last island.

She saw something inside the car shift. She winced. Her eyes warmed.

In Varanasi, she'd once seen a sitar, smashed and abandoned in an alleyway. How had it gotten there? How had it gotten so horribly broken? She'd stood looking down at it, not really knowing how or why. And she'd all but forgotten about the sitar, only now, without reason, she thought of it again.

The Camaro's back door, the tip of its antenna.

Of how it had still held a kind of beauty, though shattered. And of how some sitar maker, in some faraway place, had crafted it with love, and with a tenderness that still shone in the polish of the red cedar wood. And of how, just as she'd turned to leave, a wind had risen from the Ganga, traveled up the steps of the ghat and along the alleyway, and then, just for her, in that very instant, had skimmed across the strings and made them sing.

Epilogue

Older Brother and Younger Brother and Porcupine held steady, watching as the Camaro was pulled out. They remembered the night it had been pushed into the river; they knew who was inside. They remembered how Porcupine, at the sight of their dead bodies, had wailed with fury, his branches crashing through the night. They remembered the two boys who'd been standing on the shore, young and careless, and too foolish to know that everything we destroy destroys us in return. Even so, none of them spoke. Not a single leaf, on that cold October morning, stirred.

The back seat came into view.

They remembered, too, the little girl asleep in the truck. They'd prayed, Don't wake. Please don't wake, but she had. But she'd been a smart little girl. She'd stayed down, not screaming, not uttering a sound until the man was gone. But then, so was her mama.

The driver's side came into view.

Porcupine, his heart breaking, turned away, but Older Brother and Younger Brother refused. Younger Brother, who had himself once been a reckless boy, began to weep. Sap ran down his branches, his bark. After a long while he sniffled, stood up straight, and said, "Has She been avenged, Older Brother? The Great Gray Wolf? Is it finally done?"

"Yes," Older Brother said, as water and sediment gushed out of the car. "It's done."

Acknowledgments

For historical and contemporary perspectives of the Ganges River, the Ganges River delta, Varanasi, Montana, and the Montana Territory, I am indebted to the following research materials:

Ganges: The Many Pasts of an Indian River by Sudipta Sen
Montana: High, Wide, and Handsome by Joseph Kinsey Howard
This House of Sky: Landscapes of a Western Mind by Ivan Doig
Ganges Lament by Thomas K. Shor
Ganga: Sacred River of India by Raghubir Singh

For the story of Theo Mortimer, I was inspired by: "A Memoir of Colonel Sir Proby Cautley" by Joyce Brown, the Royal Society Publishing.

The sentiment of the Karuk Tribe, referenced on page 123, was from a quote by Karuk Tribe vice-chairman, Kenneth Brink (Associated Press, 2023).

For ushering this book into the world with great care and unerring belief, my deepest thanks to: Amy Einhorn, Lori Kusatzky, Gwyneth Stansfield, Dyana Messina, Chantelle Walker, Julie Cepler, Maureen

Clark, Abby Oladipo, Heather Williamson, Amani Shakrah, and the entire team at Crown Publishing.

For guidance, patience, and encouragement, my heartfelt appreciation to Sandy Dijkstra, Elise Capron, and my literary North Star, David Groff.

For friendship, advice, and wisdom, over all these many years, my unending gratitude to: Adam Bad Wound, Preston Taylor Stone, Laurie Frankel, Dena Afrasiabi, and, as always, Tom Doskow.

For their support and faith in me, my love to the Singiresu, Nandam, and Inguva families.

For the readers who open this book and find themselves between its lines — thank you. You are the reason for these words.

ABOUT THE AUTHOR

Shobha Rao moved to the United States from India at the age of seven. She is the author of the short story collection *An Unrestored Woman* and the novel *Girls Burn Brighter*. Rao is the winner of the Katherine Anne Porter Prize in Fiction and was a Grace Paley Teaching Fellow at The New School. Her story "Kavitha and Mustafa" was chosen by T. C. Boyle for inclusion in *Best American Short Stories*. *Girls Burn Brighter* was long-listed for the Center for Fiction First Novel Prize and was a finalist for the California Book Award and the Goodreads Choice Awards. She lives in San Francisco.